THE BANDIT'S LADY

by

Irene O'Brien

WHISKEY CREEK PRESS
www.whiskeycreekpress.com

Published by
WHISKEY CREEK PRESS

Whiskey Creek Press
PO Box 51052
Casper, WY 82605-1052
www.whiskeycreekpress.com

Copyright © 2005 by *Irene O'Brien*

Names, characters and incidents depicted in this book are products of the author's imagination or are used fictitiously. Any resemblance to actual events, locales, organizations, or persons, living or dead, is entirely coincidental and beyond the intent of the author or the publisher.

No part of this book may be reproduced or transmitted in any form or by any means, electronic or mechanical, including photocopying, recording, or by any information storage and retrieval system, without permission in writing from the publisher.

ISBN 1-59374-375-0

Credits
Cover Artist: Jinger Heaston
Editor: Melanie Billings

Printed in the United States of America

Dedication

Lovingly dedicated to the memory of my late husband, Paul, who celebrated with me the euphoria mixed with melancholy when the last word of this novel was typed.

Chapter 1

April, 1861

I hate it. I hate it, I hate it, Suzanne thought vehemently. *A war with the North will destroy us all.* With the low murmur of voices behind her, Suzanne Willoughby stood tense and restless by the large window overlooking the impeccably manicured and terraced front lawn of Royal Oaks Manor. Although huge oak trees stood like sentinels scattered across the landscape, Suzanne thought it misnamed. As far as she could see, ancient weeping willow trees, with slender pendulous branches forming a graceful and sweeping welcome, flanked either side of the long approach to the plantation. In her mind, the estate should have been forever Willoughby Heights.

The manor splashed across the horizon atop a rolling knoll overlooking the Ashley River where it met the Cooper River to form the entry, which flowed forever into the Atlantic Ocean. On a clear night, from her bedroom balcony on the second floor, Suzanne could see the lamps of Charleston glittering through the darkness.

The roof of the wide veranda stretched across the anterior of the house, supported by colonnades. The pillars and manor in addition to the slave quarters, the smokehouse, and all other buildings on the grounds, gleamed white in the sparkling sunshine of daytime. But now, the muted glow of dusk was complete. A gentle April breeze rippled through the open front door, through the foyer and into the library.

Spring was happening, but Suzanne shivered as she watched the descending darkness. It filled her with a baffling sense of dread. Their snug world had gone all wrong, Suzanne conceded, since Abe Lincoln was elected president the previous November. And especially since South Carolina seceded from the Union a month later.

A sharp oath pierced the drone of voices behind Suzanne. Startled, she turned around. Her father, Aman Willoughby, a big, rawboned man with a ruddy complexion and a head of thick, tightly curled black hair, roared again. The recipient of his wrath was their dinner guest, Thaddeus Stuart, Aman's friend and attorney, and their closest neighbor.

"Come on, you two," Suzanne said. "For months you've discussed no other subject except war between the South and the North. You've agreed and argued, by turns and dead ends. Whatever is it this time?"

Aman and Thaddeus were dressed exactly alike in black trousers, vests, and frock coats with front-pleated white shirts and black cravats. They stood at either end of the massive fieldstone fireplace. Aged oak, floor to ceiling bookshelves bordered each side of the fireplace. The library served as office and refuge to Suzanne's father.

Ignoring her, Aman waved his brandy snifter precariously. Steely gray eyes emitted sparks as he swore, softer this time. "Damn it, Thaddeus, what are you trying to tell me? I ask you for a simple favor—to see my daughter safely delivered to her grandparents in Baltimore. I've even offered you my ship, the *Annebella,* for a speedy trip.

The Bandit's Lady

Suzanne looked at Thaddeus. The recent widower had a lean middle-aged face with sunken, but flushed, smooth pink cheeks. His opaque, usually impenetrable blue eyes leered at her.

Suzanne knew she looked her best, that the green evening gown intensified the color of her eyes. Earlier, in front of the mirror, she had admired the new frock. The soft silk crossover bodice fell delicately over her breasts. Short puffed sleeves, generously trimmed with ruffled lace and worn off the shoulder, exposed smooth bare shoulders. The narrow forest green velvet trim and bow, with streamers fluttering down the front of the full gathered skirt, set off the Basque waist.

Sadie, Suzanne's beloved old nanny, had stood behind her. "Miz Suzanne, you is growin' up uncommon purty. You gonna break dem boys' hearts one of dese days. Dem little round breasts is pure seduc'ive. Dat face is a perfec' oval an' you gots a temptin' curved-up mouth."

"Oh, Sadie, go on with you. I'm skinny. I have no desire to be seductive. Anyway, tonight it will be just Thaddeus and Father."

But Sadie was not to be put off. "Anyway, you gonna give dem a run fo' it with dat chin. It gots iron in it, but you a'ways was a determin' little thing." Sadie had brushed Suzanne's coppery dark curls until they shone and drew them up on top of her head.

Now, tiny curling tendrils escaped from the combs and fell softly about her face, and Suzanne felt her face warm as Thaddeus' eyes boldly raked her over. At the Fall Harvest Ball, he had used this same rude approach. When her father was out of ear's reach, she demanded he quit ogling her.

"Don't be a prude, Suzanne," he had said arrogantly. "I am simply admiring your slim, wild beauty."

Thaddeus' eyes traveled up to Suzanne's face. She watched him moisten his lower lip with the tip of his tongue. His mouth twisted wryly. She knew he planned to marry her someday, with her father's blessing, but now he shook his head regretfully.

"I'm sorry, Aman," he said. "It's not that I don't wish to care for Suzanne's welfare. When this conflict is over, I'll make good our pact, but I, too, must attend the meeting Thursday next. I'm to introduce the recently formulated States' Rights laws to the council."

"For heaven's sake," Suzanne said, "quit talking about me as if I was a lifeless object, or a dull child. I'm leaving for Baltimore day after tomorrow without help from either of you. After all, I will celebrate my nineteenth birthday in a fortnight. I'll be safe with Grandfather and Grandmother Hanson long before then."

Suzanne felt defiance boil up inside her and she heard her voice sharpen. "You can't ask me not to travel alone, Father. It's the same trip I've taken alone for the past five summers."

Acutely aware of his scrutiny, Suzanne stood quietly while Aman recognized and acknowledged her womanhood. She was fourteen the year her mother died giving birth to a baby boy, who also died a few days later. Aman, a lonely and broken man, had sent Suzanne to her mother's parents to help comfort them. Each year after that Suzanne spent long, lazy summers with John and Margaret Hanson. She luxuriated in the warmth of her grandparents' tender love and basked in the delights of the city.

"Traveling was safer before this turmoil about war between the states," Aman said.

Then turning to his daughter with a faraway look in his eyes, his expression softened. He gave her a kind look. Her mother, Annebella, had been his bride for a full year when she was Suzanne's age. "I'll not forbid the trip, my dear," he said at length, "but I've asked your Uncle Stephen if James might accompany you. Although your cousin is only fifteen, he will be a good companion. He wants to meet his grandparents and Stephen will be occupied, as we all are with this blasted war talk. It's fitting you two travel together."

"Oh, thank you, Father. I love James like a brother." Suzanne saw the pain shoot across Aman's face. "I'll guard him with my life. You and Uncle Stephen will be free to help find a solution for this terrible dispute."

Aman shook his head, "I hope it helps, my dear. At our annual planters' meetings in February, we were all there but agreed on little. We'll try again while the men are staying in town between planting and harvest."

"Why is it so difficult, Father?"

Thaddeus gave Suzanne a look of impatience, and broke in with a sigh of resignation. "Don't you see, Suzanne? Charleston is the only important center of city life on the Atlantic seaboard below Baltimore. We can mingle with distinguished and informed people from all sections of the South, and from the North as well. Our wide range of experience in plantation management, mercantile, and political activities gives us powerful advantages for leadership. We *will* keep slavery, and expand it to the West. We are setting down rules to meet our goals. The North will concede. They know we're right."

"Anyway," Aman said, with only a hint of doubt, "we know the war won't come this far. We'll fight it where Abraham Lincoln can feel it. It will be over almost before he can start it. Still, we'll feel better when you and James are safe in Baltimore."

Suzanne swept across the room and hugged her father. "Don't give it another thought. We'll be fine. First thing in the morning, I'll ride over to tell James the good news. He can have his trunk packed at dawn of the day after."

Aman cleared his throat and held Suzanne away from him. "I have a gift for you. Since you won't be here on your birthday, I'll give it to you now. For a fact, I have two gifts." He handed her two small packages.

Suzanne flashed Aman a smile of thanks. She shook them gently. The heavier parcel, wrapped simply in brown paper, intrigued her. She tore it open quickly and lifted the lid of the box. A petite and light of weight pearl-handled pistol lay on a small powder blue velvet pouch. A vague disquieting feeling made Suzanne look up with astonishment. "A gun, Father?"

"Why so amazed, my dear?" Aman asked. "I taught you myself to shoot to the mark. When you were twelve you were a sharpshooter and begged for a gun of your own. Times are unsettled now. Carry the gun in your purse. I trust you will use it only to protect yourself." He smiled with benevolence. "Now open the other, and hurry. We must be off to the harbor meeting."

Suzanne carefully opened the smaller gift. Tears trembled on her thick eyelashes as she recognized the emeralds and diamond ring and matching pendant in exquisite, delicate gold settings. They had been her mother's.

Aman put an arm around her shoulder. "I saved them, my dear, for when you came of age. They match your eyes. Enjoy them always."

Thaddeus came to Suzanne and handed her yet another small package. "I, too, want to give you a keepsake for your birthday. When you come back this fall, I hope to offer you much more."

His gaze dropped from her eyes to her shoulders to the small mounds of her breasts. She felt ice spreading through her stomach, but remembered in time that her father had encouraged Thaddeus to pursue her. She managed to choke back her fury and to keep control of her rebellion. She vowed not to make a scene until her return and thought, *he'll never, never marry me. I'll marry for love, whatever that is.*

With as much enthusiasm as she could summon, she unwrapped the gift and politely thanked Thaddeus for the elegant gold chain necklace. He took her hand and kissed it lightly, wishing her a safe journey. Aman embraced her again. "I'll be away for a couple of days, chasing better conditions for our Confederate states. So, my dear, I must bid you farewell tonight. Give your grandparents my regards. And tell young James to protect you well, or I'll have the nape of his neck when you return."

Laughing merrily, Suzanne waved them away. She watched as they picked matching black silk top hats off the hat tree in the foyer and hurried through the double front oak doors. Then she dashed up the expansive curved stairway to her bedroom and started packing her trunks for the trip.

* * * *

As Suzanne removed the combs from her hair, Sadie—short, round and out of breath—rushed through the door. "I sorry I be late. I been seein' to de master's room. I see you is 'bout ready for de trip to your Grandpapa and Grandmama. I wish for a fact dat you wouldn't go. Dere's trouble out dere."

"Oh, Sadie, don't fuss so. Didn't you know James is going with me?"

"Lotta good dat baby'll do ya if'n things gits rough. I declare you be gonna have to take precious care o' him."

"And I can hardly wait," Suzanne said cheerfully. "Now get away with you, Sadie, and let me get my sleep."

Suzanne snuggled down in the middle of the three-quarter size feather bed only to find excitement would not let her sleep. She had wanted to take James along last year, but both fathers had refused. James, like herself, was motherless. Suzanne's Aunt Selma, always delicate, had died of malaria a year before her own mother died. Suzanne sighed. James had been only ten years old. Despite their age difference, the cousins had grown close.

James' father and Suzanne's mother, Stephen and Annebella Hanson, grew up in Baltimore. Their father, John Hanson, had left the South to study medicine. Though his father owned scores of slaves and treated them kindly, John had hated slavery and took up his practice in the North. Young Stephen, however, loved his Grandfather Hanson's land and had a penchant for the plantation. He came to Hanson Estate as a lad of sixteen and started managing it a year later when his grandfather became bedridden after a stroke.

In the spring of 1841, the young men and neighbors, Aman and Stephen, traveled to Baltimore together. Aman went there to buy a clipper ship to run his cotton north. In Baltimore, Stephen introduced Aman to his sister and Aman brought Annebella back to Charleston as his bride.

The Bandit's Lady

* * * *

Suzanne drifted into dreamless sleep, but awoke abruptly at the beginning of morning when her father shook her shoulder. "Get up and come to the nursery!" he shouted as he circled through the room.

Minutes later, clad in the breeches and shirt that she found more acceptable for everyday plantation life, Suzanne raced up the narrow steps to the third floor. "Father, Thaddeus, what is going on?" she asked as she stepped between them at the dormer window.

Peering through the moonlit darkness toward the shadowy silhouette of Fort Sumter, Aman shushed her. A moment later, Suzanne heard the deep blast of heavy mortar. Through the gray dawn sky a fiery red ball traced a gentle arc before it exploded directly over the fort.

Suzanne felt panic grab her stomach; in a burst of fear, she tasted bile in her throat. When she looked to Aman for comfort, he and Thaddeus were shaking hands, congratulating each other. Thaddeus turned gleefully to Suzanne. "Major Robert Anderson was defending the Fort for the Union while waiting for supplies from Federal ships lying offshore. Earlier, General Pierre Gustave Toutant Beauregard offered him an ultimatum to surrender the Fort. He refused. Now we'll show him we meant it."

Suzanne sucked in the acrid smell of smoke drifting up from the port. All around the harbor, people gathered on rooftops to watch the winking fiery red lights of the heavy guns. The sound of each volley drove through Suzanne like a well-honed knife. For thirty-four hours, with only brief breaks for light meals and short naps, the three of them watched the shelling until all Fort Sumter spouted smoke and flames.

Aman was the first to pinpoint a difference. "Look, Suzanne, someone's rowing out to the island. He's carrying a flag of truce."

When a cheer went up, Thaddeus said, "Major Anderson has surely surrendered."

Spirited war-fever pierced the atmosphere, but in the hush of a silent aftermath, relief flooded through Suzanne. "Oh, Father," she said, "thank our God there were no injuries. How can anyone want to go on with this? Can't we resolve our differences?"

Thaddeus said, "There's too much at stake to back away. It's time to celebrate! We'll turn those stiff tariffs against cotton inside out. The North won't dare interfere with our lives again."

Aman shook his head. "It's too early to be sure of the outcome. Our men are considering an embargo. Lincoln is threatening a blockade to turn our cotton back. The slavery abolitionists aren't likely to back down. They scheme to entice our slaves to leave their safe, comfortable homes. We can't stand for it!"

"Father, don't you think the South could survive even better with free slaves. We could pay them wages and educate them. They could be useful to our cause. Mother worked so hard to make life easy for them. Grandfather Hanson says…"

"Be damned what Grandfather Hanson says. He's like the lot of them. If we give the slaves their freedom and educate them, they'll ruin us. I treat my slaves good and fair. They've got no reason to run."

Glancing guardedly at Thaddeus, Suzanne said, "Some do have reason, Father. Mother told me some masters whip their slaves for little things, or no reason."

"Enough, Suzanne. It's none of our affair. We've exhausted the subject. When will you believe slaves aren't all the same? Some are mean. They need taming. We're lucky, that's all."

Church bells pealed. Aman and Thaddeus went downstairs to uncork a bottle of Aman's choice champaign. All Charleston celebrated the victory. Most all.

The following morning, newspapers across the land carried the news. The *Charleston Mercury* headlines screamed:

CONFEDERATE PRESIDENT JEFFERSON DAVIS TOLD CHEERING CROWDS: "OUR SEPARATION FROM THE UNION IS NOW COMPLETE, NO COMPROMISE CAN BE ENTERTAINED."

Chapter 2

Sunday morning, April 14, 1861, dawned radiant. Sunlight painted the hushed scene a vivid golden hue. Suzanne sat at the long mahogany table. The dining room was spacious and airy. Rich, ornate woodwork and baroque furnishings enhanced muted beige walls. Apricot-colored velvet drapes over wispy ecru sheers framed the windows overlooking resplendent gardens to the south of the manor.

Suzanne had vigorously attacked a generous portion of creamed eggs with sautéed mushrooms and frizzled dried beef. She finished a large piece of cornbread and a dish of strawberries, fresh picked this very morning, and with cream from old Clara Cow. Scooting back her chair, she openly adored James with tender humor.

Spindly tall, he examined the variety of savory dishes at the sideboard. He had arrived at Royal Oaks Manor the night before, russet red hair looking permanently tousled by the breeze. James' bright eager blue eyes blazed and glowed. His voice cracked between adolescence and adulthood, and he was talkative and lighthearted. He carried with him an incredible vitality that, even in his innocence, made every eye turn. Suzanne loved his gentle camaraderie, his subtle wit.

He turned toward the table, plate laden, and regarded Suzanne affectionately. She felt strangely exhilarated. "James, I feel as if we're on the edge of a most remarkable journey. Hurry, so we can be on our way. Jasper's waiting."

"Go on with you, Cousin. We strapped the trunks atop the gig. I'll be there before Jasper can get you settled." A flash of humor crossed his face as he bent his head to the task before him.

* * * *

"Miz Suzanne," Jasper said as he handed her up to the carriage, "things don't look so good down in town. I's wishin' you and young James would stay here with yore daddies. There's bad things goin' on."

"Oh, Jasper, not you, too. Your Sadie gave me the same sad lament last night and again an hour ago when she was dressing my hair. We'll be fine. It's time James met his grandparents and he'll be good company for me. You stop your fretting and take care of Sadie so she won't be so sad."

"I reckon we ain't got no choice now. Let's be off."

James bounded up the steps of the coach. "Yes," he said. And, in a singsong voice, "We're off to Charleston to catch the stagecoach. To Norfolk, Virginia, to board the steamship *Bianca*. To Baltimore, Maryland, to meet the dear Hansons, Grandmother Margaret and Grandfather John."

He smiled with beautiful boyish candor and stretched his long legs casually before him.

The days pranced by to the rhythm of the horses as the stagecoach bumped along to the beat of their hooves. Since Charleston, several passengers had left the crowded coach, leaving only the cousins and three others on board for this final day to the docks of Norfolk.

Abner Williams was fifty-ish and stout. For all their quizzing, he told them only that he had business at the shipyards, his destination. Caleb Smith, a tall, thin, razor-nosed man, dressed in a threadbare waistcoat bearing many wine and food stains, said nothing at all.

The third passenger, who insisted they call her Miss Tilly, was a tiny, old-fashioned gray-haired lady of seventy. Overtly wise, and assuredly wrinkled, she was on her way to Baltimore. She schemed to live out her years with a spinster niece. But a few minutes before she had said, "I feel spooked by my own shadow. This talk of war has shattered my common sense. Suzanne, I wish I were young and energetic like the two of you, but don't you know there are roadside bandits anticipating the likes of us? Just last week on this very same road, they killed Captain Jerome and did terrible things to his lady. We should have been at the *Bianca* dock two hours ago, before this drizzling ugly night began." Miss Tilly shivered.

Suzanne herself felt less than serene, but she leaned over and patted Miss Tilly's knee reassuringly. "I dare say, Miss Tilly, you are tired and tense. Did you forget that it took two hours to repair the wheel on this creaking coach?"

Although they traveled from daybreak to dusk, Suzanne and James had reveled in the beauty of the cloudless blue skies and lush green land of the countryside. They were excited, congenial to the other travelers and kind to old George, their driver. In their youthful enthusiasm, they savored the food at the inns in which they stopped after each long day. Bone tired but relaxed from the bath that washed away the road dust, they slept peacefully, despite the seething rumors of war. Each morning George arranged for a large basket of tempting sandwiches, fresh fruits and a surprise sweet treat for the noon meal.

The fourth and final day of the trip emerged doomed from the beginning. Morning rain drummed at the heavy curtains protecting the occupants of the coach from the wet. The rain continued all day splashing on the roof of the coach, slow and ceaseless, or pounding persistently. The road was thick with mud and rutted; the horses wary and unhurried.

Lulled now by the quiet occupants, Suzanne's thoughts lazily settled back to her visits at Hanson Estates. *Dear James,* she thought. *Cousin. Friend.* She remembered how she protected him under his bed when his tutor was searching for him and they wanted to go on a picnic. On those glorious expeditions, they ate food they stole from Cook. Together they romped with the plantation children, rode and raced their favorite horses and cooled their bare feet in the Ashley River.

One trait both got from their Grandfather Hanson was a love of poetry. She recalled how James read to her, recited choice excerpts from favorite poems, Shakespeare sonnets and burning love passages from Longfellow's "Evangeline." They had delighted in the "Miller and His Daughter" by Tennyson. James had a peculiar cadence in his voice that Suzanne found fascinating.

James, who had been dozing, woke up and drew back the curtains to look outside. Suzanne leaned her head forward slightly and peered out the small window. Before they left the protection of the abandoned barn where George fixed the wheel, he had lit the carriage lanterns. At first, until their eyes adjusted, the smoky light obscured by a sudden hard downpour of rain was all that the cousins saw. Then Suzanne sucked in her breath and tensed.

At the side of the road just ahead, she saw four men on horses quietly watching the carriage approach. Their own horses faltered as one of them tripped into a mud hole. The coach lurched and lost its rhythm. Miss Tilly fell against Suzanne and James stretched out an arm to steady her. "What was that?" Miss Tilly gasped in horror. "What?"

Suzanne gave a small involuntary shiver, but answered smoothly, "The horses got tripped up by a rut..."

But before she could finish, they heard a shot, followed by a chorus of deep voices shouting, "Halt!"

In the gloom, Suzanne caught James' eye. His natural optimism surfaced. He winked. A heartbeat later Suzanne realized the unrelenting rumble of the wheels had stopped. The door burst open to a swirl of wind and rain. The old coach shook and wobbled as a tall man wrapped in a tattered cloak pulled himself aboard and took stock of the passengers. Gleaming in the dim light and pointed straight at them from his black-gloved hand was the muzzle of a pistol.

Miss Tilly swooned and Suzanne moved closer to put an arm around her soft quivering shoulders. Her pearl-handled pistol was secure in its pouch at the bottom of her purse. *Unfortunately*, she thought, *it's underneath the seat.* "What do you want?" James asked, his voice a boyish squeak.

No answer came.

From outside, a harsh raspy voice roared, "What did you find in there? Rich folks?"

Another said, "How many women?"

Suzanne looked out again. All she could see in the faint lights of the carriage were the glint of eyes and shiny teeth.

"A fair young master," the man inside said in civilized literate tones. Looking around, he quickly assessed the rest. "A merchant, a sot and an old lady..."

Miss Tilly gasped and Suzanne squeezed her shoulder.

Stooping down, the stranger gazed at Suzanne. Even in her terror, she noted every detail of his rain-wet face. A sliver-thin scar showed above his bushy left eyebrow. He had a perfectly chiseled, handsome profile; a full, well-formed mouth; and white even teeth. His black rain-soaked hair curled around his neck. The expression in his deep-set ebony eyes immersed her. They stared at her—tormented, potent, yet curiously kind.

In the space of the moment in which they examined each other, Suzanne thought, *He's mine. I want him.* She lowered her eyes swiftly so he could not possibly guess what had startled her heart. "...and a young lady," he called out.

Among crude remarks and a brazen burst of laughter, one said, "Throw her out! We'll take our turns giving her pleasure."

Another said, "Take care of the lad and the others first. Get 'em out!"

Suzanne swallowed hard. She shuddered, remembering Miss Tilly's words. What if they kill James? Suzanne doubled over and hugged her knees. She mustn't be sick. She knew intuitively she would do anything to save James. She gently set Miss Tilly aside. Surprised at the commanding way she took control, Suzanne said, "Thieves such as yourselves must work fast on a night like this. Take what you will and let us go, for we must be at the docks midday tomorrow."

"My dear miss, you will take orders from me, not the other way around," the outlaw said, displaying an alarming flash of cold anger.

"Leave my cousin alone," James said. Then he lifted his arm to put it around Suzanne's waist, but too quickly. Surprised, the outlaw hit out with his pistol and caught James on the bone below his temple. He slid to the floor; blood gushed down the side of his cheek. Suzanne thought she saw an instant of remorse in the rogue's expression, but in a flash it had gone. She fell to her knees to cradle James' head on her lap.

With the edge of her chemise, she blotted at the flow of blood and bent down to speak softly to James. "Don't say another word. He's right. We are his prisoners."

"I'm all right," James said sheepishly.

"Not another word," Suzanne whispered.

"Silence," said the bandit. "Quit whispering, or we'll find out what it is you are saying."

"Give us the women," yelled one from the road, "and get rid of the bleedin' lad."

"It's a small cut, miss," the bandit told Suzanne in a low voice. "He'll be fine. If you will all do as I say, you will be on your way to Baltimore tomorrow."

Suzanne heard the sincerity. She looked up to find him studying her. Some kind of hurt and longing lay naked in his eyes. She looked down to find James' slash was bleeding profusely again and he had turned dangerously white. She reached below her dress and tore a wide ruffle off another petticoat and folded it into a thick bandage. In a few moments, James held it himself and Suzanne helped him back to a seat. To the bandit she said, "He will have a scar. You will pay for this."

"You are wrong, young miss. You will pay. Now, get out."

Suzanne's hand flew to her mouth. Her breast rose heavily. "You would turn me loose to that pack of mongrels?" She straightened and glared at him. "I told you to take anything but our lives. I meant it. We could as well stay here where it is dry."

The rogue nodded. "Whatever you wish."

"They're coming out," he called to the others. "I've tied the men's hands. Don't touch the old lady. She might die. The young one is mine."

A groan went up outside. Suzanne echoed it as she realized the full impact of what she had promised. *Dear James, understand,* she pleaded silently.

"We want her, too," a voice shouted.

"She's mine. Before this night, I've never picked a woman. Leave her alone." Then he turned to Suzanne. "I'll carry this coverlet under my cloak. The rain has turned to a mist. The trees will shelter us."

Suzanne half-lifted, half-pulled Miss Tilly to her feet. James rose shakily and climbed out. Holding the bloody linen to his head with one hand, he helped steady Miss Tilly with his free one. They wrapped her coat snugly around her and eased her down to the muddy ground. They had tied George to a nearby oak scrub. "Be careful, lass," he said.

Suzanne lowered herself beside him. "Did they hurt you?" she asked. Trying to forget what lay ahead for her, she fumbled with the ropes that tied him. He stopped her. "Don't. If'n you tamper with them knots, they'll turn agin us. I be all right. Go back to Miss Tilly and James. They'll protect you."

Suzanne didn't go back. She had promised her body for their lives. She watched as they ransacked the trunks and found the emerald ring and pendant that had been her mother's. They found the rest of her jewelry, too, and Miss Tilly's. They had stripped the men of their money and their gold watches and chain fobs. They had left James bleeding.

'They killed Captain Jerome and did terrible things to his lady,'

she recalled. As she ran past James and Miss Tilly, her cousin called out, "Don't let him take you. I'll kill him."

"Shush, James," Suzanne said. "I must do whatever the bandit says. I cannot put up a fight. Our lives are at stake. I must rely on his pledge to send us on our way after..." Suzanne choked back tears and ran on.

The three thieves gathered around Suzanne and roughly pushed her toward the coach. She jerked away. "Get your filthy fingers off me," she said.

Almost paralyzed with panic, yet resolute, she picked her way through the muddy ruts and puddles to the carriage. It stood intimidating in the blackness. "I'm ready," she said softly.

The bandit came to the door of the coach. "We won't need the trees. The thieves have finished with the carriage."

He reached down to help her mount the lofty step. Capturing her eyes, he studied her face with a puzzled gaze for an extra beat. Startled, she thought, *He's young, not yet thirty*.

In the muted light, his scrutiny was bold and assessed her candidly. His gaze dropped to her breasts. Then his eyes raked boldly over her until, finally, slowly and seductively his fingers slid over her with trembling eagerness. There was a tingling in the pit of her stomach and she fought an overwhelming craving to be close to him. She didn't know what was happening to her. She tried to stop the dizzying current racing through her. She felt liquid with fear, or was it anticipation?

Claiming her lips, he crushed her to him, while he yanked the door closed behind them.

Chapter 3

Suzanne and the bandit stood embraced. Rain beat on the roof of the carriage. From outside, a crass voice bellowed, "Hurry up in there. Git done with it, so we can be on our way. The rain be irksome and we got other things to do besides waitin' fer you to ravish the dame."

The bandit pulled away from Suzanne and threw his ragged cape on the seat. "Shut yourself up," he yelled back. "I'll be out when I'm ready. Go under the shelter of that grove of trees yonder."

He turned back to Suzanne and spoke in an odd, yet gentle tone. "Is this the first time?"

Suzanne wanted to throw herself on his mercy, but she had made a bargain. She responded matter-of-factly. "Let's just get on with it. My past does not concern you."

His lips recaptured hers, more demanding this time. His kiss was punishing and angry. He pulled back to whisper in her ear. "I don't intend to rape you, but I'll make you wish I had."

His tongue explored the recesses of her mouth and sent the hollow of her stomach into a wild swirl. When he broke away, Suzanne bit her lips to control threatening sobs. "Who are you?"

"More to the point, who are you, Suzanne? Who would let you travel alone with a young cousin, such a poor excuse for a protector?"

"I don't need protection. I can take care of myself." Suzanne's mouth went dry with horror. They had her gun. Without it, she couldn't take care of herself. He was toying with her.

"Who are you staying with in Baltimore? Answer me, young lady. We don't have all night."

He pulled her roughly, almost violently, to him. Twisting in his arms and arching her body, Suzanne sought to wrench free, but he easily sent her spinning to the cushions of the coach seat. He stood over her, then reached down and savagely ripped the silk, brick brown traveling dress and chemise from her shoulders. Then he stripped off his white shirt and threw it aside.

She moaned at the sense of personal violation, humiliation, but it was more than her nakedness. As he lowered his lips to tease her breasts, she felt the throbbing swell of her nipples. His tongue sent shivers of desire racing through her. Her eager response to his touch shocked her. Conflicting emotions tore at her. Although she felt an invisible web of attraction building between them, she knew he would be merely filling a moment of physical ecstasy. She would be allowing him to tear apart her soul. Suzanne knew that this act she so desperately burned for at this moment caused pain, and pregnancy. It had caused her mother's death.

Miss Abigail, Suzanne's spinster governess, had clearly conveyed the message that unless sanctified by marriage vows, the act was the deepest of shames. "Premature submission can ruin a young girl's chances of matrimony," she said often with sanctimonious firmness. With a flash of perceptive wit, Suzanne wondered if early surrender was the reason Miss Abigail had remained a spinster.

At the thought, and although Suzanne felt drugged by the bandit's manly scent and male closeness, her gentle laugh, mingled with only a tinge of hysteria, rippled through the air. The bandit stiffened. His fingers dug into her soft flesh and he regarded her quizzically for a moment before his curt voice lashed out at her. "I asked, where are you going? There's unrest in Baltimore. Your cousin and Miss Tilly are useless traveling companions. You may need help."

Sobered, Suzanne lifted her arms to cover her breasts. "Why should I tell you anything? You tell me nothing in return. Even thieves have names. How did you know my name and how did you know we are going to Baltimore?"

"Whoa, your questions come too rapidly. I asked old George. He begged me not to harm the 'young uns'. Said you and your cousin and the old lady are going to take the *Bianca*. I know her captain. Sometimes he carries cargo for me."

"Who are you?"

"My name is Tyrone Sterling. My dominant port is New York. I own the *Sea Queen*. I'm a merchantman, but the U.S. Navy has reinstated my officer status and commissioned my schooner. They're refitting and arming her to become a blockade excursion cruiser. The arrangement will better suit my purposes. Union protection and—"

Suzanne sputtered. "You're vile, loathsome, nothing but a mercenary without integrity or morals."

"It isn't true, but you must think what you will for now. We'll meet again. Depend on it."

Suzanne shivered and Tyrone lay down over her. Sliding

an arm and turning her slightly, he rubbed her back and slid his hand over her cold smooth buttocks. Involuntarily, she lifted herself to him and he pulled her closer, but said softly, "I'll help you slip into your torn dress and you can cover yourself with the blanket. No one will know I didn't rape you."

Out of the darkness a coarse voice yelled, "What's going on in there? Did ye tame the vixen?"

"Damn it, man, a minute more."

Tyrone reached down and kissed Suzanne's taut nipples, rousing a melting sweetness within her. Abruptly his arms went around her. She felt her breasts crush against the hardness of his chest and her defenses weakened. Slowly his hands moved downward, skimming either side of her body to her thighs and sliding the dress and petticoats lower. He explored her thighs then moved up to her taut stomach. Her thoughts fragmented as his hands and lips continued their hungry search of her body. Gusts of desire shook her and in a moment of uncontrolled passion, Suzanne rose to meet him. He clung to her an instant longer, then moaned and rolled away. His voice broke with huskiness, "My God, I've never taken a woman by force. I won't this night, but ever since I stepped into this coach I've wanted you, and more. I think fate has joined us."

Suzanne opened her eyes. She ached inside of her very being. His thick lashes moved up and she gazed into ebony eyes, and knew in a way she could never explain that he was not wicked and despicable, but probably honorable and sensitive. He was surely embittered, but incapable of cruelty, unable to commit evil. Suzanne's body still throbbed for his touch. Her telltale voice shook when she spoke. "I admit I shared your feeling of destiny, yet too terrified for James and the others to hope you would be lenient."

"I gave my word. Still you don't answer my question. What is your destination?"

"My grandfather is Dr. John Hanson, surgeon of Baltimore General Hospital. That's where I'm going. Satisfied?"

"We're leavin' ye, mate," called a voice from the dark. "We'll be at Cross Corner Tavern dividin' up the booty."

Tyrone shrugged. "I'll be along shortly. I'll settle for the emerald ring and pendant. You men split up the rest."

He reached under the seat and retrieved Suzanne's clutch. Returning it to her he said, "I salvaged your handbag. I stuffed a secret paper inside, which I'll be needing later. I can't take a chance that someone will find it on my person. Don't let anyone see that paper under any circumstances. I have to trust you, Suzanne. Now, do as I say. Scream as if your life depended upon it. They've got to think I raped you, or your party won't be safe. Now!"

Her eyes filled with tears of frustration. Her body fluttered with a yearning she didn't understand.

"Now!" he said.

Suzanne screamed, and screamed. Then sobbed.

The carriage door slammed shut.

Alone, Suzanne felt a wretchedness she had never imagined before. Added to the disappointment, a stab of guilt lay buried in her chest. She had wanted him desperately. She would have joyfully surrendered completely to his masterful seduction, but he left her without a backward glance.

He didn't want her.

Anguish overcame her slim thread of control, and Suzanne yielded to the compulsive sobs that shook her whole body. Then James was leaning over her, gently stroking her shoulder. "Suzanne," he said quietly, "he released us. We're ready to move out. They took four of our horses. It will slow us up, but we'll be in Norfolk in a couple of hours."

Suzanne clutched her dress and the blanket tighter. Miss Tilly was unaccountably pert and alert despite the recent terror and exposure to the wet, stormy night. She sat beside Suzanne and patted her hand. "You'll feel better after a hot bath and a good night's rest."

James said, "And, don't worry. I'll talk to Grandfather. He'll find the scoundrel and take care of him."

The carriage lurched forward. Suzanne answered James in a rush of words. "You can't tell Grandfather. You must promise me you won't. I'll talk to Grandmother, and she will decide what must be done. I'll handle this myself. Promise me, James."

Suzanne wanted to tell James that Tyrone had not raped her, but had used her unmercifully for reasons she couldn't know. He was greedy. He was using the cover of the U.S. Navy to take advantage of both honest Southern gentlemen and loyal Union men.

Tyrone was playing both sides against the Mason-Dixon Line. But she dared not confide in James until she found out what was on the paper the bandit had put in her handbag. Then she would find a way to thwart his plans. "Promise, James," she begged again.

James nodded. "But if I ever see him again..."

* * * *

For what seemed like hours of wrestling with some terrible nightmare, a stream of sunlight roused Suzanne. She dressed quickly in a fine broadcloth, grass-green morning frock. After piling her long curls on top of her head, she joined the others in the Bay View Inn dining room.

The Bandit's Lady

Breakfast was eggs over corn pone with thin slices of fried ham and curried cream sauce. The cook had fried the potatoes crisp and browned them evenly. Blueberries piled high on the hot cakes were served with rich thick cream poured over the top. A surly young barmaid slammed the plates down on the table in front of them. The coffee was strong and hot, laced with whiskey for the men. Suzanne toyed with her food. "Eat hearty, me young uns. Your trip on the *Bianca* be long, and the food, I hear tell, is not choice fare," George said.

"We're ready," James said, looking anxiously at Suzanne.

After friendly farewells all-round, she and James, Miss Tilly in tow, trailed out to the dock. The small steam frigate was ready for the passengers. The howling winds had spirited away the continuous rain that imprisoned them the previous day. The sea breeze that had knifed through the earlier cushioning silence of fog was suddenly sweet, the air pungent.

Suzanne watched curiously as a small cluster of Negroes, glancing about furtively, climbed aboard and disappeared down the hatch of the *Bianca*. Runaway slaves, she decided with a stab of confusion. She wondered briefly what manner of cargo Tyrone Sterling sent to Baltimore with Captain Neal Franklin.

* * * *

Suzanne spent the first day traveling across the Bay on her cot. She slept and cried by fits and turns. Her whole body felt heavy and sensually disturbed. Tyrone Sterling's name lingered on her lips. She knew she would not forget a single detail of his face. She hungered from the memory of his mouth on hers and recalled the ecstasy she felt when he held her nakedness against his strong, hard body. Until now, she had been unaware of the ardent passion within her. No more, she thought in agony.

By evening, Suzanne savored the simple supper served to them, a bowl of thin vegetable gruel served with corn cake. Dessert was a strongly spiced deep-dish apple pie.

In the morning, an hour before time to dock, James found Suzanne admiring the Chesapeake at the rail of the slim deck. Feeling his presence beside her, she said, "It's an amazing and magnificent intricate lacework of bays."

In his poet voice, without a crackle, he caressed her with words from their childhood, by William Bradford, *Of Plymouth Plantation:*

> *Being thus arrived in a good harbor, and brought safe to land, they fell upon their knees and blessed the God of Heaven who had brought them over the vast and furious ocean, and delivered them from all the perils and miseries thereof, again to set their feet on the firm and stable earth, their proper element.*

"Thank you, James," Suzanne said, touching his hand. "I have been acting the pampered purist. Forgive me. I'm better now."

"It's all my fault, really."

"No! You mustn't even think it. You can't understand, for I've not told you the whole of it, nor can I... Let's forget that horrible night and enjoy the rest of the voyage."

The cousins basked under the warm spring sun. It stood proud in the white sky overlooking dazzling blue water rippling gently toward the shoreline. Pointing toward the teeming piers and ramshackle commercial establishments, James said, "I see land, but listen. What's that noise?"

They stretched their ears to hear the hysterical chanting of the faceless mob. Suzanne said, "It sounds like guns."

Captain Neal Franklin came up beside them and introduced himself. He was a blue-eyed, round-faced, little man with faded freckles down his arms and haphazard sandy hair on a balding head. He wielded an unlighted pipe in his left hand. "I've been searching the coast with my eyeglass. Hostile crowds are surging toward those soldiers. It looks like a riot. You must remain on the *Bianca* until we find out what's going on."

Suzanne surveyed the dark knot of people and a horde of grimy children as they gathered on the shoreline. Then she turned back to the Captain. "But we cannot. Grandfather will be waiting for us, and Miss Tilly's niece will be there. You can't keep us here."

"It doesn't look like anyone will be meeting you. Anyhow, let us make sure it's safe for you to go ashore."

"I'm sorry, Captain. I know you mean well, but we will be on our way. Grandfather won't let anything happen to us."

Suzanne turned on her heel and disappeared rapidly down the hatch to gather up her belongings. Minutes later, she and James stood again on the deck. They studied the mob. "What do you think is happening?" James asked.

Suzanne concentrated on the scene before them. Then gesturing, she said, "I just heard that bunch yelling 'Secede! Secede!' The group over there threatened to burn the Union flag."

James pulled at Suzanne's hand, "Look, those people are throwing stones. Maybe the captain is right and we should go below until it's safer."

"But, we can't. Look," she said. "There's Grandfather

waiting for us. Let's make a dash for it."

Captain Franklin stepped between them and the gangplank. "I've sent a couple of men to see if it's safe. Stay here. We'll inform Dr. Hanson of your arrival. He can collect you when the danger is over."

Suzanne defied him with enthusiasm. "Oh, Captain, you worry too much. Grandfather is within a short sprint."

Twirling to James, she said, "Are you willing, Cousin?"

She glimpsed his unrestrained appetite for adventure light up a sly twinkle in his eyes. "Let's go!"

He grabbed her hand and they ran together down the ship's ramp to the gangway and pier. Once among the angry mass of people, Suzanne felt shoved and squeezed and pushed. Jammed against the side of a dilapidated building, James was snatched away. Suzanne screamed, but no sound came.

She gagged as the foul stench of the man who had clamped her mouth shut reached her nostrils. She was hanging sideways, clutched easily under the left arm of the kidnapper. She looked up quickly. James was nowhere in sight and Suzanne was unable to follow with her eyes the path where she had last seen their grandfather.

Suzanne hammered at the offender with quick, clumsy punches, then bit him viciously, desperately. An eruption of filthy words made her look up. She found small, snake-like black eyes glittering at her. "Leave it alone, lady," he said ruthlessly, "I'm takin' you where you won't be causin' no trouble."

Suzanne's body slumped in despair. She closed her eyes, feeling utterly miserable, as she recognized the voice of one of Tyrone Sterling's cohorts.

Chapter 4

Suzanne clutched her handbag. She still had the pistol. If she could get it out of its pouch, maybe she could escape. Her mind raced, but she decided not to make any sudden moves. She would bide her time, act when they arrived at their destination.

A second thief joined them. He placed a grubby handkerchief across her eyes and tied it around her head. He slapped a wide-brimmed hat on top of her head. It hid the dark auburn curls shining in the brilliant sunlight. "That'll keep her so they won't know who she is," he said to his companion.

Between them they half-carried, half-dragged Suzanne through the crazed crowd. When quiet reached her ears, she knew they were in back streets where the rioting had subsided, or not existed. "Are you taking me to my grandfather?"

"Shut up. If'n you're lucky, you'll see your dear grandpapa when we gets good and ready to take you there."

They stopped. A door creaked. A musky smell assailed Suzanne's nostrils as he herded her inside. The kidnapper roughly removed the hat and yanked the blindfold away. Then he pushed her onto a dirty unmade bed in a corner of the tiny room. Wrinkling her nose in disgust, she said, "This stinks." Without comment, the thieves moved through another door.

Sunshine filtered through the cracks of the primitive wooden structure. Its dust-filled rays emphasized the squalor and exposed the collection of cobwebs. Suzanne heard raised voices and put her ear to the thin partition.

"Well, wise one, what are we going to do with the dame?"

"We'll keep her for Tyrone."

"I say we pleasure her and let him have what's left."

A third voice, from a man Suzanne figured must have entered by a back door or had been waiting there for them, joined the conversation. "Ye can't take the girl. Just leave her be. Tyrone'll know what to do."

The second man said, "Maybe she's got the paper in that bag she's gripping so hard. I say we find out before he gets back. If'n she's got it, we let her go. We takes her back to the dock to find her own way and him will be none the wiser."

"Get away with you. I didn't steal the dame to be lettin' her go. I got her to trap Tyrone. You saw how he looked at her. He needs subduin'. He's gettin' out o' hand. He won't be lookin' for us fer lots o' days."

"I think he's got that paper. If we don't get hold of it, we can't find them Yankees. Tyrone's been actin' strange. I think he's got friends on both sides and is playin' us for fools."

Suzanne backed away from the wall. She opened her purse and took out the pistol. She tucked it into the waist of her crinoline and threw the handbag back on the bed.

They had reminded her of the slim bulge inside her pantalets. When she had dressed in the morning, she wrapped the paper in a linen handkerchief and tucked it inside her brown stockings. Feeling above her left knee, she found the paper intact. It didn't even crinkle.

Cautiously, Suzanne crept to the front door. She would leave and find her way to her grandfather's home. But the door was locked and no amount of pulling and tugging could jar it loose. Finally, she sat on the edge of the bed to wait.

In a very few moments the door from the back of the house opened. As the men entered, stale blue cigar smoke and the stench of stale black coffee invaded the room. The kidnapper spoke, "Okay, young lady, we want the paper. Give me your purse."

"You've no right…"

"Give it to me!" He grabbed her arm roughly.

Suzanne shrugged resignedly. Wishing she had discarded the pouch, she handed him the handbag. "There ain't no paper," he growled, looking up at the others, "but look here." He held up the velvet sack. "She's got a gun. It's probably on her. Take it!"

Suzanne felt nausea welling up inside her. With a sinking feeling of despair, she shrank away, but the third thief grasped her around the waist. "I'll be havin' the honor of findin' the gun."

The thief's hand trailed on her hair. "Soft as a feather, and the color of a copper coin."

"Ain't it a crime, saving the wench for him? Why not we all give her something to remember us by?"

"Leave her be like I said, both of you. Get the gun!"

Suzanne felt her temper flare in response to her fear. She shot him a cold look. "The bandit took the pistol on that muddy night near Norfolk. Have you already forgotten you stole all our valuables and left us with only two horses to slow us down on our way to the inn?"

"I like you, young miss. You got spunk." His arm tightened while his other hand roamed over her body searching for the weapon. When he felt a bulge at her waist, he shoved her flat on the bed and reached his hands under her ruffled green skirt. As quickly, his hands moved under her bodice to grip and roughly mash her breasts.

With her mind half-chilled with numbness, Suzanne let her body rebel against the violence. She kicked and squirmed. All at once she gave a wild kick, then saw a sudden blazing brightness across her eyes before her body went limp.

She came to on the hard, bumpy mattress of the iron bed. A gag filled her mouth. Suzanne moved tentatively. Her hands and feet were free. She gently stroked the swelling on her head. Dried blood covered the egg-shaped lump where the thief had hit her with the butt of her own pistol.

It was dark. A coarse blanket covered her. Suzanne tried to sit up, but managed only to roll over. Something crawled on her neck. She swatted it away. She cried, and remembered the night she lay in the bandit's arms.

He would come for her. Tyrone would.

* * * *

In the morning Suzanne awoke with a start. This time she propped herself up easily and looked around. Her furnishings were the bed with its smelly dingy bedclothes, a low stool on which a chipped porcelain pitcher and matching bowl sat. In the opposite corner was a battered tin chamber pot.

Suzanne carefully splashed water from the pitcher on the bruise above her temple. It's coolness was soothing. She scrubbed the rest of her as well as she could, thankful they had not violated her womanhood. She examined her hosiery. The men had overlooked the paper.

The tiny unglazed window set high in the wall admitted a little light. The day had dawned cool, but bright. Suzanne watched a graceful white-and-gray sea gull swoop and straighten and fly on its way. She thought she must be somewhere near the harbor.

Her stomach growled. She realized she had not eaten since the skimpy noon meal before the *Bianca* docked. Alone and solitary, caged, Suzanne paced the narrow room. *Grandmother, Grandfather and James must think me dead,* she thought.

Unanswerable questions clutched at her like icy fingers. Where was James? Lost in the crowd? Dead? Did he get safely to Grandfather Hanson?

Suzanne flinched. James and their grandfather knew each other only by the exchange of portraits that she had carried back and forth during the years of her visits. She felt solely responsible for James' fate and wished she had not challenged him to participate in such a reckless, irresponsible act. She knew if anything happened to him, she would never forgive herself.

* * * *

Stripped down and scrubbing her undergarments, Suzanne sighed. She had tried to keep track of the time she had spent in this dismal room. If she had counted all the days since leaving Charleston, next week would be her birthday.

Thinking there was little danger of the thieves searching her handbag again for the paper, Suzanne had carefully picked a hole in a seam of the purse and transferred the paper inside its lining. The Negro, Rufus, brought her one large meal each day.

The first day, Suzanne did not eat, but after that decided to eat the deplorable fare. It would give her strength to escape, in case she found a way. Immediately upon receiving the tin tray, she would spoon up the lukewarm soup, usually a watery-thin bean broth with a chunk of salty pork fat. The one slice of cornbread, though overly generous, lacked the thick, rich cream she dearly loved to pour over it. She dunked half of the crumbly cornmeal ration in the soup and saved the other half to eat with her morning glass of water.

The rest of the supper varied from day to day. Sometimes it was a half-baked potato and a bruised apple. At other times, a piece of undercooked beef, an overripe banana, or other equally unappetizing combinations. It didn't matter. Suzanne ate it all, and was hungry.

The first night the black man introduced himself, Suzanne looked at his face. Deep smallpox pits had scared it. He had crooked yellow teeth, and his bright eyes glittered from deep-set sockets. He was a small wiry little man, almost childish in appearance, but white hair belied that fact. "I'm Rufus," he said shyly. "I be not supposed to talk to you, but I be telling you jus' the same that you be safe."

"When can I leave? Do you know what happened to my cousin? Do my grandparents know I'm alive?"

Rufus put his fingers to his lips and silently left the shack. In the days following, Suzanne cried and paced. She counted seven steps from the bed to the window, seven steps back. She would flop on the bed and remember the summer visits with her grandparents.

* * * *

Grandmother Hanson's beloved housekeeper, Zoe Jackson, had a daughter six months older than herself. Dr. John and Margaret Hanson had bought Zoe from their neighbor, Mr. Thomas, after Zoe's husband died by a spooked horse. They gave Zoe her freedom papers immediately and Polly was born a week later. Suzanne smiled at the thought of seeing Polly again. She had grown genteel and proper under Grandmother's faithful supervision. Her dark olive skin was smooth and flawless. Her body was slender, hips slim. Her chocolate-brown fiery eyes glowed.

It was hard for Suzanne to think of Polly without chuckling at their antics. They had hidden in the hay to frighten Henry the gardener. He never got over jumping in surprise when they leaped out at him.

They climbed high in the apple trees to scare Zoe when she called them for dinner and then had to watch them scurry down. And, enjoying the lapping water caress their tender, sensuous young skin, they swam nude in the pond behind the pasture at the edge of the forest. *Thank goodness,* Suzanne thought now, *no one had caught them at that.*

Suzanne's favorite times were when she and Polly went to the city. Baltimore was full of activity and culture. Grandfather Hanson had educated Polly as if she were his child. She had attended school regularly. She could read and write and enjoy the cultural enrichment with Suzanne.

Many of their outings began with Polly saying, "Today I want to be the famous Mary Young Pickersgill. Let's go to the waterfront and stand in front of the flag house on Pratt Street."

Suzanne said, "I want to see the George Washington Monument in the city square."

Their day of sight-seeing included hours of admiring the Rembrandt and Charles Wilson Peale portraits and the rich memorabilia of the Revolutionary War collected at the Peale Museum. On the way home, the girls bought ribbons and trinkets, and munched their way along the stalls of Lexington Market. The strong fish smells were well worth the taste of delectable crab cakes made of the savory backfin meat.

On rare and beautiful occasions, Grandmother Hanson took them to a performance at the Baltimore Music Hall. Or they visited the Dickey Woolen Mill and purchased soft, exquisite pieces of wool goods at the company store for Zoe to sew into garments. On the way home they ate frog legs, delicately sautéed in buttery garlic sauce, at the Lady Baltimore Tea Room. More than once, Grandmother insisted they eat five-layer cake for dessert.

Grandfather Hanson also helped expand their horizons. He escorted them to the shipyards where they watched the shipbuilders working. Sometimes they went to the Mount Clare Railroad Station at Pratt and Poppleton Streets, where they ate fish soup while they watched the laborers loading freight. The excursion always ended with a short train ride that took them close to home. The girls would run and skip the rest of the way to Hanson Racing Stable yards, while Grandfather followed at a more leisurely pace.

* * * *

Until last night, Rufus had not spoken another word but silently delivered the meal. Then he had whispered, "Soon."

There were two wooden pegs on the wall where the sunshine was the hottest. Suzanne wrung the water out of the garments she was washing, then hung them up to dry. She would be ready, she thought, if she could leave this night. Rufus had given her a sign. Something was up.

The sun had moved to the west side of the shack when Suzanne pulled on the clean undergarments and brown cotton hose. She had begun to slip the soiled green dress over her body when she heard the key turn in the lock of the far back door.

She knew the sun was still too high for the intrusion to be Rufus. Steps pounded across the small back room—too many and not lightly enough to be Rufus'. Suzanne's heart began to throb. She tried to get the dress in place. She backed up to the wall in the shadows away from the sun and sank onto the stool. The second door swung open.

The kidnapper set down the supper tray. He gazed at Suzanne with a lust she had not seen before on his face. His eyes glittered. "We be changin' our mind. We still thinks you got the paper; it be time for a closer look."

By the look in his eyes, Suzanne did not believe that looking for the paper was the only thing they had on their minds. The other two thieves stood leering, waiting their turns, she supposed. One spoke. "No need botherin' with the fasteners on ye dress. Looks a bit like you was expectin' us, maybe anticipatin'. Ye been hankerin' for some lovin'?"

Moving toward her with slow calculation, the kidnapper traced Suzanne's cheek with his finger. Her heart banged against her chest, her throat felt like cotton, and hot tears slipped down her cheeks. "You can't. You know I don't have the paper you're looking for. Please leave."

His hand coursed down her neck, hesitating at her rapid pulse. "Ye told us the bandit took your pistol. We figure if ye lied once, ye would again."

His lips parted and he touched his lower lip with his tongue. With a quick sharp blow, he broke apart her clasped fingers and slowly raised his hands to cup her breasts.

Suzanne's gaze never left his face; she felt paralyzed, then faint with fear. The kidnapper smirked. His fingers tightened their hold. He turned to the others. "Undress her slow. Check every piece of clothin' for that scrap of paper. Then we'll decide what to do with this temptin' body."

While the kidnapper looked on, the others lifted her, almost tenderly, to the bed. One held her hands above her head. The other one slipped the dress up and over her head. Like a child too weak to resist, Suzanne lay quiet, prostrate. She thought... *and did terrible things to his lady.*

She closed her eyes and felt the considerate way they took off each piece of clothing: the dress, the chemise, petticoats, the pantalets and, finally, the brown stockings. "There ain't nothin' here," one said in disgust. "I'll take me turn."

She felt the blood drain from her face and clenched her jaw to kill the sob in her throat while she watched him through lowered lashes. He impatiently unfastened his belt and dropped his trousers.

Without warning, the front door burst open.

Chapter 5

Standing framed in the glow of the early evening sunset, Tyrone took in the whole scene at a glance. In two strides, he seized the thief by his neckerchief and pulled him upright. Suzanne's breath caught in her throat. She couldn't tear her eyes away from his magnificent profile. A delightful shiver of wanting ran through her. *My bandit.*

"What the devil's going on here? Where did you get the girl?" Tyrone said, sounding enraged.

"We was lucky to find her at the dock. She ran out on the *Binaca* to find her folks."

"Where's the boy?"

"We separated them, let him go. We want the paper. We figure she might have it."

"Do you think I'm an idiot? Get back to the house, all of you."

Suzanne swiftly pulled on her clothes. The third thief slipped her delicate, pearl-handled pistol out of his pants pocket and handed it to her. She put it at her waist where he had first found it. As respectfully as they had undressed her, he helped her off the bed and fastened the row of buttons up the back of her frock. The kidnapper held his ground. "There's three of us against you, Tyrone. We think you're pullin' somethin' over our ears. We'll keep the girl till we finds out what you're up to."

The other two men dragged Suzanne between them toward the far room, but Tyrone was quicker. He pulled out his gun and brandished it before them. "Let the girl go, or you'll be dead. I've worked with you scoundrels nearly a year. I've been more than fair and you well know it. When I want to cheat on you, I'll quit your company."

The men let Suzanne go. She fled to stand beside Tyrone.

One of them said, "He's right, ye know. We ain't got no real grumble."

The other one moaned. "I sure did want that dame. She felt real good."

The kidnapper nodded to Tyrone. "Maybe you're right, but I'll be watchin' ye. Don't pull no more funny business."

Tyrone's black eyes snapped. He smiled mischievously. "Get out of here. Have Rufus get the rig ready. I'll take Suzanne to her grandparents. We've work to do this night."

Relief flooded Suzanne's pounding heart. She struggled with the uncertainty that aroused her, but as the bandit turned to her, the lively twinkle in his eye angered her. "I suppose your work this night is marauding and stealing and molesting."

A sudden chill was in his voice as he said, "Of my work, I can speak little." His expression changed. Something disturbing replaced his smoldering look. "Let's be friends, Suzanne. We will meet often, though I can't tell you what I do. For now, I ask that you do my bidding, and trust me."

Suzanne walked across the room to the high, tiny window. All she could see was the small patch of sky. It was getting dark. Turning back, she watched Tyrone open his arms.

His voice was carefully neutral, with only a trace of intimate huskiness, "Come here, my love."

A shadow of alarm touched her. "I can't, Tyrone." The bandit's name rolled off her tongue in an awed whisper.

Tyrone took a step closer. When he spoke again, his voice was tender, almost a murmur. "Yes, you can. I won't hurt you. I won't even make love to you. We must be very careful, and we haven't the time, but let me hold you for a few minutes."

Suzanne shivered. The dark blue, double-breasted Union Navy uniform enhanced his swarthy good looks. She sensed his power. As if in a dream, she walked into his embrace. He softly touched the pale blue of the healing bruise. "Did they hurt you, my love? Did they have their way with you? If they did, I'll kill them."

She shook her head. He held her closer. He said in quiet, hushed tones in her ear, "I want you so much. I've thought of nothing else since we met."

His steady gaze, soft as a caress, traveled over her face and searched her eyes, then moved slowly over her body. Suzanne felt happiness fill her. "I, too, have thought of nothing else," she snapped. "Thanks to you, I've had no peace, but we are worlds apart. You are a Union officer. My heart is in Charleston with my father. We have nothing in common."

"Shush, my dauntless one." Tyrone bent and kissed her lips gently, passionately.

Suzanne's breasts rose and fell rapidly, taut against her gown. She knew he could feel her yearning. The moist tip of her tongue crept into his mouth. He moved his mouth over hers, devouring its softness. A fire spread through her as he pressed his hard body against hers. While they clung to each other, darkness stole over the room. Tyrone was the first to move away.

He made a queer sound deep in his throat and, although amusement flickered in the eyes that met hers in the moonlight coming from the tiny window, his voice was tight with emotion. "I've discovered why your pistol intrigued my companions. You've placed it in a fascinating position. Is the paper also protected with such care? I'll need it soon, but I dare not risk the taking of it this night."

Suzanne flinched at the puritanical, unfamiliar accent in his speech. Yet she thought how easily she could get lost in the way he looked at her. She said, "Of course, it's protected. Would you expect less of me?" Then she recovered her usual high spirits and grinned.

Tyrone's large hand took her face and held it gently. Suzanne sensed a reluctance as he spoke, this time in a dull and troubled voice. "You must be careful. Your association with me could be dangerous."

Sudden anger touched her. "How did you come to pick me on which to foist your treasured paper?"

He leaned forward. His voice dropped in volume. "I am sorry, Suzanne. I can't answer your questions. We must get you back to your grandparents before Dr. Hanson finds you here."

Pushing back a wayward strand of dark hair, Suzanne closed her other hand over his. "I'm sure he wouldn't know where to begin to search for me. If he did, he would have been here days ago. I've been a prisoner, you know. I'm ready to go now."

Brow creased with worry, Suzanne watched Tyrone open the door and pause on the threshold to look around. Then he tucked her hand under his arm and led her through the darkness. Hesitating, he halted momentarily before slipping around and through the twisted alleys. He ignored her completely as he quickly guided her along. After what seemed like hours, Tyrone stopped. "Catch your breath," he said quietly. "We're almost there. I see the coach. Rufus is waiting for us."

Then he swept her up in his arms and bolted for the carriage. A shot whistled over their heads and fear clutched at Suzanne's heart. "Hang on," Tyrone said. "They won't pursue us."

In the quiet of the night, the only sounds were those of the clip-clop of the horses' hooves on the hard dirt streets. Suzanne glanced at Tyrone. Lines of concentration lay deep along his brows and under his black eyes. "I think it's time you stopped playing games with me, Tyrone," she said softly. "There's obviously something more I should know about you."

She followed his gaze out into the night. The hour was late. They had passed through endless rows of shack-like houses. The neighborhood through which they rode now was quiet. Inside the sprawling, prosperous-looking old houses, people were extinguishing lamps. He answered wearily, "I have had a long day, Suzanne. The secessionists triggered the ruckus that caused the riots this week. It was an attack on the Sixth Massachusetts Regiment down between President and Camden Streets' railroad stations. You happened to dock during the worst of it.

"Federal soldiers have already begun searching the homes of Confederate sympathizers to confiscate weapons and documents. It's going to get rough. We don't know where it will end. Many Confederate sympathizers will be imprisoned. Your grandfather could be in difficulty."

"What kind of difficulty? Are you accusing my grandfather of being a troublemaker against the Union? How do you know my grandfather? Why do you spend your time with those despicable men?"

"You're doing it again, Suzanne. You're asking questions faster than I can answer, ones I can't answer."

Tyrone reached out and drew Suzanne into the circle of his arms. "I'm sorry I can't put your mind at rest or tell you anything that will change your mind about me. Let me hold you a moment longer. Then we must part. Be patient, my little one."

Suzanne heard a deep longing in his gentle voice. Exhausted, she leaned toward him and raised her face to his. She could feel his uneven breathing on her cheek as he held her close. Then he kissed the top of her head, and his lips grazed her earlobe. He kissed her eyes, the tip of her nose and, finally, his lips were warm and sweet on hers. The kiss left Suzanne weak and puzzled. She struggled to conquer her involuntary reactions to his tender, loving look. "How can I go on like this when I can't find reason to trust you. You steal from me, force threatening papers into my care, slander my grandfather and ignore my questions."

She jerked away from him as anger boiled up inside her. "I don't expect to see you ever again. Leave me alone now. We'll soon be at Grandfather's."

Suzanne turned toward the window and watched familiar scenes come into view, but Tyrone pulled her around to face him. "Please, listen to me, Suzanne. We're going to let you out of the carriage to finish the short way by foot. You must remember to do as I tell you. Don't let anyone know I didn't rape you the night before you boarded the *Bianca*. As for your

The Bandit's Lady

disappearance, tell your grandparents the same men kidnaped you and searched you, but tonight they grew careless. You escaped their shanty while they were discussing your fate in the back room. It's important to your safety that everyone thinks we are enemies. Don't mention my name; call me the bandit."

With an effort, Suzanne bit back a retort.

Tyrone called to Rufus. "Pull over under cover of that grove of white oaks. Miss Suzanne will get out. I'll wait in the coach while you see her safely inside the doctor's home. You know the rules; don't let anyone see you."

The carriage stopped and Suzanne started to get out, but she couldn't resist one last barb. "It is strange that a Union officer would own a slave."

Their eyes met and Suzanne felt an instant of shared passion. She quivered a little under the impact of his gaze. Tyrone leaned forward and touched her hand. "Enough tonight. Rufus will see you safe."

As she stepped out of the carriage, Suzanne thought she heard him whisper, "Thee and me will meet again."

When she looked back, he had disappeared behind the closed door.

Suzanne looked about to get her bearings. She could barely make out her grandparent's home in the distance. In the shadows of the ancient, dilapidated shade trees that protected both sides of the lane, the pathway ahead lay dark and ominous. Rufus was nowhere in sight.

As Suzanne began the long trek toward the house, she tried to swallow her fear, but her mind wouldn't relax. Panic welled up in her throat as her thoughts jumped on. She wondered why somebody had taken a shot at them earlier. She wondered who Rufus was, where he was now, and if he was stalking her. The silent figure continued to trouble her. She felt a sense of walking through a dark hostile tunnel. As if to emphasize the sensation, the night sky was strangely empty of stars. Threatening, billowing clouds rolled across the moon to cast grotesque shadows across her path.

She stopped a minute to listen to the incessant din of a million cicadas screaming into the lonely rustle of the night breeze. She envisioned all the slimy things that lived in the earth and came out at night, and the curious, squeaky animals. Suzanne inspected the trees arching thick over the lane. They seemed to reach down for her, and as she started on again a cobweb hanging from a low branch brushed her face. She recoiled, then wiped her cheek and chided herself. Where was her old, adventuresome streak? She was within five minutes of grandfather's house.

She winced at the sound of snapping twigs and the screech of a startled owl nearby. Feeling utterly alone, Suzanne stopped again to search the shadows. The warm spring air was close and moist. That, and the fear, made it hard to breathe, but she pulled her thin cape closer and broke into a run.

As she approached more familiar ground, Suzanne passed the stables and thought she heard her roan, Ginny, neighing softly. Out of breath, Suzanne slowed. Beyond the old stables, built into the rise of the hill that led to the pasture land, stood a beautiful new barn. It gleamed white in the dancing moonlight. Perplexed, she wondered why her grandmother had not mentioned the new barn in her letters, and why her grandfather needed another barn. She decided to ask him in the morning.

She reached the front lawn and paused to gaze at the house, built in the style of a Georgian mansion. Though it appeared completely dark, Suzanne saw a thin thread of light showing underneath the drape of the parlor. She again broke into a run. She took the porch steps two at a time. Even as she began to knock, the door opened and Zoe reached for Suzanne and embraced her anxiously. "Oh, Miz Suzanne, Miz Suzanne, thank de good Lord you is home. We is so scared. Dey has taken Doctor Hanson to prison. Your grandmama is plumb wore out a worryin' and a waitin' up late nights fer you. She be in the parlor."

Seconds before Suzanne entered the dim lamp-lit foyer, she glimpsed Rufus scampering away into deeper shadows. All thoughts of Rufus and the bandit vanished as Suzanne hurried to her grandmother. Kneeling before her, Suzanne put her head in Margaret Hanson's lap, exactly as when they had first met. Tears of joy and sadness flowed down her cheeks. "Oh, Grandmother, how awful for you. I'm so sorry for all your worry. Every bit of it was my fault."

"Hush, now," Margaret said, not a bit sternly. "It's nobody's fault."

"Where is James? Is he all right?"

"He's here, sleeping. He broke his leg during the revolt, but he's better now. Charlie fixed him up better than new with a crutch. You'll see for yourself tomorrow."

When she finished speaking, Suzanne felt her face flush with humiliation and anger at herself. "If only I hadn't insisted on tearing out to find Grandfather."

The tears came again. "Where is Grandfather? Zoe said they…they took him away. Who took him? Where did they take him? Where is Polly? Why didn't she come to meet me?"

Margaret Hanson burst into laughter. "Child, child, you never did quit asking nonstop questions. Your grandfather didn't come back after going to bring you and James home. A kind Negro helped James get home."

Suzanne marveled at her grandmother's serenity.

"Don't concern yourself about your grandfather; he'll be back despite my worry. We aren't sure who forced him to leave, but we think he is safe at Fort McHenry where they took the prisoners."

With tender hands, she smoothed Suzanne's dark unruly curls. "There is so much to tell you, but it's too late. It's enough that you are safe. Run up to bed. Your room is ready and Captain Neal Franklin safely delivered your trunks. You and I will have a long talk in the morning."

Finally drained, Suzanne hugged her grandmother's tiny, bony frame. Shocked to find her more frail this year, she looked up. Pure white hair softened the deep lines of Margaret Hanson's face, but tonight her bright blue eyes reflected the hours of strain. "Will you sleep, too?"

"Soon, my child. Don't fret."

Chapter 6

Without a glance at the familiar rooms, Suzanne walked to the elegant spiral staircase. She picked up a candle from the small round oak table and climbed the stairs to the bedroom she loved as her own. Chilled with exhaustion, she prepared for bed. She slipped into the pale yellow, flannelet gown Zoe had laid out for her. Its softness soothed her tired, tortured body.

Suzanne blew out the candle and stepped to the open window. She looked lovingly at her grandparents' cherished estate, bathed now in bright moonlight. She smelled the fragrant sweetness of spring earth.

Warm, happy memories flooded through her as she gazed at the paddock where Charlie trained and exercised the race horses kept by her grandfather. John had little time at home. Between the hospital and house calls he spent long busy hours with sick patients, but he loved the horses with a tender passion. Grandfather Hanson had promised her and Polly that this year they could attend the popular horse races. He did not know about the times they hid in the woods behind the track and cheered Hanson race horses to victory.

Although Suzanne had ridden a horse since she could sit on one, it was Grandfather Hanson who had patiently taught her the delicate finesse of riding and jumping. They spent many early morning hours riding together during her long summer visits. After their ride, they ate a leisurely, generous meal in the sunny east breakfast room off the kitchen. It was the same room in which the serving girls and the stable boys took their meals.

Suzanne's grandfather refused to eat in the large, formal dining room unless his wife was present. Margaret Hanson never presented herself for the day until she had her tea and toast, which was served in her bedroom.

Suzanne smiled at yet another memory. The days Grandfather Hanson had let her follow him on rounds at the hospital and on house visits were special. He often said, "You're my cheerful little helper. Someday you'll be a nurse."

She had laughed at him and said, "Oh, Grandfather, never. I'm going to live the life of a Southern belle until my coming-out party at Father's Christmas Ball. Then a handsome, young man of at least twenty and four will court me and marry me and we'll have babies. Then, my dear Grandfather, I'll spend the rest of my life being a Southern lady. I'll run a grand mansion and arrange splendid balls."

A sob caught in Suzanne's throat. She leaned on the windowpane and cradled her head in her hands. They had taken him away, put him in prison. *Oh, Grandfather, I'm so sorry. This was all my fault.*

The scene before her abruptly changed. With a pang, she realized the small figure dressed in a dark cloak was her grandmother. She was carrying a basket across the grounds from the smokehouse to the new barn. With a shake of her

The Bandit's Lady

head, she dismissed her apprehension. *That's ridiculous,* she thought. *Probably a mare is foaling and grandmother is going to see if Charlie needs help.*

Suzanne turned away from the window and crawled into bed. In the drowsy warmth of the covers, her last waking image before she drifted into sleep was of Tyrone.

* * * *

Two raps sounded on Suzanne's bedroom door. James poked his head around the corner. "Happy Birthday, sleepy head. Come on, Cousin, are you going to spend this whole day in bed?"

Suzanne pulled the covers over her head. "Go away, pest. Don't you know when to leave a sleeping lady alone?"

Then peeking out, she noticed his crutch and suddenly remembered. She leaped out of bed to stand before him. "Oh, James, do you know how I've scolded myself for my terrible foolishness? Can you forgive me?"

"Hush, silly. I was having the time of my life until they tore you from my grasp. Of course, it was a worry not knowing where you were or how you fared. But I came to tell you the good news."

"What good news? With Grandfather heaven knows where…"

James clapped his hands over his ears, his mood suddenly buoyant. "Come on, Cousin, give me a listen. Grandfather is home. That's the…"

"How did he get here? Why didn't you call me? Where is he?"

"My, how you do pump a person for details. Suzanne, there is something you should know before we go in to see Grandfather. They beat him, then somebody brought him home and dumped him on the porch. Zoe heard a disturbance early this morning and found him there."

Suzanne felt her legs grow weak. She sat in the wing-backed chair and put her face in her hands. "Oh, how beastly. How does he seem?"

"Grandmother said he's cheerful. He says the men who brought him home tried to protect him from harm, but arrived too late."

"Who brought him?"

"Zoe says she saw a stooped little Negro man disappear into the thick stand of white oaks at the lane. Grandfather wouldn't comment, except to say that he helped him get home. Come on. Let's go see him."

Suzanne thought of Rufus, then shook her head to clear it. "Give me a few minutes to get dressed, James. I'll meet you in the east breakfast room. We'll make sure he's up to seeing us before we go in."

* * * *

When Suzanne entered the bedroom an hour later, John Hanson was sitting in his favorite old black-leather rocking chair. Her grandmother had pulled a straight, fashionable, cane chair up beside him. They sat close, holding hands.

Suzanne felt both relief and joy at the sight of them. John's green eyes sparkled in spite of the ugly black bruises around them. If he was to stand up, she noted, he would stand as tall and erect as ever. His silvery hair was sparkling clean, his face shaved.

Together, Suzanne thought, *my grandparents have grown old with a silent dignity. They've aged so gracefully, so happily.* "You look for all the world like comfortable, wise old lovers," she said.

The Bandit's Lady

She dropped a light kiss on the tiny bald spot at the crown of her grandfather's head, then lowered herself opposite them on the cumbersome, antiquated, French settee.

"Grandfather, what really happened to you? Why did they hold you prisoner? Where is James? He was supposed to meet me in the breakfast room."

"Dear ones," Grandmother said, "I'll leave you alone. Suzanne will keep you busy answering questions, John, until it's time for you to rest." She gave them a slight salute and bustled out of the room.

Suzanne turned back to her grandfather. "Please tell me what is going on, Grandfather."

John's eyes flashed humor and tenderness as he looked at her. "I don't know where to begin, but it's time for you to know everything. Your grandmother and I need your help."

"You know I'll do anything…"

"Hush, my dear, until I tell you the whole of it. Life here may be very difficult for you when you learn what is going on. But first, your grandmother and I agree that James is too young to take into our confidence. He's a delightful young man, but we must protect him for now. What I will tell you must be strictly confidential."

"Of course, Grandfather. You know you can trust me."

He sighed audibly. "It's more than trust, Suzanne. Our life here is dangerous. You must leave as soon as it is possible without your departure looking suspicious. For now I will tell you what you need to know."

Thrusting his lean body forward, he touched his granddaughter's hand. When he began to speak, his voice was both warm and concerned. "They took me to prison because they think I am a Southern sympathizer. They think that because your mother and Uncle Stephen, and now of course, our grandchildren live in the South. They have assumed you and James brought us treasonous news—that we are not loyal."

"But, you freed Zoe. You pay your help. You don't have any slaves."

"In truth, many years ago your grandmother and I decided to join the fight to free mistreated slaves. We think all slaves should be free, but especially those who want freedom badly enough to run away for it. We believe the ideology that all men and women can be free and educated and earn a decent wage to support their families."

Suzanne had found it easy to suggest those ideas to her father. Now, it sounded impossible. "But, Grandfather, we take care of our slaves. Their quarters have tight roofs and plank floors. The slaves have an adequate supply of firewood and plenty of rations. Remember, Mother was also very kind to them. She insisted their rations include milk, sugar, coffee and tobacco. Father summons Doctor Tom Travis to attend a slave with symptoms he would ignore in himself.

"Samuel is a skilled leather worker. He makes and mends cowhide boots for the field hands. Old Molly and Jane, the seamstresses, fashion their clothes. Mother taught them how to sew."

"Sweetheart, we'll discuss your father's slaves later. Right now, it's important for you to learn what is going on at Hanson Racing Stable yards."

His voice was full of indulgence. She waited quietly for him to go on. "We keep a 'safe house' Suzanne. It's in the new barn. A trapdoor conceals a huge cellar where we harbor runaways. We've concealed scores of fugitives. We help arrange escape for them to Canada, but our activities must be kept secret. No one can know we are part of the Underground Railroad or the escaping slaves can't get to freedom. We can't even tell our closest neighbors. It's too dangerous."

Suzanne barely stopped a gasp of surprise. "But, Grandfather, that's wrong. Most Negroes belong to plantation owners who can't survive without them."

"I know you feel that way now, Suzanne. However, when you get used to the idea, you'll realize the slaves must be free. They are people, my dear. They laugh and cry and live and die, just like you and I. Don't you see? Think of Zoe and Polly. Think of Sadie and Jasper who love you so dearly you miss them when you come north each summer."

Suzanne felt totally bewildered by the mixed emotions that assailed her. "Oh, Grandfather, it's too confusing."

"Yes, my dear, let's not continue this conversation today. We'll talk more about it when you are feeling up to it. Besides, I must rest before your grandmother scolds me."

Later in her bedroom, Suzanne could not relax. She had always loved the wallpaper pattern of tiny yellow flower bouquets accented with lilac bows. In the past, its delicacy soothed her; it did not now. She lay across the bed deciding to tell her grandparents she would be going back to her father as soon as possible. She felt he needed her more than ever since she had opened and read the paper the bandit put in her purse.

She wondered how she could warn Aman. Almost certainly the enemy would confiscate a letter. Her mind went over the details. Then she got out the paper for a second time and tried again to decipher its meaning.

<u>S/F</u>
*Jesse Owens—Charleston, SC
Tom Bush—Myrtle Beach, SC
Jed Brown—South Point, NC
Lee Freeman—Wilmington, NC
*Tad Hooker—Hatteras
<u>E/H</u>
Thaddeus Stuart
James Scott
Grant Williams
Howard Jackson—*The Atlanta*
Charles Seward
Nathan Bedford—*Chancellor*
<u>P</u>
Aman Willoughby—*Annebella*
John Lloyd—*Steamer Lloyd*
Thomas Stone—*Sea Dog*
Judge Pope
B.E.J. Hall

The list of names was baffling and complicated. Suzanne took a sheet of paper from her small desk and separately listed the familiar names under the E/H and the P columns.

Besides her father's and Judge Pope's, several other names were familiar. Thaddeus' was at the top of the E/H list. She wondered again what the letters stood for.

Suzanne recalled that Jesse Owens of Charleston, the only name she recognized in the S/F column, was a free Negro. She had often ridden with Aman when he took their lame horses to be shod at Jesse's blacksmith shop. She remembered the easy rapport between her father and Jesse Owens.

Suzanne struggled with her memory of the tall, lanky Negro. She remembered he had been somewhat of a curiosity when he boldly set up a shop on Charleston's Harbor Road. His skin was light, and like Polly, he could read and write and understand more than one language. Stories of his birth varied. James once told her Jesse was born in Africa and had served in the crew of a slave trader. Suzanne wondered what had caused him to be on the S/F list, but she could not interpret the initials. She felt discouraged and at a disadvantage to Tyrone. Was her father in trouble? Was someone following him or pursuing him?

She longed to ask her grandfather to help, but was afraid to break the trust of the bandit. It might go sour for her grandparents. She decided there was nothing she could do until she returned home and so must put the coded lists out of her mind.

That settled, Suzanne felt relieved. She stood up, willing herself to make the most of the time she had left. She changed into a tweed cinnamon-brown riding habit. She buttoned the vest over a satin, long-sleeved, moss green waist. She tied her cascading curls at the base of her neck before putting the felt top hat upon her head. The wispy beige veil trailed behind.

Suzanne hoped a ride over the estate would restore her good humor. On impulse, she stopped in the kitchen to make up a packet of sugar for Ginny. She asked Sally for a sandwich and a piece of fruit. Sally hustled around to prepare a lunch basket. She covered it with the bright red-and-white checkered cloth that Suzanne and Polly had always used on their picnics by the pond. "Tell Grandmother I'll be home in time for dinner," Suzanne said as she picked up the basket and hurried out toward the stables.

Charlie, watching her approach, tipped his hat. "You be looking splendid, Miz Suzanne. Would you be wanting your Ginny saddled?"

"Thank you, Charlie. Yes. I feel the need for a ride and Ginny can use the exercise."

"She be missin' you for sure, Miz Suzanne," Charlie said as he disappeared to get the blanket and prepare the mount.

Wishing Polly were along to confide in, Suzanne raced over the rolling hills, through the back woods and to the far corners of the estate. Resplendent purple violets carpeted the floors of the wooded areas over which she rode. Buds dotting the many varieties of trees would burst full bloom within the week.

Looking out over the lush green acreage, Suzanne urged Ginny to a rhythmic gallop. Lulled by the warm sunshine, she relaxed. When she reached the pond, Suzanne reined in and slipped down from the horse. "Stay close, Ginny."

She walked to the edge of the pond and pulled off her boots and stockings. She let the wet mud of the narrow beach ooze between her toes. Then she held up the bottoms of her split skirts and walked into the water where the cool waves gently lapped at her ankles. *In another month,* she thought, *I will have a sinfully delicious swim.* She hoped Polly would be back by then.

Deep in contemplation, Suzanne did not hear the quiet approach of another horse until its explosive whinny brought an answering neigh from Ginny. Suzanne had not the faintest doubt who was there. Determined not to reveal her joy at seeing him, she spun around to face Tyrone.

Chapter 7

Suzanne drank in the sensuality of Tyrone's physique, savored his powerful presence. A tingling seized her as she studied his body. He was dressed neither in the blue of the Federal Navy nor in the cloak of the bandit. Tyrone's buckskin breeches fit snugly over his sturdy, muscular legs. His long-sleeved shirt, cut from homespun cotton muslin, lay open down to the third button. Suzanne was acutely aware of the thick mat of black hair peeking out above the opening.

Tyrone, mounted on a jet-black thoroughbred steed, waited motionlessly. When Suzanne's eyes locked, finally, with his, she saw desire blazing there. For a long moment she felt as if she were floating. He was so compelling, his magnetism so potent. The tenderness in his expression amazed her. Then as quickly, she remembered he was not what she wanted him to be. The shock of discovery hit her full force. She tried to relax. Drawing in a deep breath, she forbade herself to tremble. Still, when he spoke, the vibrancy in his voice surprised her. "I think our horses welcomed each other. Mine is Midnight. What's your roan's name?"

In spite of herself, Suzanne laughed. "She's Ginny, and I think you're right. They greeted each other with elation."

"And what of *your* greeting, my pretty one?"

The amusement left her. "I've read the paper you thrust at me. My father's name is on it, also many other names I recognize. What do you have to say for yourself?"

"Nothing. I have only a couple of hours in which to enjoy your company. Let's not waste time arguing about things of which I cannot speak."

Pointing to the lunch basket, he asked, "May I join you?"

Surprised again by this unpredictable man, Suzanne nodded. "I just don't know what to think. I'm frantic for my father's safety and you shrug it off as if nothing were wrong."

His dark eyes flashed a gentle but firm warning, then he smiled without malice, almost apologetically. He dismounted and walked toward her. "Come on, Suzanne. Let's see what is in your lunch basket."

Famished from her rigorous ride, Suzanne conceded. While Tyrone spread out the picnic cloth, Suzanne began digging inside the basket. "Look at the feast. How could Sally have known I wouldn't be eating alone?"

She lifted out two thick ham and cheese sandwiches, a ripe juicy tomato, tangy pickles, two red apples and four of her favorite dark, rich molasses cookies. A small bottle of red wine lay along one side of the basket.

Suzanne and Tyrone were easy with each other, talking of the horses and her grandfather's racing stables. While keeping the conversation light, they ate every crumb of the lunch. When they finished the last drop of wine, Tyrone moved closer. He gathered Suzanne into his arms and held her snugly as he gently eased her down to the soft tender shoots of new spring grass. His nearness wrapped around her like a warm blanket and Suzanne knew her feelings had nothing to do with

The Bandit's Lady

reason. She settled back, enjoying the feel of his arms around her. Then with a deliberately casual movement, she turned and faced him. Leaning slightly into him, she tilted her face toward his.

Tyrone crushed her to him and pressed his mouth to hers with a savage intensity. The touch of his lips on hers sent a shockwave through her entire body. The kiss left her mouth burning with fire. He took her hand and pressed it against the hard, warm flesh and thick mat of hair. She felt the strong rhythm of his heart. "Do you feel it?" he asked softly. "You make my blood run like falls over a beaver dam, Suzanne."

She felt lost in the gentleness of his deep voice. As her fingers lingered inside his shirt, she stroked his muscular body, liking its touch. His breath was warm and a little unsteady as his lips brushed against her forehead. Her curious fingers continued to explore his brawny chest. Emotion trembled between them. The silence was broken only by the sound of waves lapping at the shore, scurrying animals foraging in the woods behind them and the occasional trill of a songbird.

His lips caught her searching fingers and she felt the tip of his tongue moving softly against them. She looked straight into his eyes and saw the excitement in them. Silently, he examined her face. She knew she flushed. "Stand up, Suzanne," he said at last. "I want to feel you against me."

As if without a will of her own, she obeyed him. He drew her so close she felt his forceful thighs. The muscles of his chest absorbed her soft breasts. She raised her eyes to Tyrone's. "I...Tyrone, I feel..."

His fingers pressed gently against her lips. "Kiss me," he whispered. "Don't think. Don't talk. Just kiss me."

His lips teased hers delicately, softly, causing a surge of passion that drew a moan buried deep inside her constricted throat. She moved closer to help him, enticing him. Her lips parted under the passive strength of his mouth as he deepened the kiss. She felt his hands caressing her back, moving surely around to her rib cage. When he spoke again his voice was low and seductive. "There is so much more for us. I want you, all of you."

His hands rested on her shoulders, causing her flesh to quiver. Her whole body flooded with desire. She did not protest when his hands sought the buttons of her blouse. His thumbs traced the gentle slope of her full young breasts. He outlined the tips of them with his fingers, then suckled them to tautness. Suzanne stiffened instinctively as she felt his hardness brushing against her. She wanted to yield to the burning sweetness captive within her, but something held her back. She pulled away and, with a sigh of distress, turned aside. "It's all right," he whispered at her lips. "Don't pull away from me."

Her eyes opened, wide and curious, and a little frightened. "I'm...untouched," she whispered back.

His fingers moved higher and he watched her face while they found the hard peaks and traced them again tenderly. His large hands embraced their velvet softness and pressed against them with warm, sensuous movements. "How does it feel, Suzanne?" he asked in a deep-timbered voice. "Is it good?"

Suzanne, feeling faint, remained silent. Tyrone moved a step back, but she sensed the barely controlled desire coiled inside his body. His mellow baritone simmered with restrained passion. "It's too soon, but in time, we will be one."

He pulled her close, trying to ease her embarrassment. She buried her burning face against his shoulder. Cupping her chin in his hand, he sought her green eyes with his ebony ones. He seemed pensive, not disturbed or angry. She felt an extraordinary void as they stood silent together. Then Tyrone began to speak, slowly, as if to stroke her with his voice. "This night I must leave Baltimore, Suzanne. The *Sea Queen* is going on active duty. If all goes well, I will dock at Inner Harbor in December. Will you wait for me?"

"I cannot wait, Tyrone. I must go home to Father as soon as possible to warn him of the danger he and the *Annebella* may be in."

"You know Governor Hicks proclaimed martial law over the city. It's not safe for you to leave, Suzanne."

"I know that's true for now, but as soon as the security is lifted Grandfather will help me get passage to Wilmington. From there on it will be safe. I'll take the stage to Charleston."

She watched him with smug delight. "And, who knows? Maybe a handsome bandit and his thieves will stop my coach and make the trip an exciting adventure. But alas, my jewels are already gone and I have nothing left for others."

Tyrone regarded her with amusement. He picked up a dark copper curl and caressed it gently, then planted a tantalizing kiss in the hollow of her neck. "Don't ever lose your sense of humor, my dauntless lady."

A movement in the woods brought Suzanne and Tyrone instantly alert. "What was that?" Suzanne asked fearfully.

Tyrone held his finger to his lips and said, "Wait here while I look."

Before he could leave, a baby cried, a whisper-thin wail of weakness and hunger. Suzanne ran ahead. Hidden behind a thick clump of bushes, she came upon a trembling Negro woman who, except for the slight bulge of pregnancy, was painfully thin. She wore a plain frock with an apron over it and appeared half-starved. No sound came from her lips, but her bloodshot eyes gave conflicting messages. They were dull with fatigue, while terror screamed from their dark depths. The baby looked to be but a few months old. How could it be, Suzanne thought, that this poor waif of a woman is already with child again? The woman seemed to guess her dilemma. Her hoarse voice was barely above a whisper. "Dis baby be my brother's. His mama died of de coughin' consump'ion. His daddy be shot in Virginny. I promise to raise up de chil'."

Suzanne turned to Tyrone who had come up behind them. "What are we going to do with them?"

"I'll carry them with me on Midnight to the grove of trees behind your grandfather's barn. With your help, she probably can walk from there. Your grandmother will know what to do."

"But she belongs to someone who is looking for her. Maybe she's posted. It's illegal not to help find her owners."

He answered with a cold edge of irony. "She won't live long enough for you to do your duty. If you can't feel a grain of sympathy for this poor soul and this baby, I have downright misjudged you."

Suzanne watched his eyes. They were large glittering black ovals of contempt. An unwelcome heat crept into her cheeks. Before she could respond, Tyrone scooped up the woman and baby and mounted his gigantic inky horse.

His anger became a scalding fury. "They need help," he repeated. "I only hope you are up to the challenge, Miss Suzanne."

And as the trio rode away, he said, "No matter how much you try to deny me, one day I will have you with or without your consent, as I should have the first time we met."

Sitting down on the soft grass to pull on her stockings and riding boots, Suzanne wondered what she wanted of him. Her face burned as her own words returned to haunt her memory. *Slave owners be damned; the sad woman and her baby were counting on me for survival.*

She quickly stuffed the remains of the lunch things in the basket and called Ginny to her side. Galloping toward the hiding place, Suzanne wondered why she could not see the black female and the baby. Dismounting, she walked along the edge until she spotted movement in a lilac bush at the far end of the grove. When she reached the frail pair, the baby looked still, as if life had been sucked out of him. Suzanne picked him up. "Is he all right," she asked softly?

Sheer, vivid fear glittered in the colored woman's eyes. Tears rolled down her cheeks and deep sobs racked her body. "He be dead," she whispered.

Suzanne thought so, too, but she laid him gently on the ground. She swallowed hard and bit back tears. With a confidence she didn't feel, she said, "I'll get my grandmother. You stay here, and whatever you do, don't move him."

She felt a complex compassion for the troubled pair, mixed with an overwhelming shame at herself. She hurried to the big house to find Margaret.

* * * *

Two hours later, when her grandmother returned to the house, Suzanne still huddled in the deep floral cushions of the comfortable chair in the cozy parlor. "The baby will live, Suzanne," she said softly. "Run upstairs now and dress for dinner.

It's your birthday, in case you've forgotten, and we have much to celebrate."

Zoe appeared in the doorway of her bedroom as Suzanne entered. "Would you be carin' for a bath, Miz?"

"Oh, thank you, Zoe. I feel hot and terrible, and no one has told me where Polly is."

"Don't you be worryin' yourself about Polly. She'll be back 'fore you be a missin' her. I'll get Sally's Joe to bring up the tub and hot water."

Zoe disappeared before Suzanne could ask any more questions. She vowed to make them tell her at dinner what all the secrecy was about. Once in the wooden tub, Suzanne lay back. The hot water, perfumed with lavender, oozed around her neck. She closed her eyes to relax, but her blood soared with an unbidden remembrance of Tyrone's touch. Putting her finger to tingling lips, her thoughts filtered back to the day she had met him, and to each meeting since. She recalled the ecstasy when he held her against his strong body, and suffered a dull ache of desire. How could she ever hate him enough, as she must, to guard against his evil? Suzanne closed her eyes, reliving the pain of that final scene. Startled by the thought again, she knew he was kinder than he wanted anyone to know.

But what of her father? When the *Sea Queen* sailed from Baltimore, where would it go? What was its duty? Where did Tyrone the bandit fit into the total picture?

Suzanne lingered until the bath cooled. Zoe had left her a precious bar of the soap with the same faint fragrance as the water. She lathered her slim body, then rinsed it off, letting the tepid water wash away her weariness. Next she scrubbed her hair, rinsed it until it squeaked and wrapped a coarse towel around it to soak up the water.

Stepping out of the tub, Suzanne walked to the bed to see what Zoe had laid out for her to wear. Zoe was at her side before she started dressing. "Here, child, let me help like when you was a little girl."

"But, Zoe, I never saw this dress before."

"You sho didn't, honey. You grandmama bought it at Miz Millicent's Dress Shoppe down to Thames Street fo' dis very night."

Fully dressed, Suzanne stood before the mirror. She beamed. An exclamation of delight escaped her lips. The parchment cream dress was fashioned of lustrous taffeta. Its close-fitting bodice, featuring a sweetheart neckline, delicately exposed her firm rounded breasts and dainty cleavage. The slightly lowered Basque waist enhanced her own tiny waist. Violet bows-and-ruffles trim adorned the long skirt and puffed sleeves. "Oh, Zoe, it's so beautiful."

"You be de best dressed belle dis night fo' sho. You want jewelry?"

Suzanne spoke with light bitterness. "The bandit and his thieves stole my jewelry the night of the robbery, so I have none to wear."

Sudden anger lit Zoe's eyes. She took up the brush and began gently stroking Suzanne's copper curls until they gleamed in the candlelight. She lured them atop her head and trapped them with a velvet ribbon of the same color as the frills on her dress. "Be off with you, now," Zoe said, as she stood back to admire her handiwork.

Suzanne's grandparents were already seated at the large, round, oak dining table. James, who gave her a mock salute, said, "A fine cousin you are. Here it is your birthday and I expected to spirit you off for a picnic and a spot of reading. But you, my love, disappear with the lunch basket and don't return for hours. When you return, the basket is empty. Sally says you have eaten a feast all by yourself and..."

Suzanne colored fiercely with a private memory, but rapidly recovered her fragile composure and laughed infectiously. "Whoa, friend James. You were nowhere about when I rode off to feel the freedom from the last few days of confinement. Tomorrow, I shall devote myself to your every whim."

She took the familiar chair and pointing to an empty place at the table, asked, "Whose place is that?"

Before anyone could answer, Polly, dressed in a baby-blue frock of frothy tulle over silk, came gliding through the huge double archway. "Happy Birthday, Princess Suzanne."

The 'princess' from their childhood brought tears of nostalgia to Suzanne's eyes.

Chapter 8

May and June melted into July.

Polly and Suzanne had found themselves at odds the morning after the birthday party. They argued and sparred. "I don't care what you say," Polly screamed. "I won't let a bunch of self-righteous Southern plantation owners ruin the chances of freedom for my people."

"'Righteous' is the word for Northerners interfering with the rights of those plantation owners," Suzanne yelled back.

Polly's chocolate brown eyes clawed her like the beady gaze of a falcon. "You really don't know what it's all about, do you Suzanne? I've spent these past many months traveling from New York City to Cincinnati, Ohio, defending the rights of my people. The rights, my dear Suzanne, are freedom for all, or have you forgotten so soon?" Polly put her heart-shaped face close to Suzanne's. "'We hold these truths to be self-evident; that all men are created equal...endowed by their creator with certain unalienable rights...among these are life, liberty and the pursuit of happiness.'"

She stepped away and spoke more calmly, almost gently. "I've been at the Boston Faneuil Hall. Night after night, I have been speaking from the Anti-Slavery Society meeting house pulpit. I've been telling anyone who would listen how your grandparents educated me and gave me the gift of freedom. During the day, I teach black children, those denied entry into Boston's public schools. I teach them to read and to write and to enjoy some of their cultural heritage that Boston has to offer. I'm going back in the fall to help finish organizing the first all-black Civil War regiment, the Fifty-Fourth Regiment. Can't you find a pride inside yourself Suzanne that says you know a black Polly? Can't you admit you grew up with her? We love, Suzanne, like sisters, you and me."

Suzanne reacted angrily to the challenge in Polly's voice. "I never thought we'd be in conflict…"

Polly snorted. "You mean you thought I would 'stay in my place'."

"I mean that up here, in Baltimore, it's different. At home we need slaves."

"I tell you one thing, Miss Uppity. I have devoted hours and I will devote many more hours helping to send thousands of fugitive slaves to safety. They will find freedom by traveling on the Underground Railroad here and in Boston, and beyond. Who do you think taught me how, except your grandparents?"

At last the girls were silent. They avoided each other. They ate their meals separately. Without discussing it, they took turns eating the main meal with Suzanne's grandparents. It became a ritual, a pattern that let each one respect the other on her night at the big table. They didn't speak out against each other to John or Margaret. Nor did the Hansons comment on their dining arrangements, enjoying the girls in their turn.

Without Polly's companionship, Suzanne roamed quietly through the days. She spent hours riding, thinking about all the dear black friends she knew and loved. Finally, she had long talks with Grandfather Hanson, trying to find her soul of compassion. "Grandfather, I love Sadie and Jasper and Zoe and Polly, but I can't think of them as the same as me. Aren't some people meant to work, to serve, while others are to care for their needs?"

"In the North, my dear, slavery came to natural extinction. In your South, slavery has continued and spread. If slavery was only a question of economics, it would not arouse such a high flood of feeling. In the North, we will fight for an ideal; the South fights in defense of what it regards as property."

"But, Grandfather, our slaves are property. We bought them with money and care for them with money. Mother was always kind to them and I have suggested to Father that it might be better to pay them to work. He says they are like children; that they need our guardianship."

"Let it rest, my dear. One day you will know what is right. Be kind to Polly, though she is adamant and difficult just now. In the end, you will both learn what is most important."

So the weeks dragged by. Suzanne's days began in one of two ways. She went on early morning rides alongside Grandfather Hanson or she sat quietly in the cozy parlor avidly scrutinizing the *Baltimore Crier*.

In the *Crier,* she followed stories about a small band of rogues, bandits who went about the countryside robbing stagecoaches. The details of the robberies were incomplete, interspersed among the more immediate concerns of the war news. Suzanne could not satiate her curiosity.

A series of articles stated these observations:

> *As we see it, these men are Bushwhackers who loot simply for the lust of it. The bandits live dangerously on the edge of the law. Although they plunder at regular intervals, our sources tell us the authorities cannot establish a reliable pattern of their disgraceful activities.*
>
> *It is often late, even after dark, when the robberies take place. A half a dozen of them have taken place during the daylight hours. They think the piracy is being done by the same gang. The method seldom varies though the locations range from New York State, south through Pennsylvania, Maryland, Washington D.C. and Virginia.*
>
> *They take jewelry from ladies, gold watches and fobs from the gentlemen. Also, of course, they take money when it exists.*

More than once, when an account alluded to the rape of a lady, Suzanne recalled Miss Tilly's words. "Just last week, on this very same road, they killed Captain Jerome and did terrible things to his lady."

She would remember her bandit. She wondered if it were his men who were marauding, and for what they were using the bounty. Too often Suzanne remembered Tyrone. The disturbing and exciting emotions he aroused whenever they met haunted, tormented her. She visualized the tenderness of his gaze and felt again the sexual magnetism he evoked when his eyes raked boldly over her body. She dreamed of him crushing her again in his embrace. Suzanne felt certain Tyrone was not habitually with the bandits, for she also anxiously followed accounts of the *Sea Queen*. The *Crier* reported:

The Bandit's Lady

> *Ships in alien waters are leaving for home as quickly as possible. Those in dry dock are getting prepared for sea duty. In coastal waters, the Sea Queen, one of a small group of vessels put out to protect the Union blockade, appears everywhere.*

Suzanne supposed Tyrone had become a creature of the dark. She knew by all accounts he worked on the brink of danger, probably with a burning zeal and cold courage, she concluded. Something was strange in the arrangement. There were six ships in the "Chesapeake Bay Half Dozen." They were the *Lady Maria, New Yorker, Trenton, El Rose* and *King Baltic*. These ships were all praised for their action against the ports they were protecting or gaining. The *Sea Queen* seemed to be in the middle of every skirmish.

Southern ships that encountered the *Sea Queen* were often damaged, but never destroyed. Sometimes crew members took the sailors into custody, but more often they escaped. One item in the *Crier* mentioned Tyrone by name. The writer hinted the *Sea Queen's* crew might be shirking its duty:

> *...since this war must be ended quickly, it is urgent the Sea Queen begin using its strength to better advantage. Her captain Tyrone Sterling is surely aware of the vast responsibility he carries. Without the cooperation of the whole Chesapeake Bay Half Dozen our cause is lost.*

They contradicted the content of the paper in her possession. In mid-July, a small news item startled Suzanne's eye:

The Annebella, a sturdy, recently armed pirate ship seized the Trenton on the twelfth day of July. Its prisoners disembarked at Hatteras Inlet. Afterward, the Annebella's captain, Aman Willoughby, a prominent Charleston plantation owner, confiscated the contents of the hold. He and his crew escaped undetected through the stormy waters.

Captain Warren of the Trenton told newsmen the cargo deck contained valuable medicines, munitions and weapons. He said there was also miscellany, such as razors, buckets and boots. "His luck seems uncanny," Captain Warren declared. "The Sea Queen passed by the scene only moments before the Annebella vanished into the night."

It leads this writer to wonder yet again at the allegiance of Captain Sterling. However, to accuse one of treason or, heaven forbid, spying against one's Union, would bode no goodwill.

A few days later, a short commentary signed A. Nonymous scalded the accusing offender of the *Sea Queen*. He wrote these words:

Watch your venomous pen, you who would besmirch the Sea Queen. Her captain knows ways to get quick revenge. Your apology should be forthcoming immediately. P.S. I love you, SW.

Suzanne froze, mind and body. She drew her legs up and hugged her knees to her. It couldn't be, but she knew it was. *Tyrone wrote that message,* she thought. She lingered over the paper unseeing, trapped by the memory of her emotions. The memory, pure and unsullied, of his sensuous kisses made her lips tingle. She hungered from the memory of his mouth on hers until every fiber of her being ached for his touch.

The following day, the retraction-apology shattered her nearly unbearable entrancement of the past twenty-four hours. It read:

> *This writer has made a terrible mistake against the honorable intentions of the Sea Queen captain. My apology is sincere. This is not because of an anonymous threat of retaliation, you understand. New evidence has clearly exonerated Captain Tyrone Sterling and his crew. The wire service praises the Sea Queen. Said it was responsible for destroying the Atlanta and Chancellor. Mr. Howard Jackson and Mr. Nathan Bedford, respectively, captained these southern contraband ships.*
>
> *Having watched the incident from the shore, a spokesman said the crews and their captains disappeared in skiffs. Billows of smoke swallowed them from view, he said. No one knows who may have rescued them. However, the consensus agrees that two powerful enemy ships were spotted near the scene just before the event. The Sea Dog and the Annebella, may have waited to guarantee the crews' safety.*
>
> *"Regretfully," Captain Sterling said, "we could not salvage the spoils. The holds contained precious cotton, tobacco, rice, sugarcane and other valuable cargo."*

Suzanne's sorrow was huge. A flash of wild grief ripped through the painful knot forming inside her. "*Blast!*" she whispered. "*Oh, Father, why are you doing this? Be careful. He's after you, too.*"

* * * *

Grandfather Hanson had fully recovered his normal exuberant good health. He resumed his grueling schedule and added the extra work of attending prisoners at Fort McHenry. He had quit asking Suzanne to accompany him after their early morning rides. "You're too young to take up nurses' training," he told her. "And, for decency's sake, you're too old to follow me around as you did when you were a child."

Surprised, Suzanne said, "Why am I too young for nurses' training?"

"Miss Dorothea Dix, organizer of the Women's Nurse Corps, has approved volunteer women nurses who have received previous training. They must be thirty years old or more."

"But, Grandfather, that's years away for me. The prisoners at Fort McHenry need help now. I'm sure no one would bother me if I wrote letters to their families. I could read to them or perform other non-nursing tasks for them."

"I'm afraid, my dear, someone might question your motives because you are from the South."

Suzanne glared at her grandfather. "Most of the prisoners are also from the South; the others are sympathizers. What harm could be done? No one would have to know, would they?"

"Now, Suzanne, try to have fun until this military problem is officially over. Then I'll arrange for you to go back to your father."

Suzanne tried to fill the days with the same excitement of other summers. She and James walked the streets of Baltimore and the dockside streets: Thames, Fleet, and Shakespeare. They returned to the same historical sites she and Polly had relished in summers gone by, but it wasn't the same for Suzanne. The luster was gone.

When Grandfather Hanson introduced James to David Adams, a young man his age, he soon found other interests. The Adams lived on a nearby estate. David's father was a fellow doctor and friend of the Hanson's.

The social life of a Baltimore lad was not less exhilarating because of the war. At dinner, James breathlessly described their activities in detail. His eyes sparkled and he waved his arms as he told how they played billiards and bowled. They went to horse races, cockfights and quoit pitching.

James occasionally joined Suzanne and their grandfather for their early morning rides. His horsemanship began to improve immensely by practicing John Hanson's tips. But more often he rode alone with Suzanne. They packed a lunch and explored the estate. They ended at the pond to wade and relax before returning to the manor for Grandmother's afternoon tea. "We can go swimming in the nude, Suzanne," James said, while wading one sweet, warm summer day. "After all, we are cousins."

Suzanne looked lovingly at James. His bright ruffled red hair blew in the brisk breeze. His twinkling blue eyes looked at her candidly. Without offense, she said, "I didn't tell you the story of Polly and me to tempt you to tease me. We were young and healthy. It made us feel naughty and sophisticated."

Suddenly all pleasure left Suzanne. Biting her lip, she turned away. Her eyes glazed with tears. "Oh, how I miss those carefree days with Polly."

James quickly caught her hand in his. "I didn't mean to make you feel sad. Come on, let's eat that scrumptious lunch Sally packed for us."

Suzanne often stood at her bedroom window watching the comings and goings at the new barn. Every Thursday, she noted, Margaret left the estate. She dressed in a simple day dress. She tied the matching bonnet under her chin with a wide ribbon bow. She drove the creaky old wagon filled with straw toward town.

When she returned two hours later, as few as two or as many as twenty black people scrambled out of the straw and invaded the barn. The farm buzzed then, but quietly, as Sally prepared food and the hands carried it to the barn, with other supplies. Suzanne knew the Negroes would stay in the barn until nightfall, or for several nights until it was safe for them to travel. "Where do you go to collect the Negroes?" Suzanne asked her grandmother one evening at dinner.

"To the docks. I meet the *Bianca*. Captain Neal picks them up in Wilmington and Norfolk."

"Where do they go from here? Grandfather tells me it's dangerous for you to transport illegal cargo. What would happen to you if the authorities caught you, or investigated you?"

Grandmother Hanson's blue eyes sparkled. She held up a small wrinkled hand. "Stop, child. I can only answer one question at a time. There's a station twenty miles from here. Sometimes Charlie delivers them there. Other times he takes them to the railroad. There are people to care for them and see they get out where it's safe. It's some dangerous, but your grandfather and I try not to think about that part of it."

Suzanne shook her head. "I just don't know how you can be so calm about something so hazardous."

Margaret said, simply, "We think it's right."

The first day of August 1861 arrived on a sticky, sweltering Thursday. Zoe had opened the parlor windows in an attempt to capture any stray wisp of a breeze. Sitting alone, Suzanne read a recap of war events in the *Baltimore Crier*:

> *Isolated incidents in Virginia are whetting the Union's appetite for victory. Slashing their way through a band of Confederate soldiers at Fairfax, some fifty men became instant heros. More serious was a battle at Big Bethel, where Union troops suffered about a hundred casualties...*
>
> *Federal troops came from Ohio and Indiana to protect the Baltimore and Ohio Railroad from Confederate damage...*
>
> *Weary, disheartened and terrorized Union soldiers faded away, leaving the battlefield of Bull Run and the victory to the South.*

Zoe stood at the doorway, holding out an envelope. "Miz Suzanne. You got a letter from you daddy."

Suzanne jumped up to take the letter. Her hand shook. "Oh, thank goodness. I just bet he has found a way to get me home."

Chapter 9

Only this morning, Suzanne and Polly had surrendered to an easy harmony. "Forgive me, Suzanne, for all the terrible things I said to you. We are different, you and I. It's our color, of course, and our upbringing. I was born free, thanks only to your grandparents. I naturally thought you felt the same way about slavery as I do." Tears sparkled on her black cheeks.

"My parents always treat our slaves kindly, Polly, but Father needs them to work the plantation. You can't know how difficult and impossible the work of cotton would be without our rugged, faithful workers."

Wiping the tears from her own face, Suzanne continued, "But I'm sorry, too, for the way we've hurt each other. I always thought of you as my friend, the sister I never had."

The two girls clung to each other briefly before going their separate ways. Now, Suzanne hugged her father's letter close to her heart and snuggled up in her favorite chair to read it. The parchment dated six weeks before was written in Aman Willoughby's tiny familiar script:

The Bandit's Lady

My dearest Suzanne,

You have no doubt heard that our illustrious President Lincoln has blockaded our port. A farce, indeed! On the third day, the British ship Delmat and the freighter Airo ran the gauntlet. The next day two more vessels passed safely. It will be only a matter of time before the British and French will come fully to our aid. Meanwhile, the Annebella is faring well on the seas.

Jefferson Davis invited shipowners to apply for Confederate letters of marque and reprisal. These licenses authorize the bearers to turn privateer and, acting as Navy vessels, capture Union merchantmen. We sell the loot for profit as contraband of war. As volunteers, we also collect twenty percent of the value of any Federal warship we destroy.

Thaddeus advised me and my group of Charleston gentlemen to take the risk for a chance at the huge profits. We've refitted the Annebella and converted her into a little five-gun steam sloop. We've hired extra hands, but I insist on manning the helm myself, except during very short periods of relief.

In the early morning darkness of May 10, the Annebella slipped past the Federal warships blockading Charleston Harbor. It was less than a month after the victory of Fort Sumter, and our top speed is six knots. Can you imagine it, Suzanne?

At dawn, a week ago, I spied a sail on the horizon and ordered the crew to give chase. It turned out to be a sluggish ship with a dullard of a merchantman. Within the next forty-eight hours, my crew captured three Yankee Union merchantmen. The haul was astounding—sugar, barrels of lime and precious tea.

    I dare not speak of other plans. You must not know more than is good for you. I will be in touch as often as is possible, and Suzanne, you must not worry about me. I have a network, of sorts, supporting my activities. Someday I will tell you everything, things I probably should have told you years ago.

    But it is a hazardous business. As I have no immediate plans to return to Royal Oaks, I have turned the plantation over to Luke Henry. Our overseer has always been a capable manager whenever I've been away. He is sure to be loyal and steady as I have promised him a cash settlement and a parcel of land when things get back to normal. It will give him a fresh start when this war is over.

    I can check on the progress of the plantation from time to time. Your Uncle Stephen, who abhors the sea, is looking out for it, too. The point is, my dear, although I miss you terribly and need you desperately at Royal Oaks Manor, you must stay with Margaret and John until things simmer down a bit. James, too, as traveling is far too precarious right now.
Your loving father, Aman.

Disappointment washed over Suzanne and for another hour she sat quietly in the big flowered chintz chair trying to think what she must do. Then she stood up and paced the small room. *If I must stay in Baltimore, it's time to find something worthwhile to occupy my time*, she decided. *I won't tell anyone, not even Grandmother.*

Resolutely, Suzanne walked upstairs to her bedroom and put the letter in her desk drawer. She changed into a pale yellow silk dress with matching bonnet. She retraced her steps to the foyer and went out the front door. Although she often strolled around the grounds, Suzanne felt guilty and glanced quickly around to make sure no one was watching her. She was oblivious of the heat, yet beads of sweat trickled down her back as she sauntered down the lane and turned toward town.

Once away from sight of the house, she thought back to the night she had arrived at Hanson Racing Stable yards, and the bandit who drove her home. She felt peculiar physical waves pulling at her as a queer passion surged up inside her. It was a dizzying, powerful feeling.

As quickly, her feelings revolted. Rekindled were the suspicions, and an awful hopelessness invaded her mind. Suzanne shook her head to clear the profound muddle forming there. So many mysterious things had happened since she met the bandit. Tyrone had asked her to pretend he had raped her, yet no one, not even her grandmother, had mentioned the incident. While her grandparents had been kind and considerate, they had not asked about her captivity either. James, too, had kept quiet about the episode.

From what were they shielding her? Why did they completely ignore what could have been the most horrible event in a young girl's life? Unable to answer the questions, her senses turned outward to enjoy the smells of the estate's newly-mowed, fragrant hay. She treasured the solitude of the late morning quiet where nothing stirred, and took the time to devise a plan for entering the hospital when she arrived there. Lost in thought, Suzanne walked briskly and the five miles to Fort McHenry passed quickly.

Thick ivy clinging to its side and across the door header obscured the entrance. "It's a secret doorway, girls," Grandfather Hanson had told her and Polly on days they visited the old Fort. It had made them feel clandestine and John Hanson perpetuated it with a mischievous wink. Suzanne stepped over the threshold and into the huge brick edifice through the small back door.

Today, obscurity was important. Being too young to join the nurses' training program rankled Suzanne and she resolved to show them she could do the job efficiently. Suzanne innocently walked into the enormous room. She gasped. Row upon row, hundreds of soldiers lay sprawled across the floor. They lay on flimsy blankets or beds of straw or pine needles. Some had pillows; most did not.

The sickening sour stench made Suzanne reel and lean against the rough-hewn pine door casing. The room reeked of the smells of antiseptic and whiskey. They were mixed with the foul pungent odor of decaying, rotting bodies, moldy straw and a mingling of smoke and sweat. Suzanne fled back down the short hallway through which she had entered the improvised hospital. In the privacy of the sweltering midday heat and the ivy, she vomited until she was weak and empty. While catching her breath, a sound pierced the edge of her mind. It was a horrible scream of tormented agony, followed by the silence of death. The awful sound drove through her like a blade.

But then, squaring her small thin shoulders, Suzanne walked slowly and painfully back into the close, dank-smelling room. Two men in bloodstained shirts were lifting the dead soldier from his makeshift bed to a stretcher for removal. As Suzanne approached the first row of men, a silence of futility assailed her senses. The only sound was her shoes clicking softly on the floor.

She looked around and saw several preoccupied women dressed in drab grays and browns. They were quietly talking to, or tending patients. Beside her, a rough croaking noise caught her attention. Another nearby sound, a tiny moan, intruded the strange eerie stillness. Suzanne bent to the task of making the lonely and the injured and dying men more comfortable, less frightened.

* * * *

Hours later, alone in her bath, she wept aloud, rocking back and forth. At dinner, Polly asked, "Where were you all day, Suzanne? I declare I looked everywhere, including the pond. I really expected to find you there. I took my bathing dress."

Suzanne managed a small, tired grin. "I had a sad day. After father's letter arrived, I didn't feel like playing. Maybe tomorrow."

James burst into the conversation to taunt them. "Oh, great! May I join you?"

Polly and Suzanne broke out laughing. But Suzanne knew that tomorrow she would go back to the hospital. There were so many wounded men, so much to do. She couldn't stay away from their terrible needs. She must go back every day. Polly would soon tire of looking for her because she was too busy with the underground work in the big barn. James, absorbed with his new friend, would forget. Never again would any of them capture the magic of their childhood delights. She sighed.

Margaret said. "It's so lovely to have both of our girls at the table tonight. We've missed you and are proud you have resolved your differences."

Suzanne said, "We haven't really resolved our differences, Grandmother, but we have determined not to let the antagonism grow bitter between us."

"Yes," Polly said quickly, "we love each other. We can begin the peace right here—the peace that will soon prevail throughout the nation."

John, who had been unusually silent during the meal, changed the subject abruptly. "A very strange thing happened at Fort McHenry this afternoon. Nurse Manner told me about it when I went there on my late afternoon rounds."

"Whatever is it that makes you so distracted, John?" Margaret asked.

"The nurses saw a young girl talking to and comforting the soldiers. She was not much older than our Suzanne."

"Whatever is wrong with that? You often say you need help so very much."

Suzanne, thankful she had changed into an aqua-blue dinner dress, waited with fluttering breath. Her cheeks burned. She hoped the dim glow of the kerosene lamps would mercifully hide the extent of her feelings. Would he never answer? Suzanne looked fleetingly at Polly who briefly caught her eye, but turned her attention briskly back to her food. John said, "You're right, of course. We need help badly, but the inexperienced intruder is not old enough to be a nurse. It's not proper for a young lady to take on chores of that magnitude. Truth is, it's downright indecent."

"Why didn't someone stop her?"

"I guess no one thought to. They were too busy themselves to take the time. There had been a nasty death, you see, and the unrest was too acute."

"But after the crisis. What of then?"

"I don't know. Mrs. Townsend, head of the nurses, said the girl just disappeared. No one had got close to her. She seemed to do no harm."

"Did anyone talk to the men she helped?"

"Oh, yes. One Southern boy, no older than the young girl, said she was an angel of compassion dressed in yellow fluff. Another said she promised to come again."

"Well, then, what's all the flurry? Surely someone can speak to her about the impropriety of the visits when she returns."

"I suppose you are right, Margaret. I just think it's curious someone so young is free to visit the Fort un-chaperoned."

Polly interrupted the prolonged hush that hung awkwardly around the table. "It appears to me that someone doing such a good deed should be praised, not criticized. Heaven knows, before this war is over we are going to need help from anyone who is willing and able to volunteer their services."

"In my heart, I agree with you, Polly," Margaret said. "But young ladies must protect their reputations, you know."

"I know, Grandmama, but it won't always be so. Women are naturally capable of helping in a crisis. I, for one, applaud the young lady. Someday our individual abilities will be recognized. People will not judge us by our gender or age."

"You are luckier in that way, Polly. You can choose what you do and where to go. It is simply not true for young girls of Suzanne's station."

James saw Zoe standing by the table ready to serve dessert. He said, "Come on, you two. Quit being serious and let Zoe serve up this delectable-looking vanilla blancmange. I'll have two scoops of whipped cream, Zoe."

Suzanne, grateful for the interruption, fondly watched James attack his cake. When she reached her room to get ready for bed, Polly, clad in a plain pink nightdress, lounged comfortably in the middle of her canopied, four-poster bed. Devilment twinkled in her eyes. "Here arrives 'the angel of compassion dressed in yellow fluff.'"

Suzanne knew she turned crimson, yet experienced an odd feeling of satisfaction. She smiled faintly. "How did you know, Polly? Did I give myself away at dinner?"

"I don't believe the others caught it, but I happened a glance at you before you covered your emotions. I couldn't wait to hear about it."

"Oh, Polly, it was awful! There are so many boys, so young and so far from home. There are not enough doctors to go around, nor medicine to cure them. I've got to help them. I don't care what anyone says!"

"Well, the first thing you have to do is find yourself a different dress. What possessed you to wear yellow? Those copper curls of yours will be a dead giveaway."

"I didn't think. Father's letter said I must stay here indefinitely. I have to do something to help the cause and to keep me busy."

"I can solve the clothes problem. Mama Zoe has two dreary gray dresses and a matching bonnet hanging in her cabinet. I checked before I came down here. She only wears them when she goes to Lexington Market, and I think we could have one. She might not notice if we took it."

"Do you think not?" Suzanne asked. "Let's get it now, before the maids go to the attic for the night."

"I have one other suggestion first, Suzanne. I'm going to leave again in September."

"Oh, but you can't leave before the Septemberfest Horse Races. Grandfather said he would take us this year."

"I wouldn't dream of deserting you before the races, but afterward I must go to Boston to get on with my work. Your grandmother needs someone here to help with the underground. She's getting fragile, Suzanne. Don't you think it would be better for you to help here where no one would worry about your age?"

"I can't, Polly. Anyway, what does it matter where I help, if I'm doing it for the cause?"

"It matters because Grandpapa and Grandmama need you here. Besides, they will soon catch you and scold you for going to Fort McHenry. They'll make you quit."

Suzanne grew somber. "I'm sorry, Polly. I can't. Not now. Please forgive me and wish me luck."

She knew Polly watched the play of confused emotions flash across her face. "Okay, my friend. I wish you luck. What you are doing is really generous. Let's sneak upstairs and steal a dress."

Arm in arm and giggling, the girls left Suzanne's room.

Chapter 10

Suzanne was careful to leave her grandparents' house by different doors and at different times of the morning. She always entered the Fort by the back door and performed her self-imposed duties away from the nurses and trainees. Many tasks were difficult, some degrading. She changed bandages, emptied slops and bathed blood and sweat from the despondent or crippled bodies. But, she also wrote letters to the prisoners' families, often trying to give encouragement without false hope.

Suzanne stood in long lines to get bowls of thin soup to feed the incapacitated men who could not, or the indifferent who would not, feed themselves. She felt safe in the food lines because everybody was too busy to pay attention to her. She discreetly watched the other women and imitated their actions. If one of them started toward her, she moved to a more secluded part of the room. Day after day, she sidestepped the threat of discovery; it was more exhausting than the physical chores. She decided the rewards were worth it.

The men she tended were grateful. They quickly comprehended Suzanne's predicament and even the weakest prisoners found ways to warn her if the other women started their way. "Miss Angel, come here. Quick!"

The Bandit's Lady

She rushed to the scene of the call. "What can I do for you, William?"

His silver gray eyes softened at the sight of her. "Nothing for me, miss," the chunky young lieutenant answered. "But if I didn't call you away from that rascal over there, Mrs. Townsend would have intercepted you and challenged your right to be here."

Suzanne looked back at Danny Fletcher who laid on his bed of straw. He gave them a small salute and squeezed his eyes shut against the pain. William said, "His suffering has not let up since Dr. John amputated his left leg three days ago. He signaled me to rescue you. We ain't going to let anyone make you leave us. You're too good for us. Last night we got the word around to all the guys in this end of the room."

Suzanne felt a warm glow flow through her. "Thank you, William. I don't want to quit coming, but I don't know how much longer I can avoid the ladies."

"By the way," William said, "since you are here, there is something you can do for me." His square jaw tensed visibly and his face took on a determined expression. He reached out, caught her hand in his and stared at her with rounded eyes. "Promise me a dance at the Governor's Christmas Ball."

Suzanne made no effort to retrieve her hand, but threw back her head and laughed in sheer joy. "If, by some magical means we should both go to the most grandiose event of the season, I shall be delighted and honored to grant you a dance."

* * * *

Suzanne worked at least six hours, and up to ten hours, each day. But she knew two things for sure—she must never be at Fort McHenry when Grandfather Hanson arrived for evening rounds and she must never be late for dinner. The first would mean instant discovery and the second might cause her grandparents to question her activities. That she could not work on Sundays was another fact.

Suzanne loved Sundays when the whole family, followed by Zoe and Polly, Sally, Charlie, Henry and the others, walked to town. They attended services at the majestic five-year-old St. Paul's Episcopal Church. The Sabbath reminded Suzanne of home, where the slaves followed Aman and her to their Episcopal Church and were allowed to worship upstairs in the balcony.

Each afternoon when Suzanne arrived home from the fort, she asked Zoe for a bath. Having none other, she used the lavender-scented soap to scrub the stains out of her dress. She wrung it out by hand as well as she could and hung it in her dressing room to dry for the next day. Then she eased her tired body into the tepid water.

After three weeks Zoe met her at the bedroom door with fire in her black eyes. "Your bath is ready, Miz Suzanne. What be the matter with you, not lettin' Zoe take care o' you? You give me dat dress. From now on I be gettin' it ready for you to wear next day. Polly fin'ly tole me what you was doin'. I's shamed o' you fo' not tellin' me."

When Suzanne came out of Fort McHenry the following afternoon, Rufus sat on the ground by the back door. When she saw him she froze, then ran, but stumbled. Rufus, quicker, closed a hand over her right shoulder to stop her fall. "I got to see you, Miz Suzanne. It be Mr. Tyrone. He say for you to meet him at the townhouse."

She shook her head violently. "No!"

Drops of perspiration clung to Rufus' forehead. "It's important, Miz. Mr. Tyrone says he needs the paper. He say you bring it. I be takin' you."

The Bandit's Lady

Suzanne studied him. She pushed back a wayward strand of hair and straightened to relieve the ache in her shoulders. "When?" she asked, scarcely aware of her own voice.

The muscles in Rufus' face relaxed and his smile widened in approval. "Tomorrow. Here. Two 'clock. I have you home by dinner time."

The struggle between reluctance and willingness raged in Suzanne's mind. Would giving him the paper work against her Father? Or, if she agreed to see Tyrone one more time, could she convince him to tell her what was going on? Then again it might be a trap set by the thieves to kidnap her again. A mixture of turmoil caused by both fear and trust assailed her. Her eyes met Rufus'; they probed, pleaded. "Nothin' won't happen to you, Miz. I promise dat."

Suzanne recalled the passion that smoldered within her and thrilled her whenever she was with Tyrone. She turned her face away from Rufus' steady gaze. In a voice that seemed to come from a long way off, she said, "I'll be here."

Suzanne whirled toward home, but not before she heard Rufus let out a long, audible breath.

* * * *

At dinner, John opened the conversation brusquely. "The girl comes everyday."

"What girl?" his wife asked sharply.

"The young girl who plays nursemaid to the soldiers at Fort McHenry."

"You get so riled up, John. What is really bothering you?"

"Today, Nurse Townsend told me the young lady called Angel was not behaving at all like a proper lady."

Suzanne stifled a denial and a giggle. "Whatever do you mean, Grandfather?"

John looked at Suzanne sternly, as if he had forgotten her presence. "Oh, well, now, this isn't exactly conversation for the dinner hour. Excuse me for bringing up an awkward subject. We will talk of other things."

Suzanne silently pleaded with Polly. Using the pet name he taught her to call him, Polly said, "Come on, Granddaddy Hanson, you can't leave us with questions. Whatever did Miss Angel do?"

Innocently, Margaret also came to Suzanne's aid. "Yes, John, I dare say you wanted to talk about it before you roused our curiosity. Now finish your story."

He looked acutely embarrassed. "I wish I had restrained my tongue, but if I must tell it—this 'angel' was on the verge of getting caught by Mrs. Townsend..."

"What do you mean, getting caught, John?"

"All the ladies have been instructed to try to talk to the young girl about the indelicacy of her working among the men. You know, because of her age, although she does dress properly now.

"It seems she is always on the lookout for the women. She darts away to another area whenever one of them gets too close to her."

"But what of today, John?"

"I was getting to that. When Clara got within speaking distance of her, Lieutenant William Barclay summoned her to another part of the room. This time Clara kept a close eye on her. He called her over to him, no doubt, on purpose. While she was there, he took hold of her hand. She laughed, but did not pull away. She was coquettish, you see, although I don't like to use the word in front of the girls. I don't like to think of what Mrs. Townsend told me later, either."

"But you must, of course," Margaret said with obvious pleasure. "You have us all on the edge of our seats."

"She said the men are conspiring against the other women to keep the young one out of their clutches."

"Oh, what a splendid story, John. Frankly, I hope they can do it. The young girl, an angel indeed, is doing a fine job of helping to keep the wounded prisoners' spirits high. Since they have something to keep their minds occupied, they will recover their health much faster. Haven't you said the same thing many times, John?" She did not wait for an answer. "If I had the time, I would go to Fort McHenry and help that young girl myself."

Black eyes sparkling, Polly said, "I wonder if Angel has found her true love. What do you think, Suzanne?"

I think, she thought, *she has, but it has nothing to do with William.* How could she get the bandit out of her mind forever? Impatiently, she pulled her drifting thoughts together and answered somewhat testily. "How should I know? My guess is she was only enjoying a cheerful moment, especially since she had escaped those bothersome women who continually stalk her. If this angel attended the soldiers at Fort McHenry every day since you first told us of her, and has done no harm, then why, dear grandfather, don't you tell them to leave her alone?"

"A good point, Suzanne. I am inclined to agree with you, but first I want to meet her to assure myself she is sincere. If she is, then I will try to get one of the better nurses to take her under her care."

Suddenly anxious to escape this disturbing conversation, Suzanne caught herself glancing uneasily at Polly. Polly said to Margaret, "I hate to shift this fascinating discussion, but

Grandmama, I heard the *Bianca* is docking tomorrow, a day early. Would you like me to meet the steamer?"

"Thank you, yes. Maybe Suzanne would like to go with you."

On safer ground at last, Suzanne said, "I can't go tomorrow, Grandmother. I have an errand in town, but I am truly struggling to make more sense of this Underground Railroad business. Maybe I could begin by helping out at the big barn sometimes."

Polly shot her a grateful look. Margaret's blue eyes glistened with emotion. "My darling granddaughter, you are perfectly welcome to come with me whenever you wish. Day after tomorrow, there will be many things to do. The children and babies always need extra care between trips. You might like to help us get them ready for travel."

"I'll think about it, Grandmother, but for now, let's all enjoy Sally's chocolate mousse." She turned to Polly's mother. "I'll have a large helping, Zoe."

* * * *

"What will you do," Polly asked that night, from the center of Suzanne's bed.

"I don't know. I've considered letting Grandfather discover me. Then I get goose bumps thinking he may find out the truth. At any rate, tomorrow I will be safe, for I really do have an errand in town. I will not take any risks until after the weekend. By then I shall think of something."

"Now," Polly said, with mock seriousness, "tell me all about your devoted Lieutenant William Barclay."

"Oh, Polly, he's so sweet, but it's not what you think. Quite by guess, and by accident, he and the others have found out my plight and have vowed to save me."

"But he held your hand and you allowed it?"

"That was completely innocent. In jest, he asked me for a dance at the Governor's Christmas Ball. I accepted of course, knowing full well neither of us would be invited. We had a good laugh. The men, boys really, need laughter and light."

"Be careful, Suzanne. You are far more attractive to the opposite sex than you can even imagine. And don't be so sure you won't be invited to the Christmas Ball. Your grandfather and grandmother attend every year. It's the event of the season. I must leave you now, my friend. I have a big day tomorrow."

* * * *

After a restless night, Suzanne arose before daylight. She took particular pains to get ready for her meeting with Tyrone.

She was happy to see Zoe had used a hot iron to smooth the wrinkles out of the smoke gray dress. She had also starched the matching bonnet and replaced the frayed ribbon with one of pale yellow. She grinned as she thought about dressing in yellow fluff.

Suzanne brushed her hair until it shone, caught it up with combs and hid it beneath the bonnet. A few heedless loose tendrils swirled softly around her face.

In the faint light of dawn, she stood before the mirror and decided the pallor of her face showed the strain of her fitful night. While she applied a tiny tinge of rouge to her cheekbones, she recalled Miss Abigail's earthy advice. "Rouge is for harlots, ladies of the night. Nice girls don't wear it."

Suzanne smiled at the memory. Outspoken as she was, on the side of risqué, Miss Abigail wore the rouge herself, no matter how she tried to conceal it.

Suzanne took the bandit's paper from its hiding place in the secret compartment of the bottom desk drawer. She slipped it back into the tiny slit in the lining of her clutch. The pearl-handled pistol was secure in its pouch in the bottom of the purse. On top, she placed a dainty linen handkerchief trimmed in yellow lace. She left the house by the side door and inhaled the delicate sweet smell of the rose garden as she passed by it on the way to the lane.

The hours at Fort McHenry rushed by and dragged in turns. Suzanne checked, fed, comforted and wrote letters for two dozen soldiers. She cried out in utter despair when she discovered Danny Fletcher's empty bed. Tears coursed down her cheeks as she made her way to William's side. "What happened to Private Fletcher?"

"The gangrene had already set in by the time they operated. There wasn't enough medicine. They could've heard his screams across the bay." A shudder passed through him. "Twelve died last night." He put his head in his hands. "Oh, my God, Angel, what are we going to do?"

Suzanne flinched at the agony in his voice. She sat gingerly on the edge of his bed and reached an arm around his shoulders. He clung to her for comfort. She spoke with a deceptive calmness. "I don't know, William, but we'll think of something. Where do the medical supplies come from?"

"I don't know. I think from up north. They're swapped for other goods and filched and misappropriated. I'll be out of here in a few days. I got lead in my thigh, but I was luckier than some. I'll get those bastards, pardon my language, Angel, who seize the stuff."

"Is it awful here, William?"

"It's okay. It's worse in the field. We're always short of surgeons. There's never enough morphine or quinine. The guys in the swamps get malaria. We sleep on the hard ground and drink bad water. We get dysentery—it spreads. Meal after meal, we eat hardtack and drink coffee made of roasted wheat. Bacon is a treat."

"I've got to leave early, today, William, but I might know someone who can help get medical supplies out to the field."

"It's okay, Angel. The ones who care are doing all they can. I'm just discouraged. It's so damned hard to see 'em die because somebody stole stuff for them Union scoundrels. You better get out of here. Old lady Townsend is hustling this way."

Suzanne gave William a pat on the back for encouragement, and fled.

Rufus was sitting in the carriage. It was the same buggy that took Suzanne home the night Tyrone rescued her from the kidnappers. The whole evening flooded back in her memory, raced through her mind. Her heart thundered crazily. It had been so comfortable and cozy. Her private pleasure sent a small thrill coursing through her.

Rufus' black face lit up at the sight of her. She remembered in time the stranded, left-alone feeling when Tyrone let her out to fend for herself in the half-light and grotesque shadows. She retreated a step. "I'm sorry, Rufus, I can't go with you today. I must find my grandfather. Those sick and wounded soldiers need help and I promised Lieutenant Barclay I'd try to find that help. I'll come with you tomorrow."

The coach door opened. Tyrone leaned forward. He shot her a dazzling smile. When he spoke, his tone was velvet, yet edged with steel. "I thought you might decide to change your mind, Suzanne. I came along to make sure you didn't. Get in!"

Chapter 11

More surprised than frightened, Suzanne looked up. As their eyes met, she felt shock run through her. It made her want to hurt him and, at the same time, make him want her. She shrugged and reached for the bandit's hand. Careful not to let her fingers linger on his, she sat across from him. "Take me home, Tyrone. I must get there quickly to get Grandfather's help."

His left eyebrow rose a fraction. "Really Suzanne, will one night make a difference? Whatever the problem, your grandfather will probably need time to work out a solution. Besides, I want you to meet a friend of mine."

Suzanne leaned back against the soft cushion and closed her eyes. She felt spent, defeated. "You win, of course. I want to talk to you anyway."

The coach grew quiet. Tyrone moved across the aisle to gather Suzanne in his arms. "How long do we have to go on like this, my love? I know you feel the same way I do. I dare you to tell me otherwise. Look at me, Suzanne."

The look on his face mingled eagerness and tenderness and an almost imperceptible note of pleading. Her arm tingled as his hand slid down and tightened around her wrist. A shaft of sun struck his black hair; it gleamed in the light. A swath of wavy hair fell casually on his forehead, accenting the thin scar. His well-groomed appearance seemed out of character with his weathered, sun-bronzed skin. Suzanne smiled. "I wish so hard I could deny what I feel. Since I cannot, I must stick to my plan of not giving in to my emotions."

Tyrone lifted her hand and kissed her fingertips. He reached up and untied the yellow ribbon under her chin and in one quick motion removed the curved combs that held the silky ringlets. Released, her hair tumbled carelessly down her back. His smile sent her pulses racing. "Ah, Suzanne, it is enough for now that we feel the same for each other. Would that I could indulge your curiosity, but the mystery will clear up in time."

"Not likely, Bandit. The war gets worse, and bitter. How can you pretend that you will absolve whatever it is you are about? I read every issue of the *Crier*; I know the objectives of your corrupt crew. They intimidate and steal and rape and you're their leader."

"If you would only trust me, Suzanne..." His voice was husky with emotion.

"I can't and well you know it."

"Then let me hold you." His hint of meaning was unmistakable, but the force of his appealing smile caused her defenses to fade away. She longed to feel his arms around her and swayed toward him. Tyron's steady gaze bore into her in silent expectation, before his arms enveloped her. He bent and kissed her gently. At last her lips parted. The moist tip of his tongue crept into her mouth. Suzanne felt her breasts swell beneath the plain gown she was wearing. Her arms crept around his neck. She felt the rippling movements of powerful back muscles and was fully conscious of every contact where warm flesh touched her and the occasional jolt caused by Tyron's thigh brushing her hip. She held him fiercely, ached for him, let his vitality seep through her entire body. There was a dreamy intimacy to their kiss now. Suzanne yearned to give him more, but with difficulty struggled back to reality. Painfully she withdrew from his arms and moved to the right. Choosing the words carefully and as casually as she could manage, she asked, "When the war is over, will we see each other?"

She turned away without waiting for an answer, anxious now to escape from his disturbing presence. She realized that each time they were together, the pull toward him was stronger. She blinked her eyes shut against the flash of loneliness that stabbed at her. Her whole being filled with the agony of waiting.

"By then, we'll be fighting for the same cause," he said, as his steady gaze traveled over her face and searched her eyes. His invitation was open and passionate. His large hands took her face and held it gently.

The carriage came to an unnerving halt. "What's going on out there, Rufus?"

"We be there, Mr. Tyrone."

"Damn," Tyrone said, under his breath as he caught Suzanne to him again.

She felt the excitement in his restless flesh. For a few final minutes, they clung to each other in the semi-darkness of the rig. Tyrone's voice was low and seductive. "We will much more than see each other when this war is over, believe me, Suzanne. Come with me now. I promised to get you home by the dinner hour. Time is wasting."

He jumped lightly to the ground and spoke quietly to Rufus. Then he helped Suzanne to the ground and led her up the brick walkway to a modest, narrow, three-story town house. "Who lives here?" Suzanne asked.

Tyrone grinned. He spoke in a carefree, jesting way. "It's the perfect refuge for a *Sea Queen* captain/bandit, don't you think?"

"This is your home?"

"Yes. Come on, Suzanne. Tea will be ready."

Tyrone led her up the steps. A long L-shaped porch fronted the frame house. A small entrance hall led into a comfortable all-purpose sitting room. At the door, Tyrone said, "Rufus has told me there is pressing business I must take care of at the shack. Make yourself at home, Suzanne. Faith will bring refreshment."

She shuddered as she remembered the shack and caught the look of amusement in Tyrone's eyes. His mouth curved with tenderness. "Don't worry, my dear," he said, calmly. "I'll be back within the hour."

Suzanne stepped into the room and looked around curiously. The room, a study in blues, had a rich masculine décor. She suspected it reflected Tyrone's concept of a warm, traditional life-style richly woven with stories and artifacts. Accented with high-beamed ceilings, the towering, elongated windows had wooden shutters instead of drapes. A small drop-leaf table with a captain and its mate chairs were placed by the window that overlooked a tiny flower garden. A small fish pond, complete with three quacking ducks, rounded out the scene.

A braided oval rag rug covered the center of the polished oak floor. A roll-top desk dominated one wall and massive bookcases surrounded an unlit fireplace in the center of a second wall. The bookcases overflowed with classics, including a thick red volume of *Uncle Tom's Cabin*. Suzanne recalled the row they'd had when Miss Abigail had snatched the book away from her. "You're too young to read that trash," she had said.

Suzanne retrieved the book later from her father's library and hid it beneath her bed. As she read the story she had thought of Polly, free and happy in her grandfather's home.

Suzanne's eyes traveled to the plump, skipper blue davenport with pudgy, squashy cushions. The only other pieces of furniture that graced the room were a matching set of flowered chintz-covered armchairs.

Surprised, she spied Captain Neal Franklin sitting in the chair facing the door, cradling the unlit pipe in his left hand,. A devilish light blazed in his blue eyes as he offered Suzanne a half-salute with his free hand and greeted her with a chuckle. "How be ye, mate?" he asked in mock seriousness.

He was teasing her affectionately, mischievously. Suzanne felt her cheeks burn in remembrance, but she fondly returned his disarming smile. She took the armchair facing him. "I should be mortified, but I've already paid dearly for my reckless blunder."

A tall angular lady bustled fussily into the room. She carried a teapot and a tray filled with a variety of tiny, exquisitely decorated cakes. Setting them down, she looked at Suzanne for instructions. "I'll pour, Faith. Thank you."

Suzanne looked at the captain. "I'll have my tea black and sweet. Two, heaping, please," he said.

The tea was hot and strong. To hers, Suzanne added the juice from a wedge of lemon and bit into a warm sugary cake before she spoke. "Tyrone said he wanted me to get acquainted with a friend. I conclude it is you, since he left us alone. What does he want me to hear from you?"

Captain Franklin's eyes were bright with merriment. "I must say, Suzanne, you do get right to the point. Before I begin, I must tell you that I think you are a gutsy young lady, but it shouldn't surprise me. You are, after all, your grandmother's flesh and blood."

She smiled comfortably. "Yes, I am. Now, tell me about Tyrone."

He eyed her with a critical squint. "You know I carry cargo for Tyrone and you know I deliver cargo to your grandmother each Thursday. What you may have guessed is that the cargo is the same."

"Runaways?"

"Tyrone is a very complicated man. I cannot explain him except to tell you he delivers medicines and munitions to army camps and prison hospitals, in both the North and the South. He brings rice, sugar, tobacco and cotton North. He seeks and aids runaways coming up to the safety of the Underground and freedom."

"But why? The newspapers are full of his Chesapeake Bay activities. He turns blockaders back. He hunts for Confederate ships."

"Ah, so you keep track of him."

Seeing the enjoyment in his eyes, she laughed. "But of course. Didn't he terrorize me, rob me and torment me?"

She wondered if she should confide in him about the fake rape, confess her doubts to him, tell him of her fears for her father. The moment passed.

"Let me tell you a story about your bandit. Tyrone brings the Negroes to Norfolk from ports such as Charleston and

Wilmington and sometimes as far south as Savannah. The captain of the *Sea Queen* is careful. Last week the ship stood off the coast all one long day. At night, Tyrone sent skiffs ashore to leave off twenty blacks. My mate, Tim, worried himself puny that at any moment a revenue cutter following in the steamer's wake would overtake us."

Suzanne enjoyed a gentle sparring with Captain Franklin. "I suppose you weren't one particle afraid yourself."

His face split into a wide grin. "Nah. I told Tim nothing but gulls would follow us. I might have felt different if I had risked taking runaways aboard in the Charleston Harbor, but I gave up doing that a long time ago. Tyrone is a patrol for the Union. Because he does the job expected of him, he hasn't been searched in years. The Charleston authorities have come to regard both of us as safe men."

"How does Tyrone get the Negroes aboard the *Sea Queen?*"

"I can't tell you something that you could use against him. We're on different sides of this war, remember?"

"Of course I remember, but I wouldn't do anything to hurt my grandparents. You can trust me."

Captain Franklin lit his pipe. He took a long drag and gave Suzanne a steady look. "I guess you are right."

He continued more confidently, his eyes alight and his features more animated, "Tyrone devised the system. When the steamer is ashore at night and the landing dances in the light of pitch-pine flares, it's impossible to tell one hurrying figure from another. Black hands snatch the piled wood and set it down with a thud on the rough wharf before the steamboat has run out her two gangplanks. A stream of burdened Negroes lopes up the first, staggering with the weight of the wood in their arms. They soon trot down the second, empty-handed. They don't all come back down that second gangplank. When the boat starts up the dark river again, the flares burn out at the landing. In that blackness as many as five or six runaways might be on their way to freedom. Escape by sea requires the sympathy and help of ships' officers, usually Yankees. Occasionally a Southerner opposes slavery, too; they're the best help."

"How does Tyrone find the runaways?"

"The *Sea Queen* had a strong hold on a shipping route that served the South before the war. Through friends along the route, Tyrone knows all the contacts he needs. Most of your grandparents' slaves come to them by the sea."

Suzanne struggled with the uncertainty the words aroused in her. She knew now she would have to be doubly careful of her actions. What if Tyrone and her grandparents knew each other? Something cautioned her not to ask. If he did not ask for it, she would not give Tyrone the list. That paper might be her father's undoing. *On the other hand,* she thought, *maybe he can help me get the medicines we need at Fort McHenry.*

Aloud, she said, "He trades blockade runners for runaways. He has friends on both sides. He's a hard man to believe."

Behind her, coming through the doorway, Tyrone spoke without a hint of boastfulness, "But that's not true, Suzanne. I am meticulously scrupulous and entirely dependable to whatever cause I dedicate myself."

Suzanne's temper flared. "Your causes appear to be many. You attack and pilfer blockaders. You seek runaways and aid them when they leave their plantation owners. You steal precious medicines and munitions from your people." She spat out the words contemptuously.

When Tyrone did not answer, fury almost choked her, and she knew sarcasm sharpened her voice. "When you are not otherwise occupied, you rob people on stagecoaches and rape the ladies."

Suzanne picked up her clutch bag and moved to the edge of the chair. "Take me home, Tyrone. I'm weary of this discussion of your virtues."

Eyes sparkling with mirth, Tyrone turned to the captain. "I'm sorry, Neal, that you are here to witness this disclosure of my wickedness. Maybe we can discuss our mutual problem better at another time."

Captain Neal stood up and walked over to lay a hand gently on Suzanne's shoulder. Giving it a little squeeze, he said, "It has been a delightful afternoon, my dear."

Then, for her ears only, "Don't be too hard on your bandit. He's compassionate for the good of the whole human race. If he has a fault, it's his inability to control his zeal."

He turned to Tyrone and the men walked to the door talking softly. But Suzanne's mind went repeatedly over the captain's words to her. She thought, *yes, my bandit. Dear God, what am I going to do about my bandit?*

When Tyrone came back in the room, his annoyance was visible. "I am sorry our afternoon ended on such a hostile note, Suzanne. I had such high expectations." He faltered in the silence that engulfed them. "Suzanne, can't you say anything?"

She said, "The captain is perfectly congenial. I really had a lovely afternoon, thank you, but I must go now. Will you take me?" He shot her a penetrating look as she started to rise. "Suzanne, I must have the list. Did you bring it?"

A wave of apprehension swept through her. "Yes, but I've changed my mind about giving it to you."

He glared at her, frowning. She felt her lower lip tremble as she returned his stare. The strange surge of affection she felt frightened her. "I could, of course, take you apart, piece by piece, as my friends did. The ones you call the thieves. Or you could give me the list peaceably. Either way, I will not take you home until I have the paper in my possession."

He walked across the room and sat on the edge of the desk looking down at her. His eyes were as dark and commanding as he was. They never left her face. Suzanne cast her eyes downward. He waited quietly for a moment while he regarded her quizzically. "Well, what will it be?"

She became increasingly uneasy under his scrutiny. She found his nearness both disturbing and exciting, but she did not doubt he would carry out his threat. "If I give you the list, will you take my father's name off of it? You've already demolished two of his friends' ships, the *Atlanta* and the *Chancellor*. Thanks to my father, the *Annebella* crew rescued the captains, Howard Jackson and Nathan Bedford, and their crews."

He looked at her in surprise, but said in a low and composed voice, "Suzanne, you don't fully know what you're talking about or what you are asking. I will promise to do everything in my power to see that no harm comes to your father. Now, may I have the list?"

Suzanne looked up in time to see the sincerity in Tyrone's eyes before his expression changed. She saw a lazily seductive look flit across his face before Tyrone's lids came down swiftly over his eyes. She went on eagerly. "And what about Thaddeus Stuart?"

"Who is Thaddeus Stuart?"

"He owns the plantation next to Royal Oaks Manor and is a Charleston attorney. "And," she teased lightly, "is my father's choice of a husband for me."

"What of your choice?"

"That has nothing to do with this conversation. Do you want the list or not? If so, please answer the question."

Tyrone leaped off the desk and swept her weightlessly into his arms. His rich-timbered voice was sensual, husky with emotion. "My preference of your future husband has everything to do with this conversation."

His breath was warm and moist against her face and her heart raced. She settled back to enjoy the feel of his arms around her. "But as God is my witness," he murmured in her ear, "I can't speak of it now."

The magic shattered.

Chapter 12

Suzanne wrenched herself free. "I'll give you the list. You give me no other option. Then I'll thank you to take me home."

Tyrone's eyes blazed with humor. "You've forgotten something, Suzanne. Maybe I can help you. Didn't you intend to bargain with me? The list, for medicine for your soldiers at the fort?"

She looked at him with amused wonder. Without a trace of embarrassment, she said, "I'd almost forgotten. Of course I meant to bargain with you. Could you? Would you help me?"

Tyrone sobered. "Yes. I'll see that medicine gets to the fort, but you must not get involved. It's still important not to admit knowing me. Don't, under any circumstances admit you know about the supplies that will arrive there from time to time."

"I don't know why that's so important."

"Everything we do in Maryland is precarious, Suzanne. We're a border state, and although we didn't secede, there is a strong element of slave holders. No matter what your personal convictions are, you must be very careful with whom you associate. Believe me, I'm not a good risk for you."

An easy smile played at the corners of his mouth. He scooped her up in his arms again and swung her around. "For another thing, my sweet, no one has formally introduced us."

* * * *

"Tyrone! Whatever are you doing? Come, give me a kiss."

The voice, like a silken thread, held a challenge. Suzanne stiffened, and felt lucky to have landed on her feet. Tyrone rushed across the room. "I didn't know you were leaving Philadelphia. What a delightful surprise. We have so much catching up to do. Oh, ladies, forgive me."

Tyrone turned to Suzanne. An excited light glowed in his ebony eyes. "Suzanne, this is Bridget, an old friend of the family."

Suzanne nodded in a small gesture of greeting. Bridget acknowledged her with polite indifference as her brilliant black eyes fixed on Tyrone. They had forgotten her. Suzanne noted every detail of Bridget's tall graceful form. The sweetheart neckline of her gown revealed full, firm, high-perched breasts. Even the color of the periwinkle frock looked especially fashioned for this very room. Bridget's hair, a cobweb of silvery gold, lay satiny soft about her proud shoulders. She had delicately carved facial bones and a full mouth. Her sweet, low voice was soft and clear.

Suzanne stood motionless in the middle of the room, willing her composure to return and steady her voice. Then she reached out and placed her hand on Tyrone's forearm. "Forgive the interruption," she said firmly, "but I must be going now."

His muscles tensed under her fingertips; hastily she drew her hand away. He glanced sideways in surprise. His eyes met hers. The expression in them brimmed with tenderness and seemed to plead for understanding. They filled her with a curious deep longing. He said, "Yes, of course. Rufus will take you home." He turned to the newcomer. "Excuse me, Bridget. I'll see to Suzanne. Make yourself at home. I'll send Faith to show you to your room."

Standing by the carriage, Tyrone said, with a tinge of impatience, I'm so sorry, Suzanne. I was looking forward to taking you home, myself. Please give me the list before you leave."

Without speaking, she pulled the paper out of its hiding place and handed it to him. "I pray to God you keep your promise to protect my father."

Tyrone gave her a gentle smile. He stepped away. The carriage lurched forward.

Suzanne leaned back and closed her eyes, reliving the pain of that final scene. She held back tears of frustration. A bitterness stirred inside her. Her mind churned. Her misery was so acute it was a physical pain. Sensations of intense sickness and desolation swept over her. By turns, disbelief and rage mingled as she struggled to understand. She wondered how he could pretend to care for her, then decided it was only carnal need. The next instant, she admitted Bridget was probably an old friend as he had said she was.

The simple explanation of Bridget would not drive away the thoughts. She visualized their black eyes locked together as their breathing came in unison. The scene played over and over like a bad dream. She felt a cold despair spreading through her stomach. *Please, God, don't let me love him,* she thought, but knew the plea came too late.

When the carriage stopped at the far end of the estate, Rufus took charge with quiet assurance. He opened the door and helped her to the ground. "Miz Suzanne, 'member when you was a prisoner in the shack an' I told you you'd be out soon? I did not lie then. I don't now. Everything be okay. That Miz Bridget mean nothin' to the boss."

Suzanne managed a small, tentative smile. "It's all right, Rufus. It's not likely I will see him again. Thank you for bringing me home. Hurry away now, before someone discovers you."

The next two days passed quickly. The *Baltimore Crier* reported the seizure of two wagon loads of medical supplies bound for Richmond, Virginia:

> *The robbery was obviously performed by an experienced group of thieves. The authorities have not found even one clue at the site of the robberies. It's as if the priceless shipment simply disappeared like invisible vapor.*

* * * *

Because Suzanne feared her grandfather would discover her, she worked at the fort in the early mornings, keeping careful watch for his unscheduled visits. In the afternoons she helped her grandmother in the big barn. Margaret Hanson, wisely, Suzanne realized later, gave her the job of caring for the sweet, innocent babies who traveled in baskets. She fed them, wrapped them in warm flannel and stupefied them with the paregoric that kept them silent and safe for the next phase of the trip north.

At the dinner table Friday night, Margaret's eyes sparkled at her husband. "Well, John, tell us about Angel."

Suzanne watched her grandfather guardedly. He glowered at his wife. "I've not seen her. I've missed her three days running, but her influence is everywhere. Two wagon loads of prized medicines mysteriously appeared at Fort McHenry today."

"Why are you so disturbed? What does the delivery of precious medicines have to do with the angel?" Margaret asked.

"We think it was the same medications the bandits looted just day before yesterday."

"That still doesn't seem to have anything to do with this angel."

"Lieutenant Barclay says Angel promised to find a way to help them. We haven't sent the medicines on to their original destination, because heaven knows we are in desperate need of them. But we don't want stolen goods either. I feel stronger than ever that we must catch this angel and put a stop to any more criminal schemes."

Suzanne was puzzled and more than a little nervous. She shot Polly a questioning look. Polly's brow creased with worry. Almost undetectable, she shook her head negatively. Suzanne swallowed her confession.

Later, from the middle of Suzanne's bed, Polly asked, "For goodness sakes, girl, who do you know that would steal to help you?"

Relieved to have somebody to talk to, Suzanne said, "The bandit—the one who robbed the stage and let his partners snatch our jewelry."

"And raped you?"

"Polly, that's what I don't understand. He didn't rape me, but made me tell everybody he did. He ordered me to scream so the thieves thought he had. He was loathsome."

"What's his name?"

"Tyrone Sterling."

Polly began to laugh, softly at first. Then she threw back her head and let out a joyous peal of laughter. Howling with mirth, she rocked back and forth. Tears coursed down her cheeks. "What's so funny?"

Polly wiped her eyes. With an effort she sobered a little. "Honey, Tyrone wouldn't hurt a fly."

"You know him?"

"He's a friend of Captain Neal. We been picking up Tyrone's cargo from the *Bianca* for three years." Polly grew quiet. "He's right, though. You can't let on you know him. You could get him killed and get yourself in trouble, too."

"In what way? Besides, he may be dangerous to my father."

"That's another reason not to mention that you know him. He's not exactly playing straight on the right side of the law. I can't tell you more. Just promise to be careful, Suzanne."

"You're not telling me anything, are you?"

"No. The less you know, the better. Hey Princess, the big races are next weekend. I'm getting really excited, but for now, let's get some sleep."

Polly scrambled off the bed and reached out to put her hand on Suzanne's arm. Deep concern showed in her snappy black eyes. "Take care, Suzanne. War is a terrible business."

* * * *

The September Saturday, in full bloom of autumn, was bursting with golden grains and trees laden with bountiful ripened fruits. Suzanne and her grandfather rode past the orchard and leisurely surveyed the estate. They cantered around the two-mile racetrack that was a part of the land John had donated to the city for the annual horse races. They reined in their horses and looked out over the course. When John turned to Suzanne, excitement shimmered in his eyes. "The other two races, the one at the end of May and the one on Independence Day, are fine races, but this one is famous. The finest horseflesh in these parts come here year after year to compete in the Septemberfest Races. Next week we'll have three horses from our own stable vying for honors: Sir Billy Blue Belle, Lady Jane and Miss Mary-Mary. That's the most we have ever entered all at once. We're hoping for some wins. Charlie started giving the racehorses extra oats a month ago. He put them in special training, watching them through their paces with a keen eye. He's been working long extra hours with the young jockeys. We're all ready for the big event."

Affection for her grandfather swelled in Suzanne's heart. She felt eager and alive with delight and mischievousness. "Don't worry, Grandfather. Polly and I will cheer them to victory as we did when we were too young to attend the races."

"How was that, my dear?"

"We stood in that grove of trees over there and..."

"You didn't! You mean you sneaked to watch the races?"

Suzanne laughed at his surprise. "We couldn't resist. Oh, Grandfather, it was such fun! We are both wild to sit properly in the new stands at our very first real races."

"I will forgive your childish escapades and escort you both, one on each arm. James will squire your grandmother. It will be great sport."

They returned to the house and ate a huge breakfast in friendly companionable silence. After John left to tend his patients, Suzanne walked through the cheery dining room and down the long hallway to the parlor. She let out a small squeak when she saw the envelope with its familiar script lying on the tea table beside the morning *Crier*. Aman's letter was full of his activities.

>*My dearest Suzanne:*
>
>*This war is so discouraging. It is difficult for me to report anything of consequence to you for fear the enemy will confiscate the mails. If that should happen, you could be put in unnecessary danger, but I will update you to a small degree. Our group is still operating the Annebella. Very successfully, I might add, but it continues to get more dangerous.*
>
>*Our leaders declared a voluntary cotton embargo in hopes a cotton shortage will speed the day when Great Britain and France intervene on our behalf. They can do it easily by dispatching a fleet of ships to break the stranglehold of the blockade that has choked off Confederate exports. England owes nothing to the North and it would be to her economic interest to be the guardian of the South's independence. After all, we produce half the world's output of the cotton that is processed in English mills—abundantly and profitably, truth be known.*
>
>*I find time to visit Royal Oaks about every six weeks. The Yankees built a tower encircled by a stockade for defense against enemy attack, right on the plantation. I am told that seven such towers have been built between Folly Island and fifty-five miles south to Hilton Head. Their sole purpose is to relay messages within minutes from one end of the line to the other. Thaddeus is studying the signals. He plans to figure out the code and report it to General Pierce.*

They use two simple flag movements, made in differing combinations to represent each letter of the alphabet.

Luke Henry tells me it is quite unnerving for the laboring slaves. Thaddeus is always after me for spoiling my Negroes, but they repay us year after year with profuse productivity. Thaddeus says our generous ways are causing discontent among his slaves. His are restless and getting belligerent, but I say it's his own fault. Royal Oaks is doing much better than many plantations in the surrounding area. Nevertheless, I wish it could have your gentle touch to assure our people continued contentment.

One Union ship, Sea Queen, is often in the vicinity of our own maneuvers. She has not hurt us, nor have I been close enough to attack the she-devil, but I stay wary. Her captain has a reputation for avoiding out-and-out combat, but still stalks us constantly.

I find I have said more than I intended. With all my heart I pray this brutal war will come to an end in a short time, so we can all be together. Give my regards to your grandparents and keep James with you. It is not yet safe to travel.

Your loving Father, Aman

Suzanne reread the letter again, and read the part about the *Sea Queen yet again. Why would Tyrone continually give chase to the Annebella,* she wondered? Suzanne's glance fell on the front page of the *Baltimore Crier*. Its large black headline fairly jumped off the page.

Brilliant Union Victory
(Both forts, 630 Prisoners)

A major flaw in President Lincoln's coastal blockade has persisted in and around Hatteras Inlet. Little was done, until yesterday, at either Fort Hatteras or Fort Clark to shield the inlet. Blockade runners, rebel traders and privateer ventures, have continued to slip through the barrier almost at will.

Once beyond the protective barricade, the vessels are free to take the Pamlico Sound. They travel up Neuse River to New York, up Pamlico River to Washington, through Dismal Swamp, and by the back way to Norfolk.

This paper criticized the Sea Queen on more than one occasion, but she played an indispensable roll for the fleet by taking measures that successfully shut off the fort's outlets. Her captain captured some 630 volunteer defenders, planters, shipowners, tar boilers, proprietors. The list goes on and on.

The Sea Queen filled every available space with prisoners. And, because her captain is a compassionate man, he gave prisoners all the freshwater they wanted to drink; they used up all the ship's ice. A spokesman said the captives had nothing but unfit water for weeks, even months, before their arrest.

Thanks to the Sea Queen's crew, Hatteras Inlet is entirely shut off from Confederate trade. Although it was a major victory, there was one biting incident to mar the triumphant affair. The long-sought-after Annebella escaped again. Her disappearance was blamed on the prevailing southwest gales and a heavy surf breaking on the beach. The fleet of boats picking up the offenders simply didn't reach her in time. Captain Sterling, of the Sea Queen, was not available for comment."

Suzanne curled her legs up underneath her and closed her eyes. She recalled how the bandit had swept her into his strong, gentle arms. She could almost feel the tingling of her lips when he kissed her. In the stillness of remembering, she visualized the soft, penetrating grip of his hand on her arm. A brief shiver rippled through her. She knew an undeniable web of magnetism was building between them. *Is the bandit the man I have dreamed of—the kind of love I must know before I can marry?*

Suzanne's mind wandered. She remembered the day she had enjoyed the restful banter and the comfort of Captain Neal Franklin's company. Her heart gloried in the warmth of feelings that surrounded her when Tyrone had called her 'my sweet'. Unbidden, a stab of pain so sharp she winced, reached through her brain as she recalled Bridget's unannounced entrance. The jealousy she recognized was as alien to her as the love that trembled through her body whenever she thought of Tyrone. She had known from the beginning she should not love a man like Tyrone. She decided she must concentrate on Thaddeus or William. *Yes, maybe the Lieutenant*, she thought.

Chapter 13

Suzanne's eyes popped open. She had dozed. She had promised Private George Johnston she would change his bandages and she told Sergeant Tim Yancey she would write a letter to his girlfriend. She had given William her word she would escort him to his sister's house. He planned to recover fully before going back to the front lines. Suzanne dashed up the wide spiral staircase to her bedroom to change into her gray dress and bonnet.

* * * *

As William manipulated the cumbersome, improvised crutch under his right arm, the mid-afternoon sunshine vanished. Lightning illuminated the horizon with eerie flashes. Thunder grumbled as the first plump raindrops began to spatter down, making fat dark blotches on the dirt streets.

Suzanne took William's other arm and helped him awkwardly out the back door of Fort McHenry and down the path to the waiting gig. "My brother-in-law sent the carriage," William said as they settled down comfortably behind the driver.

He gestured. "That's Noah. He came from my parents' tobacco plantation in Virginia and has been with my sister Julia and her Tom since they married. Julia couldn't come for me

The Bandit's Lady

because of their three little ones. Tom works down at the shipyards; he is a shipbuilder."

"Where do your parents live in Virginia?"

"Our folks are dead."

"Oh. I'm so sorry."

"It happened a long time ago."

Suzanne sat back and regarded the rain anxiously. It was falling steadily now. The Septemberfest Races were but a week away and she hoped the worst of the autumn rains would hold off until after the lively holiday. Startled, she looked over at William. "I'm sorry. I didn't hear you."

"I asked if you knew about the large delivery of medicines, blankets and other scarce supplies that mysteriously arrived at Fort McHenry yesterday morning."

"Yes, I knew, but I can't tell you how."

"Dr. Hanson was asking after you, Angel. He thinks it's time to meet you. Now that I have left the hospital ward, you must be extra careful. I won't be there to help organize your protection."

"Don't fret, William. I can't go there so often now. My grandmother needs me at the estate. I'll only be at the hospital for short periods in the mornings and I promise to be careful."

Noah reined in the horses at the front of a big square frame house. The yard was small, but well kept. "Uncle Willy! Uncle Willy! Mama said you were coming to stay with us for a long time."

Two freckle-faced children with carrot red hair stood on the front stoop waiting for William to alight. "Your mama is right, but you rascals stay back. I've hurt my leg and won't have you climbing all over me."

He turned to Suzanne. "These are the twins, Laura and Lief. They're four and a half, and a captivating handful. Say hello to Miss Angel, children."

Two pair of identical bright blue eyes looked up to inspect their guest. "Are you a real angel?" Lief asked in awe.

"She ain't no real angel, silly," his sister said. "Real angels have wings and long white gowns and a gold circle above their heads."

Suzanne laughed. "Hello, Laura. You're right. I'm not a real angel. Hello, Lief."

William's gray eyes bathed Suzanne in admiration. They exchanged a subtle look of amusement as they walked slowly up the short footpath to the front door. "I was happy to see you home, William, but I must leave now. I dare not be late for dinner."

"You can't leave yet. Julia is eager to meet you. Please stay for tea."

"Yes, please, do stay."

Suzanne looked up. Framed in the doorway stood a young girl not much older than herself. She was the feminine version of her brother, slightly plump with direct silver gray eyes. Behind her, a baby cried. Beside her, a small white-and-black spotted dog yelped to get out-of-doors. *How does she manage?* Suzanne wondered. Julia answered as if she had asked the question aloud.

"I know it looks like an impossible task, but the puppy is really good company for the twins, and the baby is only fussing. She has just suckled and will be asleep in moments. Come in, do. I adore adult visitors after being with the children all day. I'm Julia."

Julia's voice was smooth, but insistent. She had an air of calm and self-confidence Suzanne liked. "And no matter what you may have heard about an angel, I'm Suzanne. Suzanne Willoughby."

The twins lost interest and scampered across the porch to a wooden swing suspended from rafter beams. Julia led her brother and Suzanne into a square, plainly furnished parlor. It was small and windowless, but like the yard it was neat and immaculately clean. William sat on a blue velvet settee. With a sigh of gratitude, he lifted his wounded leg to rest on one end of a wiggly tea table. Julia motioned for Suzanne to sit across from him in the only easy chair.

Julia quickly returned from the kitchen with the tea service and spicy apple tarts, each topped with a thin slab of cheese. She sat on the edge of the Boston rocker to pour the hot, aromatic liquid. "Tell us about yourself, Suzanne. What William has been saying about you may or may not be reliable. Although, I will grant he was telling the truth when he said you are seductively petite and flower like."

Suzanne felt her face grow hot. She flashed William a small, shy smile. A wry but indulgent glint appeared in his gray eyes. He said, "Tell us about the angel part. You're too young to be a nurse. How do you get away from your family? You spoke of a grandmother."

"My grandfather is a doctor, both in private practice and as a war volunteer. Grandmother volunteers her services to the war effort in...in other ways. I want to be a nurse, but I'm too young, so I decided to sneak away and do my part."

William turned to Julia. "You should have seen Angel—Suzanne—dodging those women. What do you mean, your grandfather is a doctor? Can't you accompany him to learn until you're old enough to be a nurse?"

"I wish it was that easy, but I'm visiting from the South, you see. In these troubled times, Grandfather thinks it would be unwise for me to go on rounds with him."

Julia asked, "Who is your grandfather?"

Suzanne looked straight at William and smiled. She anticipated his reaction with delight. "My grandfather is Doctor John Hanson." William gawked comically. Then his undiluted laughter was triumphant.

"Oh, dear God in His heaven, that is rich." His shoulders shook with laughter. "I told you Angel is a saucy one, didn't I, Julia? Then a melancholy frown flitted across his features. "And I was about to ask if I could escort you to the big races Saturday."

Suzanne flashed a smile of thanks. "I wish you could, but of course that would give away my little game. Grandfather would know immediately how and where I met you."

William's eyes glistened as yet another spasm of laughter quivered through him. "It's okay. I'll wrangle an introduction out of your grandfather. Then we can spend part of the afternoon together. When we meet at the Christmas Ball, you will naturally save three or more dances for me."

Julia gave a peal of laughter. "My dear brother, you most probably will meet Suzanne at the races, but you, go to the Governor's Christmas Ball?"

"You two listen up. I'll be there."

The three young people chatted excitedly about the forthcoming races until the clock standing in one corner of the room struck four o'clock. Suzanne jumped up. "Julia, this has been great fun, but I must get home and changed in time for dinner, to avoid suspicion."

She purposely gave William an impish smile. "I do hope you'll find a way to make my acquaintance Saturday next."

Julia reached out and touched Suzanne lightly on the arm. "Thank you for taking such good care of my brother. Do promise to stop by again. You can rest assured your secret is safe with us. Noah will take you home now."

* * * *

When Suzanne walked up the lane and reached her bedroom, her bath was ready. She sank into its steamy, lilac fragrance to relax, but Zoe bustled into the room.

"You's got to hurry or you be late fo' dinner. Let me fix dat achin' back." She leaned over the tub and took the cloth out of Suzanne's hand.

"Zoe, I know you're free and Grandfather pays you a wage, but where did you come from? How does it feel different to be free instead of a slave when you do the same chores and work such long, hard hours?"

"Honey, somebody yanked me away from me mama befo' I kin be rememberin'. I went from cotton fields to tobacco fields. Seems ever' year I got sold agin till I ends at mercy of Maser Thomas. He fetched me fo' to teach the housekeepin'. Said I was tall 'n a might graceful and would look dignified for his callers. He taught me himself to carry a book on top of me head so's not to stoop my shoulders."

"But why did he let Grandfather and Grandmother buy you?"

"He be lettin' my Job and me marry up, but he don' like it. When Job be dead, I lost me heart 'n it seem I couldn't serve him well. I been whipped plenty, but Maser Thomas was too kindly. He never beat at me. He jus' give up on me. Let me go."

Zoe straightened and wiped a tear from the corner of her eye. "This ain't a gettin' you ready fo' supper. We gots to hurry now, else you be late. Yore grandmama and grandpappa gonna be wonderin' where you be so long."

Dressed in peacock blue with matching bows around the ring of ribbon drawing up her curls, Suzanne hurriedly slipped into her place at the table. Polly gave her a quick, secret, relieved look.

James said, "Well, Grandfather, let's hear the continuing saga of "Angel." Did you meet her today?"

John's blue eyes crinkled at the corners. He chuckled heartily. "No, but I saw the backside of her leaving out the back door."

"Couldn't you catch her?"

"I was just coming in the big double front doors. By the time Mrs. Townsend told me and I reached the back door, a carriage was disappearing around the corner."

"Didn't you try to chase it?"

"If I were your age, my boy, I might have, but of course I am not. My mount was out front, so the chance was lost. It is doubtful she will be back."

"But why ever not," Margaret joined in.

"Because she brazenly left in the company of that young lieutenant, William Barclay. Can you beat that? A young girl, not chaperoned…"

Polly sent Suzanne a charming smile. She said, "I think it's most exciting. Do you think young love is in the making, Granddaddy?"

John's quiet severity forbid further conversation. "This is not a discussion worthy of our time at the dinner table."

Margaret smiled sweetly at the girls, who had all they could do to keep from giggling. James swiftly turned his grandfather's attention to a tale about his afternoon at the cockfights.

* * * *

The week of the races sped by. Although more and more men were being taken prisoner and the sick and the wounded wards were growing in numbers, Suzanne spent less time at Fort McHenry. She spent more time helping her grandmother move the runaways out of the barn to make room for their guests' racehorses.

Margaret had cleared the big barn of any signs of its normal activities. Henry and the handymen removed the hinges on the trapdoors and replaced the doors with solid wood planks. They installed twenty temporary cubicles and Charlie moved the Hanson racehorses inside. By midweek the rest of the empty stalls were full, as were all the stables at the track site.

The guest rooms at the house were full as well and, although Margaret was not serving formal meals, Sally and her staff kept the sideboard replete with tempting foods for each meal. Breakfast featured eggs, bacon, ham, sausages, fried potatoes, gravies, hot-cakes, grits and cornbread. At noon, the fare changed to fresh salad vegetables, sliced turkey, roast beef, pork cuts, and loaves of hot baked breads with rich, creamy, freshly churned butter, and jellies. The evening feast included oysters and clams and crab cakes, platters of roast duck and quail. There were large bowls of honey-glazed carrots, baby whole potatoes cooked with tiny tender onions, and peas. The fresh green beans were seasoned with bacon bits.

Added to every meal, from their own harvest were succulent deep pink watermelon, sweet muskmelon and honeydew. From the orchard were bright red and golden yellow apples and perfectly ripened pears.

In town, every hotel overflowed with horsemen. Lexington Market swarmed with people. Suzanne and Polly mingled with the crowd. Suzanne said, "Oh, Polly, it's so exciting. In past years, I've always been back in the classroom with Miss Abigail. But I'm sad, too. This is our last afternoon together."

"Do not brood, my friend. My plans include the Governor's Christmas Ball. Did your grandmother tell you we are all invited?"

"Are you serious? No. She didn't mention it."

"We are all so busy I expect it slipped her mind. She told me to get myself home for the ball and to celebrate the season with the family. She'll remember to tell you when the excitement of the races is over."

"Well, I'm not going any place, so I have plenty of time to hear the news."

"Are you sad, Suzanne, because you can't go home?"

"It disturbs me not knowing whether Father is safe. I know he needs me at Royal Oaks, but I love it here, too. I'm patient to wait. Let's buy a crab cake to eat on the way home."

"You get one. I'm going to have a cherry tart."

Elbow to elbow with the crowds of people enjoying Septemberfest and looking forward to the big races, Polly and Suzanne walked on, each savoring her chosen delicacy. Polly asked, "Do you plan to continue working at Fort McHenry?"

"Yes, but not so much as before. I'm going to help Grandmother more now that you will be gone."

"I'm proud of you, Suzanne. Will you tell your grandfather of your little adventure at the Fort?"

"Yes, but not yet. He's angry again because he doesn't know who is responsible for the provisions. There's time enough to tell him, but I dearly hope he doesn't catch me on the job. Besides, Lieutenant William Barclay is going to beg an introduction tomorrow so we can see each other on occasion. And, since they saw me helping him home."

"Is a romance budding?"

Suzanne walked slowly on without answering. She wished the bandit could be the one to ask for permission to court her. She sighed. *Bridget, of course, will have Tyrone,* she thought. Polly's laughter filled the air. "I do believe you are smitten, my friend."

* * * *

In her free time, Suzanne helped Polly pack her trunks for her trip back to Boston. She searched the *Crier* in vain for word of *Annebella* and *Sea Queen* activities. On Friday morning, the day before the races, two small news items gave her a clue to the whereabouts of Tyrone. A third piece worried her over the safety of her father.

> *The war robbers, the small band of mystery thieves is still at large. In their latest escapade, they plundered a stagecoach just outside Annapolis. Jake Tipton, of Tipton Ships Company, told this reporter that every valuable on the carriage disappeared with the polite scoundrels. "Although," he said, "thank God, they left our women alone."*

> Somebody deposited a second shipment of medical supplies and miscellaneous goods at the kitchen door of Fort McHenry early this morning. Included in the crates was enough chocolate to give each man a sweet treat.
>
> Two well-known slave finders were apprehended and sentenced to prison, for an indefinite period of time. They are Tom Bush, Myrtle Beach, SC, and Tad Hooker, Hatteras. Both men are on a long list of most wanted men. Often, the southern plantation owners and the Union profiteers seeking bounty are looking for the same men.

Suzanne remembered that those same two men were on the bandit's list.

Chapter 14

The morning of the big races erupted in brilliant sunlight. Suzanne bounded out of bed and called Zoe for her bath. Snuggled down in the steamy fragrant lilac water, she anticipated the glorious day ahead. Then she scrubbed herself vigorously and stepped out into the large fluffy towel Zoe was holding. Zoe dried Suzanne and helped her dress in the sheer cotton stockings, drawers, camisole, chemise and petticoats.

Suzanne's high-waist lisle dress was the color of rich sea coral. Its long sleeves had a slight fluffy swell at the shoulders and were fitted at the wrist. Although Suzanne feared it showed too much of her small round breasts, the low neckline was the latest style. A full skirt billowed gracefully over three petticoats. Lace ruffles, evenly spaced from the hips to the hemline, gave emphasis to Suzanne's slim curves. The ribbon that captured the curls on top of her head, a slightly deeper shade of sea coral, enhanced the copper highlights of Suzanne's hair.

Suzanne breakfasted on sausages and hot-cakes, dripping with sweet maple syrup and washed down with hot spicy cider. Afterward, she went outside to admire the flower gardens while she waited for the rest of the family.

The brisk air, just above a frost, gave promise of a perfect day that would turn warm in the middle. Fall flowers—asters, marigolds, geraniums, nasturtiums and chrysanthemums—brimmed with a myriad of colors. They flaunted golds, burnt and tangerine oranges, amber, reddish browns and other autumn hues. Songbirds twittered. Suzanne watched the stable boys scampering about doing their chores. This morning they were clean and neatly dressed, and energetic and cheerful.

Suzanne knew the splendor of the season was often deliberately fickle. She felt thankful that this day had dawned magnificently. James walked quietly up beside her and touched her hand. He said, "Remember Longfellow's *Autumn*?

'And, from a beaker full of richest dyes,
Pouring new glory on the autumn woods…'"

Without turning, Suzanne said, "Yes, of course, I remember. Are you homesick, James?"

"A little…sometimes. Are you?"

"I love it here, but I've never stayed so long and I don't like the way this war is going. It will destroy our old way of life."

"Nonsense. We're winning most of the skirmishes. There will be a truce in no time. When I get back to Hanson Estates, I'll have to go to work, and I would much prefer to be the gentleman playboy." He smiled easily. "Let's walk out to the racetrack and look at the horses. We can get there long before the others arrive in the carriage."

Suzanne looked up at his beaming face. "I can see you have already forgotten your duty. Grandfather said you would escort Grandmother."

"Truth, and I will, as soon as they arrive on the scene. Coming?"

Suzanne tucked her hand through James' arm and turned him toward the house. "Not until we tell someone we will be there ahead of them, so they will not have to hunt for us."

* * * *

At the racetrack, Suzanne and James watched the sea of bubbly faces. Coming toward them was a cavalcade of horses and wagon loads of enthusiastic families. Most of them had probably slept little and left their homes before dawn.

Excitement was at a fever pitch.

Long-time rivals greeted each other congenially and friends hailed each other with elation. No matter what other harvest activities the shortened days of the season brought, the Baltimore Hanson Septemberfest Races were most important. Many horses entered in this race also raced in various other meets from New York to South Carolina.

Though not Grandfather's, thought Suzanne. *He keeps his horses for pleasure only, and for this Septemberfest.*

Suzanne turned to James and said proudly, "Grandfather planned the whole layout of this racetrack and its stables for the convenience of fellow race patrons. This event is the most popular one on the circuit. Although no more spirited than some others they participate in, Grandfather created it strictly for lovers of the race. Winners of the Hanson races now bring their owners' prestigious honors."

Eyes sparkling, James said, "I, too, have followed the history of Hanson races. Did you know that many winning horses become famous breeders or studs when they leave active racing and go out to pasture? The small purse offered the owners after each heat is almost always donated back to the track fund. Our grandfather used it to buy the lumber for the new bleachers everybody is admiring this year."

James and Suzanne walked slowly along the stable aisle admiring the handsome horses that would compete. Then, as they strolled over the grounds toward the wagon path to greet the arrival of their grandparents, they came upon Mr. Peters.

Mr. Peters was a small, potbellied man with blunt-fingered hands. His hair, neatly parted in the middle, was well groomed and starched. A stall owner at Lexington Market, he was setting up a stand from which to sell lemonade, hot cider and other tempting refreshments. He was famous for sweet treats—tiny fruit-filled tarts and small cakes with nuts, coconut and other delectable tidbits baked inside.

"Watch what you say, James," Suzanne whispered as they neared the table. "Mr. Peters is a nosey goose and a terrible gossip."

"Hello, Miss Suzanne," he said as they approached. "And might this be your cousin come all the way from Charleston with you?"

"Yes, Mr. Peters. This is James."

"I heard you all got separated in the riot. How did you come to find your way home?"

"It's a long story," Suzanne said, "and I think I see Grandmother and Grandfather Hanson and Polly coming now. We promised to meet them…"

Mr. Peters said. "Didn't you think it strange that your grandfather did not allow you to come to the races before this year?"

"Oh, Mr. Peters, we never gave it much thought. I think when we were younger, Grandfather was just trying to protect us from the rough wagering men."

Mr. Peters looked at her with a scorn that belied the distorted grin. "You girls came anyway, didn't you?"

Suzanne's green eyes never blinked. "Oh, yes, Mr. Peters. How could we resist?" Then innocently and before he could respond, she said, "I told Grandfather about it the other day and we had a good laugh. We really must go now."

Mr. Peters laid his stubby fingers on Suzanne's arm. "Don't you think it's curious that your grandparents raised Polly like a white girl?"

"Mr. Peters, you are out of place," James said sternly. "Come, Suzanne, we don't have time for this man's petty interrogation. Good day, sir."

He took Suzanne's hand and swung her around. As they moved away, he said, "I think I won't be welcome to buy goodies of Mr. Peters."

Suzanne giggled. "Well done, cousin, and you won't need to buy from him. Sally will have packed enough food for even your enormous appetite."

Then she sobered. "James, do you think Mr. Peters may be right about Polly? I can't get the confusion about slaves and free Negroes out of my mind."

"It's easy, Suzanne. People here are getting used to free Negroes. Back home we shall always have slaves. Nothing is going to change that. I like Polly, but I don't want her kind to come to our home and give the slaves any ideas. Did you notice she doesn't talk about going South? Even she knows better than that. Hey, there's Grandfather and Grandmother. I'll race you."

Breathless, the cousins reached the carriage in a dead heat. Charlie was pulling it up under the shade of a gigantic and ancient white oak tree. James handed his grandmother down, bowed good-naturedly and took her arm. "May I have the pleasure of escorting you, my lady?"

Face flushed, Margaret proudly beamed at her grandson. Eyes aglow with unashamed affection, she curtsied. "Oh, James, I'm so happy you came to us at last. Let us go and cheer Hanson horses on to victory."

John offered Polly and Suzanne each an arm. "Yes. Come, girls. The races are about to begin and I don't want to miss a minute of them."

The lighthearted party made their way to the best seats in the new grandstand. Track workers had roped off the center section for the many participants who could afford to pay a fee for the privilege of sitting in the fashionable box seats. The colorfully-clad race fans filled the stands to its capacity. As the Hansons and Polly sat down, the trumpeter boldly blared the theme on his horn, announcing the beginning of the races.

The jockeys paraded the horses around the track in a gentle canter. Their brightly colored shirts and the matching streamers tied to the horses represented the owners' private stables. Stopping in front of the family, all three Hanson jockeys dismounted and came to stand in front of them. Jake Miller bowed low and handed Mary-Mary's brilliant scarlet streamers to Margaret. "That's for good luck," he said.

Following his example, the other two jockeys, brothers Tad and Ned Edwards handed streamers to Polly and also Suzanne, who said, "Look, Polly, my very own horse is Lady Jane. Yours is Billy Blue Belle."

Then the rest of the jockeys joined the ceremonies. They handed their ladies a kaleidoscopic of streamers, vibrant in turquoise, Kelly green, shades of reds, oranges, blues and purple.

The races began.

The Bandit's Lady

Suzanne, wide-eyed, sat on the edge of her seat and watched the two-mile heats. When Lady Jane came down the homestretch to win the heat, she stood with the others and cheered at the top of her lungs.

Then across the crowd she caught a glimpse of dark curly hair. She felt a tug of emotion infused by a feeling of warmth. Tyrone turned and captured her green eyes with a look that touched a deep wellspring of passion within her. But as quickly, something seemed to turn and break inside her. Admiration and desire gave way to a sharp prick of jealously as Bridget stood up to stand beside Tyrone. With a loving motion, she put her hand on his cheek and turned it toward herself, until he bent his head and said something. He was smiling.

From where Suzanne stood, frozen, it looked special, intimate. She turned away.

"Suzanne," her grandfather was saying, "I've got someone here I want you to meet. Lieutenant William Barclay was recently released from Fort McHenry. This is my granddaughter Suzanne, Lieutenant."

Suzanne looked up into dancing gray eyes. "Yes, I remember, Grandfather," she said, looking back at John. "He's the one with an angel."

William saw her for the first time in fashionable clothes. His eyes never left her face as he said, "An angel who reminds me of you. It's my pleasure to meet you, Suzanne."

Suzanne smiled coyly. "Thank you, and this is Polly, a dear friend."

Polly's snappy brown eyes sparkled with mirth. "How do, sir. We have had many a discussion over our dinner table about you and the angel. We feel we know you both personally."

"Whatever you have heard about my angel is not nearly enough," William said, looking directly at Polly. "I do believe I have fallen in love with her."

Polly gave Suzanne a look of amused understanding. Suzanne tried not to respond, but her body would not obey. She felt herself grow hot and turned to William. "You surely cannot know such a serious feeling after so short a time. You must have fallen in love with a nurse, a passion that passes quickly…"

John said, "I hope, then, you will make an honest woman of her. I saw her leave with you a week ago Friday. She is mighty young to be so exposed and unchaperoned."

"I agree, sir, but she was merely helping me home because my family could not come for me. Let's not pursue this subject. I wish permission to take these delightful young ladies to Mr. Peters' stand for a refreshing lemonade. Would you allow it, Doctor Hanson?"

"Of course, my boy. Have fun, children." He waved them away and turned to concentrate again on the sport at hand.

"Come with us, James," Suzanne said, tugging on his shirt sleeve.

The four young people headed toward the stand. "I didn't know I offered to take you, lad," William said. "But I'm sure you have some merit, or Miss Suzanne would not have brought you along."

"It's simple, William. James is my cousin from Charleston. We traveled here together and I wish for him to have a good time."

"Not to worry, my pet. I was only kidding. Good to know your acquaintance, James."

William turned back to Suzanne and asked quietly, "Do they know?"

She put her finger to her lips and cautioned him to silence.

Mr. Peters, watching them coming, gave James an odious look. James grinned. "I'm sorry if I offended you earlier, sir, but would it interfere with our buying refreshments from you now?"

Mr. Peters grudgingly gave his unspoken consent and the foursome looked over the trays of mouth-watering treats. James chose a spicy cinnamon apple tart with a slice of cheese. William selected a cherry tart with a dab of soft whipped cream. The girls, afraid of spoiling their lunch, each opted for a small lemonade.

"Julia said I must bring you over to see her, Suzanne," William whispered in her ear. "Can we get rid of the others? The twins will surely let the truth out."

"In a few moments, please. Otherwise James may be suspicious. We are childhood friends. We have a sixth sense about each other."

Polly and James skipped on ahead and William and Suzanne found themselves alone. "It looks as if we are safe to go to wherever we wish," she said.

"Suzanne, I'm glad we have these few moments alone. It is true that I think I have fallen in love with the angel. I hope you will tell your grandfather about your work at the prison very soon, so I may court you properly."

"I do plan to tell Grandfather soon. I need his help to find someone to teach me to be a nurse. But, William, don't get your hopes up. We've only just met. You don't even know me. My heart is not ready for love, nor is it ready to settle down."

William's gray eyes couldn't conceal his fondness. He said, "Poof. That doesn't bother me in the least. I'll make it ready."

"But you don't understand."

"Hmm, do not worry. We won't speak of it now."

They walked on. In the silence between them, Suzanne wished she could learn to love this comfortable man. She knew she could not.

The visit with the family was delightful; the conversation easy. Laura and Lief solemnly asked her if she knew the real angel. Julia's Tom told them they had been wrong to declare Suzanne a non-angel. They all laughed. Julia again asked Suzanne to visit her at home, where they could chat without the interference of the men.

"I promise to call on you soon, Julia, but now I must get back to my grandparents. They will be missing me and it is almost lunch time."

William said, "May I see you back to your seat?"

"Please, no. I'm going to stop at Miss Bee's booth to pick up a souvenir for Grandmother."

Featherlike laugh lines crinkled around William's eyes. His voice was low and purposefully seductive. "We will let you go this time, but I assure you, someday I will make you want to stay." Then lightly, "I'll see you at the Christmas Ball."

Suzanne laughed and waved good-bye. "Till then."

* * * *

She saw his hands first. They held a brooch with the head of a thoroughbred painted on its surface and framed within a chaplet of vibrant flowers. The bandit's voice was unmistakable. "If I were to choose a memento of this day for my lady, it would be this splendid piece."

Suzanne swallowed the despair in her throat. She answered quickly, softly, over her hammering heart. "I'm sure Bridget would adore it."

He answered in a tone filled with a gentle huskiness. "I was thinking of you. I can't linger here now, but meet me after lunch at the pond back yonder. Please, Suzanne."

Suzanne straightened herself with dignity. She had no intention of permitting herself to fall under his spell. She looked up to refuse his invitation.

Tyrone had disappeared into the crowd.

Chapter 15

Silent denial flew from her. *I will not appear at your rendezvous, my bandit,* Suzanne thought. Determination was like a rock inside of her. She twirled around to Miss Bee and bought the brooch Captain Tyrone Sterling had picked out for "his lady."

As she walked back to her grandparent's box seat, a shadow fell across her path. Suzanne looked up. It was the thief who had returned her gun and helped her to dress those many weeks ago. His eyes swept over her appreciatively and he gave her a conspiratorial wink.

"Oh, no," she murmured.

"Miss Suzanne," he said raising his hand. "I be here to see ye get to the pond at the appointed time. If you go yourself ye'll not be seein' me agin; if not, I be takin' ye; 'tis up to ye." He looked her up and down lustfully.

Suzanne gave him a withering glance. "All right, thief. I understand."

She walked on without looking back in his direction, but out of the corner of her eye she saw the other thief and the kidnapper. A shudder rushed through her as she hurried along to the grandstand and her grandparents.

The Bandit's Lady

At the wagon, protected by the noonday sun, supper was grand. There were tiny sandwiches filled with various combinations of cheeses and thin slices of creamed cucumbers, or jellies with ground peanuts. Chickens, fried to a golden brown, served as the main dish. The vegetable was teeny June peas laced with baby pearl onions. The dessert, moist soft gingerbread squares, was still slightly warm. Suzanne dribbled Sally's thin sweet lemony sauce over the top. The selected wines were light, delicate.

John Hanson looked lovingly at Suzanne. "My dear, you missed a good part of the races, so deep in conversation were you with the lieutenant and his family."

"Not really, Grandfather. I know Grandmother's Miss Mary-Mary and my Lady Jane will both be in the final races this afternoon. It's too bad about Billy Blue Belle, Polly."

"It's all right. Next year, Granddaddy promised to have Sir President John ready to compete. I picked her two years ago as my very own. She'll win next year; you watch and see."

Eyes sparkling, John rose. "Let's get back to our seats. I for one am going to carry my pillow to the bleachers this afternoon. Everyone ready?"

"I'm begging off, Grandfather. I feel like taking a long walk after that huge supper. Besides, I want to buy a bauble to remember this day. I'll be along in time for the final races."

She gave Polly a silent communication. It was, as she had hoped, misinterpreted as a plea for time to spend alone with William. Before James could decide to walk with Suzanne, Polly grabbed his hand.

"Come on, I'll race you across the back of the stables to that dilapidated oak tree and back. By then we'll be ready to settle down for the afternoon races."

James raised his hand in a half-salute and dashed away behind Polly. John and Margaret walked hand in hand toward their seats. Watching them, Suzanne sighed and turned toward the pond. *I might as well get it over,* she thought.

She walked listlessly. Her mind swirled with memories of Tyrone that still lurked in the secret places of her being. She struggled with the contradictions in her heart as she tried to study the situation dispassionately. As much as she struggled to pretend indifference, it was obvious they attracted each other. He could be the answer to all her longings, but she knew it was a hopeless love. Suzanne's stomach churned with anxiety, half in anticipation and half in dread of seeing him. Her eyes filled with blinding tears of frustration. She stopped to catch her breath and collect her jagged painful thoughts.

By the edge of the pond, Suzanne pulled her skirts up and tucked them behind her knees as she crouched at the water's edge. She felt the lazy breeze come off the water. She spattered cupped handfuls of water against her face. Behind her, Tyrone's low and troubled voice cut through her thoughts. "Feeling better?"

At the sound of him, she lifted her head and stood up reluctantly. She swung around to face him and heard the bitterness spill over into her words. "Actually, I'm feeling wretched."

He eyed her with concern, pulled her to him. She knew she made a perfect fit inside his arms. If only she could let her feelings flow. He turned her slightly and led her into the deep shade. Under the low-hanging limbs of a weeping willow tree that was drooping its branches in the pond, he pulled her again into the circle of his arms. His cheek gently caressed her hair.

With his mouth next to her ear, he said, "Is there anything I can do to help make you feel better?"

"In fact, you make me feel worse."

Still holding her close, he pulled back a few inches and looked directly into her eyes. There was a slight tinge of wonder in his voice. "How can that be, since I don't know what troubles you?"

Suzanne felt her breath cut off, but she was determined to get this out. "I can't see you anymore. It's too painful for me. You see, I have grown to care for you. There's too much between us that can't be repaired: the war, the destruction of those ships and the capture of the men on the list...and Bridget."

Sobbing, she spun around, but he caught her and whirled her back into his arms. She struggled wildly while he gently tugged the ribbon out of her hair and buried his face in the tumbling curls. Whispering words of endearment, he rocked her back and forth. When she quieted, he asked in a voice filled with awe, "Don't you know I love you? Don't you know I've loved you from the moment I first laid eyes on you? Let me love you!"

"Bridget—"

"Shush. Bridget does not have anything to do with us. I've already told you she's a friend, nothing more. Oh, yes, more, she's a house guest." Tyrone's mouth twitched with amusement. His laugh, low and throaty, broke off as his eyes smoldered and probed her very soul. Suzanne watched his tender glance travel from her tiny walking boots to her sea coral dress, to the too-low neckline.

"It's flawless." His eyes flashed in a familiar display of humor. Suzanne blinked, feeling lightheaded. She tried unsuccessfully to weigh the whole structure of events, but she was swimming through a cloud of feelings and desires. He was so disturbing to her that she froze in limbo where decisions and actions were impossible.

"Let's walk." Tyrone took Suzanne's small hand in his large one. Together they ventured farther and deeper into the woods. The carpet of crisp fallen leaves crackled under their feet. Tiny creatures scampered out of sight. She was enjoying his closeness as he checked his long stride to match hers. When he finally spoke again, Tyrone's voice held more than a hint of excitement. "How soon do you have to be back?"

"In a couple of hours. I promised to watch the final races. It's an exhilarating day for my grandparents. By the way, I bought the brooch for Grandmother Hanson."

Tyrone grinned. "An excellent choice, my dear. Did you have a good advisor?"

Suzanne stared at the twinkling lights in his ebony eyes and could barely keep the laughter from her voice. "The best. A stranger came out of nowhere to recommend the keepsake. 'The very one,' says he, 'that I would choose for my lady.' I thought it charming of him. Don't you think so, too?"

Their soft laughter took on a new significance. His gaze, soothing as a caress and riveted to her face, now moved slowly over her body. The smoldering flame she saw in his eyes startled her, but he drew her to him tenderly. "You are the charming one, my sweet. Let's not waste precious time in idle prattle."

Suzanne's heart jolted and her pulse pounded. She felt herself drifting along in a trance. Just when she thought she would faint, Tyrone laid his coat at the base of a tree and pulled her down beside him. His appeal was devastating; the very air around them felt electrified. She could feel his heart beat against her as he unbuttoned the back of her dress and began caressing her soft skin. His touch sent ripples down her spine. She closed her eyes and lay very still. "Although I do not know what it means, I want you with my whole heart and spirit. But I cannot come to you without marriage. Do you understand? Will you wait for me?"

"Loath as I am to wait, I promised long ago I would not take you by force. I stand by that vow."

They shared an intense physical awareness of each other as he lifted her into the cradle of his arms and molded her soft curves to the contours of his lean body. She leaned against him with a sigh of pleasure. His kiss was slow, unhurried. His lips pressed against hers, then gently covered her mouth, devouring its softness. The touch was a delicious sensation.

His tongue traced the soft fullness of her lips, delicately pried them open and explored the recesses of her mouth. It sent shivers of desire racing through her. His lips left hers to nibble at her earlobe. Then they seared a path down her neck and shoulders as they continued to explore her ivory skin. Finally, his lips recaptured hers, more demanding this time. Parting her own lips, she raised herself to meet his kiss. She gasped at her eager response. His ardor was surprisingly, touchingly, restrained. He moved slightly away and helped her sit up. He whispered in her hair, "I can't keep touching you. I want you too much."

"What will happen to us, Tyrone?"

"Someday we'll be together for good, but tomorrow I must go back to duty. The *Sea Queen* has been in dry-dock for repairs these past many weeks. You must not worry about supplies at Fort McHenry. I've arranged for regular deliveries."

"There is so much speculation. Where do you get the stuff? Where are you going? When will I see you again?"

When he spoke again, his tone was warm, with a trace of laughter in his voice. "If I had a silver coin for every question you ask, I'd be a rich man this day. I can't answer your first two questions. Ah, but you will see me again at the Christmas Ball. I wish I could escort you, but that is impossible. Will you go to the dance with the young man I saw you with this morning?"

Suzanne knew she colored slightly under his gaze. "No. The man you saw me with is Lieutenant William Barclay. He was one of my patients at the prison, released, now, to recuperate at home. It will be a long and tedious recovery before his leg is back to normal. He wants to court me, but I've already explained to him I'm not ready for love."

Desire brightened Tyrone's dark eyes before his glance filled with amusement. "Did you know you lied?"

Suzanne felt a sudden shyness. She dropped her eyes before his steady gaze. "No...well, at the time, with him, it was not an untruth. I must confess, however, I agreed to three dances if he gets an invitation to the Ball."

"And how many will you promise me, my sweet love?"

She relaxed, and teased, "Not more than one, as it wouldn't do for people to see us too often together. Besides, we are not properly introduced."

"I'll get us introduced, no fear!"

His arms tightened around her again. She sighed. "I feel so warm and loved in your embrace, but when we are apart I have many doubts. You never put me at ease about your work and my father."

"I can't, dear Suzanne. You must trust me. Please, trust me."

She felt his maleness pressed against her as he bent his head and kissed her hungrily. For a few precious moments their hearts, their bodies and their pounding breasts fused together. They dreamed someday they would consummate their love. Finally, Tyrone turned Suzanne around and buttoned her dress. He helped straighten her hair and confine the curls within the ribbon. His smile was as intimate as a kiss.

"You must go," he whispered in her ear. "Forever remember this day. Hold it deep inside your heart until we meet again."

Suzanne tilted her head back and peered at his face. She knew her smile contained a passion that had been missing too long. She touched his cheek a final time and slipped away.

* * * *

As Suzanne slid into place beside her grandfather, he patted her hand. "You are in time for the last two races. Your Lady Jane will be pitted next against Sami Jo and your Grandmother's Miss Mary-Mary is to be in the final race. She will compete with Queen Olivia Prudence."

Her grandfather's enthusiasm captured Suzanne. She looked around at the rapt faces of silent watchers. The grandstand was full. Beyond the benches happy crowds of eager people jostled for the choice places to get the finest view. Carriages, too, had been pulled up close to the track.

Suzanne said, "Lady Jane has shown so much flair she has the admiration of the spectators. William told me she has drawn a large betting purse."

John pointed. "Look, they're off!"

The crowd jabbered with excitement as Lady Jane fell behind Sami Jo. "Grandfather," Suzanne yelled over the noise, "Ned is urging her on. She's gaining slightly; do they have time?"

The fans came to their feet yelling, coaxing. Lady Jane and Sami Jo flew over the finish line so close no one knew which horse won. The hysterical crowd waited for a decision from the judges. They quieted when the head judge walked to the fore, megaphone in hand. "The winner is...by a vote of two to one, Sami Jo."

A cheer went up from one sector of the stands, a groan from another.

The race master announced the final heat. "Miss Mary-Mary stands sixteen hands high. Her jockey, Jake Miller is bringing her from the paddock to the starting line. Billy-Bob Jones is leading Queen Olivia Prudence, who stands at fifteen and one-half hands. The race will begin."

"Look at her," John said to Suzanne. "Miss Mary-Mary stepped out to the starting line as fresh as she did this morning."

Prancing slightly, tall and proud, the two horses waited for the starting gun. They began racing to tumultuous cheering. It was obvious to the onlookers that both horses were raised to race, but Miss Mary-Mary looked magnificent. Her bloodline was impeccable, her jockey skillful.

Nose to nose, they came down the homestretch in strides that were no longer smooth, both horses showing the effects of the long contest. For an instant Miss Mary-Mary veered dangerously. But Jake Miller, using the whip to keep the horse into top speed without hurting her, checked her in time to

The Bandit's Lady

keep her on course. The wasted motion cost them dearly, but Miss Mary-Mary suddenly leaped forward. In a final burst of speed, she closed the distance between them. She finished the race a half body length in front of Queen Olivia Prudence.

As one, the crowd stood for the finish that put the Hanson horse in line for the highest honors of the 1861 Septemberfest Races. Well-wishers swarmed around. John smiled broadly as he bowed and waved to the crowd, conceding victory.

Then, with every eye upon them, he tilted Margaret's face up so he could see her. Taking his time about it, he kissed her until a warm blush colored her cheeks. "Let's go home, my dear," he said taking her hand.

Coaches rumbled. It had been a long, exhausting, but triumphant day for all of them. Inside, the Hanson carriage was quiet, each content with his or her thoughts. Suzanne felt a certain sadness that their day was ending. Tyrone had unlocked her heart and being, her spirit and core. Her mind relived the velvet warmth of his kisses. Even in remembrance she felt the intimacy of them and experienced a curious swooping pull at her innards.

She had grown up. The knowledge enveloped her like a cozy warm robe.

Chapter 16

It had been nearly four weeks since Polly went to Boston. On Fridays she wrote a brief, pithy note relating her progress and the needs of her people. She included detailed descriptions of the growing support for their freedom. Suzanne read the letters with interest and inner conflict. This late October morning, she sat at the breakfast table with John. "Grandfather, I'm ready to talk about Father and slavery. Father's attitude confuses me."

"Your parents were of one mind, as are your grandmother and I. Our disagreement was a technicality. Your father is different. He's special, but he still thinks he can own men."

"But, Grandfather, he lives at peace with his conscience. He is honest in his inability to understand the rising clamor against slavery."

"That is true and it's because he stays at the plantation during the summer instead of going to the Charleston house. His overseer is strictly an aide. Suzanne, your father loves his fields and knows them far better than any hired hand. But because he is a successful planter, he is the worst kind of enemy of the South. The appalling significance is that the virtues of a good master serve to mask the vices of many bad masters. Can you understand?"

"Father would never understand. On our plantation, life for the slaves is tolerable, even easy. They have their gardens. They fish. They have a pig and chickens. They attend worship services with us. Father says it's illegal, under any circumstances, to set a slave free. The slaves are his property from birth to death. They don't have to worry about holding a job, probably couldn't survive away from the plantation."

"But in reality, Suzanne, the job holds the slave."

"I, too, have known bad masters, but Father says some slaves are unmanageable."

"True, but does a bad master make unmanageable slaves or does a bad slave make a bad master? Your grandmother and I believe the slave is a human being. Some slaves are bad and some are good, as are all human beings, including masters."

"I think Father is what he can hear and see, and above all what he feels. He feels freer and leads a better life than many Northerners who accuse him of evil doing."

"It's the idea of owning men and the evil slave holders who degrade humanity that we are fighting. Can you find it in your heart to work with us, my dear?"

"I'm ready to help, but Father needs me at Royal Oaks. Uncle Stephen needs James, too. Can you help us find a way to go back, Grandfather?"

"Charleston is the hub of Confederate privateer activities. Your father is obviously in the thick of it. It appears you and James will have to stay for the duration of the war. So let's get to work here."

"What can I do?"

"For starters, your grandmother is not feeling well today and there is a shipment due this afternoon. Would you meet the *Bianca?*"

* * * *

Suzanne's days took on new dimensions. A stomach malady was making Margaret weak. "Old age, my granddaughter." She answered Suzanne's question with a glint of the old sparkle in her blue eyes. But Suzanne was saddened.

Mornings, after the long companionable rides with her grandfather, Suzanne hurried to Fort McHenry. The hospital wing was so full the nurses stopped pursuing her. They were afraid to question her, Suzanne decided, because there was so much suffering and work to do. They did not want to force her to quit helping them. She continued to work only in the section near the back door where she had begun. She listened to the soldiers—heard about their families, their fears and their dreams. She comforted them, helped to keep their spirits up, even nursed them, but she never told them her name. She was "Angel."

Afternoons, Suzanne worked in the big barn. Each day she scouted the area for stray runaways. She often found confused, single slaves in bushes, clumps of grass, or in the wooded areas of the estate clinging to high branches in trees. They were usually worn out and half-starved and always afraid it was not safe to stop.

Terrorized, there was not much difference between day and night to them. In the bright sunlight, the runaway lay paralyzed, imagining all kinds of things. At night they sneaked and stumbled through the darkness, each moment fearing being traced by the warning bark of a dog, the squawk of barnyard animals, or the hoot of an owl.

Lightheaded from fright and hunger, they were never quite sure if they had made progress or not. Suzanne coaxed the drifters into the big barn where she gave them a large tin cup of milk laced with whisky. "Sip slowly," she told them, "while Sally fixes you a hot supper."

The petrified Negroes were typically quiet, so Suzanne learned little of their former life. When she asked Grandfather Hanson why people took such chances to help the slaves escape, he said, "The underground deals extensively in swamps and woods, barns, footpaths, farm wagons and by common people touched by the spirit of adventure. Thousands of nameless men and women work on the underground. They are backed by nothing but their enduring consciences and because it makes them feel good. It becomes a hobby, an avocation. Its lawlessness adds a stimulating dimension to many lives that otherwise might be dull."

Sally's Joe filled the wooden tubs with water. Suzanne helped scrub the women and children. And, gritting her teeth, she took special care to rid their heads of lice. She exchanged their tattered clothes for simple loose-fitting gowns tied at the waist with a wide sash, made for them by other underground volunteers. The men and boys wore a shorter version of the same crude style. A rope belt held up their homespun trousers.

* * * *

Three weeks after their grandmother took to her bed, James carried her down to the dinner table. In the atmosphere of celebration and the intimacy of the scene, Margaret smiled innocently. She said, "Bring us up to date on Angel, John."

"She comes everyday without fail, except Sundays."

"Did she ever get caught?"

"The nurses have decided she's invaluable to them. She's young, but sensible and extremely conscientious. She seems devoted to the patients' healing and happiness.

"Will they help her to become a nurse?"

"Unfortunately, it's out of the question. She is much too young."

"That's not true, Grandfather. If I can help those men…"

"Cousin, do you know…what you…just…said?" James' young voice cracked as he began to laugh.

With a pang, Suzanne realized what she had done. John and Margaret looked from one young person to the other in obvious genuine astonishment and Suzanne regretted her long weeks of deception. Nervously, she bit her lip, then swallowed with difficulty and found her voice. "I'm so sorry… I should have… I didn't think you'd let me continue if you knew."

John recovered first. "Of course, we would not have let you continue." His green eyes flashed with a satisfied light. "I might have known. I thought that young girl leaving with Lieutenant Barclay looked a bit familiar, but I never dreamed it was you. John chuckled. "You knew him even before I introduced you at the races."

"Yes, Grandfather, I knew him. He wants to court me, so he asked you to present me to him. Although he is a congenial young man, and I adore his sister and the twins, I'm honestly not interested in him that way. I was truly just helping him home."

Margaret chuckled. "Oh, my dear, you do have mettle. James, I feel overtired. Will you help me back to my bed?"

James unwound his long legs and stood up. Looking at Suzanne, he said, "My cousin, you never cease to amaze me with your adventurous spirit. Would that I could have your fervor, but I must leave you all now. My friend David Adams and I have a date with a billiard table and a pair of cue sticks." He gave them an exaggerated bow and tenderly picked up his grandmother.

When they were alone, John said in a puzzled tone, "Suzanne, do you know where the medicines and supplies are coming from?"

Suzanne steeled herself to keep her voice steady. She looked directly at her grandfather. "I know who is responsible, but I really don't know where they come from."

"Will you tell me?"

"Tyrone Sterling."

"Ah, yes, it figures."

Nothing more. Suzanne looked at him expectantly, then said, "Grandfather, did you know that Tyrone faked a rape of me as we were coming to visit you? He and his gang robbed the stage and treated us roughly, but they really didn't hurt us and they let us go quickly.

Without further comment, John said, "I think I'll see to your grandmother now, Suzanne. I'll be waiting for you in the morning. We will ride as usual."

Alone, Suzanne wondered at the strange expression on her grandfather's face. She walked to the foyer, picked up her candle and went to her bedroom. In her four-poster feather bed, she dreamed confused and baffling fantasies of her bandit.

The following morning, John accompanied Suzanne to the Fort and introduced her to Clara Townsend, and the others. "I declare," Mrs. Townsend said, "you have gumption. Welcome. I will teach you myself to be the best nurse I know how."

Eyes sparkling with mirth, she turned to John. "My dear Dr. John, if you find any more granddaughters like this one, bring them to me. The injured boys are coming in here faster than we can nurse them back to health."

* * * *

Suzanne eyed the weekly *Bianca* delivery. Studying them without seeming to, her mind focused on a boy and a girl with light complexions. They were about eighteen or nineteen years old, not older than herself. The girl would be worth more in the South, because of her color. "Gentlemen of fashion," Miss Abigail had said to Suzanne, "have an eye for a girl who could almost pass for white."

The boy, on the other hand, would be worth considerable less than the third passenger, a full-blooded Negro. Mixed blood males were often troublemakers. These thoughts echoed snatches of conversation she had heard between her father and Thaddeus.

Too bad there were three of them, she thought idly. If it were just two single men, they could get food and directions and take themselves to the next station. Now, Charlie would have to hitch up this night and drive twenty miles before he slept. Suzanne felt a queer little excitement stealing over her. She was beginning to enjoy participating, even in any small way, in the freedom of slaves.

Some runaways she had befriended had been mean and would have been mean no matter what their color. Some had been cringing and embarrassing in their appreciation. Most were good, plain, troubled people, like the quiet male Negro in this group. This other pair was different and it didn't take Suzanne long to figure out why. Anybody could see they weren't brother and sister, but sweethearts. They had the need common to all escapees, plus a private need of their own.

Charlie would deliver them to the next station keeper near Philadelphia. There, they would hide all day and leave the following night. Charlie would get back to Hanson Race Stable Yards about dawn. He would cut three more notches on the post in the new stable where he kept the records.

When Suzanne tried to sympathize with Charlie for the long night ahead, he denied it with a wave of his hand. "Aw, Miz Suzanne, dese ol' ho'ses know de road well by now. I gets me a few winks on de way back."

* * * *

The mid-November Friday morning dawned bleak. It had cold that soaked through to the skin. Despite the fire, the parlor felt damp. Suzanne, dressed except for her navy woolen cloak, was ready for her trip to the Fort. She sat down to scan the *Baltimore Crier* before braving the winter elements. From her grandfather's study, she heard a soft moan turn into a sorrowful wail. Suzanne dropped the paper and ran to find Zoe doubled over. Tears streamed down her troubled face. John stood awkwardly over her. He handed Suzanne the piece of mail he was holding. "It's Polly. They've seized her. Look, here."

The paper, a printed handbill with a description of Polly had been posted as proof of ownership of an alleged fugitive. It read:

> Wanted!
> Alive, if possible, one slave girl, Polly Jackson, of Baltimore, Maryland. Five feet tall, she has burn scars across her left knuckles. Well dressed and somehow educated, her

present activities consist of speaking out at abolitionist rallies and writing and passing out leaflets and pamphlets that conflict with confederate slave-owner policies. Last seen in Boston, but has been spotted in New York City, Philadelphia, and as far west as Cincinnati, Ohio. Owner, Seth Byron, Raleigh, North Carolina offers for her return: $575

Suzanne knelt down and put comforting arms around Zoe. John handed Suzanne another scrap of paper. The short message was in Polly's handwriting.

Dr. John Hanson: Please help! I must appear before the magistrate Monday, a week hence, November 25, 1861. To disprove this dreadful mistake, I will need at least one witness who can attest to my identity. It cannot be my mother as she is a Negro and not a reliable witness according to their strict rules. Please come yourself, or send Suzanne with the proper papers. I am in prison until a judge makes a decision and it will not go well with me if I remain to face these charges alone.
As ever, Polly.

Suzanne looked at her grandfather. "How can this be? What will happen to her? What can we do?"

"Not so fast, child. I will have my solicitor send a wire to the authorities stating that Polly's papers will be coming directly. I cannot leave your grandmother, so I must ask you to make the trip by train."

"Will I travel alone, then?"

The Bandit's Lady

"Positively not, but I have not solved the matter concerning who will accompany you. James is too young; you are too impetuous to travel alone." John scratched his white head in thoughtful concentration.

Suzanne patted Zoe's shoulder and giggled. "I may be 'impetuous,' but I just bet I can get the job done." She sobered, then asked, "Grandfather, do you know Tyrone?"

Suzanne watched her grandfather hesitate. Conflicting emotions crossed his face. She thought he was going to deny knowing him. "Yes, of course. What are you thinking?"

"He is probably out with the *Sea Queen* right now, but I think I know someone who would help us. Tyrone's man Rufus seems trustworthy. If he could travel to Boston, he could keep an eye on me without anyone knowing he is escorting me. He could protect Polly and me on our return trip."

"What makes you think he would consent to such a plan?"

"Why don't I drive the gig over and ask him?"

He shot her a penetrating look. "You are a treasure box of surprises, my dear. I can't imagine where you met those people."

Suzanne spoke with a sense of confidence she didn't feel. "Never mind, Grandfather. It's a long story. Suffice to know Tyrone is a friend. If Rufus can help us, he will."

Then, to Suzanne's ears, her grandfather said a strange thing, softly, almost to himself. "Yes, Tyrone is our friend. I will leave it to you to arrange the trip, but let Charlie drive you."

Zoe got up and put her arms around Suzanne. "You be careful in dat side of de town. Don't get youse'f in no trouble. Polly wouldn't be likin' it."

"Don't worry, Zoe. I'll be in Boston to help Polly and we'll be back in time for the Christmas Ball."

When she got to Tyrone's house, Charlie helped her down from the carriage. "You wantin' me to come?"

"Thanks, but I'll be fine. You wait here; I will be ready to return home within the hour."

Faith opened the door and led Suzanne inside Tyrone's town house. "De mas'er not be home, Miz Suzanne."

"I know, Faith. I came to see Rufus. Is he here?"

"No, but I be sendin' someone to fetch him at de shack if ye be waitin'."

"Thank you. I'll wait by the fire in the blue room."

Faith gave her a puzzled look, but took her cloak and ushered her to the door of the familiar room. She hurried away to send an errand boy for Rufus. Too late, Suzanne saw Bridget sitting in the blue flowered chintz chair facing the door.

Bridget's eyes filled with resentment and shone like chips of onyx. "Do come in, Suzanne. I welcome this opportunity to get better acquainted."

Chapter 17

Suzanne moved slowly into the comfortable room and sat gingerly on the edge of the chair facing Bridget. The flames in the fireplace gave the blue hues a warmth that were not present the first time she visited. Her eyes moved to Bridget. She wore the same blue dress as on the day they met. Once again, Suzanne thought it had been a deliberately calculated part of Bridget's wardrobe. The golden mist of her hair hung in long graceful curves over her shoulders.

Memories flashed through Suzanne's mind and left a sensation full of sweetness and pain. Then she remembered meeting with Tyrone during the races and his plea not to forget that day, "Hold it deep inside your heart," he'd said.

Suddenly feeling entirely at ease, Suzanne smiled. Her eyes met Bridget's in a direct and challenging way. "I am sorry to barge in this way. I came to see Rufus. Faith didn't tell me you were here, or I would not have disturbed you; I would have had her show me into the parlor."

Her light tone did not relieve the tension. Bridget gave an impatient little sniff. "Let's get straight to the point. I am more than Tyrone's 'old friend'. I expect to marry him. You have delayed his proposal."

Suzanne felt laughter bubble up inside her. She stifled a giggle. "I have what? He told me nothing of his intention to marry you."

"Well, I'm telling you he is planning to marry me and I expect you to get out of his life, and quickly."

Her undertone of meaning was unmistakable, but Suzanne decided to ignore it. She chose her words carefully. "You must forgive me for not understanding your meaning. I could not possibly have delayed a proposal; either he was going to ask you or not. And apparently he has not."

Bridget's eyes glistened with unshed tears. "Believe me, you are not his kind of people. Please, Suzanne, I'm begging you to leave him alone."

Suzanne felt a prick of sympathy. "I think you really love him, Bridget. I am genuinely sorry for you, but I cannot decide Tyrone's future. He will do that for himself."

Rufus darted through the doorway. "Miz Suzanne, be there somethin' I can do for you?"

"Please, Rufus, is there somewhere we can talk?"

Bridget stood up. Her faint smile held a touch of contempt. "I was just leaving. I hope you'll remember I warned you, Suzanne. I will have Tyrone."

When she left the room, Rufus started to speak, but Suzanne stopped him. "It's all right, Rufus. Bridget must fight her own battles."

She told Rufus about Polly and they agreed to leave for Boston on Wednesday. That would give Suzanne time to get settled and to see the magistrate. She would visit Polly and enjoy a weekend of sight-seeing.

Rufus said, "Don't you worry your head. You trust Rufus to take care of everything."

The Bandit's Lady

* * * *

The next few days were a frenzy of preparations. Suzanne lined up nurses at the Fort to care for her station while she was in Boston. She turned her Underground duties over to Zoe and Jeanne. Charlie would collect the delivery for them.

The evening before she left, Suzanne kissed her grandmother good-bye. "Don't worry about a thing, Grandmother. Polly and I will be fine. We will come back together the end of next week."

In the early hours of the dark cold morning, Zoe helped Suzanne into a sturdy moss green traveling dress of smooth, dense, woolen material. "Dat dress won't be showin' travelin' dust, Miz Suzanne."

"It will be warm, too. Please hurry with my cloak and bonnet, Zoe. I don't want to keep Grandfather waiting."

"I's so happy you be goin' to get my Polly. Please be car'ful. I's scairt fo' her."

"Don't worry, Zoe. Rufus and I will get her if we have to kidnap her."

Zoe snorted. "Dat Rufus don' know nothin' 'bout carryin' away the wash water, let alone kidnappin'. You believe me, he gonna be useless."

"Zoe, you sound like you know Rufus."

"He didn' fool me none de night you come home from dat shack. I seen him scurryin' away to de dark of dem trees."

"Zoe, does everybody know everything that happened to me during that time?"

"Not ever'thing, but I knowed Rufus fo' a long time. We ain't got no more time to talk. Git along with ye. Jus' be car'ful."

The Bandit's Lady

Sally had packed Suzanne a basket of food. She served a breakfast of biscuits and honey with a cup of black coffee. John drove Suzanne to meet the four thirty a.m. northbound train. He bought her ticket, and they sat on the wooden bench to await its arrival. John turned to Suzanne and in a strained tone, he said, "I wish I were going to Boston instead of you, my dear."

As he spoke she noticed a look of tired sadness pass over his features. She felt excitement welling up inside her. "I'll be fine; but, Grandfather, what's really troubling you? Is it Grandmother?"

"Partly, but it's this whole affair with Polly and what Tyrone's gang did to you. And because now we have to rely on Rufus to protect you girls and return you safely."

"Grandfather, how well do you know Tyrone and the rest of them?"

"Tyrone is our friend, but he's dangerous."

"Alllll ab o a r d. Alllll a b o a r d! Train leaves in three minutes. Alllll a b o a r d!"

As they jerked to their feet, John asked, "Have you seen Rufus, Suzanne?"

"No, but he'll be there. He promised." She threw her arms around John's neck, tipped her face up to his and looked directly into eyes the image of her own. "Don't worry, Grandfather, I'll be fine."

"Alllll aboard."

Suzanne pulled her skirts above her ankles and ran to the steps of the train. Inside, she took a seat by the window and waved until her grandfather was only a speck in the distance. Then she settled back to enjoy the countryside flying past the window.

The Bandit's Lady

A shadow fell across her view and when she looked up the thief was sitting down beside her. She looked for Rufus, but saw only the kidnapper and the other thief. When she opened her mouth to scream, the thief's fingers clamped over her trembling chin. "Don't! We ain't here to hurt ye."

"Then why are you here? Where is Rufus?"

"Rufus be nigger. He obviously can't travel with ye. He be in another car."

He grinned briefly with no trace of his former animosity. "I won the longest straw. Ye be stuck with me." He quirked his eyebrow questioningly.

Suzanne bit her lip to squelch a grin. Although she couldn't define its source, a feeling of trust came over her. She looked him over critically. She knew he towered over the other men by several inches. He had a powerful set of shoulders and carried himself with a commanding air of self-confidence. And, for a change, he was tastefully dressed in a pair of clean buckskin trousers. Tucked into them was a black cotton shirt and over it all he wore a rust-colored, woolen overcoat. There was an inherent strength in his face. She looked into dark gray-green eyes. They showed intelligence and independence of spirit. He winked broadly. "Okay, thief, you won. Do you have a name, or must I continue to call you thief?"

His smile widened in approval. "I'm Frank Reilly."

"And the others?"

"The one you call the kidnapper is Will Snooks. The other one is Clay Long."

"What's your game?"

"We be basically good. Will, he's the gutsy one and Clay be on the mean side. We play the Robin Hood gig."

"You mean you take from the rich and give to the poor?"

"Yeah."

"But," Suzanne felt her face grow warm, "what about the rapes?"

"We get a yen for a woman sometimes. Clay can't be denied. Anyway, it keeps the authorities a guessin'."

"What about me?"

"Ye be a lady! Tyrone had ye. Ye be the first one he ever took. He would kill us if'n we let anythin' happen to ye." He looked at her almost hungrily, then snapped his attention back to the task at hand. "Rufus be watchin' us, but we be taken care of ye. We decided you should have a proper escort. I told ye before. I won." Frank Reilly chuckled and folded his hands together in a comfortable gesture.

Suzanne responded to his disarming good nature. She smiled easily, then leaned back to look out the window. At noon, Suzanne shared her basket of food with the four men. They promised to get out at the next station to buy sandwiches and tea for supper. The clattering train droned on. Night and darkness came to the coach and the passengers made themselves as comfortable as possible to catch a few hours of sleep. Frank said, "Ye can lean on me shoulder, if ye wants to."

"I think we'll both be more comfortable if you move into the empty seat over there and stretch out," Suzanne said.

The sun was setting the following afternoon when they arrived at Boston's South Station. Frank and Suzanne took a carriage to the Bostonian Hotel located near Faneuil Hall where Polly had been seized when she spoke out against the sins of slavery. Rufus saw to Suzanne's small trunk while she arranged for a room. Will Snooks and Clay Long had disappeared. "They be seein' to their ale and pleasure. We're not

The Bandit's Lady

likely to see them again till mornin'," Frank said in answer to Suzanne's question.

After a luxurious bath and a good night's sleep, Suzanne arrived at the magistrate's office at seven a.m. A clerk heard her request and pointed her to a row of hard wooden benches. She counted thirty others already waiting to see the judge.

Frank and Rufus decided there was nothing for them to do and disappeared to pursue their own interests. Suzanne felt the hours drag by. She was hungry and hot and out of sorts when the bailiff called her at three-thirty in the afternoon. She stood before Judge Boyd Jenkins. He was a glum-faced man—plump, well-dressed, but slightly wrinkled, with a balding head and beady, darting eyes. "Miss Suzanne Willoughby. What do you want of this office?"

"I came to take Polly Jackson back home to Baltimore. She was falsely accused of being a slave."

"There's a wanted poster out for her return. You, yourself, by sound of your accent, are a Southerner. Why does this slave girl interest you?"

"John and Margaret Hanson, my grandparents, raised Polly Jackson as their granddaughter. She was born free. They educated her."

"Her hearing is not until Monday morning. Why do you come this day?"

"I want her released in my custody until her appointed court time Monday morning."

"This is highly unusual."

Suzanne could feel his sharp steel blue eyes boring into her. She felt her temper rise in response, but silently vowed not to give in to the tension that had been building all day. She forced a bold smile and her old spirit of confidence returned.

"Polly is highly unusual. She is not, nor has she ever been a slave. Please, sir, I beg your indulgence."

Her directness obviously startled him. "Well, this is extremely unorthodox. Bailiff, where is the prisoner, Polly Jackson?"

"She's in women's, east ward, sir."

"Take this young lady down to see the prisoner."

Suzanne barely suppressed her annoyance. "But I want her released, sir."

"Hmm, well, yes, I know that. Go with Bailiff Sterns. Bring the prisoner back here so I may speak directly with her before making my decision."

Stirring his papers, Judge Jenkins said, "Thomas Sundry. You may approach the bench."

Suzanne had to speed up to keep close to the tall, lanky bailiff. Past the main hallway, he led her through a narrow hall. An occasional single candle-filled sconce hanging on the walls gave out an eerie feeble light. Suzanne shivered in the cold, dank walkway; her insides felt frozen. She had only an unfocused awareness of the sordid conditions inside the small rooms. A feeling of sorrow slowly reached her as the realities and the stench of crowded humanity claimed her mind.

Four to six women occupied each cell. Bars covered the tiny two-by-two-foot openings to the hall. Guards shoved plates full of tasteless-looking bowls of gruel through a slot. Crude bunk beds with gray sheets and thin blankets filled most of the existing floor space. Two slops stood in opposite corners of each room.

The tunnel-like hall turned and twisted. When Suzanne thought she could stand it no longer, Bailiff Sterns walked to a tiny window. "Polly Jackson. You have a visitor."

The Bandit's Lady

No one answered or stirred.

Suzanne moved to the window and looked inside. Four women, sitting on the edge of the bunks, slowly raised their eyes. None was Polly. A fifth figure facing the wall sat cross-legged at the far side of the room. She muttered something unintelligible.

"These women aren't Polly. You've brought me to the wrong cell."

"This is the cell. If your friend isn't here, someone released her for some reason."

"What do you mean, released? Where is she? Where have they taken her?"

"Lady, it's not my job to know what happens to 'em."

"Make it your job. Where could they have taken her?"

"If she's not here and not in solitary, she might be in the infirmary. Sometimes they take them there if they get sick like that one in the corner."

Suzanne turned back to the prisoners. Trying to keep hysteria out of her voice, she asked, "Did the other one, Polly, get sick?"

One woman stood up and came closer. She pointed to the figure on the floor. "Dat be Polly."

Suzanne looked closer. A crazy mixture of hope and fear assailed her. She began to shake as a flicker of recognition swept through her. "Oh, my dear God," she whispered, "that is Polly."

The bailiff put his hand on Suzanne's shoulder. She turned to him. "What will happen to her? Can I take her with me?"

He quietly took charge. "I'll order her to the infirmary. Come back Monday with her papers; she'll be ready to go home."

"But I can't just leave her here. What's the matter with her?"

"Sometimes they get like this, the ones who have never been deprived or known hardships. She probably wouldn't eat. They get chilled clear through and without nourishment their bodies can't fight it. We call it the 'prison pits'."

Bailiff Sterns' face split in a wide grin. "If she has as much gumption as you, Miss Suzanne, she'll come around real good in a couple of days."

Suzanne felt a strange numbed comfort. "What shall I tell Judge Jenkins?"

"Leave everything to me. I know a shortcut to the front door."

In the late afternoon dusk, Suzanne stood quietly in the doorway of the State House. She drew a deep breath and fought for self-control as she watched Frank Reilly coming toward her to escort her back to the hotel.

Chapter 18

Suzanne loved Boston.

She bought a lunch basket packed by the cooks in the Bostonian Hotel Tea Room and hired a carriage. Accompanied by Frank, she began the day by driving to the outskirts of town to gaze at the home of her favorite poet, Henry Wadsworth Longfellow.

It was the historic house that had been Washington's headquarters during the siege of Boston. Mrs. Andrew Craigie, widow of a commissary officer in the American army who bore the distinguished title Apothecary-general, had lived there.

Suzanne was sad as she turned away. She wished James could share these moments. On the way back to town, she and Frank stood in awe on the front lawn of Harvard University grounds.

* * * *

Later, they followed the familiar story of Boston's freedom trail. They spoke in soft voices while standing on the site of the Boston massacre and gaped in awe at Benjamin Franklin's birthplace on Milk Street.

They visited the home of Paul Revere and walked through Old North Church where the lanterns had hung to warn patriots of an attack by the British. They visited Paul Revere's grave, Samuel Adams', in Old Granary Burying Ground. They passed America's first public school, the Boston Latin School, and Suzanne spent a silent reverent hour in the nation's first free public library. Then Suzanne insisted they stop for tea at the Old Corner Book Store. It was a meeting place of Boston writers, where Suzanne hoped for a glimpse of Longfellow. She was not disappointed. He sat quietly, alone, in a far corner of the room. "Oh, Frank, wait until I tell James," she said excitedly.

"How 'bout I get ye an introduction?"

"Oh, no, I couldn't disturb him. I saw him. That's enough."

At noon, Suzanne and Frank ate lunch in the old public park. She said, "Did you know that women found guilty of witchcraft in the late sixteen hundreds were hanged in the Commons? And did you know Benjamin Franklin grazed his family's cow here during his boyhood?"

"No, me lovely, I didn't know. But ye must be careful in Boston, for surely you are the witch who captured Tyrone Sterling. Pull your cloak around you tight; let's walk over to the garden lake."

Suzanne gloried briefly in the shared moment, then sighed. *If only my bandit could be with me now,* she thought.

Later the curious twosome discovered the Back Bay area, a recent landfill development of a marshy section by the Charles River. The elegant, extravagant houses stood all along the neighborhood's tree-lined streets. They walked around the Beacon Hill vicinity, a fashionable older neighborhood with gaslights and narrow cobblestone streets. Luxurious brick town houses surrounded the park in Louisburg Square.

* * * *

On Sunday morning, Suzanne worshiped in the Park Street Church where US military forces had stored gunpowder during the War of 1812. She ate lunch alone in the hotel tea room and spent the afternoon reading Longfellow's *The Courtship of Miles Standish*.

Suzanne had only heard of the poem, but yesterday had found and purchased the three-year-old volume at a little shop on Market Street. Besides the idyll of old colony times, the tiny book contained a collection of the author's recent short poems. She would give the book to James as a memento of her trip, but she knew he wouldn't mind if she read it first. By the end of the day, the question of Polly and getting her back home hung heavily on Suzanne's mind. She poured over the affidavit and other papers given to her by John Hanson's solicitor and, finally, slid into a thin sleep.

* * * *

Judge Boyd Jenkins' cold steel blue eyes gave Suzanne a brutal, unfriendly stare. "My dear Miss Willoughby, where is the prisoner, Polly Jackson?" The question brought a hushed silence to the courtroom.

Suzanne felt surprise siphon the blood from her face. She swallowed hard and boldly lifted her chin to meet his icy gaze straight on. "I...I don't know. H...how would I know? She was ill. Bailiff Sterns assured me he would see to her care until I arrived back today." Startled at her voice, she glanced up. His accusing gaze riveted on her face.

"She's gone." He ripped out the words impatiently.

Anxiety spurted through her. She felt tears gather in the corners of her eyes. "I...I thought...she would be here," she said in a choked voice.

His expression was a mask of stone. "This is not a game, miss."

Suzanne shuddered inwardly. Her mind was spinning with bewilderment. "I didn't think it was," she said in a dull and troubled voice. "I don't know where Polly is."

Judge Jenkins gave her a courteous, almost forgiving smile. "It's obvious I cannot decide in favor of a prisoner's freedom without a prisoner and without proper evidence. Frankly, Miss Willoughby, I see no reason to continue this hearing."

"But, please, sir, let me present her papers and the affidavit. The authorities will surely find her. If we complete these details, she can return home with me."

Suzanne waited quietly, then felt her flesh prickle with goose bumps. Wanting to put all the pieces together, she said, "What if that Seth Byron...that plantation owner from North Carolina kidnapped..." Her voice trailed off. A glimmer of an idea, still naked, lay in the recesses of her brain before the stunning recognition hit. Suzanne knew instinctively that Will Snooks and Clay Long had kidnapped Polly from the prison infirmary. She bowed her head so the magistrate wouldn't see her startled deduction.

Relief and pain, so closely tied she didn't know which one was worse, surged through her. *What would they do to Polly? Where would they take her? How could she find her?* The questions whirled through Suzanne's thoughts.

She stole a glance at Judge Jenkins, but he had taken her silence for fear. He gazed at her sympathetically and cleared his throat. "This is very unusual, but let us determine if the late prisoner is indeed slave or free. Will you please submit the evidence to the court, Miss Willoughby?"

Suzanne handed the papers up to him and begged him with her eyes. She was suddenly anxious to get away from his disturbing courtroom and make private inquiries about Polly. Judge Jenkins studied the papers, then pausing, gazed at her speculatively. He said, "These seem in good order. She is, no doubt, a free Negro."

He turned to the court stenographer. "George, fill out the usual forms for liberating Polly Jackson. Send one public notice to the *Boston Morning Globe* and make a duplicate one for safe keeping with her other papers. Miss Willoughby will be responsible for returning them to their Baltimore solicitor."

Suzanne smiled. "Thank you, Judge. Will the authorities search for Polly?"

"They will make certain she is not in Mr. Seth Bryon's custody. Beyond that, no. It is our experience in cases such as this, that your Polly will soon find her way home. You are dismissed."

Outside a wind had come up—a fierce, steady wind with a promise of snow. Suzanne pulled her cloak tighter around her. When she saw Frank's tall figure turn the corner and head toward her to escort her back to the hotel, she fairly flew at him. "They've taken Polly. You know she's sick. Why didn't you tell me where she was, so I could nurse her over the weekend? Where did they take her? When can I see her?"

Firmly, he propelled her around and walked her quickly into the nearby Commons Tea Shoppe. "Now," he said, "what's this all about? Who has taken Polly?"

"Will and Clay, of course. You've got to answer me. Where is she?"

A young lady dressed in a long black dress and dainty white apron stood beside them. Absently, Frank ordered two hot chocolates. "Skip the cakes," he snapped.

He turned back to Suzanne. His eyes were sharp and assessing. "Ye be wrong. They can't have taken her. I ain't seen 'em since yesterday."

"There! That proves it. If they didn't take her, where are they?" she said in a shrill voice.

"Shush. Keep ye voice down. Let's find Rufus. He can settle this for certain." He picked up his cup and downed the scalding liquid. Suzanne left her chocolate untouched as she hurried after him. Rufus was no help at all. They found him passing time with the hotel stable hands. He had made arrangements for a carriage to take them to the six o'clock train back to Baltimore. "I ain't seen Will and Clay since we got here, Miz Suzanne. Dey been stayin' down to de Tremont Inn. I don' speck dey be kidnappin' Polly."

"Somebody did. She's gone, just disappeared from the jail. If they didn't do it, who did?"

Frank said, "They could o' done it. I told 'em about her predicament when I seen 'em yesterday. They come along to help if we needed 'em. Ma'be they paid her a call."

"It might o' been dat Seth fella," Rufus said.

Suzanne felt things spin out of control. Why hadn't she insisted on taking Polly with her on Friday? The thought made her throat ache. *Dear God, now what?*

Rufus asked, "What you be gonna do, Miz Suzanne?"

The question hung between them. Suzanne looked out through the open stable doors. It was snowing. The snow-chilled wind whipped at her ankles. She wanted to go home, but she wouldn't forgive herself if she didn't take Polly home with her. "I've got to try to find Polly. Rufus, you go to the Tremont, find Will and Clay and bring them back here. They can help us search. Frank and I will eat supper at the hotel, then go over to Faneuil Hall. There is an abolitionist rally tonight. Polly has friends there. We'll look for somebody who might know where she is. Meet us there."

When they arrived, the lecture hall was filled. Suzanne and Frank stood in the back of the room and watched the proceedings. Four speakers sat in straight chairs on the small platform. After the first speaker finished, Suzanne wove her way through the crowded side aisle to wait in line for a private word with her. The moderator introduced her simply, "Mrs. Jane." She was a tall, slender, dark-haired woman in a modest dark gray frock and apron. Obviously born of plain homey kindness, there was a quiet and deep inbred force about her. It was difficult to guess her age.

When her turn came, Suzanne looked into serene ebony eyes. An instant of recognition swept through her, but she couldn't know why. *She's genteel*, Suzanne thought, then shook her head to clear her musings. She said, "Forgive me for staring. For a moment, I thought we may have met."

Mrs. Jane looked at her kindly. Her voice, when she spoke, was silky with warmth. "That happens to all of us sometimes, my dear. What can I do for you?"

Suzanne found it easy to confide in this stranger. "It's Polly Jackson. She disappeared and I'm trying to find her. I thought someone here might know of her whereabouts."

Suzanne watched a melancholy frown flit across Mrs. Jane's features and quickly continued. "I'm sorry. I didn't introduce myself. I'm Suzanne Willoughby. I came from my grandparents' home in Baltimore to clear her name."

"I might have known," Mrs. Jane said softly to herself. To Suzanne, she said, "I wish I could help you, but I haven't seen her since they arrested her. Did you clear her name?"

"Yes, and I'm grateful to the judge. He's putting out a public notice, but Polly is sick and now we can't find her. Do you know anyplace I could look for her?"

"Seth Byron is staying at the Commons Tavern. They say he's waiting for her. She might be at one of her students' homes. You could check with Millie Brown at the school over on Market Street. She might be hiding out at the recruiting offices. Find Otto Warren; he'll help you."

Suzanne felt hope when she looked into Mrs. Jane's dark, doelike eyes. "Oh, thank you. Tomorrow I shall find her and take her home. I promised my grandmother and Zoe. That's Polly's mother."

Mrs. Jane touched Suzanne's cheek with her fingertips. "Thee is such a pretty child. Be careful, my dear."

"I will. I have help. If we find her, we'll be on the train for home tomorrow evening." With a wave of her hand, Suzanne fled the hall.

* * * *

Rufus had not found Will and Clay, but promised to search them out in the morning. For the second night, Suzanne slept fitfully.

The storm that had raged most of the night was quiet. The drab city of yesterday sparkled in the brilliant sunlight that spilled across the frozen wonderland. Frank handed Suzanne into the carriage and covered her with a woolen blanket. Their first stop was the telegraph office. The wire Suzanne sent to her grandfather was brief:

Polly cleared Stop Small Delay Stop Home soon Stop Suzanne

Suzanne's inquiries received negative responses. Otto Warren shook his head sadly. "She got a head for leadin' the men to hep the cause. We needs her bad. If'n you see her, tell her to come back."

"I will tell her," Suzanne said. "But first she will go to Baltimore for the holidays and a good rest."

"Ever'body here be wishin' you good luck."

When Suzanne told Millie Brown what she wanted, Millie said, "Oh, Miz Suzanne, we love our Polly. Nothing bad will be happening to her. When you find her, give her our love. We will be waiting for her to come back. She's the best teacher in the whole world."

In spite of Millie Brown's enthusiasm and optimism, Suzanne's own spirits sank to a new low as the carriage moved toward the Commons. She felt a creeping uneasiness at the pit of her heart. "Frank, I'm frightened. What if Seth Byron has Polly and won't let her go?"

"You don't be worryin' your head 'bout that. If she be there, we'll get her, or the authorities will. I'll go up to that door. You wait in the carriage."

Impulsively, she took his gloved hand in hers. She felt her lust for life flood back through her. "You are more than sweet, Frank, but this is one man I will meet."

Ten minutes later, Suzanne watched Seth Byron coming across the Commons lobby toward her. He was a small, potbellied man with wide shoulders and a heavy, squarish jaw. His greasy hair shone in the sunlight that came through the big front window. He had a jaded surliness about him. His eyes, shrewd little chips of quartz, pierced the distance between them. He spoke in a thick, raspy voice. "What's your game lady?"

"I came for Polly Jackson, or at least to find out if you've got her."

"That nigger got her freedom, thanks to your smart aleck obnoxious cleverness. It's Southern pieces like you who should have your plantations burned. Niggers is slaves and slaves is only as good as them that controls 'em. Polly's a slut. She shouldn't be ramblin' and roarin' and makin' other slaves discontent. If'n I get hold of her, I'll get her out of circulation in a big hurry. As for you—"

Frank circled around to stand behind Suzanne. He put a gentle hand on the small of her back. Towering over Seth Byron, his voice deadly cold, he said, "That's enough! If'n ye be seein' Miss Polly today, ye better get her over to the Bostonian Hotel in one short time, or I'll be seein' to your discomfort personally."

Frank stepped out and leaned over the small man. "If it's after today, you will see that she gets home. Understand? Is it perfectly clear?"

Seth Byron blanched. He slurred some words between his teeth.

"What say ye?" Frank Reilly spat out.

"I gotcha."

* * * *

"I don' know where dey be, Miz Suzanne," Rufus said sorrowfully. "I be lookin' all de day. Nobody be rememberin' seein' dem since Satu'day night."

Suzanne said, "I'm sure Will and Clay have taken Polly back to Baltimore. They probably thought it was safer to take her away in case she couldn't get cleared and they decided not to disturb us in the middle of the night. Rufus, go to my room and get my trunk. Frank, get the carriage. We must be on that six o'clock train. I've got to go to her."

Chapter 19

Suzanne tried to get comfortable. Sick at heart and scared for Polly, she dreaded the long train ride home. For the past twenty-four hours, sound sleep had eluded her. They would arrive in Baltimore before dawn. She would go straight to the shack. She was certain Will and Clay would have taken Polly there. They would not have thought to take her to Tyrone's, or home. They would have thought the shack was safer. She remembered the hot wind whistling through the cracks of the wooden structure when she was prisoner there after her arrival to Baltimore.

Suzanne shivered. The passenger car was drafty; the wind in the shack would be cold. She hoped Will and Clay would think to give Polly extra blankets and take good care of her. She thought of Polly's Boston friends. How kind they had been; they loved Polly. Suzanne recalled Mrs. Jane's serene ebony eyes. They were the eyes of a woman with a deep faith in God.

Unbidden, thoughts of Tyrone floated into her mind. Memories so vivid, they came crowding back like a hidden current, an electrifying lure. She loved him with a queer mixture of anxiety and passion. His arresting good looks totally captivated her. She liked the curve of his mouth, the gentleness in his eyes, the graceful strength of his hands. Why could the touch of his hand send fire through every nerve of her body?

She had felt crushed by his strength and a longing for his embrace sent waves of warmth through her. Fleeting thoughts of sleeping with him skipped through her head. Sparks of unwanted excitement shot through her. Common sense attacked her fantasies. Their differences about the war probably would keep her and Tyrone apart. Although she loved his quiet air of authority and rare warmth, she saw his drive and temper and shrewd intuitions. *Oh, dear God, don't let Tyrone harm my father*, she thought.

Her senses still reached out for him into the night. Suzanne drifted into a placid dreamless sleep. Later, the noise of the train engine rose and rose, passing through a cry and into a scream against the crush of steel wheels against steel rails. She woke up with a start. The raw burr of the whistle came spiraling down as the train screeched to a stop. "Where are we?" Suzanne asked.

Frank stood above her. "Home, Suzanne. Rufus is already on his way to get the carriage. We be waitin' for him inside the station. Come."

He took her hand and guided her to the dim candle-lit room. Suzanne's trunks stood at the door. "What time is it?"

"It be almost mornin'. Rufus will be takin' ye to Tyrone's for the rest of this night."

Suzanne rubbed the sleep out of her eyes. "Not until I see Polly. I'll stay with her."

"We ain't found her yet."

"We will. She's at the shack."

"If she be there, I'll take you back to Boston. Remember, they hang witches at the Commons."

Suzanne grinned. "She'll be there."

At Suzanne's insistence, Rufus drove directly to the shack. "Let me be takin' a look, Miz Suzanne. I goes in de back door."

"I'm going with you." Suzanne let Frank help her scramble out of the carriage. Inside, Rufus handed Suzanne a candle. Cautiously she opened the inner door. A tattered piece of canvas was tacked to the tiny window. Polly lay huddled in the middle of the bed. A thick feather quilt covered her. Suzanne leaned over her and touched her dark cheek tenderly. Polly's eyes popped open. For an instant they filled with terror, then went blank and stared unseeing at Suzanne. "It's all right now, honey," Suzanne said. "I'll take care of you."

She turned to Rufus. "Wrap her up and carry her to the carriage; we'll take her to Tyrone's. I don't want to worry Zoe and Grandmother until she's better."

"I done tol' Faith to get a room ready for yous."

Holding Polly to quiet her tremors, Suzanne slept. Faith brought their meals. Late the following afternoon, while Polly slept quietly, Rufus drove Suzanne to the Fort to meet with her grandfather. John Hanson's face was full of concern as he walked toward Suzanne. "What happened, my dear? Why didn't you come home? Where is Polly?"

Suzanne felt tears spring to the corners of her eyes as she buried her face in her grandfather's embrace. She laughed and cried. "Oh, Grandfather, you sound just like me, asking so many questions, but it's all right now, or soon will be."

She explained what had happened. "I didn't want to worry Zoe and Grandmother. Maybe you could tell them we decided to stay on for a while and will be home next week. I think Polly will recover rapidly when she knows where she is. She's sleeping now, but I won't leave her for a minute after I get back. Rufus is waiting for me outside."

John wiped her tears away with his handkerchief. His own eyes were moist. "I'm glad you are both home safe. I'll stop by in the morning to check on Polly."

* * * *

Polly gained strength each day. "It was so terrible, Suzanne. I just couldn't stand the squalor, the suffering. My mind simply escaped the only way it knew how."

"How did Will and Clay come to find you and bring you here?"

"They heard Seth Byron talking to friends down at the tavern at the Tremont Inn. He was planning my escape. Will and Clay came straight away and plucked me out of my bed. They put me in a coach and got me out of there."

"Did you know them? Were they kind to you?"

"I tried to think who they were, but they didn't harm me, or rape me, if that's what you're asking. I was too out of it to ask any questions. I guess they were kind. They took me away before Seth Byron could get to me."

"Anyway, it's all right now. I think you'll be ready to go home tomorrow."

Polly laughed. "It sounded to me as if we didn't have a choice."

"What are you talking about?"

"You know very well what I'm talking about. I heard Bridget. I expect everybody in the house heard Bridget."

Suzanne felt sheepish. She embraced Polly and giggled. "Do you think so? She really let me have it in clear terms, didn't she?"

"Is it true?"

"That Tyrone is coming home tomorrow? I suppose it is, or she wouldn't have said so."

"Not that, silly. Is it true you are a threat to her happiness?"

Suzanne shrugged. "How should I know? Besides, she didn't say that."

"She might as well have." Polly threw her head back and laughed. "I would have loved to see your face when she told you to get out because Tyrone would feel compelled to be friendly to you. What's the story, my friend?"

"She thinks he would have asked her to marry him if he hadn't seen me at the races."

"What do you think? What is between you and Tyrone?"

Keenly aware of Polly's scrutiny, Suzanne kept her gaze unblinking and her features deceptively composed. "Oh, Polly, the sea and the war, and who knows, maybe there is nothing between us. At any rate, I won't be here tomorrow. Remember, there's still William lurking in the unknown."

Polly grinned and patted Suzanne on the shoulder. "You are a mysterious lady. Let's leave now. We'll be home in time for dinner and can start planning what we will wear to the Christmas Ball."

"Good idea. I'll get Rufus. You start packing."

* * * *

Dinner was a gala affair. Zoe and Margaret, frail now from the illness that was slowly eating away at her life, were unaware of the trauma that had recently taken place in the

The Bandit's Lady

girls' lives. Suzanne handed James the small volume of Longfellow poetry as she told him an exaggerated version of her seeing the poet. "And I talked to him in person," she concluded.

"You didn't, Cousin. I can see that in your mischievous eyes."

"You're right, I didn't, but Frank Reilly offered to get me an introduction. I would have let him, but Mr. Longfellow looked so sad. He lost his wife in a fire last summer. I couldn't find it in my heart to disturb him. I heard he stays in seclusion most of the time, so I felt extra honored to see him."

Zoe stayed in the dining room as the girls described their sightseeing trips, using Suzanne's recent experiences and Polly's memories. They explained in detail about Polly's release, except the one fact that Polly wasn't present and couldn't be found.

Margaret said, "No matter what that old judge put you through, we're glad to have you home. Tomorrow Zoe will take you both to Miss Millicent's to choose your gowns for the ball. I only wish I could take you myself."

John said, "Girls, it's time for your grandmother to go to her bed. Polly, I have the clipping from the paper announcing your legal freedom, and Suzanne, I have saved this letter for you. It's from your father, I believe."

Suzanne hurried to the parlor and her favorite chair, but the note from Aman was brief.

> *My dear Suzanne,*
>
> *It is nearing the end of 1861. My crew and I have searched boldly for prey off New York City and Boston and as far south as Florida and the Gulf states, but we have re-*

cently quit the hazardous privateer activities. Mostly we are unable to penetrate the blockade. With so few ports open for the sale of prizes and with so much risk for doubtful profits, we have decided to switch over to the more lucrative occupation of blockade running. You will not be hearing from me again for many months as it is highly dangerous for me to be in contact with you by letter. May your New Year be joyous. I will see you again when this tragic war comes to its close.

Your loving father, Aman

* * * *

The following morning at Miss Millicent's, Polly gazed happily at Suzanne. "Oh, Suzanne, it's beautiful. You look just like a real princess."

Suzanne laughed. "Thank you, Polly. Frank Reilly called me a witch and threatened to take me back to Boston to be hanged at the Commons. I would rather be a princess. Your dress is gorgeous, too. Let's not tell a soul what they look like. We'll make them wait until we put them on the night of the dance."

"Oh, I agree, but I can't wait."

Zoe's eyes shone with pride. "You don' hab no choice but to wait. It be only a week, me daughter."

Polly put her arms around her. "I know, Mama, but it's so exciting this year because Suzanne is with me."

* * * *

Suzanne spent the next couple of mornings catching up on the war news in the *Baltimore Crier*. In the back issue of November 11, she read:

> *Last week a Union victory far more important than Hatteras took place. A fleet under Flag Officer Samuel Francis DuPont and 12,000 troops commanded by Brigadier General Thomas W. Sherman captured Forts Beauregard and Walker in Port Royal Sound, South Carolina. In the thick of things was the Chesapeake Bay Half Dozen, including the controversial Sea Queen, who came through for the Union with sails a whipping.*

Zoe stuck her head in the door. "Charlie jus' brung de mail and dis here's a letter fo' you, Miz Suzanne."

"That's strange, Zoe. I received a letter from Father the other day."

Handing her the letter, Zoe said, "It don' look de same, Miz."

Suzanne studied the unfamiliar handwriting, then carefully opened the envelope. She quickly turned to the signature to discover that the message was from Thaddeus.

> *My Dear Suzanne,*
>
> *I heard a distressing piece of news from your father's closest friend on the pirate seas, Captain John Lloyd of Steamer Lloyd. It seems that in late October, an imposing fleet of warships and troops set sail for Fort Monroe with orders to secure Port Royal Sound. Several of our Confederate steamer fighters rushed to the scene to help defend our vested interests. Your father, on the Annebella, was among them. On November 7 the sixty-six warships steamed into the bay. They sailed around it battering at Fort Walker and Fort Beauregard with dozens of shells per minute.*

Captain Lloyd's account described the sad affair in detail. "The rounds fired kicked up pillars of smoke on shore that looked as if hundreds of racing stagecoaches were raising the dust of the land. The confederates dauntlessly fired back, but found their armament sadly unequal to the charge. Some guns were defunct by outsized shells, overcome by their own recoil or ruptured by defective fuses. Many companies plainly ran out of munitions altogether. But worse, the enemy's circling tactic stripped our fighters of solid targets. When all ended, the Annebella was nowhere in sight."

Now, Suzanne, I do not wish to be the carrier of bad news and I do not want you to worry unnecessarily, but it seems your father has disappeared. He had told the good Captain Lloyd it was his last run as a pirate.

My point being, Suzanne, although the folks at Royal Oaks sorely need you, it is not wise for you to come back now. I will make it my business to come for you in the spring after the muddy season. You may look forward to my arrival on or around April 15, 1862. Then we will have a serious discussion about what is best for your future. My regards and warmest wishes for your holidays.

Respectfully,
Thaddeus Stuart

Suzanne's heart went into sudden shock. Fear like the quick hot touch of searing, spitting embers shot through her. A scream clawed in her throat as she ran up the stairs to her bedroom and fell sobbing on the big soft bed. She had a feeling of having to hold herself, not to let go. Polly stood beside the bed. "It was bad news?"

Suzanne nodded.

Polly sat down on the edge of the bed. "Tell me about it."

"Oh, Polly, it's a nightmare beyond anything I have ever imagined. My father...my father..." After that she uttered only disjointed sounds and strangled groans.

When Zoe came into the room, Suzanne caught a whiff of the zesty smell of lemons and hot tea. She knew nothing could calm her nerves, but she sat up. Her words were sudden and raw. "He will pay; it's that bandit, Tyrone Sterling. He promised not to harm my father. Now Father's gone. No one has seen him since the Port Royal Sound battle."

"Tyrone will undoubtedly be at the ball Friday night. It's only three days away. You can ask him about it then."

"Oh, Polly, I couldn't go to the ball. My father may be...dead."

Polly took on a practical, no-nonsense tone. "Come on, Suzanne, there could be any number of reasons why your father disappeared. Don't dwell on the worst."

"But Thaddeus said..."

"Who is this Thaddeus? Why wouldn't he investigate your father's whereabouts before scaring you to death, maybe unnecessarily?"

In spite of herself, Suzanne chuckled. "Thaddeus wants to marry me. He hasn't been out of Charleston, and he didn't know for sure."

"There, you see, you were only jumping to conclusions."

"Maybe. Anyway, thank you, Polly. I feel much better. I will go to the ball and I will ask Tyrone if he knows anything."

Over the next few days, Suzanne tried to relax, but a sense of everything going wrong obsessed her. A nervous fluttering prickled at her chest. Whenever she thought of her father, fear and anger knotted inside her. No matter what Polly said, she was scared. *Thaddeus wouldn't be so careless about anything so serious*, she decided.

She would go to the ball. She went over and over what she would say to Tyrone. The afternoon of the ball, an idea slowly germinated within her. Suzanne took the pearl-handled gun from its pouch and fingered it gingerly, getting the feel of it. Deep inside she loved Tyrone, but she had tried to get the truth from him without success. *This time I will get the truth,* she thought.

Chapter 20

Fresh from a lavender-scented bath and dressed, Suzanne stood at the mirror. Zoe pulled back her shining copper curls and tied them with a bow at the nap of her neck. Her new frock was of creamy satin with a deep V-neckline, a smooth-fitted midriff and dramatic puffed sleeves. A gossamer overskirt, gathered into sheer flounces, was secured with tiny pearl clusters in the center of each swirl. "Zoe, it's the most beautiful gown I ever owned."

"I was thinking the very same thing about my dress," Polly said from the doorway. She came through the door with the rustling of taffeta and a flourish of ruffles and stood beside Suzanne at the mirror.

Polly wore her long black hair exactly like Suzanne's, although her bow was dusty rose, matching the color of her own frock. The gown had a scoop neckline and puffed sleeves trimmed with a frilly ruffle. The full skirt fell from a Basque waist and featured two large back bows and a ruffled hem.

Zoe said, "You two goin' to be de purtiest of dem all. Now quit admirin' and get away with you. James done already got your grandmama into de carriage. Shoo!"

Suzanne picked up her small beaded purse. Hand in hand, the girls left to put on their wraps and hurry to the waiting coach.

* * * *

Inside the grandiose mansion, they were directed to the upper rooms where they laid their cloaks on the bed in a guest room and made last-minute repairs on their hair before going downstairs. Suzanne caught her breath as she stood on the balcony overlooking the ballroom.

The twinkle of the massive crystal chandelier illuminating the scene caught her attention. The twelve-light burner was of gold gilt material, artistically embellished. A tripod of figures, exquisitely proportioned and symbolic of the first white settlers, supported the columns. A finely molded Baltimore Oriole complimented each figurine. Within the three columns stood a carved replica of a 1776 patriot, dressed in the splendid regalia of an officer of his day. Immediately above the three columns, the cornice, the Maryland coat of arms adorned the crowning piece of the work.

The room below held the lingering smells of the crisp winter air coming through the open doors with the guests. Mixed with its freshness, was the scent of fresh flowers placed around the huge ballroom. Dignified dowagers and elderly gentlemen sat in straight chairs along the sides waiting patiently for the young people to start dancing.

In a far corner the orchestra was warming up. At the other end of the room a long buffet table was laden with every delicacy Suzanne could imagine. She moved slowly down the massive spiral staircase. The ornate handrail was of smooth black walnut; the stairs were a polished, darkly stained oak. William Barclay waited for her at the bottom. "You are the most ravishing young lady I have ever known in my life, Miss Suzanne." He gave her a lopsided grin. "I came to collect my dances."

"However did you secure an invitation?"

"Oh, my dear, didn't you know? I have friends in high places. I warned you I would be here."

Suzanne felt joy bubble in her laugh. "And so you did. Yes, you may have this dance."

The couple whirled away, keeping perfect step to the beat of the music. *William moves with grace despite his stocky build*, Suzanne thought, as she closed her eyes to enjoy the flow of the dance and the music. William spoke softly in her ear. "You dance like a dream. Do you like the music?"

"Oh, yes; the waltz is so easy. Did you know it evolved from the German *Ländler?* It became popular almost a century ago."

"With you in my arms, it doesn't matter from where the waltz came. I don't care whether it's the one-step or the jig."

He leaned her back for a final bob, then gently encircled her waist and brought her up to stand beside him. His cheeks were flushed. "I fell in love with my nurse again. Can't you admit you love me a little, my angel?"

Before she could answer, a new partner whisked Suzanne away to a new tune. He was handsome enough, but gangly and awkward and one of a string of young men whose names she would not remember when the evening was over. Nevertheless, the dancing was exhilarating and somewhere in the middle, William, pouting, claimed her again.

He said, "You didn't answer my question and you seemed not to miss me at all. I could hardly concentrate on dancing with those other girls, for watching you, but you were laughing and gay and oblivious of me."

"I don't mean to be rude, William, but I promised you three dances only. The question will have to wait until we get better acquainted."

Suzanne saw his face fall in disappointment. Recognizing his despondency, she smiled brightly. "Maybe we could sit out this one. My feet feel abused and your leg must be hurting unmercifully."

His mood changed abruptly. He tenderly touched her cheek. "May I get you something to eat, or a cool drink?"

"Yes, thank you. I am starved. An icy fruit punch sounds delicious. I'll wait here."

Alone, Suzanne surveyed the room. The uneasiness about her father and about Tyrone returned. Where was he, anyway? Polly came up behind her and touched her shoulder. "Whom are you looking for?"

Suzanne swung around. Polly's eyes sparkled as though she was playing a game. "Your sweet William is at the buffet table piling food upon two plates. You will never be able to eat it all, and your Tyrone is over by the door. He has somebody very handsome with him. Would you care to get me an introduction?"

Suzanne spun towards the door. Her breath caught in her throat. Tyrone had on a black formal, three-piece suit with tails off the sides of the short coat. His shirt, tucked and starched, was adorned with a black bow-tie scarf. There was a curious old-fashioned dignity about him.

Bridget, on his arm, had an exquisite, fragile beauty, Suzanne admitted to herself. She watched Bridget say something to Tyrone and move sensuously to the stairs. Suzanne switched her attention back to Tyrone. He hadn't bothered watching Bridget saunter away. *Too bad,* Suzanne mused, *she was walking like that to entice you, my bandit.*

Tyrone was scanning the room and a moment later his ebony eyes softened at the sight of her. Suzanne felt the power of his gaze as she watched his eyes grow hungry. Tenderly, they probed her very soul, caressed her. The woman inside of her started to come alive and she felt herself flowing toward him. She was halfway across the room before a confusing rush of anticipation and dread whirled inside her. Polly, following close behind, must have seen her hesitate. "Go on, Suzanne. Enjoy yourself. You can talk to him later," Polly whispered.

Tyrone grabbed Polly in a brotherly hug. "Oh, Polly, I have somebody with me I want you to meet. Suzanne, too, of course. Girls, this is Jesse Owens of Charleston."

Jesse gave Suzanne a kindly look. She examined gentle smoke-gray eyes and felt like they had been friends for many long years. He said, easily, "We have met, but it was such a long time ago. You grew up beautiful, Miss Suzanne."

"Thank you. It's nice to see somebody from home. Have you seen my father lately?"

"No, not recently. War keeps friends apart, but we'll meet again someday."

Suzanne looked at Polly who shook her head, reminding her to refrain from asking the one question burning inside of her. She wondered again where Jesse Owens fit into Tyrone's plans, what the S/F on the paper had stood for and about Jesse's heritage.

Prim Miss Abigail had delighted in her version of his parentage. "Suzanne, you hear my words," she had said with relish, "that man's a griff. He was born of a slave girl, but his father was a plantation owner. He's an upstart, bound to cause trouble someday. He's too smart to stay in his place. When he decides, everybody in Charleston will know his story."

Suzanne came back to the present. Polly and Jesse were deep in conversation as the next musical selection began. Jesse opened his arms and they floated away to the dance floor. Tyrone was speaking. His voice brimmed with a husky excitement. "May I have this dance, my sweet?"

Suzanne started toward him, but Bridget stepped between them. "But of course you may," she said in her silky, throaty voice. "I've waited a lifetime for this very night."

When they left, Suzanne felt the cutting edge of loneliness. She spotted William on the far side of the room. He was hunting for her and juggling two unmanageable-looking plates. Guilt assailed her as she hurried to his rescue, but at the same time she could feel Tyrone's sharp eyes boring into her. "There you are," William said with relief, handing Suzanne a plate. "I don't know how much longer I could have held these plates without dropping one of them."

"Let's take them to one of the small tables set up in the dining room, Suzanne said."

She toyed with her food, pushing it around and rearranging it on the plate.

"I thought you were hungry."

"I thought so too, but I find I am not."

"Let me get you a glass of champagne. It will relax you."

"Oh, thank you, William. You are so kind to me. I wish I could be better company."

"Does it have anything to do with that rogue I saw with you?"

"If you mean Tyrone, what makes you call him a rogue?"

The Bandit's Lady

"I didn't like the way he looked at you. Come on, Angel. Cheer up. Let's dance."

Suzanne gave herself to the music. She would not allow Tyrone to spoil her evening, she decided. *He'll think I am having a glorious time.* She took a deep breath and adjusted her smile.

The evening was almost over. Suzanne stood beside William whose leg was throbbing from too many dances. She was trying to figure out a way to lure Tyrone to the library for the talk she had so carefully rehearsed when the music maestro held up his hand for silence.

"Ladies and gentlemen," he said, "it is our pleasure to introduce the newest romantic dance in triple time. We dedicate it to Baltimore, Maryland, at this Christmas Ball on Saturday, the twenty-first day of December, 1861. It was recently presented in the United States to New York City's highest society dancing circles. The orchestra will now take a five-minute recess and then we will end the evening with the magnificent and splendid Viennese waltz by Johann Strauss."

Suzanne sensed Tyrone behind her. She could feel the heat in her face as she turned to look full in his face. His eyes never left hers. "I believe, Miss Suzanne, this is my dance."

Suzanne lowered her eyes and consulted her dance card. It was blank. "I believe," she said in mock seriousness, "you are right."

When Bridget tried to step between them again, Tyrone turned to her graciously. "I am afraid I must leave you, my dear. You may be pleased to meet Lieutenant William Barclay. He will accompany you while I fulfill my obligation to this young lady. Since I have business later, I will not return to escort you home. Rufus will be waiting for you out front."

He nodded to William. "Would you be kind enough, Lieutenant, to see Miss Bridget to the carriage?"

Without waiting for an answer, Tyrone leaned toward Suzanne with a casual air of ownership. He picked up her right hand and brushed the back of it with his lips. His other arm came around her waist as he led her to the dance floor. "Thee is mine at last," he whispered into her ear as they twirled.

Suzanne looked at him with frank admiration. "And just what is your business this night, my bandit, to keep you from the chic and lovely Miss Bridget?"

His eyes had a sheen of purpose. "Well, certainly not to roam about and raid in search of plunder. No. Tonight my ambition is to woo a desirable and enchanting, willing maiden. What say, my sweet?"

Lending herself to the magic of the moment, Suzanne felt herself soaring within the circle of his embrace. His hand tightened on the small of her back. She looked up, wishing the rapture of the rhythm would never end. "Have you noticed that Polly and your Jesse Owens have not let each other out of their sight since you introduced them? I believe they have danced every dance."

"I would not know. I have seen nothing except your exquisite form dancing all over this ballroom with dashing young men. I've been green with jealousy."

Suzanne felt like he was smiling into her heart. Eyes locked, they were one with the music and each other. As they swirled and spun, the other dancers gradually stopped and moved away to form a circle around them. When the dance ended, Tyrone swooped and arched Suzanne backwards. He held her tenderly in a deep low dip for breathless moments as the final notes of the waltz melted into silence. In the astonished hush, when at last he lifted her effortlessly to stand beside him, applause rose in great waves and filled the room.

The ball was over.

"I must talk to you, Tyrone," Suzanne said as they walked off the dance floor.

"Come into the library, my sweet. Nobody will bother us there."

Closing the door she leaned her back against it. "My father is missing and I think you know why. Maybe you are responsible."

His body became taut and he stood hovering over her, hands on hips. Suzanne reached into the small beaded purse. When she pulled her hand out, she clutched the tiny pistol tight, pointing it straight at this man who was her father's enemy. Quickly, but gently he reached out and grasped her wrist. Thrusting the small gun easily across the space to the small settee, he drew her into his arms. "Don't be afraid. I won't leave, though I could do so quite easily. Suzanne; what can I do to get you to trust me?"

"Tell me my father is safe and that you will not harm him."

"I can't guarantee his safety, but I will not harm him. You have my word."

Suddenly Suzanne found herself clutching him as to a column of strength in her whirling world. She felt blissful, knowing the arms that held her loved her. She smelled the clean aroma of soap, felt the smoothness of his recently shaved cheeks, his lips upon her hair and the spontaneous hard tensing of his muscles. Every curve of her body was molded against his.

He guided her over to the fireplace, nuzzling her throat and kissing the softness of her exposed cleavage. His fingers circled her breasts; the tiny tips puckered and ached with desire. A small sound of wonder came from her throat. With a lazy, sensuous movement, his tongue entered her mouth. While it ravaged the sweetness of her mouth, she tasted him with a new hunger. She clung to him, wanting the kiss to go on.

The door burst open and James stood on the threshold. Her cousin was a study of hate and in that frozen moment, Suzanne knew what it meant to be condemned without investigation. James lunged for the gun. The rage in him was a livid, living thing. His voice cracked as he said, "Move away, Suzanne."

Tyrone thrust her aside and moved toward James. Two explosions shattered the air. Tyrone slumped to the floor in a pool of gushing blood. He seemed to stop breathing.

Suzanne heard screams like the roaring of blood in her ears. She realized the screams and a guttural cry of terror were hers. Finally she sank to the floor in a stunned tangle and cradled Tyrone's still form in her lap.

Chapter 21

Like an echo from an empty tomb, James' voice sounded far away. It was emotionless. "What should I do?"

The words chilled Suzanne. An icy fear twisted around her heart. Through the roaring din in her head, she said, "Get Grandfather."

The shots had electrified the lingering guests. The rapt faces of silent watchers occupied all available space. Once again they formed a circle around the couple. This time the quiet was deafening. John Hanson had already been summoned. Despite his slight frame and usually quiet demeanor, he charged through the door. "Move aside."

Steadfast eyes swept the onlookers with a piercing glance. He said in a voice that left no room for defiance. "Please leave quietly. This man is seriously wounded. He needs air. Suzanne, undo his tie. Loosen his shirt."

She saw the snap of his impatient green eyes. Given something definite to do startled her out of hysterical panic. She obeyed without question. John leaned over the prostrate figure. "He lives," he said shortly.

Those who loitered around the edges of the room watched the predictable chain reaction of events. John Hanson barked out orders. Suzanne tore the ruffle off her petticoat. James rushed to the kitchen for a knife and boiling water. Polly went to the carriage to get the doctor's bag.

Through a dizzy, spinning nausea in her stomach, Suzanne, by turns, helped her grandfather and watched helplessly as the relentless hours dragged along. When the flow of blood finally ceased, Tyrone's jagged, shallow breath rasped in his chest. His eyes remained closed.

John spoke in a weary voice, "That's all we can do tonight. We can't take a chance of removing the bullet right now. We will take him home where I can watch him."

Suzanne heard her own voice, stifled and unnatural. "Grandfather, will he live?"

He looked her straight in the eye. "It's not probable. Maybe a miracle..." he said wearily.

Rufus, Frank Reilly and Jesse Owens stepped out of the shadows from the far corner of the room. Rufus said, "We be takin' him to you' place, doc'or."

Suzanne was touched by the tenderness with which they lifted him onto the improvised stretcher, a slab of wood covered with a sheet. They carried him to the carriage. William came up beside Suzanne. He helped her into her cloak and pulled it close to cover her bloody gown. "Is there anything I can do?" he asked humbly.

His voice seemed unnaturally loud in the stillness that had invaded the room. Suzanne hurried to the door. On the threshold of the mansion, she paused to take in a long breath of the cold air. She focused on the swirls of powdery snow kicked up by intermittent gusts of wind. She was remotely conscious of the cracking of the huge wind-whipped flag somewhere above. William gripped her arms; his face was bleak with sorrow. "Suzanne, say something. Answer me."

She flung out her hands in simple despair. She felt guilty and selfish. She swallowed hard and bit back the tears. "Thank you, William. There is nothing. I must get home to help take care of him."

"He's the reason you can't love me, isn't he?"

Too exhausted to argue or rationalize, weariness tinged her voice. "Yes. I'm sorry."

Hurt and longing lay naked in William's eyes. He stepped forward and clasped her body tightly to his. His lips brushed against hers as he spoke. "If he lives, he's the luckiest man alive. If you ever need me..." His eyes drank her up. Then brusquely, he said, "Come on. I'll take you home."

* * * *

Zoe met Suzanne at the front door and led her to her bedroom. "We gets you out o' dat dress, Miz Suzanne."

"I'll wear the gray one."

"You better get you'self to bed, so you be mo' able to help tomorrow."

Suzanne had already stepped out of the soiled, bloodstained gown and petticoats. She stood in the middle of the room with only a chemise and drawers to cover her. She shivered and heard her voice sharpen, "Don't argue; I'm freezing. Get the gray dress out of the closet."

* * * *

Hands clasped tightly in her lap, Suzanne sat motionless on the straight chair beside Tyrone's bed. Her heart ached with the pain; she felt a suffocating sensation tighten her throat. Memory closed around her and filled her with a longing to change the whole scene in the library. After what seemed like many frozen hours, Suzanne roused herself from the numbness that weighed her down. She pressed both hands over her eyes; they burned with weariness and despair. Tyrone had not stirred. Suzanne touched his cheeks; the hot skin beneath her fingertips raged with fever. She jumped as if bitten.

Blinded by tears, she ran up the narrow stairway to the maids' quarters and pounded on Jeanne's door. She knew a faint thread of hysteria was back in her voice. "Get up! I need help!"

She heard Jeanne scurry around and ran back to Tyrone's side. Finally, after what seemed like an eternity, Jeanne carried a bucket of cold water into the sick room.

Every few minutes, Suzanne wrung out and held a fresh cold compress on Tyrone's forehead. She put another behind the back of his neck. Once she thought he winced slightly, but she quickly sensed it had been a figment of her imagination, a hope. The endless night finally grayed into dawn and John stood beside the bed shaking his head.

"It's not working, Grandfather. Nothing is working."

"Go get some rest, my dear," he said gently.

"You know I couldn't." Suzanne walked to the window overlooking the front lane. She turned her back to her grandfather. "It was all my fault," she said in a strangled voice.

He went to stand beside her. "Don't blame yourself, Suzanne. James told me the whole story."

"Only what he knew, Grandfather. I've never told him everything and the gun is mine. I threatened Tyrone with it to find out what he did with Father. He took it away from me and threw it on the davenport. We..."

"Don't torture yourself. Let's concentrate on saving his life."

The Bandit's Lady

He walked back to the inert figure. "We can't operate. He's already full of infection. We have to lower the fever."

He showed her how to blend and apply the healing compound. He said, "We will use this powdered lobelia and slippery elm poultice to draw the poison from the wound. Mix it into a thick paste with very hot water—like this. Now put it full-strength onto the wound, enough to cover the bullet hole completely. Then put a plain bandage on it and tape it into place. Give him this sulfur compound every six hours. You'll have to force it down his throat. If he...when he is better, we'll operate then."

"You were going to say, if he lives, weren't you, Grandfather?"

"It looks very bad, but I've seen worse. He's young and strong"

"Why doesn't he move? He hasn't even moaned."

"He's in a coma. The second bullet glazed the base of his skull. I don't think it did permanent damage. He is not in any pain now; it's the fever that keeps him in a coma. Now, you go get some rest, Suzanne. You can visit him later. I'll have Jeanne stay with him."

"Not yet, Grandfather. She can take turns with me, relieve me for a few hours at night. I'll stay with him during the days."

John looked at his granddaughter. "Keep bathing him with cold compresses. Dribble liquid, both the tepid water and the slippery elm tea, down his throat every ten minutes. If you don't, he will dehydrate. I'll have Zoe keep you supplied with the things you'll need. Send Charlie to get me if there's any change for the worse in his condition."

* * * *

Three days passed slowly into two weeks, and in a frenzy of helplessness, Suzanne sat quietly, holding Tyrone's hand. Tears of frustration streamed down her face. She was ever conscious of the dull throb of grief in her mind. *Tomorrow is Christmas,* she thought sadly. Jeanne flew through the door to the sick room. "Zoe waked me up and tol' me to come back here. She say you got company in de parlor."

"I can't go down there. I'm not dressed for company."

"She say, 'tell her forgit how she be dressed. Miz Suzanne got nothing to 'pologize fo'."

"Who is it? Do you know, Jeanne?"

"No, Miz, I don' know. Hurry now. I be takin' care of de sick one. He be goin' to be better soon. I feels it in me bones."

"I will be back as soon as I can, Jeanne, so you can get your sleep."

"Be takin' your time, Miz. I be fine."

Bridget, pathetically pale, was sitting on the edge of Suzanne's favorite chair. Across the room, William had his bad leg propped on the tea table. When Suzanne approached, Bridget jumped up. Her black eyes blazed. "What have you done to him? I want to see him."

Suzanne closed her eyes and sighed. "Of course, you may see him, but he has not regained consciousness. He can't talk. He won't know you're here."

It was Bridget's turn to sigh. "I know, Suzanne. Zoe told me. In fact, she has told me every day since the accident. I just want to see him. Have Zoe take me to him. You can stay here and talk to William."

As if on cue, Zoe came into the room with a tea tray. "I be takin' Miz Bridget upstairs. You relax here with Mis'er William."

Suzanne looked absently at William. "Lieutenant, Zoe."

"Yes, um, Miz," she said as she turned and led Bridget out of the room.

"What is this all about?" Suzanne asked William.

William looked at her with a wry smile. "It's about two people who love two people who love each other."

Suzanne went quickly to sit beside him. A flash of wild grief ripped through her. "Oh, William, what a mess humans make of things. Can you ever forgive me? Can Bridget?"

"There is nothing to forgive, my angel. None of us plan to fall in love with a certain someone to hurt another. It just happens. The love and the hurt just happen," he said softly, almost to himself.

The pent-up tears rolled down her cheeks and suddenly Suzanne yielded to compulsive sobs, buried sobs that shook her whole body. William held her tenderly until they gradually abated. She took deep breaths until she was strong enough to raise her head and meet the bleak sorrow in his eyes. "You know I wouldn't have hurt you for anything on earth if I could have helped it."

William rocked her gently. "I know."

"Tell me about Bridget."

"Bridget came to say good-bye to Tyrone. She's going back home. She decided to leave for Philadelphia this afternoon, in time to spend Christmas with her family."

"What about you?"

"My stay here is short. I'm going to spend the holidays with Julia and Tom." He grinned, "And the mischievous monster twins. I will rejoin my regiment the middle of January."

"Do you know where?"

"In the Shenandoah Valley with T.J. Jackson's outfit."

"And afterward?"

"I don't know for sure," he said. But as he continued, his face came alive. "I find I have an extraordinary curiosity about, and an abundance of ideas for, improving the commercial banking industry. The best place to investigate and satisfy my inquisitiveness is the North American Bank of Philadelphia. I had secured a minor position there before this war split men apart."

"But you are a Confederate. How can you possibly find peace in the north?"

"After the war, when things settle down, the United States will stand strong. Differences die hard, but they will die."

The sheer logic of what he said was convincing. "William, you amaze me." She reached out, lacing his fingers with her own. "You'll be fine. Once this war is over, you will find yourself a city girl to share your dreams and your life. I wish you well."

His free hand moved to her face. He tenderly traced the line of her cheekbone and jaw, then brushed the hair from her neck. His fingers curved under her chin. His eyes caught hers. He studied her thoughtfully for a moment, but when he spoke, his voice was resigned. "I hoped it could be you." The next moment he offered her a light, forgiving smile. "But I know it can't. Just never ask me to forget my beautiful and incredibly fearless angel, for you will always hold a very special place in my heart."

"And you in mine," Suzanne said as Bridget reentered the room.

Bridget's eyes shone with unshed tears. Suzanne felt another pang of guilt. "Bridget, I'm so sorry."

"So am I, Suzanne, but it's not what you think. I have believed myself in love with Tyrone since we were children. He has always had a masculine force about him, a great presence born of certainty."

"You don't have to explain..."

"Please. I want to. He never encouraged me. I've tried everything. I realized the first time I saw the two of you together that he loves you, really loves you, with a rare and tender love."

"But..."

"I know you think you have problems, but he'll work them out. He fought for everything he ever got, except his mother's love. He sees in you her gentleness and other special traits she possesses."

Bridget's black eyes snapped. She walked gracefully over to Suzanne and helped her to her feet. "I'm not giving up entirely, but I'll leave him to your care for now. It's too bad we love the same man. I think we could have been friends under other circumstances."

Suzanne reached out and hugged her. "Thank you for your trust. I'll take very good care of him."

Before Bridget and William were in the carriage, James stood at the window behind Suzanne. He put his hands on her shoulders and massaged the tense muscles.

"Cousin, I've caused you so much pain. Can you ever forgive me?"

"It seems the whole world is asking for forgiveness today." Suzanne walked back into the parlor to sit by the fireplace. "You did what you thought best to protect me. If I had been square with you from the beginning, none of this would have happened. Now, think of it no more. Our only concern is to get Tyrone well."

"Let me take a shift," James said. "I can take care of him as well as you and Jeanne."

"Thank you, James. Indeed I will. You can have the eleven P.M. to seven A.M. shift. That way, both Jeanne and I will be able to sleep and she can relieve me for meals during the day."

"Gee, Cousin, you really know how to punish a fellow." But James' irresistible boyish smile spilled over, denying his words.

Suzanne turned to him and smiled. "Of course, I do. You can start tonight."

James sobered. He kneeled and put his head on Suzanne's lap. "What if he dies?" he asked in a muffled voice.

Suzanne tousled his hair softly. "He won't die. Grandfather won't let him. We've got to have faith. Dear James, I'd give anything if you didn't have to go through this. I will tell you everything as soon as Tyrone is better. I've got to get back there, now. I'll see you at Christmas dinner."

* * * *

Suzanne looked around the small room. The parlor was full; Polly and her guest Jesse Owens were talking quietly in front of the fireplace. James and Grandfather, looking out of the front window, were discussing the weather and the possibility of going rabbit hunting, Suzanne supposed. Margaret, looking frail, but alert, sat contentedly in the big easy chair. She had picked up her knitting for the first time in months. "You look beautiful, Grandmother," Suzanne said as she planted a kiss on her soft, wrinkled cheek.

The Bandit's Lady

Margaret chuckled. "You lie with charm, my dear granddaughter, but I love it. John, please pour the eggnog. I think I'll join you in a glass."

There was a flurry of exclamations as they exchanged gifts and enjoyed easy banter. Suzanne's gifts to the others were a small pearl-beaded purse for Polly, plaid woolen mufflers for James and her grandfather and the pendant she had bought at the races for her grandmother.

In return she received a small volume of Shakespeare's sonnets from James, a green velvet riding hood from Polly, a gold chain with an emerald drop from her grandfather and two linen handkerchiefs with her grandmother's special tat edging. Feeling special, Suzanne thanked each one with a kiss.

"I have a greater gift for you, my dear," John said when she stood before him. "We are going to do the surgery on Tyrone tomorrow morning. Mrs. Townsend will come over to help us."

"But he hasn't regained consciousness yet, Grandfather."

"I think he will soon. At any rate, his temperature is almost normal. I believe he is strong enough to have the bullet removed."

* * * *

Late afternoon sunshine splashed across the dazzling white world as Suzanne stood by the window in the sick room. *Christmas, 1861*, she thought; *it is almost the new year; I am still in Baltimore and there has been no word from Father.*

Before Tyrone spoke, Suzanne heard his quick intake of breath. She whirled around. "You are the most beautiful vision in all the world," he said, and closed his eyes in a natural sleep.

Chapter 22

"Grandfather, Grandfather, he opened his eyes. He spoke. Where are you?" Suzanne ran down the curved stairway and poked her head into doors until she found him reading a book in his study. "Did you hear me, Grandfather?"

"Of course, I heard you, my dear." His eyes sparkled. "I expect Charlie heard you out in the barn, too. Tell me how he is."

"I don't know. He mumbled a few words and fell into sleep again."

"Good. That is exactly what I hoped would happen. After the surgery, he should recover rapidly and be able to leave here within a few weeks. You go upstairs and get a good night's rest. Tomorrow will be your first day as a real nurse. Mrs. Townsend sent word she is shorthanded at the fort and can't come. She assured me you are capable of doing a superb job in her stead."

* * * *

The days ran together in a swirl of snow. Suzanne looked out into the white wonderland of mid-January. She had just spoon-fed the patient a bowl of thick vegetable broth. Tyrone had continued to sleep most of his days and nights, waking only for meals, bathing and other necessities. Suzanne was in a light mood. The surgery had gone well. He was healing and his strength was coming back. He was lucid more and more often. She winced. He could have died, and that sobering thought made her throat ache with despair. "Sit here, Suzanne. Talk to me." Behind her, Tyrone's voice was like a warm embrace.

She went to sit in the old Boston rocker James had brought in for the long watchful hours. Tyrone reached out and caught her hand in his. A faint light twinkled in the depths of his black eyes. "Pull the chair closer. I want to thank you for saving my life. I think I always knew you were here. You willed me to live."

Then his mouth quirked with humor. "I was only afraid the first time I sensed James in the room."

"James wouldn't hurt you," she said before she saw the irony of it. "Oh," she sputtered, "you know what I mean."

Amusement flickered in the eyes that met hers. He was teasing her affectionately. Then he grew pensive. "You remind me of my mother."

"Bridget told me. Why?"

"Let's lay Bridget to rest first."

"That's not necessary. She gave you into my care, Tyrone. She left for home in time for Christmas. Tell me about your mother."

"She's very gentle, very loving, but so stubborn. You have all those qualities, too."

"What does she do with her life?"

"Mother is a Quaker. She's hated slavery since she was very young. When my grandparents came to America, she was seventeen. There were slaves aboard the *Delta Prince,* the vessel on which they came to the States. The slaves had been picked up weeks before and packed in tight to grovel in the bowels of the ship."

"For a sensitive young lady that must have been terrible."

"Mother vowed to do something about it. Her family settled in Philadelphia, later a natural crossroads for slaves escaping from Maryland. The Pennsylvania Abolition Society had an active Chapter in the city. She was seventeen when she joined the society and quickly won a reputation for enthusiasm, resourcefulness and availability at all hours of the day or night. She had a zealous dedication to the task and an extreme hatred of injustice and oppression. She headed a group of Quakers and free Negroes who would shelter escaping slaves. She's so gentle she could slip through loopholes." Tyrone paused to reflect with amusement. "But she has became extremely troublesome, especially to irate slave holders."

"I met a woman like that in Boston. She spoke at Faneuil Hall. She harbors runaways in her Philadelphia home. She was advocating a boycott against the agricultural products of slavery."

"Did you enjoy her speech?"

"Frankly, Tyrone, I was a little uncomfortable with the speech. They introduced her as Mrs. Jane. She said she would use any tactic except outright violence to oppose injustices to slaves. She said she was no advocate to passivity and that Quakerism did not mean quietism. She attributed her choice of words to Lucretia Mott. You would have loved her, Tyrone. She was tall and slender and held herself like a queen. She had a quiet air of authority and yet of rare warmth."

Suzanne rocked gently back and forth trying to recapture the dimly remembered gentility. A fragment of an idea slowly germinated within her. Suzanne felt the memory of Mrs.

Jane's ink black eyes ruffle through her mind. "Tyrone, I've met your mother, haven't I?"

He tried to look indifferent. She loved him for the humor that glinted behind his eyes. He said, "Yes, she told me."

"Why didn't you tell me, or why didn't she?"

"She approved of you. I had told her I will marry you one day. She knows Polly, of course, and remembered your name. She was inspecting you."

Suzanne giggled, then leaned over, embraced him and kissed him on the cheek. Her arms were solid and strong around him. Tyrone leaned back and closed his eyes. Suzanne stroked his hair with her hand and loved him with her eyes. "Sleep now, my love. We'll talk again later."

He sighed and rolled over.

* * * *

"Okay, Tyrone," Suzanne said cheerfully as she entered the room the following morning. "It's time for you to get out of that bed. Today, you will sit in the rocker while I make your bed."

"You are one cruel lady. I want to spend the rest of my life lolling in this bed, watching you glide through my dreams, my fantasies and my life."

"Ah, ha, it is as I thought. You are taking advantage of my good nature, but no more."

"I'll faint."

Suzanne brought her hand up to stifle her giggles. "You better concentrate on staying on your feet, for if you pass out you'll have to spend the day on the floor until somebody comes to help you back to bed."

"Then I won't faint."

"That's better. Come on, I'll help you."

The Bandit's Lady

* * * *

A few days later, when Suzanne started down the hallway, Tyrone lounged casually against the door frame. "I think I'll get some fresh air today, my sweet. I do need to get back to duty, and I can't get my strength back unless I begin. Will you walk with me?"

The day had dawned dull gray and unseasonably warm. A spring-like thaw had distracted the death clutch of winter. Hand in hand, they walked down the lane. Suzanne said, "Tell me, Tyrone, how you met my grandparents."

"My mother and your grandparents met when Mother was speaking at the music hall. Your grandparents were easily convinced to join the Underground. Did you know your grandfather helped organize the use of the railroads as another means for the slaves to escape? He convinced key people to instruct the crews about the trains' unscheduled stops. Today they can stop anywhere along the way to pick up Negroes. It was also through your grandfather's ingenuity that Negroes are hidden in packing cases, hogsheads, or even temporarily in gunny sacks."

"Yes, but where did you meet them?"

Tyrone's laugh was deep, warm, and rich. "I was the delivery boy. Mother also organized sewing circles, as did your grandmother, to sew travel outfits to replace the tattered clothes of the slaves. Your grandmother asked Captain Neal to find her a dress from a Quaker woman so she could make copies to keep on hand as disguises. He talked to me about it and I brought your grandmother a supply of the dove-gray gowns, kerchiefs, bonnets and the heavy veils. That's when it started. Later, when Captain Neal needed someone to care for my cargo, he asked your grandparents to help out."

"You knew Polly, too. You hugged her the night of the ball."

"She's a dear. I've been wanting to introduce her to Jesse for a long time."

"I think you made a good match. They seem to be infatuated with each other. How did you meet Jesse?"

"Oh, my Suzanne, you do ask questions." Tyrone turned back towards the house. "Unfortunately, I'm still a dangerous man to you and your household. I must leave here soon and get back to this business of war. Come upstairs and put me to bed. I'm purely exhausted."

An inexplicable look of withdrawal came over his face. This time Suzanne kept her expression under stern restraint. There would be another day to learn his story. She leaned lightly into him. Tilting her face towards his, her delight grew when his heartbeat throbbed against her ear. "Come on," she said, putting her face devilishly close to his. Let's find out how weary you really are."

Later, in his room, his face filled with love. He said, "You've got to stop teasing me, Suzanne. A man can take only so much torture."

Suzanne buried her burning face against his shoulder. Her excitement embarrassed her and she was ashamed at having taken advantage of his male appetite. "I didn't intend to torment you, Tyrone, but I've watched you sleep and fight for your life these many weeks. I've agonized over you and I love you. I'm mortified to be so bold, but I can't seem to help myself."

Despite her confession, she felt a warm glow of joy flow through her. She looked up. Tyrone's eyes contained a sensuous flame. He opened his arms and she walked into them. For precious moments, wrapped in each other's arms, they surrendered to the crush of feelings that drew them together. She was aware of the hunger in him. She wanted to yield to the burning sweetness that seemed captive within her. She felt her knees weaken as his mouth descended and his kiss sent new spirals of ecstasy through her. Gently he eased her down on the bed and wrapped his arms around her waist. "Please lie next to me while I fall asleep," Tyrone whispered, his breath hot against her ear.

* * * *

Suzanne awoke with a start. Dusk was settling. She eased herself out of Tyrone's embrace and hurried down the hall to dress for dinner.

The following morning, Suzanne found Tyrone's room empty and decided to see what was going on in the big barn. She slipped into her heavy cloak and hurried across the path Henry had cleared of snow. As she opened the trapdoor, she heard a young boy whimper. "It hu'ts, mas'er, sir."

Tyrone responded in a quiet, comforting voice. "I know, Jethro, but it will feel much better after we set the arm. In a few days it will be healing nicely. Hold still now."

Suzanne took in the scene. A thin trembling young black boy of about nine years of age, cheeks streaked with tears, faced Tyrone. "Can I help?" she asked.

Tyrone looked up gratefully and smiled over the boy's head. "Hold him steady. Jethro is a brave lad. He's going to be fine."

They worked silently until the splint was properly positioned and secure. Then Suzanne washed the tiny face with warm water and fixed him a cup of hot chocolate. By the time he drank the soothing liquid, Jethro's eyes were heavy with sleep. Tyrone picked him up and carried him to a cot where he covered him up with a thick quilt. Suzanne whispered, "I don't see anyone with him. Where did he come from?"

Tyrone motioned her outdoors and led her across the grounds to the small barn where they sat on a mound of sweet-smelling straw. "We won't bother him here. He should sleep for hours, and Charlie will look in on him from time to time until he is moved upstate."

"Where are his folks?"

"I found him in the woods this morning when I was giving Midnight a bit of exercise. He had fallen out of an overturned wagon I found nearby. He said slave hunters snatched his mother, but he hid under an evergreen tree."

"What will happen to him?"

"When he wakes up, Charlie will take him to the train and find somebody to watch over him until he can get to the Canadian border, via Boston. There's an orphanage across the border near Sherbrooke. The nuns will keep him until they can find someone to raise him."

Suzanne settled back into a more comfortable position. "Tyrone, you are a study of inconsistencies. Tell me more about yourself. You haven't spoken of your father."

The same hurt, tormented expression she had seen on their first meeting flitted across his face. He spoke slowly, as if considering each word. "I barely knew my father. He died when I was eight. He was a slave trader."

"How could your mother marry a man with ideals so different from her own?"

"She met him on the same ship that brought her to this country. He was handsome and glamorous; he swept her off her feet. She didn't know his real business until it was too late.

After that, he stayed away from home much of the time. He loved her in his own way, left her well off, but he died a horrible death. A black slave stabbed him, then escaped during the commotion that followed."

"You were so young when he died. Why didn't she protect you from the truth?"

"In fact, she insisted I learn the harsh facts for my own good."

Suzanne heard the bitterness spill over in his voice.

"Mother's brother, Uncle Jacob Yoder, took me to New Orleans with him when he went there to settle my father's affairs."

"Tell me about it," Suzanne said softly.

Suddenly his face went grim. "We stayed at my Grandfather Sterling's home for two weeks until the day of the sale. Always inquisitive, I set out to learn as much as I could about this plantation life that my mother spurned with such savage hatred."

Looking as anxious as if he were still the child who had stumbled on something he didn't understand, Tyrone lowered his voice. "I saw young women strung up by their wrists and whipped on their bare backs until the blood ran. I saw a male slave shot dead by an overseer for trying to run away from a flogging. In addition to the physical cruelty, was the miserable food, clothing and lodging given them. The food allowance for a field hand for a whole month was eight pounds of pickled pork or fish, a bushel of cornmeal and a pint of salt. The pork was often tainted, the fish of the coarsest kind and the meal of the same quality as that slopped to the hogs. The slaves didn't have garden patches, hen houses, or pigsties. They allowed an adult male two flax or hemp-linen shirts and a pair of tow-linen trousers for summer. He had one pair of woolen trousers and a woolen jacket for winter. They gave him one pair of yarn stockings and one pair of ill-fitting, rough shoes. Children under ten had nothing to wear all year but two shirts. When they wore out or were outgrown, they went naked until the next allowance day."

Tyrone shuddered. Suzanne reached out and put her hand over his. "They gave men and women one rough blanket. They cuddled up with the children, who had none, and huddled together in feed bags or sacks in which corn was carried to the mill. During the day, the slaves kept to the sunny side of the house, or crouched in a corner of the kitchen chimney; at night there was nothing but the floor of trodden earth. There was not even loose straw to lie on, though the horses in the stables had it. On sale day, we went to the ship and watched the slaves being deloused and scrubbed with a crude scrub brush. Then the slave master drove them to the auction block, nipping at their heels with a whip. They were frightened, utterly degraded."

He shook off Suzanne's hand and shoved his own hands in his pockets and hunched forward. Tyrone held his head high with pride, his profile was strong and rigid, but there was a restless energy about his movements. Suzanne moved to comfort him, but his dark angry expression silenced her. "Before they went on the block, they were forced to parade in front of white 'shoppers,' and jump or dance to show their liveliness. They usually stripped the younger ones to prove they had not been damaged by whipping. Buyers probed their bodies. They felt them, pinched them and crammed filthy fingers down their throats to examine their teeth."

Suzanne visualized a young sympathetic Tyrone painfully observing the demeaning humiliation thrust upon poor, powerless human beings. "It was too hard a lesson for a small boy. But now, why are you willing to save people of enemy camps with food and medicines and munitions? You've let shiploads of crews from battered vessels slip away into foggy darkness. You oversee medicines delivered to wounded troops at Fort McHenry to men you know will go back and fight the Union. It doesn't make sense."

With a pensive gesture, Tyrone touched her cheek and pushed away stray tendrils of hair. There was a caustic tinge of cynicism in his voice. "The slave master in charge was my father's brother. Uncle Jacob sold him out, left my father's family flat broke, bereft. I feel a certain responsibility to them. There is another reason. The United States Union soldiers will win this war. That doesn't mean killing is right on either side. What I do for the wounded, the sick, the hungry and the defenseless, I am willing to do for either side equally, for humanity."

His voice faded, losing its steely edge. "Besides, I only told you the agonizing side of the visit and sale day. I saw good too. Someday I'll tell you the rest of the story."

Suzanne watched his pained expression of confusion and grief turn to desire as he put the last of his agonizing childhood resentment and recollections behind. He swung her into the circle of his arms.

Chapter 23

The smoldering flame Suzanne saw in Tyrone's eyes aroused her curiosity. He didn't smile, but his dark eyes narrowed, spearing her with an intensity that made flames kindle in her own blood. His hands stroked her hair lightly. Then he turned over, pulling her under him, and the weight of him crushed her yielding body down into the hay.

His eyes held hers while his body eased completely over hers. "Now I can feel you totally, perfectly," he whispered, "and you can feel me. We can't hide anything from each other when we touch like this. You know how much I want you, don't you, Suzanne?"

Her fingers touched his face, his mouth, his thick black brows and trailed down the thin thread of a scar. When she breathed, she was even more aware of the warmth and weight of his hair-roughened chest. Her arms went up to hold him even closer as he bent to take her mouth in his. She opened her lips; her fingers twisted in his thick hair as the kiss lingered and deepened. His tongue darted into her mouth, demanding, tormenting. His hands slid under her thighs and lifted her body up against his. Pleasure surged through her like a well of spring water and she sensed again her own awakening emotions and sensations that still waited for fulfillment. "I feel so inadequate for you, Tyrone," she said softly. "I wish I could come to you, proud and willing. I dream about how it would be with you."

She shifted fitfully under the crush of his body. A hard groan tore out of his throat as he rolled away. "Hush, my sweet. You shall. But for now we must say good-bye once more. I'm taking Midnight home this afternoon and leaving at first light in the morning."

"What are you going to do after the war, my bandit and captain?"

Tyrone smiled warmly. "I want to divide my energies. I have always dreamed of designing and building a great ocean liner to carry my mother in style back to visit England, her homeland. I want to resume commercial shipping. Those ventures can best be done here in Baltimore."

"And the other?"

"I have vowed to help Jesse Owens. When this war is over, he will devote the rest of his life helping liberate the blacks, cleaning up the mess, and educating the children." He grinned. "That, my prying southern beauty, will best be accomplished in Charleston" He bent his dark head and brushed his mouth against hers. A whisper of delicious sensation quickened her pulse, her breathing. "Go now," he said, but not before his hungry passion blazed between them afresh.

She stopped trying to understand and melted into him. She felt the hungry crush of his mouth. His arms held her body against his long, hard form. The contact with his powerful body, the warmth of him seemed to burn everywhere they touched. She didn't want the kiss to end. She wanted to spend the rest of her life in his arms, holding him, loving him. Loving him. She shifted her body sensuously against his. The thought of how scandalized Miss Abigail would have been flitted delightfully through her mind. "I...I like the way it feels to lie with you like this," she said.

"Oh, my dear God, I like it, too." He caught her wrists abruptly and tore her clinging hands away from his back. He looked down at her as if he had only just realized what he was doing. He shook his dark head to clear it, then stood, pulling her with him to an upright position. He backed away. "Please, go now. When next we see each other, it will be forever. God willing, before the year ends."

* * * *

Suzanne dawdled over dinner. A desolate sense of unrest and discontent had assaulted her these past weeks. She exhausted herself by working long hours at the Fort. Each night she read until the candle burned low and she was finally able to fall into troubled sleep. She knew part of her emptiness was the absence of Tyrone. When he left, a piece of her went with him, although they had not yet fulfilled their love. She deliberately, and often, let her mind run backwards, searching to relive the memories. She felt as if they were the only solid reality in her shifting world.

Since Thaddeus' letter had arrived a week ago, those memories were the fantasies that made her life bearable. The letter had informed her, almost coldly she concluded, that her father had probably run away from the South, the war efforts of the Confederates and the plantation. It had read, in part:

>...*I have not seen, or spoken to your father personally, but I have it on good authority he may have headed toward South America. Although I am glad your father's*

ship was spotted, I am certain he has abandoned the war and his duty to help its bid for independence for the South. The why of his decision baffles me. I wouldn't falsely charge your father of being disloyal without speaking to him, but many men cannot face and fight this war to its painful end.

But, my dear, you mustn't worry overly about it. When I bring you home in the spring, I will care for you. We will find happiness together, even as I protect you and see to your interests on the plantation. You may depend on it.

Respectfully,
Thaddeus

Polly comforted Suzanne as she ranted and raved against the accusations Thaddeus had implied. She went over and over her father's last letter and could find no hint of him quitting. Had he in fact given up? Her depression caused a solid hollow spot deep inside her, like a stone that would not move . Finally, she clung to the knowledge that her father was alive. Someday Tyrone would help her find him and they would put the whole affair behind them. Tonight, determined not to dwell on an uncertain future, she tried to concentrate on the discussion at hand.

Margaret, looking perkier than she had in months, turned to Polly. "Tell me, honey, how are things going in the big barn? I think I feel well enough to help out a little bit this week."

Polly looked first at Jesse, who had joined the family for dinner, then back. "Actually, Grandmama, things are very slow right now. The snow and cold discourage travelers.

When they can't sleep under bushes or travel barefoot or survive at all without full protection and daily refuge, they aren't as likely to make the trip north. Jesse and I have been taking care of things easily, but by spring we'll both be gone. Jesse is going back to Charleston next week. I plan to go back to Boston when Suzanne leaves in April. Why don't you take another month off?"

John said, "I'm going to get you some permanent help, Margaret. With the girls gone, Zoe won't need Jeanne to help in the house. She has offered to work in the big barn and I've hired Frank Reilly. Polly and Jesse will start training him tomorrow so he can take over when he comes back from seeing Suzanne safely home to Royal Oak."

Suzanne said, "Grandfather, Frank doesn't have to go with me. Thaddeus is coming to get me. He won't harm me."

John chuckled. "I know, my dear, but Frank says that Tyrone demanded he make the trip. Says he paid him well and threatened his life if anything happens to you. I'm an old man, but I think it's quite romantic."

Suzanne felt her face grow warm before she broke into a wide, open smile. "Oh, Grandfather, you are a dear, but if you knew Thaddeus." She laughed outright. "Thaddeus wants to marry me and Father has encouraged him. He'll refuse to have Frank along to thwart his attempts at courting."

"You needn't worry about that. Frank will be discreetly invisible. He said he was to watch, not interfere."

Polly's mirth was uncontrollable. "Suzanne, how many hearts are you going to break before we get you to the altar. First you scorned the Lieutenant. Now Thaddeus is going to try to capture your heart, a heart that belongs to another. I am sure of that by the way you have been moping around here since Tyrone left."

Suzanne smiled. "Thaddeus doesn't plan to capture my heart. He plans to marry me, by force if necessary. In any case, James will be chaperon enough. Maybe you could persuade Frank to stay behind. He would be much happier here and far more useful. Where is James, anyway?"

"He's with David, of course," John said good-naturedly. They've gone to play billiards." He turned serious. "James would have told you himself, but since it came up, I'll announce the good news. James has chosen to stay with your grandmother and me. He wrote to his father and received permission to go to West Point. After he graduates, he plans to become a physician."

"Oh, Grandfather, how wonderful. Will he practice with you?"

"That would indeed be a dream come true, but he's too young to make such a serious decision. It's possible he will want to go back to the South to heal his own people. But, of course, he will be welcome to carry on my practice if he chooses to do so. Why don't you young people run along to the library now? I'll see your grandmother upstairs and join you later for a glass of sherry."

* * * *

Suzanne and Polly sat on the comfortable old leather divan in front of the blazing fire. After pouring the girls a sherry and himself a brandy, Jesse left John's black leather wingback chair empty and selected instead a small rocker next to Polly.

"Jesse," Suzanne said, "do you think my father is in danger?"

The Bandit's Lady

"I don't believe a word of what Thaddeus said about Aman running away. That wouldn't be the least bit characteristic of your father."

"I don't believe so either, not for a minute. What do you think happened to him?"

"I wouldn't hazard a guess. There's so much to do out there. He said he was going to deal in merchandising. Merchants can buy precious commodities in warmer climates during the winter months and sell them later in the north. Maybe he went to Brazil, the West Indies, Jamaica, Mexico, or Texas. But one thing is for sure," he winked broadly at Polly. "You should read the *Crier* carefully. I noticed that wherever the *Sea Queen* is the *Annebella* is usually close by."

"Is there a reason for that? How did you get to know my father so well? For that matter, how did you meet Tyrone?"

"My, you are an inquisitive young lady. Instead of talking about those two, I have a far more interesting story that links your life to mine. Can you guess what it is?"

"I can't imagine. It seems we are all mixed up in knowing the same people for very different reasons. I first remember you as an excellent blacksmith. I used to go to your shop with Father."

"And I remember you, too, especially your dark copper curls. I thought you would be a heartbreaker when you grew up and I see I was right."

Suzanne felt her eyebrows shoot up in surprise. "The first time I came into your shop, I must have only been about six years old. You couldn't have been over seventeen or eighteen yourself. I remember the gossip, too."

Jesse threw back his head and let out a peal of laughter. "Now we're getting somewhere. Tell me the gossip." His eyes swept over her face approvingly as he leaned back in his chair and contentedly sipped his brandy.

"I remember your mother, too. She was a dressmaker; everyone called her Prissy. Is she well?"

Jesse sobered slightly. "She died of the fever a few years ago, but she had a good life. Come on, tell me the slander."

"It wasn't that bad. It was merely speculation about where you came from and why you got a generous education . My governess, Miss Abigail, loved to venture guesses and theorize about people. It was a game. She used her imagination to strengthen her opinions. She was marvelously entertaining."

Suzanne watched the play of emotions on Jesse's face before she heard his deep, triumphant chuckle. "What a splendid description of Miss Abigail. It's even better than I could have concocted. You must have loved her very much."

"Did you know her?"

"Oh, yes. Miss Abigail LaFontaine was sweet, saucy, individualistic and unconstrained. She tutored me for years, from the rudiments of education through the embodiment of culture and literature and three languages."

Suzanne looked at Jesse with amused wonder. "Do you mean to say even though she was your teacher, she was pondering your ancestry?"

"Isn't that hilarious? The happenstance of fate we have in common is that she taught us both."

"But, of course, I am not nearly as well educated, for I am female and it is disallowed."

"Nonsense, bright is bright, and knowing Miss Abigail, she must have taught you the joys of the challenge of pursuing knowledge to the best of your capabilities. But did she know my parentage, or was she simply guessing?"

"If she knew, or suspected your true identity, she didn't tell me."

A strange, quizzical expression, almost relief, Suzanne thought, briefly crossed Jesse's face. He said, "I love her, too. And so shall you, Polly, when you meet her."

John came through the door. "And how is our Polly to accomplish that?"

Polly looked shyly around the room. Suzanne saw a flash, like sunlight on rippling water, when Polly's dark eyes brushed Jesse's. Joy bubbled in her voice. "Jesse and I are going to marry," she said simply.

Suzanne reached over and hugged her friend. Polly, looking elated by her new resolve, said quickly, "Now, don't go asking all of those questions that are boiling up inside of you. We don't have any answers. Jesse just proposed today. I've only had time to tell Mama Zoe."

John stood up and poured each of them a second small glass of sherry. Holding his out, he said, "Here's to your happiness, my darling Polly, and to yours, Jesse."

After they sipped, he said wistfully, "I hope Margaret will see the two of you married. Maybe you will chose to have the ceremony at St. Paul's Church and a small reception back here at the estate. Margaret and I will always be your folks, Polly. Promise me that wherever life takes you, you will visit us often. Now, I think I've had enough excitement for one evening. How about the rest of you?"

Suzanne nodded. "Yes, Grandfather. I, too, shall go to my bed." She blew Jesse and Polly a kiss as she followed her grandfather from the room.

* * * *

The Bandit's Lady

Polly joined Suzanne and John for their early morning ride. The last of the snow had melted in the warmth of mid-March. As they cantered off, Polly said, "Last night Jesse and I decided to get married before he leaves for Charleston. It will mean a few months of separation and loneliness, but we want to belong, really belong, to each other. Grandpapa, when you said you hoped Grandmama would see us married that settled it."

Suzanne reached out to grab Polly's hand. "What good news! But how can we arrange a wedding within a week?"

Polly giggled. "Jesse has postponed his departure for another week. That will give us plenty of time. Grandpapa, would it be all right with you if we get married in the parlor on Saturday? Then Grandmama won't have to leave the house at all."

John's eyes misted over. "How thoughtful. I'll tell her as soon as she has had her breakfast."

"How will Miss Millicent get a dress fit and sewed for you on such short notice?" Suzanne asked.

"Jesse has decided I shall wear the dress I wore to the Christmas Ball. He says he fell in love with me that night. Besides, there's a war going on; we don't want to be extravagant. We'd rather spend our money helping slaves get their freedom, and educating them."

"Come on, girls," John said, "you have much to do. I'll race you back to the stables."

The week whirled by.

* * * *

Zoe and Jeanne cleaned and polished the downstairs rooms from the floors to the ceilings. In the bright vivid sunlight and the warmth of early spring, they beat the winter dust out of the carpets and washed the windows until they sparkled. From the kitchens came the delectable smells of cooking turkeys, and roasting beef and pork. Sally's fresh baked breads, pies, cookies, and cakes smelled as delicious as walking past Mr. Peter's Bakery in town.

Suzanne and Polly spent long hours shopping for a simple trousseau. Suzanne bought a travel trunk and began to fill it with pretty household wares. "Stop," Polly cried three days before her wedding day, "you are spoiling me to distraction."

"You will thank me well enough when you cook your first breakfast for your good-looking new husband."

"That's true. Oh, Suzanne, I'm awfully excited, but..." a troubled expression flitted across her face; pain showed in her eyes, "the months will be long until we can settle down in Charleston."

"Must you go back to Boston?"

"I must. I promised. As soon as President Lincoln frees the slaves, I can join Jesse. In the meantime, we'll see each other whenever possible. He has his own work to do."

* * * *

The parlor was filled. Margaret, pale but radiant, quietly watched the activity around her. John greeted the guests as they arrived, including Rufus and Frank Reilly. Charlie, Henry, Sally, Joe, Jeanne, and Zoe, proud as any mother of the bride, sat in straight chairs around the room waiting for the ceremony to begin.

Chapter 24

Captain Neal Franklin bowed low over Margaret and took her hand in his. "You look marvelous, Margaret. Any day now, I expect to see you pull up to the docks to pick up a delivery."

"Ah, Captain Neal, I think my pick-up days are over, but it is so very good to see you."

"And what a glorious occasion this is. I've known Polly and Jesse since they were both knee-high to a filly. What a nice surprise, their wedding announcement. The bride and her spunky attendant are lovely."

Margaret's soft blue eyes laughed with him. "They certainly are. Thank you, Captain Neal."

Suzanne was dressed in a modestly cut pale lavender silk gown. Her shining curls were piled high on her head. She stood calmly beside the glowing bride, while the couple exchanged vows.

Suzanne tried to keep her mind on the simple, sacred wedding ritual as the deep, rich voice of the Right Reverend Ambrose Malone began: "Dearly beloved, we are gathered this day in the presence of God..." But an intricate lace of confused but pleasant thoughts of Tyrone filled Suzanne's mind. She remembered his chest, a thatch of black curls. She remembered his large gentle hands holding her in a caress. She could almost feel their bodies welded together, and wedded to the music as they spun to the rhythm of the final dance at the Christmas Ball.

She recalled the hardness of the body that held hers, spoon fashion, the afternoon they slept together when Tyrone was recovering from his gunshot wound. She recalled the smile that lighted him up from the inside whenever he glimpsed her from afar. *Like candles in a lantern*, she thought. She had memorized the loving look Tyrone gave her when she had found him with Jethro in big barn. And Suzanne recalled the bold masculine smell of his freshly bathed body, and the magic of his mouth and fingers.

"...I now pronounce you man and wife. Jesse, you may kiss the bride."

Tears that mingled sorrow and happiness came unbidden to Suzanne's eyes. They distorted the scene into a hazy blur as she drew Polly into her arms and gave her a hug. "I wish you all the happiness in the world."

Polly grinned. "You quit those tears, you hear? Your bandit will be your husband before you know it."

Then Jesse placed his big hands, one on each of Suzanne's shoulders. His steel gray eyes, like silver lightning, caught and held hers. There was a gentle softness in his voice that lulled her into a relaxed mood. "This war won't last forever. The last words Tyrone said to me before he left were, 'Tell Suzanne I love her. I'll be back for her, and soon.'"

Suzanne felt complete trust in Polly's new husband, and more, an uncanny familiar relationship. She wondered idly why she should feel so close to a man she barely knew. She brushed it off as a sister love for Polly that included her choice of husband. She brushed away her tears. "I know, but I won't be here. Since Father is missing, I've got to get back to the plantation. I'm sorry, Jesse. I didn't mean to get all weepy and I certainly don't plan to get morbid, but there is one favor I want to ask of you."

"Anything, my dear Miss Suzanne. Name it."

"I still don't know where Father is or if he's safe. If you learn anything about him, will you be sure to get a message to me?"

Jesse's voice was calm, his gaze steady as he replied with warmth and concern. "You know I will. Please try not to worry. A man knows his business. He'll survive."

The hours following the wedding sped by. Played by Margaret's favorite string trio, strains of soft background music enhanced the mood of the gala affair. His plate brimming with all manner of delicious-looking finger foods, Captain Neal pulled up a chair beside Suzanne. He said, "I hear I'll be carrying you back to Norfolk within a fortnight."

Suzanne felt a tug of regret at the thought of leaving Baltimore and her grandparents, but a part of her felt a rush of elation in anticipation of going home. "At least within the month. Thaddeus Stuart has written that he will come to escort me home."

The captain's smile held a tinge of devilishness. "And how is your adventuresome spirit? Will you be content to have an uneventful trip home, or will this Thaddeus keep you in tow?"

A surge of affection for this fatherly figure spread through Suzanne, but she pretended to ignore his subtle teasing. "I can't imagine what you might be thinking."

His smile became genuine, his voice cheerful and booming. "I'll bet you cannot, Miss Suzanne. But no matter, I'm

The Bandit's Lady

looking forward to your company. Together we will cross the big and dazzling bay. Together we will admire its long fingers of islands that stretch out to meet the sea, and its coves that hold secrets too ancient to recall."

Suzanne grew serious, without being apologetic. "And, I, sir, agree to behave myself. It is obvious you are in love with the Chesapeake. We shall stand on deck to savor the smells of pungent sea air. The wind will fill our sails and nuzzle our hair. That will be excitement enough for me this trip."

"That is, of course, if an intriguing combination of a brisk wind and a warm sun favors us."

Suzanne laughed, then, knowing her eyes danced with mirth. "Besides, Thaddeus would dissolve in embarrassment right before our very eyes if I so much as hinted that I might enjoy a bit of fanciful amusement."

Captain Neal joined her merry mood. "You were lucky the last time you chose a risky venture. This time I'll tie you up myself if you seek trouble over safety. And what of your cousin?"

"He stands behind you, sir," James said, coming around to join the conversation. "And what about me?"

"I was just asking if you are returning South with Suzanne."

James beamed. "No, sir, I am not. I'll be entering West Point in the fall."

Captain Neal reached out to shake his hand. "Good luck, my boy, but who will protect our Suzanne on her trip home."

James' boyish voice cracked with gaiety. "Not to worry about our Suzanne. She is a particularly shy, fainthearted young lady. She'll never cause you a minute's worth of difficulty."

"Of course. Of course. How impertinent of me to imagine her bold and capable of craving adventure."

"And what is all the uproarious laughter about over here?" Jesse asked as he and Polly approached the trio.

Captain Neal, a twinkle in his eye, waved his unlit pipe toward Suzanne. "It's about a young lady who is an escapade waiting to happen."

Polly and Jesse left with the last of the guests.

"Jesse booked rooms at one of the Nation's most prestigious inns, The Washington. We'll explore every nook and cranny of the capital and be back in five days' time. I'll tell you all about it when we get home," Polly said as she squeezed Suzanne in a fond embrace.

While the world still slept, in the lonely black before dawn, John's voice, filled with anguish, brought Suzanne instantly awake. "Suzanne, it's your grandmother." He shook her shoulder gently.

Fully aware of her surroundings, Suzanne sat bolt upright. She saw the excruciating pain in her grandfather's eyes. "I'll get dressed and go to her immediately."

"There is nothing we can do, my dear. We can't prolong life; we can only try to keep her comfortable while she lives. Just hold her hand, console her. I am going to the hospital to get a supply of quinine. She'll rest better."

James brought the rocker, from the guest room Tyrone had occupied, into their grandmother's room. He rested a hand on Suzanne's back. "I heard you all getting up. If there is any way I can help, call me. Tomorrow night I'll take my turn."

Suzanne sat silently by her grandmother's side. The endless waves of pain had drained away her health and vitality. She rested, half-swooning. As the sunlight of dawn swept across the eastern sky and flooded the room, Margaret roused. She spoke with labored breath. "It's so lovely to have you by my side, dear granddaughter. You can't know how forlorn one feels when they lose a child. Your mother was such a love, and you have become the daughter who was taken from us."

"Hush, now, Grandmother. You must save your strength. I'll sit here quietly. Grandfather will be back soon with something to ease your pain."

"Its too late, my dear. The pain won't go away until the blessed relief of death."

When Suzanne would protest, Margaret gestured her away. "It's all right. I'm ready. Your grandfather and I have had a wonderful long life together. Tell me about your mother. We missed her so."

"I suppose, Grandmother, I must have felt some of the same things you did when Mother died. From a child's viewpoint, I, too, felt desolate, abandoned really."

"Well of course you did, my dear. How insensitive of me to think only of myself."

Suzanne gently touched her shoulder. "It's all right. You mustn't grieve for me. We both despaired, but differently. We were so lucky to have each other and Father, who understood enough to allow my visits." She said sadly, "I think he never recovered from her death. Else why would he not have married again."

"I don't know why he didn't marry again, but you are right about us being lucky. He could have kept us apart, for personal reasons...reasons you don't even know," she added softly to herself.

Suzanne didn't want her grandmother to dwell on past unpleasant things. She soothed, "Mother was the most beautiful woman I ever knew. Besides pretty, she was serene, and at peace inside. I'm sure she was much like you, Grandmother."

"And yet we disagreed so strongly on the slavery issue."

"I don't believe that is really true, Grandmother. She felt as you and Grandfather do. I didn't know it then, but she lived it. The only difference was that she loved my father, who also protects his slaves. Although his viewpoint seems sterner, it is not at all. One day I will question my father and learn the whole story. But I am beginning to understand that my parents, though plantation and slave owners, have been rebels among their people."

* * * *

As the days rolled together, the effectiveness of Margaret's medications decreased. John went sadly about his daily business of healing other patients. Even as he brought new lives into the world and restored others with his surgeon's knife, his wife's days dwindled. Her complexion took on an unhealthy pallor, her form a crumpled and listless posture.

Suzanne and James, with Jeannie's help, took their turns. They held her hand, or read her favorite passages from the Bible or from the *Canterbury Tales*. Although inert much of the time, as consciousness began to leave the bent, pain-wracked figure, she often babbled. The memories spawned from the delirium of sickness often kept her oblivious of the family's loving vigil. In the last hours, John stood silently by the east window. The brightening day touched his wrinkled cheeks and forehead. Polly, who had arrived home the evening before, and Zoe and James stood watch at the foot of Margaret's bed.

The Bandit's Lady

Suzanne alone sat in the chair beside her grandmother's bed. While Margaret breathed in shallow, quick gasps, Suzanne tried to keep her own fragile control. She stroked the frail, withered hand, and reached out to caress the soft cheek in a wistful gesture. There was no final moment of recognition when her grandmother's eyes looked upward with a light of joy. Her breathing ceased quietly. Suzanne pushed back a wayward strand of silver hair and gently closed the unseeing eyes.

Sweet death had come at last.

Tears streamed down Suzanne's cheeks as she went to stand beside her grandfather. Unable to lift her voice above a whisper, she put an arm around his bent form. "The pain is over, Grandfather. Grandmother is at peace. She is gone now, to meet her God."

* * * *

As Suzanne and Polly walked to Miss Millicent's to purchase proper mourning frocks, Polly's voice was full of concern. "What are you going to do, Suzanne?"

"I have no choice. I must go home and see to the plantation. Thaddeus' wire said he would delay a week, no more."

"What about your grandfather?"

Suzanne felt her voice choke. "Oh, Polly, he's such a dear. He said he'd be fine. James will be here during the summer months. The Underground is running smoothly, thanks to you and Frank and Jeannie. I will try to come back here for a month in the fall. We'll just have to come as often as we can. You'll help, too, won't you, Polly?"

"You know I will. Jesse says we can meet here sometimes, instead of me going to Charleston every time or him coming to Boston. What a mess this war makes."

"Polly, I haven't told a living soul, and I cannot talk to Grandfather now while he's grieving so, but I'm afraid of Thaddeus."

"Whatever are you talking about?"

"He's got an evil streak. I know he's mean to his slaves. I...I suspect he may be dishonest. As you know, Thaddeus says he thinks Father ran away. I'm certain he didn't, but something isn't right. I can't know what it is. I can't imagine what it might be."

"Isn't Thaddeus your father's closest friend and confidant? How could your father condone or be friends with a man who is cruel or unscrupulous?"

Suzanne smiled with fondness. "Father doesn't see bad in people. But there's more." She knew a trace of hysteria was back in her voice. "I think Tyrone is also involved. He gave me a paper for safekeeping. It had Father's name, Thaddeus' name, and your Jesse's name on it. It was in code, somehow. Why are they all involved with each other, and why can't Tyrone, tell me about it? What do you think the danger might be? Some of the men whose names are on the list have already been captured; some of the ships have been destroyed. Jesse shows up; he and the bandit are friends. Frank Reilly and associates appear to be reasonably decent. Oh, Polly, I can't make sense out of any of it."

"I really can't answer any of your questions. Why don't you ask Jesse, or better yet, ask Thaddeus? You will have plenty of time to pump him while you travel home."

Suzanne felt the heat burn in her cheeks and knew she turned crimson. "He's not comfortable to be with. He has been after me since his wife died. He plans to marry me, but he wants more. Father approved; he promoted the idea in the first place."

"Do you think your father is serious about you marrying him? Would he insist if he knew you really loved another?"

"He was enthusiastic at first. He felt sorry for Thaddeus, and he thought I needed someone to take care of me. That was before he discovered I had grown up. We really haven't discussed it, but if I could talk to him now I'm sure he would see I don't love Thaddeus and can't marry him. Meanwhile…" Her voice trailed off.

Polly turned to look at her. "Meanwhile, with your father missing, Thaddeus could take advantage of you. That's it, isn't it?"

Suzanne cast her eyes downward. "Yes. And, since Grandfather needs Frank here, I won't be safe."

"Don't give it another thought. I'll have Will Snooks and Clay Long follow discreetly along and take care of you. They are truly the most loyal men you'd ever want to meet. Just leave it to me. When you get back to Royal Oaks, Sadie and Jasper will look after you."

"Oh, Polly, thank you."

On the morning of the funeral, Suzanne sat in the sunny breakfast nook feeling many mixed emotions: gladness that she and her grandmother had the years to get to know each other, sadness and loss at her passing and an ache for the forlorn, bewildered look in her grandfather's eyes. *At most, I have a week with him,* she thought regretfully. *How can I help him in so short a time?*

Clearly reading her mind as he joined her, John said, "Do not worry so my dear. I know you must get back home. Life here will continue. It's natural to be lonely, but your grandmother is out of her pain. We had many wonderful years upon which my memories will feed."

Tears filled Suzanne's eyes. "Thank you, Grandfather. You are kind to comfort me when your own heart grieves."

He patted her shoulder. "Come with me now to the cemetery. I want you to help me pick the perfect grave site. During his spare winter hours, Henry builds the pine coffins and sells them to the undertaker in town for the price of the lumber. He told me he fashioned a special one this winter, 'for the mistress.'"

They finished their tea in silence and rose together to go to the stables. Charlie had expected their errand. John's stallion, Samson, and Suzanne's roan, Ginny, were saddled and waiting for their morning exercise.

The Hanson cemetery of family members and faithful servants was on a knoll in the far corner of the estate. The trees that had been planted in loving memory of the deceased after each death shaded the burial plot. John's parents, who had arrived in the new world just prior to the Revolutionary War, were buried side by side at the top of the designated tract of land. His twin brothers had died of the fever when they were infants. A sister, a few years older than John, had died the year before Suzanne began making her yearly visits. Margaret and John's first and second-born infants completed the family segment of the cemetery.

"What do you think, Suzanne?"

"Beside the babies' graves, Grandfather. When your time comes, there will be room for you on the other side of Grandmother."

"Yes. I will instruct Henry." He turned Samson toward home without another word.

The Bandit's Lady

Zoe and Jeannie had laid Margaret out in the parlor. For the second time that month, the tiny parlor filled up. And, again, The Right Reverend Ambrose Malone began the service.

"Dearly beloved, we are gathered this day to pay tribute to God's loyal servant, Margaret Hanson, who devoted her long life to the comfort of others..."

Later, under the brilliant blue of the midmorning April sunshine, family, friends, and domestics, all clad in black, stood silently giving homage to Margaret. Henry and Charlie gently lowered the simply made pine coffin into the ground.

A stir in the crowd caused Suzanne to look up. A coach stopped a few yards away. The forbidding figure stepped down with a crisp authoritative air and strode purposely to her side. Suzanne felt goose bumps rash out over her entire body. Unnerved by his presence, she felt more than a vague foreboding. Possessively, the man put an arm around her waist. Suzanne felt an almost tangible, clear vision of his terrible power.

Chapter 25

By sheer will of effort, Suzanne kept her expression deceptively composed as she stepped away from the fraudulently protective embrace of Thaddeus Stuart. His electric blue eyes gave her a narrowed glinting glance. A thinly disguised leer touched his lips. She watched him warily as he stepped back a pace, seeming to respect her grief.

The mood was broken. The mourners began moving away from the area, collecting in small curious groups. John and Polly came quickly to Suzanne's side. She introduced Thaddeus with a gesture. Then she turned to him. Her misgivings increased. She felt herself shrinking from his cold watchful smile. "You're early. You promised to give me an extra week with my grandfather."

"And so I shall, my dear. I must travel to Boston to take care of pressing business. I decided in the light of your grievous loss to stop by and offer my condolences. I will take the afternoon train out, and return on Tuesday next, if that will suit you."

She was grateful for the short reprieve. "Thank you. I shall be ready to go home when you return."

At bedtime, in the center of Suzanne's deep feather bed, Polly sat clad in a pink flannel nightgown. A tinge of despair touched her voice. "Oh, Suzanne, you were right not to trust Thaddeus. I don't like him at all. He's despicable. What is he up to, anyway?"

Suzanne chuckled. "Grandfather expressed those exact sentiments, only with a much more subtle approach. He said, 'My dear Suzanne, I cannot find it in my heart to want you in that man's care and company for the duration of the long trip home.'"

"What will you do?"

"I will go and trust Will Snooks and Clay Long to take care of me as you promised."

"I will give them extra instructions not to let you out of their sight for a moment."

"Thaddeus should be ecstatic when he finds out he can't get me alone." Suzanne giggled at the thought, then turned somber. "Polly, tell me about Jesse. There's something about him. Somewhere in the corner of my brain I feel like something has escaped me—something that I should know or be told. Did you ever feel that way?"

Suzanne watched Polly closely. She thought acknowledgment raced through her eyes, but it passed so quickly she decided she had imagined it. Polly said, "I felt that way when I met Tyrone's mother. Although they don't look alike, there is something about them. It's a quiet decency, honesty, maybe even a common mannerism. Did you feel it when you met Mrs. Jane?"

Suzanne couldn't control a burst of laughter. "My first meeting with Tyrone and my first meeting with Mrs. Jane could not have been linked in any way. Yet later I figured it out, and Tyrone admitted I had met his mother. Yes, Polly, it's something like that I sense in Jesse."

Polly's eyebrows rose a fraction, but again Suzanne thought she must have imagined the slight hesitation. "All I know about Jesse is that a cruel master took him and his mother to New Orleans and sold them," Polly said.

"For goodness sake, how did they get back to Charleston?"

"Patience, Miss Curiosity, I was coming to that. The strange part of it, he told me, was he had been born on a plantation near Charleston. The man who bought him and his mother took them back to Charleston. He set them up in their respective businesses, and Miss Abigail began to educate him. He never saw the man who actually paid for those things. It was a Judge Pete, or Poke—"

"Judge Pope."

"That was it, Pope. Do you know him?"

Suzanne nodded. His name was on the secret paper, with her father's, under the P column. "I've known the judge since I was a little girl. He and his beautiful wife, Amelia, went to all the same social gatherings Father and I attended."

"Anyway," Polly said, "he took care of all the details. He helped Jesse's mother select a location and secured the house for them. It was a duplex; they lived in one-half and rented out the other half. That, with her seamstress work and Jesse's blacksmith shop, kept them very well, he says."

"Did Jesse ever find out who his benefactor was? Didn't his mother ever tell him who his father was? If they returned to Charleston, they must have been near the man who fathered him. Everybody supposed his father was a local plantation owner or gentleman farmer, but I never heard anyone accused by name. If it was well-known, it was certainly a guarded piece of information."

Polly said, "But why was it such an isolated case? There have been mulattoes, since the beginning of slavery."

"I think it was because he and Prissy were free, and Jesse educated, that made them open to speculation. In the South, free Negroes are extremely rare. Did he tell you anything else?"

Polly grinned disarmingly. "Sure. Jesse told me what you are dying to hear. He met Tyrone at the auction in New Orleans. They were about the same age and Tyrone sneaked all kinds of goodies into their stall. Tyrone was out on his own when he was seventeen years old. He stopped in Charleston on one of his first trips south and looked up Jesse. They've been working together ever since. When the war came along, Jesse became a slave finder. They don't force slaves, or encourage them to run away, but they help those they hear about that want to run."

Polly paused and then said proudly, "Tyrone told me Jesse became a remarkable power to arouse and inspire others, and he used his network to become a contact man for Tyrone. He picks up Negroes in both Charleston and Wilmington, as you know by now."

Suzanne was thoughtful. The S/F probably stood for slave finder. Dressed now for bed, she walked over to pull the covers back. "I still think there's more to Jesse's story than I know, but I'm too tired right now to think. Tomorrow I'm going to sleep until I wake up, even if I lose the whole morning."

"Good idea, my friend. I think I'll do the same."

"When are you leaving?"

"I'll wait until you and Thaddeus are safely on your way. It will be easier for Granddaddy if I wait for a couple of days after you leave."

Suzanne put her arms around her friend. "Thank you. Get some rest now. I'll see you tomorrow."

* * * *

Suzanne wandered through the next few days. Her trunks were packed. Her twentieth birthday, two days before, had gone virtually unnoticed. It was Monday. She and her grandfather had taken a long, early morning ride, the first since Margaret's funeral. They'd eaten breakfast together in the small, cheerful breakfast room.

A soft April breeze brought the sweet smell of violets through the parlor window. Suzanne, curled up in the chair she had come to think of as her own, was reminiscing. It had been over a year ago since she sat at the long dining room table at Royal Oaks eating breakfast with James and anticipating their trip north. The events of the year flashed through Suzanne's mind. So much had happened in so short a time, but best of all, she conceded, she had fallen in love. She closed her eyes and pictured her bandit as she had first seen him. His cape flying, his gun pointed at them and his haunted eyes had implored her. *For what,* she wondered?

After lunch, on the afternoon he had ridden off on Midnight, Suzanne had hurried back to the barn for one last stolen kiss. His passionate ardor flared once again like wildfire between them. He had scooped her up, carried her back into the shadows and laid her down in the soft haystack.

With a violent movement he had stood up and pulled off his shirt. She had stared at his broad back incredulously before he turned and gathered her into his arms. While her nails dug into his chest involuntarily, he unbuttoned her bodice. "Slip your dress down, Suzanne," he whispered sensuously.

"I shouldn't...let you," she whispered.

"No, you shouldn't," he said, moving closer. "Tell me to stop, Suzanne. Tell me you hate it."

"I wish I could."

His mouth was on her closed eyelids, then the tip of her nose. His mouth bit at hers tenderly in a succession of teasing kisses that made her want to cry out. "My dear love, you're so sweet. Let me help you." He brushed his mouth across hers as he tried to remove her bodice. "Help me."

She gasped against his invading mouth, felt his hot skin searing her. As the magic worked on her, she whispered, "I feel...heat in your body."

He lifted his head, captured her eyes, and grinned. "It's not heat, my love. It's fire. I'm burning alive. Move against me with nothing between us."

Her trembling fingers had savored the warm, hard muscles under his mat of crisp black hair. She moved slightly and felt him ease down against her until her taut nipples vanished into the dark pelt of his chest. She shuddered with pleasure. "This is ecstasy," he whispered tensely. He had shifted his long powerful torso slowly, seductively, full length on hers until she felt dizzy, her need matching his. His lips burned on hers, his fingers flamed where they touched her skin. Torrents of desire she had never known stirred to life through her and there seemed to be no will inside of her to resist their blissful passion.

It all seemed so long ago.

Now, she sat in lonely silence a few moments more before she picked up a *Crier* from the bottom of the stack, to catch up on the war news that she had neglected for many weeks. She read official accounts of the February surrender of Fort Henry in the movement up the Tennessee River. She read about the gunboats that took Fort Donelson some days later with fifteen thousand prisoners and three thousand horses. She read:

> *The rebels lost forty-eight field pieces, seventeen heavy guns, twenty-thousand stand of arms, besides a large quantity of commissary stores. The rebel troops are completely demoralized and have lost confidence in their leaders. On the Washington home front, soldiers fired salutes last night, this morning, and at noon today at the arsenal and Navy yard in honor of the successes of our arms...*

In other accounts:

> *On the eve of Fort Henry's capture, the White House was the scene of a gala social event. The President and Mrs. Lincoln were not to be outdone by the drama of the war. They entertained in the East room. It was a brilliant spectacle indeed. A sense of obligation to our lady readers chides us to allude to the fact that Mrs. Lincoln was well-dressed (according to the verdict of qualified female critics). She appeared in white satin with black lace flounces. Perhaps half a yard or more in width, the flounces were fastened up with black and white ribbon. She wore pearl adornments, an attractive Parisian headdress with clusters of crape myrtle and a bouquet to match. The delicacies and luxuries appeared in such profusion that the thousand or*

The Bandit's Lady

more guests did not deplete the array. Champagne and other costly wines and liquors flowed freely...

On February 22, 1862, the 129th anniversary of George Washington's birth, both North and South—two peoples and two governments—honored the father of their countries. On this day the Confederate States inaugurated its own President, Jefferson Davis, who took over his appointment in Richmond, Virginia.

Suzanne sorrowfully read of battles in Texas, New Mexico, Kansas, and Rocky Mountain country. The Union declared victory after victory. When she scanned the latest news, naval engagements seemed highlighted: the *Merrimac* and her success in crippling the rebel steamers. The war was simmering in the Ozark region of Arkansas and Springfield, Missouri, and a siege had been directed at Yorktown.

Suzanne read the ghastly details of the battle at Pittsburgh, Tennessee. It was of one of the bloodiest battles of modern times, where the slaughter on both sides was immense. The enemy's loss (South) was an estimated thirty-five to forty thousand. The Union's loss was from eighteen to twenty thousand. Both sides claimed victory at Shiloh.

Then she saw it.

Suzanne picked up the day's early morning *Crier*, dated Wednesday, April 30, 1862.

The Enemy takes New Orleans
City surrenders to Farragut

Great destruction of property and cotton and steamboats has been the result of the latest bloody campaign.

There is immense confusion and agitation among the inhabitants. Farragut steamed ahead past enemy land guns, gunboats, and a variety of water obstacles, including barges, purposely set afire to trap him.

Then highlighted within an ominous black box, another headline captured Suzanne's attention:

Ship Captain Sees Fiery Collision

Many steamboats were saved to take away the ammunition, but the flames of one massive explosion seemed to devour in a burst two rival ships. Although for months the Annebella has been rumored missing, she was seen briefly this morning by a witness to the disaster.

The captains Tyrone Sterling and Aman Willoughby, of the Sea Queen and the Annebella, respectively, clearly had no time to signal for help after colliding. The ships vanished in a huge eruption of fire.

Captain John Lloyd of the Steamer Lloyd was first to reach the scene. He said the flames were so huge he could not make out, even with the telescope, either of the ships, or a third ship that disappeared over the horizon between the glow of the blaze and the radiance of the sunrise.

There were an estimated one hundred sixty-three men listed missing and presumed dead in the disaster, although no one knows exactly how many men were aboard the Annebella.

"My ship was steaming toward the New Orleans conflict when one of my lookouts spotted fire and thick smoke and made out the names of the two ships. We arrived on the

scene about forty-five minutes later to help rescue the survivors, but too late."

Captain Lloyd said by the time he was alerted and picked up the telescope the stricken vessels appeared intertwined into one blazing mass. He could not see either of them plainly because the fire had erupted as high as one hundred and twenty feet.

"At 5:58 a.m., a big ball of flame shot up into the sky," Lloyd said. "When the blaze subsided, the object in the telescope was gone."

Lloyd said his ship and at least four other vessels searched the area for two more hours but found nothing. "All we saw were particles of debris," he added.

The captain said only eleven bodies had been recovered.

Suzanne read the account again. And again.

A cold shiver spread through her as the memory of her desires and emotions trapped her. She cringed even now at the thought of those keen, imploring black eyes that had begged her. Yet in the end, on that last precious afternoon, she had refused his request.

She had put her arms around his neck. A golden wave of passion and love flowed between them. He had whispered her name over and over like a song of love before he stopped abruptly and pulled away. "Please, Suzanne, let me love you. Let me fill you with the wholeness of our desire and satiate your body."

His lips had continued to explore her soft flesh, sending tingles of delicious sensations through her. Her body craved his hands, ached for his touch, but reluctantly she had moved away. Her denial returned now to haunt her. "I can't. Not yet."

Suzanne felt the squeezing hurt like a painful bruise knotting itself around her heart. Why hadn't she let him love her? Was something wrong with her? She doubled over, wrapping her arms around her waist, and rocked back and forth.

The *Baltimore Crier* fell to the floor. She was conscious only of a low, tortured sob. "It's over," she moaned. "My life is finished. Done."

The pain in her heart was a sick, burning gnawing.

Tyrone was dead.

Never again would she see her beloved parent.

A terrible sense of bitterness assailed her. Like a child suddenly finding herself alone in an empty and strange room, Suzanne could see nothing familiar in her future. She went to the stables. Neither Charlie nor Henry was about. As she saddled Ginny, she felt icy fingers seep into every pore of her body. Her teeth chattered; her body trembled.

She rode. She kneeled beside Margaret's grave and babbled to the dead woman, words she would never know or recall. She cried hysterically, begging her grandmother to come back. She would never remember how long she stayed there.

She rode to the pond, stripped off her boots and walked into its icy spring waters until its depth soaked the clothes around her waist. When the freezing wetness penetrated her consciousness, Suzanne clambered back upon Ginny and continued her lonely trek. She shivered uncontrollably as the frigid cold and sheer black terror swept through her. Frightening images built in her mind. She entered the track at the racecourse. Sobs racked her body. She urged Ginny faster and faster around the dirt track.

The Bandit's Lady

Dust from the horse's hooves swirled backward as Suzanne galloped out through the gate. Body hunched forward, she coaxed her mount even faster. The uneven road dipped, rose again, curved through the small wooded area around the pond, then plunged into a ravine. Suzanne was totally unprepared when the roan stumbled. She lay unconscious in a sodden heap in the low-slanting light of late afternoon.

Chapter 26

April 1863

> Wandering between two worlds,
> one dead,
> The other powerless to be born.
> ~~Matthew Arnold,
> "Grande Chartreuse"

Her daily walk had become as indispensable to Suzanne as her morning cup of sweet black coffee, two small realities to cling to. About a half mile from the house was a small hollow where she often sat, even as she did now, staring off into space. It was a peaceful retreat enclosed at her back by heavy shrubbery, yet close enough to the Ashley River to hear the slap of the waves on the rocks. Sitting on a tree stump, Suzanne absently watched the withered leaves drift slowly downstream. She relived her sadness each day.

Although Suzanne had suffered multiple bruises over most of her body from the fall off her beloved Ginny almost one year ago, neither she nor the roan had been seriously injured.

The Bandit's Lady

Ginny had limped back to the stables, arriving at dusk, alone and neighing a tortured cry of anguish.

All Hanson hands, armed with lanterns, combed the estate for hours before a tormented shivering Charlie stumbled upon Suzanne near midnight. John had soon concluded the reason Suzanne wouldn't open her eyes and would not talk was not because of a head injury, but because of a broken heart.

But when pneumonia set in, caused from exposure to the chilly spring air, Polly canceled her plans to return to Boston. She stayed by Suzanne's side day and night and applied hot poultices to her rasping chest.

In her fevered state, Suzanne went over and over the fiery description, screaming and sobbing and moaning in frenzied spasms and hysterical outbursts. When finally her breathing evened out, she slept—still and coma-like—for another fortnight.

By the time she acknowledged her surroundings, it was mid-May. Thaddeus had come for her, and left. "He was angry, like a small boy," Polly said. "He said he'd come for you again, that you are to wait for him."

"It doesn't matter," Suzanne said. "I'll wait."

"What will you do?"

"I'll stay with Grandfather, of course. But you must go back to Boston to get your job done, so you can join Jesse in Charleston."

"Yes, I'm leaving at the end of the week, but promise me you won't leave here without me. I'm stopping back to see Granddaddy on my way to Charleston to live with my husband. No matter what happens, I will be leaving here next spring. Lincoln promises emancipation of the slaves by the end of the year. Thaddeus is coming April next. I'll go with the two of you. Don't go alone with him. It's too dangerous. Will and Clay have promised to chaperon us."

Suzanne had waited. Devoid of feeling, her days passed without incident. She had quit reading the *Crier* or listening to any talk of war news. She had not gone back to Fort McHenry or ridden Ginny in the glorious early mornings. She had avoided her grandfather after he told her, "The hurting stops eventually. You have to fill the emptiness with happy memories."

"Is that how you got over Grandmother's death so easily," she asked sarcastically.

She regretted the remark when the pain reached his eyes and had flung her arms around his neck. Sobbing, she said, "I'm so sorry, Grandfather."

"It's all right, child. I understand. You've lost so much, but you are young; you will mend."

But she hadn't mended.

* * * *

The seasons rumbled on. Julia had visited once with the twins, but Suzanne couldn't keep her mind on the conversation. Shades pulled, she sat in the dim, shadowy parlor while her grandfather and James went to the Septemberfest to cheer Polly's Sir President John to championship victory.

Except one night at dinner the week after the races, Suzanne left the room whenever the subject of the war came up. On that night, James asked, "What in the devil happened at Antietam, Grandfather? It was a bloody bath."

Suzanne watched her grandfather's green eyes fill with sadness. "War is always bloody," he said. "Nearly twenty-five thousand men were lost, but there was a decent ending. Our

The Bandit's Lady

President has declared the Union victorious. He has issued a proclamation that declares the abolition of slavery."

"What does it mean to my father and to Suzanne, owners of slaves?" James demanded.

"It's an attempt to make it easy for slave states to reunite with the United States after they voluntarily adopt immediate or gradual abolition of slavery within their respective limits."

"That's idiotic, Grandfather. We'll never abolish slavery."

John looked kindly at James. "Never is a long time, son. The North will win this war, and recovery will take a very long time. It's the only humane outcome."

James snorted. Suzanne excused herself.

* * * *

Polly arrived home for the holidays, but no amount of begging had any effect on Suzanne. She had stayed home from the Christmas Ball.

When Thaddeus arrived to escort Suzanne home, she had very little packing to do. Except the necessities and three plain dresses, including the gray dress she had worn to nurse the soldiers at Fort McHenry, the trunks were untouched from the year before.

On the trip South, Thaddeus tried everything in his power to get Suzanne to respond to his ardor. He coaxed her with boxes of candies she left unopened. He maneuvered to sit close, stealing an arm around her whenever Polly was looking another way. On more than one occasion, he pleaded for her hand in marriage. "Suzanne, you make this so hard for me. You know your father wanted us to wed. I will make you a good husband. I will help you run the plantation; it's not a job for a woman. We will have children, boys to carry on my name."

The Bandit's Lady

Even then, she knew that someday she would agree to marry Thaddeus, but not yet. She was silent.

On the way across the Chesapeake Bay, Suzanne made good her earlier promise to Captain Neal Franklin. They stood on deck in the glorious sunshine. "Suzanne, is there anything I can do for you?" Captain Neal asked as the *Bianca* sailed along through the glistening waters.

She sat down suddenly on the small wooden bench and swallowed tightly as he squatted beside her. A flash of wild grief ripped through her. Then as her eyes met his squarely, she felt there a tangible bond between them. She searched anxiously for the meaning behind his words. "I wish you could, Captain Neal. I feel so helpless, but I can't find a way to face this world. It's too big, too cruel."

Captain Neal looked away to the east. As if speaking to himself, his voice filled with an anguish that seemed as fresh as though he had just learned of his own disaster this very moment. "I lost the only women I ever loved. I was twenty-two. Kathleen was twenty. The velvet warmth of her kiss sang through my veins. The flames of passion burned within us. The wedding mass was set for a week hence."

A glazed look of despair spread over Captain Neal's face. "She took an arrow meant for me from an Indian. She died in my arms those forty years ago."

A raw and primitive grief overwhelmed Suzanne. All her pent-up loneliness and confusion melted together in one upsurge of devouring yearning. Caught unaware when his eyes suddenly filled with fierce sparkling, she went in his arms to comfort him and be comforted. "Thank you," she said softly.

Captain Neal cleared his throat. His voice was normal when he spoke again. "One does go on. Don't rush the grieving. It's the healing."

During the rest of the two-day crossing, Suzanne aroused herself from the numbness that weighted her down. She felt more like her old self than since she had read about the explosion.

But the night the *Bianca* docked in Norfolk, Thaddeus had grabbed her and pulled her roughly to him. His mouth had covered hers hungrily, brutally. His kiss was punishing and angry. Suzanne struggled for air. He released her so suddenly, she staggered back. His eyes raked boldly over her. "Tonight I will announce our betrothal," he said savagely.

He looked at her, and the double meaning of his gaze was obvious. She could feel her throat closing up. She tried to hide her inner misery from his probing stare. How she felt was not his concern, she decided. "You take too much for granted," she said scathingly. "I have not consented to marry you." She closed her eyes, reliving the pain of that final scene with Tyrone. With a moan of distress she turned away.

Thaddeus was unaware of her turmoil, unaware he had sliced open the healing wound. His offending hands gripped her upper arms. His angry gaze swung over her, but in spite of his anger, his tone was relatively civil. "I've waited long enough for your phony grief to waste itself. You act like you're the only one in the world to have ever lost a parent."

"It is more than that."

"Of course, my dear. It is the bandit, the thief who stole your maidenhood, for whom you pine. Consider yourself lucky I will still have you after you let him take your virginity."

"I loved him. He was more a man than you will ever be." She threw the words at him like stones, ignoring his false accusation.

"He's dead. I will have you now."

Thaddeus had invited everyone. He invited the serving girls, the stable boys, guests of the Inn, and Captain Neal and his crew to a gala celebration in honor of Suzanne's twenty-first birthday. He fully intended to declare their engagement. Suzanne had come of age. She ignored Thaddeus' attempts to be seated at her table. Sitting beside Captain Neal, she drank three glasses of the rich bubbly red wine in quick succession. Polly had helped her upstairs to bed.

Will Snooks had heard of Thaddeus' plans, and when the stagecoach left Norfolk, he and Clay were passengers. Their horses, tethered behind, trotted along beside Suzanne's Ginny. Will winked at Suzanne and slapped his hat over his eyes as he leaned back to doze.

The rest of the trip was uneventful. Suzanne closed her mind to Thaddeus, and as she settled back to endure the trip, she began to see the country as it really was. Thoughtfully, she noted the expansive stretches of forest. She felt sad that abandoned fields were growing up again in weeds and brush and young trees, the first stages of a return to the forest that had once covered the land. Parts of it were hilly or mountainous, some of it was pine barrens and here and there were long tracts of treacherous swamps. She recalled her grandfather saying, "The Underground deals extensively in swamps and woods, barns and footpaths, farm wagons and common people touched by the spirit of adventure."

It's all here, she thought. So enormous and varied and sparsely settled a land as the South could never be sealed off, or even thoroughly policed. Negroes left at will, just as abolitionists and paid abductors crossed its boarders to come in.

* * * *

It was spring. Green buds revealed themselves on oranges and jasmine. Camellia and japonicas were in full bloom. Suzanne stood up slowly. She was stiff from sitting in one position on the tree stump for so long. As she stretched, she chided herself. She had been home two weeks. Sadie and Jasper had fussed over her long enough. The plantation needed her attention. *It's time for spring planting and I can help,* she thought.

Suzanne went straight to Sadie. "Get Jasper, Sadie. I need to talk to both of you."

Big tears rolled down Sadie's fat black cheeks. "Oh, praise de Lord, Miz Suzanne. You is a gonna be yo'r ol' se'f. I can see it in dem spunky green eyes."

Suzanne gave herself freely to the passion of Sadie's hug. "Somehow, I've got to get on with the business of living. Father would not have wanted me to mourn my life away, but I'm so alone, Sadie. I lost my true love *and* my father in that fire."

Her voice broke. She turned away. "But enough of that for now. Someday when I can, I'll tell you about it. For now, get Jasper. We've work to do."

An hour later, Sadie and Jasper found Suzanne in her father's study poring over the plantation books. She looked up, anxiously. "Where is Luke Henry? I need him to help me figure out these books."

Sadie and Jasper exchanged a guarded look. Jasper spoke timidly. "I reckon' he be gone, Miz."

"Where? How long has he been gone? What's going on around here? I know we've lost some field hands, but how bad is it?"

"Beggin' yo'r pardon, Miz, but yo'r questions is gettin' ahead of my answers."

Suzanne couldn't help herself. She burst out laughing. "I must be getting back to normal. I think I've always been too curious for my own good. Okay, I'll be patient while you tell me everything I should know."

"It ain't no purty picture, Miz Suzanne. Luke Henry left and took a bunch of dem others with him, too. We got 'bout nine'y of 'em left, litt'e less than ha'f. We can't get none of de work all done."

"How about the house slaves, Sadie?"

"Li'l better, Miz. But me and Josy, we do real good."

"Jasper, ring the dinner bell in half an hour. I want every man, women, and child at the porch steps by noon. Sadie, come with me. Help me dress."

Suzanne, dressed simply in a blue cotton dress and a matching bonnet, stood as tall as her slim five-foot, two-inch stature allowed and looked over the familiar black faces. She suddenly knew she was a woman facing the harsh realities of loneliness. The knowledge twisted and turned inside her.

Staring back at her from frightened dark eyes were grayhaired men and women, and younger ones. She recognized a few of them as former pickaninnies with whom she and James had frolicked. Their youngsters stood beside them. She closed her eyes, not able to bear the misery showing on their faces. Although she couldn't identify it, something more than their fear and despair penetrated Suzanne's consciousness. Facing them again, her eyes darted nervously around the group.

There was a restlessness and at the same time a detachment, an isolation between them and herself. Suzanne managed a friendly smile.

When she spoke, she was pleased that her voice sounded eager and alive with affection to her own ears. "We have all had a very great loss. My father's death came at an extremely inopportune time, but we must get back to the business of the plantation. It's planting season and we have lost our foreman and almost half of our fellow laborers. I need all of you who are willing to stay on here at Royal Oaks. I will pay you twenty cents in cash for each day you work, beginning tomorrow, until the end of the war. Your pay will be here at the porch on the first day of each month. The rest of your life will go on as before. Your clothes, food, tobacco and land will be provided as usual. If you would rather have all your money at one time, I will record the amount each month and give it to you when the war is over. At that time you may decide to remain here or to take your money and move on. You are free.

"One more thing. For every new laborer you bring to work with us, or for any former hands you persuade to come back, I will add fifty cents to your bank account. Now, how many of you will stay here under these conditions?"

Every head dropped to the ground, or moved to look away; not one would meet her eye. Nobody answered. "What's the matter? Have I not offered you enough? Tell me what you think is fair. Jimbo, will you speak for the group, and will you be the newly appointed overseer?"

Jimbo had always loved the plantation. Even when a child, he had told Suzanne that someday he would be her father's right-hand man. Now he stood tall and straight beside his wife. Four little barefoot children clung around their knees. His powerful, well-muscled body twitched. He shuffled his feet and looked at the ground, and answered in a low awkward voice.

"Yez, ma'am, I speaks. We cannot a'cept you' offer, even tho it be gen'rous. Der's tro'ble ahaid. I cain't say no mor'. We bes' be gettin' bac' to wo'k. We starts de plantin' in de mornin'."

Suzanne watched them turn as if one and move silently across the land toward their quarters. She clenched her jaw to kill the sob in her throat and fought against the tears she refused to let fall. Sadie led her back through the veranda door. "Get Jasper, Sadie," Suzanne said. "I'll be in the library." She vowed to build a new life for herself. *I'll make them want to stay and help,* she thought.

When Jasper returned, Suzanne heard her voice squeak with impatience, "What is going on around here? Who is going to tell me?"

Sadie spoke up. "Der's tro'ble in de big house ober at Mas'er Thaddeus' place."

"What does that have to do with our slaves?"

"When tro'ble is in de big house, it alwa's mean tro'ble in de slave quarters. Prob'em is he been actin' nasty to you' slaves, too. He sayin' deys haf to min' him, dat he be in charge now dat our own mas'er be daid. He be mean one."

"I don't understand. Jimbo said they will be starting the planting tomorrow."

Jasper finally found his tongue. "Yez 'um, Miz Suzanne, dat be de truth, but he be meanin' dey is goin' to be plantin' over at Stuart Place Plantation."

Suzanne's breath burned in her throat. She felt suddenly weak and vulnerable in the face of her own anger. "I'll see to

Thaddeus. Tell Jimbo to report to me at the seed shed at daylight. Tell him to have every able-bodied Royal Oaks worker with him. You may go now."

For the rest of the day, Suzanne buried herself in the plantation record books. She ignored Sadie's call to supper. She left the tray Josy brought, and set on the small round table beside her, untouched.

Only when the candle sputtered, threatening to darken the room, did Suzanne stretch and stand and move out to the veranda. As she paced back and forth on the wooden porch and stared out into the darkness, Suzanne thought only about how to get the spring planting finished on time.

Chapter 27

The days turned into weeks. Suzanne tied her hair back with a crinkled velvet ribbon and stuffed it under her father's old straw hat. She labored in the cotton field alongside the slaves. They planted and tilled.

So much a part of the scene was she, the slaves soon forgot she was their mistress and began to talk naturally among themselves. Suzanne listened appalled when the talk turned to the frequent uprisings at Thaddeus Stuart's plantation. She asked Jimbo about it one day.

"Dey is fo'bidden to carry fir' arms, o'course, but them niggers kin a'ways lay dey han's on axes an' scythes and clubs."

"Whatever are they going to do?"

"Dey's fo'bidden to 'semble, but you jus' watch an' see. Dey kin git word from one to de other quicker den a blink by the graveyard rabbit. Dey's gittin' angry. Dem what ain't gon' yet is gettin' ready to do somethin' terrible."

"What's their real problem, Jimbo, outside the fact that Mister Thaddeus is a bit harsh?"

"He be more den a bit harsh, Miz Suzanne. He be downright mean. He threatens de punishment. Dem black bucks dey get plumb sullen. What's lef' is gonna turn into rebels or run."

"Where would they run?"

"Dey don' be carin', Miz Suzanne. Dey got nothin' to look forward to, no hope until in de full of time de sweet chariot should swing low. Frosty mornin' or swelterin' mornin', der is always work, but de only reward dey expec' is to escape de punishment."

"But they have their evenings and weekends, don't they?"

"Dey got a curfew—gots to be in by nine 'clock. Dat nigger overseer, he poun's on ever' cabin to make sure all dem slaves is 'counted fo' de fires is banked fo' de night. He don't even let 'em go to church no more."

Later, Suzanne tried to talk to Thaddeus on behalf of the slaves, but he laughed. "You wait until your own precious niggers get on a rampage. They all get uppity; it's just a matter of time."

Suzanne kept her silence but worked the harder beside her slaves. Perspiration poured down her heat-reddened face and between her breasts. Her hands calloused over, and her feet and legs ached and cramped.

Each afternoon before dinner, Suzanne sank gratefully into a warm lilac bath and wished the slaves could do the same. But the slaves splashed off with cool water from the well or played in one of the backwater pools. Saturday night they took their baths in the river, before going to church Sunday morning.

Suzanne continued to keep meticulous plantation books. She had first made a list of the field hands. She and Jimbo had divided them into crews of fifteen. Each crew had a charge leader responsible for reporting the number of workers each day. The slaves' cash earnings were adding up to a tremendous sum. After six weeks, eighty-one laborers had earned their full pay equal to seven dollars and twenty cents. Twenty-two of the field hands had brought in an extra worker who had been hiding out in the swamps. That was another eleven dollars.

Suzanne stared at the bottom line. It totaled up to six hundred seventy-four dollars and twenty cents. She smiled, wondering what her father would have said of her extravagance. She fervently hoped that come fall she could find a buyer for the crop. *We have one hundred and three workers. We will survive,* she thought.

In work she found a mindless solidity that helped camouflage the anger and deep despair of loneliness that seethed inside her. As the cool darkness of deep night brought an end to long exhausting days, Suzanne carried a glass of sherry to the veranda. Pacing back and forth, while sipping the cool, soothing liquid, she planned the work for the next day.

One such a night in late June, Suzanne became aware of an eerie light off to the west, but it was several moments before the reason penetrated her consciousness. Even as her mind leaped to the sickening truth, Thaddeus Stuart's plantation buildings burst into brilliant flames.

Suzanne watched in terror as Thaddeus and his friends, armed and on horseback, and silhouetted against the orange-red sky, sprinted toward the scene from the direction of town. She felt her body stiffen as she recalled the description of another fire, but she quickly shook free from the memory and ran toward the house calling for Sadie. She found her in the kitchen. "Sadie," she said as she whirled around and headed for the stairway. "Get Josy in here to make sandwiches and set the coffee to boiling. You come with me."

"Where's you be off to, Miz?" Sadie said as she panted along behind her.

"Jasper and I will go over to Thaddeus' place to see what we can do. Come! Help me get out of this dress and into a pair of breeches."

At the sound of a carriage, Sadie rushed over to pull the drape back. "You can't be leavin' now, Miz Suzanne. You be gettin' company."

Pulling one of her father's old shirts over her head, Suzanne went to the window. "Who in the world can be visiting at this time of night? Whose carriage is that, Sadie?"

"I dunno, Miz, but I bes' be gettin' down to answer de do'r."

Suzanne finished dressing, tied her hair atop her head and grabbed the mud-splattered straw hat as she left the room.

"I declare, Miss Suzanne, how often do I have to tell you to dress like a lady no matter what. Where do you think you are going?"

Miss Abigail, dressed in a cotton twill, burnished gold dress, stood hands on hips at the bottom of the curved stairway. As she stopped to survey the older woman, Suzanne noted that Miss Abigail stood as tall and slender as ever, and with the same careful elegant grooming. The only thing that gave away the passing years of this vividly attractive lady was the full dark head of hair, graying slightly at the temples. Pulled back lightly into a soft bun at the nap of her neck, it was a perfect style for the richness of her clothes. Suzanne thought the clean purity of her profile was classic. The slightly arched nose and high cheekbones accentuated the rare beauty of her violet eyes. Suzanne saw sadness in them and felt a strong tug of emotion.

It triggered the emotions of her own year of terror, still locked deep inside her. All the pain resurfaced as she realized how she missed her father and the life they had before Miss Abigail left them. Suzanne nimbly sprinted down the stairs into the cradle of her former governess's arms. "Oh, Miss Abigail, I thought I would die when you and Father decided I was too old for a governess. You went away when I was barely sixteen. But what made you come back now?"

A soothing voice nudged her back to the present. "I came back because of our tragedy, but we will have plenty of time later to talk." Then her eyes squinted with amusement. "For now, let's debate why you dressed like that—why you think Thaddeus needs you personally to fight the fire."

Thinking Miss Abigail had responded with her usual refreshing and ingenious capacity of warmth, Suzanne grinned. She felt again like a child who had been caught stealing a piece of Josey's poppy-seed cake. Impulsively, she hugged her again. "I'm so glad to see you. Where did you come from? How did you know I was home?"

Miss Abigail laughed gently. "Ah, Suzanne, you have not changed at all. You are altogether inquisitive, but there's trouble brewing. Can you find me an outfit like the one you are wearing?"

Suzanne felt a ripple of mirth before her amusement swiftly died. "Come. We haven't a moment to lose."

At Sadie's bidding, Jasper had saddled two horses, a gentle mare for Miss Abigail, and Ginny, whom had not been ridden since Suzanne returned home. "All the mens dat be stayin' to work fo' you' is over at de fire, Miz Suzanne," Jasper said as the two women mounted the horses. "De rest is gone."

"I see four fires out there, Jasper. Can the men save any of the buildings?"

"Dey got de bes' chance over at Cypress Pine Plantation. Dat's where all de mens is. Dey gots the river water nearby. B.J. Hall be kind to his slaves—dey be stayin' to help."

Nobody recognized the two disguised women as they took their places, relieving two men that needed rest. Hours later, in the crisp predawn, the sounds of the screaming, escaping animals were quiet. The mingled stench of smoke and sweat hung heavily in the air. Faces streaked with soot, and in some cases blistered, the fire fighters sat around in small somber groups.

They had saved most of B.J.'s buildings. The other burning plantation structures had disappeared, crumbling to hot cinders, and finally ashes. Miss Abigail and Suzanne, aching with fatigue and strained muscles, left the scene to go back to Royal Oaks, and to soak briefly in the tubs of steamy water Sadie prepared for them.

Daintily dressed, they returned to the site by carriage. Josy had prepared a large urn of scalding coffee and an assortment of roast beef, turkey, and ham sandwiches. Annie Hall helped the hungry men fill their plates as the three women worked quietly side by side. When Suzanne turned to Jasper to ask him to load up the empty urn, Thaddeus stepped up beside her.

"When can I see you alone, Suzanne? It's urgent." She looked up to see him staring at her. His eyes, little blue chinks in a set face, took in every detail of the closely fitted bodice and narrow waist of her creamy white morning dress.

Choosing to ignore the vicious glint and the sly intimacy, Suzanne answered in a low, neutral voice. "First you must sleep. You are welcome at Royal Oaks. Sadie will make up a room for you. I'll see you in Father's study after dinner."

As the carriage pulled away, Miss Abigail asked, "Whatever possessed you to invite that contemptible man to stay in your home?"

"He won't stay long, but I can't be inhospitable. He lost everything, and is—was Father's friend."

"Did you see the way he looked at you?"

In a dull voice, empty of emotion, Suzanne said, "He wants to marry me."

"Surely you aren't considering such a foolish proposition," Miss Abigail burst out.

Suzanne realized with numb astonishment she was doing just that. She was contemplating the absurd proposal as a possible solution to her future. Biting her lip, she looked away. "I'm really too tired to think right now. Please, let's discuss this tomorrow after I hear what Thaddeus has to say. He's had a terrible loss. I doubt he's thinking of wedding bells today."

Miss Abigail took her hand. As they rode on in silence, Suzanne's mind reeled with bewilderment. She felt her feelings toward Thaddeus becoming confused. Every fiber in her body warned her against him, yet the nagging in the back of her mind refused to be still. He had been her father's friend. Aman had wanted her to marry him.

Her love was dead. A strange, cold excitement filled her whole being. The sensations Tyrone had awakened made a peculiar yearning flow through her in heated waves. Hunger rose and flared in her like a savage animal. She had only sensed love, never daring to claim it. There was always an excitement and an invitation in the smoldering depths of Thaddeus' eyes.

Maybe she could learn to love him. *I am a fool to think happiness will always surge through me,* she thought.

She felt the stillness and looked up. Jasper was handing Miss Abigail down from the carriage. "Give the hands the day off, Jasper," she said as he also helped her to the ground. "Tell them to sleep or have a holiday. Tomorrow I'll have no nonsense. We'll work as usual at Royal Oaks."

"Yes, Miz. I be tellin' Jimbo to pass de word."

Suzanne walked Miss Abigail to the door of her old bedroom. She embraced her and said, "It's wonderful to have you here. It's comforting. But why *did* you come?"

Miss Abigail's eyes clouded over. Unshed tears glistened in the violet eyes that darkened with pain. "It's too complicated. Let's get some sleep. I promise we'll talk tomorrow."

Seeing the hurt and longing that lay naked in her eyes, Suzanne wanted to reach out, but stopped herself. "You're right, of course. I'll see you at dinner. You don't dare leave me alone with Thaddeus. It's bad enough I will have to face him later."

Suzanne thought she would wrestle with the problem of Abigail when she lay down, but the fatigue caused by the terrible night of fire pulled her immediately into a deep sleep.

* * * *

Dinner was almost a silent affair and when it was over Thaddeus walked around the table to help Suzanne to her feet. "Excuse us, Abigail," he said as he led her toward the door. "Suzanne and I have much to discuss."

Without ceremony, Thaddeus went to Aman's liquor cabinet and poured one large glass of red sherry and a snifter of brandy. Suzanne noted his set face, clamped mouth and fixed eyes. A muscle flicked angrily at his jaw. She felt anger also rising within her. How dare he act as though it was his right to serve cordials without asking permission? She said, "I think you are taking much for granted."

His blue eyes blazed. His voice was cold when he answered. "I have been excessively patient with you, my dear. We both know what your father wanted for your future. He intended for you to marry me. And, although he foolishly threw his life away or ran away, he knew you would obey him in the end. It's time you decided."

"What are you saying? I won't have you speaking ill of my father. I have always intended to marry for love. Father would have agreed to that, had he lived."

"But he didn't live, and neither did your scheming bandit. When will you forget this nonsense about marrying for love? It's expedient for you to marry as quickly as possible. A young woman alone cannot conceivably run a plantation, and I am quite capable of doing that for you."

Thaddeus set his glass down and went to sit beside Suzanne on the settee. She shifted uneasily. "I've been alone these five years. Madeline May was barren. I want children. Now with the house and buildings burned, I have no place to go. I aim to marry you immediately."

He draped an arm roughly about her shoulders, handling her as if he owned her. She flinched, resenting his familiarity, but his mouth claimed hers in savage command. He kissed with a punishing insistence as his tongue moved into her mouth with urgent passion.

Tyrone's name echoed in the black stillness of her mind. His face haunted her, smiling, serious, thoughtful. Thaddeus' sensuousness threatened to rekindle old forgotten feelings. Suzanne froze as her senses leapt to life; her heartbeat throbbed in her ears. Despite herself she found herself responding to Thaddeus' harsh actions. She resisted with every means in her power and yanked away from him. She would not be manipulated by this brute. He grinned and straightened his shoulders.

His burning eyes prolonged the moment, holding her still. "You might as well admit it, Suzanne," Thaddeus said softly, mockingly. "You are as ready for the marriage bed as I am. Let's save time and tempers. Name a date. You can't go on like you have been. Working in the fields is shocking and unladylike. It's time you began to act with more prudence. I also understand you are paying those damn slaves. That's despicable. I will not tolerate it after we marry and merge our holdings. After all, those niggers are nothing but animals."

Suzanne felt anger threaten to choke her. She gave him a stony look. "I will run *my* plantation *my* way. I will never agree to join our property. You may stay at Royal Oaks as long as you need to, but stay out of my business. Whether we marry or not, you have your own work in the city. Mine is here."

A hope that surprised her flashed in his expression. "Does that mean you'll marry me?"

Suzanne took a deep breath. She sighed, weary of the argument. She knew she must marry him. She couldn't go on alone much longer. After a long pause, during which she fought for self-control, she nodded. "But not until after harvest. I have spent too much time establishing harmony among my slaves to quit now. By winter, if we still feel the same, we can get married."

Thaddeus put one hand on her shoulder, his fingers digging into her flesh in a possessive gesture. The fingers of his other hand touched hers, and she fought a wild urge to jump back. He said, "I was really hoping we could marry right away."

A vision of Tyrone flickered through Suzanne's mind, and she pressed both hands over her eyes as if they burned with weariness. "I'm sorry, Thaddeus. A bride has much to do to prepare for her wedding. I will shop for my trousseau in Charleston when I open the town house in August. I can't be ready before winter. The wedding will take place the day after Christmas." She watched a play of emotions cross Thaddeus' face.

"I guess I must be content with that, my dear," he said as his gaze lazily appraised her.

Suzanne stood. "Good night, Thaddeus. We have had a long and tiring couple of days. I must retire."

He, too, stood, and walked across the room to retrieve his drink, making no comment as she left the room.

Chapter 28

"What do you mean, you consented to marry Thaddeus?" Miss Abigail asked sharply as she poured a second cup of coffee from the coffeepot at the sideboard.

Out of the corner of her eye, Suzanne saw Miss Abigail's expression of disbelief. Suzanne closed her eyes, feeling utterly miserable. She shrugged. "It doesn't matter. I lost the only man I ever loved in the fire when the ships exploded."

Miss Abigail walked to the table and sat across the corner of the long table from Suzanne. She reached out to lace Suzanne's fingers with her own. "I don't understand. You loved your father, but the death of a parent shouldn't..."

"*You* don't understand. It isn't my father. Although I miss him terribly, it is not his death I'm speaking of. It's the bandit. Tyrone Sterling, the love of my life, died in that fire."

Suzanne bowed her head to protect the place in her heart that only Tyrone had ever touched. Memory closed around her and filled her with a longing to turn back. It had been a long time since she had let herself reminisce, but suddenly remembered the day he pressed every inch of her body to his. His powerful body had rippled with tension. The lips that brushed hers held a tempting invitation for more. She could almost smell the tantalizing scent of his masculinity. She had denied him. Suzanne realized her taut nipples were straining against the thin fabric of her cool cotton summer dress and crossed her arms around her breasts. She groaned.

Miss Abigail's voice was barely above a whisper. "Tell me about him."

Suzanne talked. She started at the beginning, leaving nothing out, and when she had spent herself, she lapsed into an uneasy silence. She pushed loose wisps of hair away from her face. A puzzling thought assailed her. Why couldn't she put the pieces together? Her mind bulged with unasked questions. "But you referred to our tragedy. Why?"

She watched Miss Abigail lean back and sip the coffee that had grown cold in her cup. Abigail looked at Suzanne quickly, then spoke in an odd, yet gentle tone. "Because I loved your father. I have loved him since I was a young girl."

"But how could you have?"

"My parents died on the ship that brought us to America. It was the French *Princess Dion*. The plague took sixty-three of its passengers. I watched my mother and father, and my two little brothers die."

"What did you do when you got here? How old were you?"

"I was thirteen. My father had been a British naval officer. We had traveled all over Europe where I learned many languages, both modern and ancient. I came here able to teach Greek and Latin as easily as French, German, Spanish, Italian, and Russian. When I arrived in the States, I telegraphed my uncle in Charleston. He arranged for my transportation south, but he died before I arrived. I lived with his wife. She was grieving and never recovered, and could not love me. She died a year later."

"What did you do?"

"I had a little money. I continued to live in the little house in Charleston. When I was sixteen, I began teaching Judge Pope's two youngest children."

"How did you meet Father?"

"Aman used to come to visit Malcolm Pope. They were great friends. After my daily duties were over, Malcolm insisted I join him on the porch for a lemonade. He was sweet on me, but once I met your father, my heart was only for him."

"What happened?"

"Nothing. Your father left to purchase the *Annebella*. He named the ship after he met and married your mother. I was crushed, but it was too late. I didn't see him again until after your mother died. He remembered me then and looked me up to ask me to be your governess. When Judge Pope was looking for a tutor for Jesse Owens, he suggested I could share my time between the two of you."

"What happened to you after Jesse finished his lessons and after you left here?"

"I went to Columbia as governess for a family named Johansen. When those children were grown, I came back and taught John Will's two boys."

"Did Father ever know you loved him?"

A blush like a shadow ran over Miss Abigail's cheeks. "Years later, yes. Before he left, we accidentally met at the Harvest Ball and again at the social hour following Thanksgiving services at St. Paul's Episcopal Church. It was there he noticed me as a woman who might fill his lonely years."

"What happened?"

"I'm not sure. He said he was in some kind of difficulty and was leaving for the duration of the war. He said he had a good friend, even called him by name. It was your young man, Tyrone Sterling. He said Tyrone would help see him through, that he was on Tyrone's protection list."

Suzanne stiffened, then nodded woodenly. A stab of guilt lay buried in her breast. "I wish I had trusted Tyrone. He told me to, but I couldn't. He thrust a list into my care the night we were robbed. I thought he was hunting for Father. He wouldn't deny it. Oh, Miss Abigail, I'm so miserable."

Suzanne buried her head in her hands as she was once again assaulted by a sick yearning. Miss Abigail stroked her hair. Then she stood up and said brusquely, "Enough of this for now. Are you really planning to marry Thaddeus?"

Suzanne nodded glumly.

"I think it's a mistake. I've managed to live all of my life without a man. You could certainly wait until you find one more suitable."

Suzanne flung out her hands in simple despair. "I know Father would approve. It really doesn't matter anymore, and I will try to be a good wife to Thaddeus."

She stole a glance at Miss Abigail's face. Her violet eyes regarded her with a speculative gaze, but when she spoke her voice was once more full of affectionate concern. "I'll not say more then, but Christmas is a long way off. You need a chaperon. I'll move in with you until after the wedding. Please, honey, call me Abigail. The 'Miss' sounds so stuffy."

Suzanne felt a warm glow bubble up inside of her. She walked over and threw an arm around her friend. "'Stuffy' is not a word I would ever associate with you, dear Abigail. Thank you for your offer to live here. Oh, how I need you. We will get your things today."

* * * *

"And just when did you plan to get around to it, my dear?" Thaddeus stood at one end of the fireplace that evening, pointing his brandy snifter at Suzanne. "You look terrible. Your skin is as dark as a nigger's. If you didn't have freckles, I couldn't tell you apart from them."

He pouted. "I want a party, a Ball, to announce our engagement. What's so wrong with that? Why won't you quit working in the cotton fields long enough to start planning for a Ball, and the wedding?"

Abigail and Thaddeus had been living at Royal Oaks three full weeks. The only two concessions Suzanne had given to the house guests were a long, leisurely breakfast hour, usually alone with Abigail, and a couple of hours after dinner with Thaddeus. Outside of those times she spent her days exactly as before, with the slaves in the fields during the day, and kept track of the enormous details of running the plantation and the small dairy barn at night. Suzanne loved the dairy barn. It produced enough milk for all of the needs of the big house and the slaves' quarters, with a little left over now that so many of the slaves were gone. She took the remainder of the milk to Charleston and gave it to Polly and Jesse to distribute to the children Polly was teaching.

Suzanne basked in her newly awakened sense of life. She felt elated by her new objectivity and impatient with Thaddeus' whining tone. "In case you haven't noticed, there's a war going on," she said sharply. "Right now I'm doing my best to keep my plantation intact. We've plenty of time to go through the proper formalities."

Thaddeus' voice grated harshly. "But when?"

Suzanne could feel his ice blue eyes boring into her as she walked to the window. She looked out over the vast cotton fields spreading across the rolling land to the west. She had helped plant the seeds and had watched the shrubby plants grow up to her shoulders. The creamy-white flowers that formed had quickly turned a deep and glorious pink before they began to fall off, leaving the small cotton bolls containing the seeds.

She knew she should make the decision to open up the town house during the humid, stifling heat of late summer or to stick it out here until harvest. In Charleston, the breezes off the ocean cooled the air and lessened the threat of malaria that lay in the sultry swampland near the rivers. Jasper and Sadie were already badgering her to close up the big house. "Time be 'nuff den to git in the cotton durin' harves' season," Sadie had said. "You workin' too hard fo' a white lady. If'n you don' gits some rest, you be takin' sick fo' sure."

Thinking about it made Suzanne smile. As she turned back to Thaddeus, she came to a final conclusion. Her smile was disarmingly generous. "You're right, of course. I've been so busy I put off thinking about the wedding. I'll open up the town house the first of August. While Abigail and I are in Charleston, I'll shop for my trousseau. You can announce our betrothal at the Harvest Ball. This year, it's going to be at Judge Pope's."

His admiring gaze gratified her, and she suddenly found him disturbingly attractive. His eyes glinted with an intensity, a pure masculine hunger that unnerved her as his hands spanned her waist to draw her to him. She felt heat in her face as sparks of unwanted excitement shot through her. Thaddeus' smile came to life on his lips, and she watched his sultry gaze rest briefly on her breasts. An unexpected tremor of pleasure raced through her and Suzanne knew she coveted him with a queer mixture of contempt and desire. His hand swept to the back of her neck, and he kissed her in the moist hollow of her throat, then moved to press his lips to hers in a primitive act of domination.

Suzanne felt the drumbeat of his heart. As she moved against him in a suggestive body caress, her own hunger came on in a heated gush. She felt crushed by his strength and pulled away, flustered by the extended contact, uneasy at the sudden physical intimacy. She shuddered and turned away. Thaddeus twirled her back to face him. The blue eyes that met hers were filled with desire. He let them roam over her figure, then raked her with a fiercely possessive look. When he spoke, his voice cracked with a sardonic weariness. "You cannot deny it. You want me as much as I want you. Come upstairs with me now. I'll show you more about making love than your bandit ever could know."

Suzanne was instantly filled with resentment and humiliation. She felt her throat closing up. He had broken through her fragile control. It was pointless to deny her attraction to him, but she knew in the privacy of her own heart she could never love this man as she had Tyrone. "Not now," she said, recovering her good humor enough to taunt him. "You'll have to resort to the waiting game. You've won yourself a virgin, and I plan to give myself to you only after the marriage vows are performed."

His face was a glowering mask of rage. "I detest liars, my dear. I suggest you don't try to deceive me again."

Not caring what he thought, Suzanne shrugged. "Please leave me now. I've work to do."

Thaddeus frowned at her and walked away.

* * * *

In the following weeks, Suzanne stayed away from the fields more and more, going only on morning and evening rounds. Stray slaves continued to return, and new ones, abandoned because of the fires and encouraged by others eager to earn the bonus, signed on. Under Jimbo's shrewd supervision, the plantation was finally running smoothly, and Suzanne and Abigail began making plans for the move to Charleston. "I promised Polly that while I'm in town I'll help her smuggle the children to their house, and help teach them," Abigail said one morning at breakfast. "Will you help, too?"

"When I have time, but I must catch up on my correspondence. I want to arrange for Grandfather's trip to Royal Oaks. He's coming for the wedding. Also, I gave my word to Thaddeus I would purchase my trousseau and new gowns for the holiday season."

"Oh, what fun. Can I help?"

"Of course. Polly, too. We loved to shop together at Miss Millicent's in Baltimore, but I'm not sure where to go. Winfrey Whitney is getting on in years. Materials are scarce, too."

"Jesse suggested his mother's protégée, Phoebe. Why don't you give her a try?"

"Good idea. I need to make a visit to John Will's Jewelry Store, too, to replace some of the jewelry that was stolen the night the coach was robbed. Mr. Will was Father's friend. He'll help me make wise decisions."

Later, a few days before her departure, she asked, "Thaddeus, where will you be staying while I'm in Charleston?"

"I have business at the state house in Columbia. I'll be gone for several weeks, but I will be back in time for the Harvest Ball in October."

Suzanne felt her cheeks grow warm as Thaddeus' eyes swept over her slender figure. An invitation lurked in their smoldering depths. "I trust you'll be ready for the big night, and you will stay out of the field altogether after we are married."

Suzanne felt anger rising inside her, but she answered calmly. "I fully intend to help with the harvest, and I shall always do as I please in my fields."

"Don't count on that, my dear. I have a plan to keep you permanently occupied. Babies take a great deal of care and time."

Something seemed to turn and break inside of her. There was only room for one man in Suzanne's thoughts. *If only Tyrone and I could have had a child,* she mused silently, *he wouldn't be quite so dead.* "Please don't talk like that, Thaddeus. I'm fond of you. Nothing more. You'll have to settle for that."

"I will for now, but once you are mine, you'll come around. Wait and see."

* * * *

Suzanne stepped into the deep shadows of the Charleston town house, reveling in the cool sensation of its interior. Featured throughout was rich mahogany furniture. Katrina, Suzanne's housemaid, had opened the east, west, and north windows at dusk in order to catch the ocean and river breezes. At dawn she closed the heavy brocade drapes against the torrid heat of the summer.

The days in Charleston took on a pleasant uniformity. Abigail and Suzanne breakfasted together. Then Abigail hurried to Jesse and Polly's where the students met secretly in the small home behind the blacksmith shop. The three friends often spent their afternoons together. They sat sipping lemonade or went to Phoebe's for the gown-fitting sessions.

Phoebe had bought up materials before the war-torn city was occupied by enemy soldiers. She had stowed them in two trunks in the guest room of her home, which she used for a sewing room. Suzanne first selected a frock for the Harvest Ball. The French beige gown had a low-cut lace bodice laced up the front with a delicate satin ribbon. The modified Elizabethan sleeves and full skirt with tiers of lace ruffles were made of the same color of satin silk.

In complete accord, the women chose a lush opal-white satin taffeta for Suzanne's wedding dress. The frothy lace overdress was adorned with tiny pearls and crisscross lace trim from the fitted bodice to the slightly dropped waistline. Lace ruffles trimmed the sweetheart neckline, and matched the lace of the tapered sleeves. The tiers of lace extending down the flowing skirt covered layers and layers of petticoats.

Standing in front of the mirror during the final fittings, Suzanne was momentarily lost in her own fantasies. She closed her eyes to imagine Tyrone beside her. She felt transported on a soft and wispy cloud, and as her thoughts spun, her emotions whirled and skidded.

Her wedding day should have been their wedding day. Oh how she had loved that maddening hint of arrogance about him, and his gaze that traveled over her face and searched her very soul, and how she had dreamed of being crushed within his embrace.

She wondered idly what he would have thought of her gown. Suzanne opened her eyes to take in the details of the dress once more. He would have adored it, she decided. She knew she had selected it with Tyrone in mind. Suzanne came back to reality with a strange restless unease. She and Thaddeus had never been more than careful strangers to each other, no matter how he looked at her, or tried to dominate her life.

Chapter 29

The days lazed along. Abigail and Suzanne made plans to go back to the plantation in two weeks, in time for harvest. The note from the bank had arrived yesterday. Suzanne was dressing for a fitting at Phoebe's when she heard voices in the foyer. She ran down the long, straight stairs and Katrina handed her a small piece of paper. "Wait a moment," Suzanne told the young man who had delivered the message. "I may want to send an answer in return."

She moved into the parlor and sat down in front of the large window overlooking the gardens, still resplendent with the rare beauty of lush hibiscus, roses, magnolia, and larkspur. Without, for once, noticing their delicate bouquet that wafted into the room, she hurriedly opened the note:

> *My Dear Miss Willoughby,*
> Before you return to Royal Oaks, I trust you will visit the Charleston Institute of Banking. I will be most happy to meet with you at your convenience and look forward to seeing you again.
> Sincerely,
> *Jules Johnston*

Suzanne had planned to go to the bank before she returned to the plantation, but she dreaded it. She knew her father had probably left a will, and the business must be taken care of. She felt sad.

As she slipped on a pale-yellow silk dress in preparation for her visit with Mr. Johnston, she paced the floor of the small bedroom. She was anxious to get back to Royal Oaks, back to work. When she finished at the bank, she would meet Abigail and Polly at their favorite haunt, the popular Planters Hotel where they would savor the specialty of the kitchen: Planters Punch and sliver-thin sugar cookies, delicately browned. Suzanne sighed. It was getting more and more difficult to meet with Polly and Jesse. Although Charleston had a small constituent of free Negroes, they were not welcome in public. The sympathetic proprietor of the hotel put them in a dark, out-of-the-way corner nook so they would be undisturbed and seldom harassed.

Tomorrow, Suzanne decided, as she poked her dark curls into the bonnet, she would visit Mr. Will's Jewelry Store and then pick up the last two gowns at Phoebe's.

* * * *

"Mr. Stanton, at your service, Miss Willoughby. I will escort you to Mr. Johnston's office."

"Thank you, sir," Suzanne said to the tall figure who led her across the marble floor.

Mr. Johnston scurried to his feet to greet Suzanne. He was a vigorous, elfin man. "Well, well, young lady, I've been expecting you ever since your return, but I hear stories about you. Folks are saying you spend as much time in the fields as your daddy used to. I see it's true. You are as brown and healthy as a hazelnut."

Suzanne burst out laughing. She recalled she had always liked this outspoken, zealous man. His voice was gusty, and she saw only friendliness in his smile. "I'm sorry I didn't visit you sooner. I knew there would be business to take care of, but I've been putting it off. It seems...so final. I...have only recently taken over the management of Royal Oaks." She smiled. "Anyway, now that I'm here, I will need a little extra cash for the expenses of the wedding."

Jules Johnston peered at Suzanne over the top of glasses that had slid down his nose. "You may have the cash you need, of course, but I thought Mr. Stuart was taking care of everything as he has since your father's death."

He paused for a moment, as if reluctant to voice his next thought. "He has been cashing in your late father's railroad holdings at quite an alarming rate."

Suzanne listened with rising dismay. She clasped her hands together and moved forward to the edge of her chair. "I don't altogether know what you are trying to tell me."

"He was your father's solicitor. He had a letter signed by your father stating that in the event of your father's death he was to be your guardian until you came of age."

Suzanne felt sour bile come into the pit of her stomach. "Father never mentioned such an arrangement to me. Thaddeus has not given me any money at all and I am of age. Whatever is he using the certificates for? How long has he been cashing in Father's savings? Why wasn't I informed of the transactions?"

She stopped abruptly when Jules flung out his hands in simple surrender. "I'm sorry, Mr. Johnston. I always ask questions faster than anyone can answer."

He hesitated, measuring her. "I will try to answer all your questions, my dear. Thaddeus came to me over a year ago, right after the fiery explosion that took your father's life. He said your condition was so grave after the loss of your father you had to be hospitalized and the funds were required to pay for your care."

"He what? Of all the impertinent gall. I was sorely distressed, but I was not ever hospitalized, and there were no expenses. I was living with Grandfather Hanson."

"Oh, dear. This is unpardonable. He told me... I thought you were not able to be informed of the transactions. I see now I was very wrong. However, I must tell all. He used nearly fifteen thousand dollars of the certificates; there is a scant nine thousand in reserve. Ah...there are other funds, Suzanne. You will never be destitute, but the railroad stocks were easy to use because they were Bearer Bonds, the money could be awarded to the bearer."

Suzanne blinked, then focused her gaze on Mr. Johnston. She felt a shadow of alarm welling up inside her. "How could he?" she said, scarcely aware of her own voice. "He stole Father's money, or rather my money, on the pretense I was not capable."

"I'm terribly sorry. I feel responsible, negligent."

"It's all right, Mr. Johnston. It wasn't your fault. I will deal with Thaddeus, but can you help me put the rest of Father's money into a trust so he cannot use it for frivolous purposes? Father would want his money to be used for the preservation of our plantation and...and for his grandchildren."

An hour later, dazed, but satisfied that Aman Willoughby's funds were safe for her own prudent disbursement, Suzanne left the bank to join her friends in the high-ceilinged dining room of the Planter's Hotel. "What's the matter?" Polly asked as she seated herself at the table. "You look like you swallowed a thorn."

"It's been a long morning. I have much to think about, not the least of which is what I will do about my future with Thaddeus."

Abigail, clearly unable to contain her disapproval for another instant broke into the conversation. "Are you finally coming to your senses? Will you truly break off this ridiculous relationship, this engagement that is so ghastly irrational?"

"I agree with Miss Abigail. May I join you, ladies?" Jesse had escorted his wife and former tutor to the Planters Hotel. Without an apology for breaking into their plans, he sat between Polly and Suzanne.

Suzanne nodded absently. "Of course, Jesse, it's good to see you, but why all of this sudden concern about my decision? I think I must have brides' jitters."

While the waitress took their order from Abigail, Suzanne bent her head and studied her hands. She shyly looked up into Jesse's gray compassionate eyes, the same gray eyes she had known somewhere before, but where? Without pausing to think, she asked, "Why do you seem so close to me, Jesse? It's more than my love for Polly, much more. Can you tell me what it is?"

He reached out and touched her arm. "I suppose I must, though I wish your father were here to enjoy the moment. We were going to tell you together, when you came of age."

"Tell me what?"

"Aman and I were half brothers. Your grandfather was my father."

"But that means…"

"It means I and my mother Prissy were deliberately followed and purchased from Thaddeus' father in New Orleans. We were purposely brought back here, myself to be educated by your grandfather and Prissy to be freed and set up so she could live a reasonably luxurious life."

"Did you know your father? When did you find out my father was your brother? Why do I feel this has something to do with my father's disappearance?"

Jesse threw up his hands. "Stop! I can't keep up with you. Your grandfather and my mother were very discreet, for obvious reasons. They met after your Grandmother Willoughby died. I knew your grandfather was my father, but not until after his death. As he lay dying, he explained everything to Aman and asked him to make sure my mother didn't want for anything while she lived. Aman came to me then; we loved each other from our first meeting."

"How does all of this tie in with the war and my father's name on that awful list of Tyrone's?"

"The truth is, my dear niece, Aman and Tyrone were working together. The three of us created the list. The S/F stood for slave finders. Those men are our friends, fighting for our cause. The middle column, the E/H, stood for an enemy of the abolitionist; they were to be watched, hunted down if possible, and controlled. The P simply meant protect; as they, too, are on our side."

Suzanne felt elated by the relief that filled her. "That explains why the *Sea Queen* and the *Annebella* were always seen together. I thought Tyrone was trying to capture Father's ship."

"In fact, the *Sea Queen* was a much stronger ship, and the two of them often traveled the same course so Tyrone could help protect the *Annebella* and her crew."

"Then, when the *Sea Queen* helped to destroy the *Atlanta* and *Chancellor*, why did he save their crews?"

"You should have figured that out for yourself. By his mother's influence, Tyrone was a gentle Quaker. He could put the ships out of commission without a sense of guilt. Remember, he was for the North and freedom of slavery, but his conscience would never let him murder human beings."

Suzanne felt tears sting the corners of her eyes. "Why couldn't he have told me? Why couldn't he have lived? I loved him."

"He couldn't tell you, Suzanne, because it was too dangerous for your father. There is a certain group of men who would dearly love to spring into action against those who are suspected of being sympathetic to the abolitionist cause."

Abigail, whose own eyes shone with unshed tears, reached across the table to touch Suzanne's hand. "I loved your father, too, my dear, but we must go on. Please say you'll break off this senseless entanglement with Thaddeus."

When Suzanne didn't answer, the others let the conversation drift back to their tiny pupils who were eagerly learning to read and write. Suzanne allowed her mind to float backwards to the moments during the Christmas Ball when there were no shadows across her heart. She knew joy had bubbled in her laugh and shone in her eyes as she and Tyrone had swirled and turned and dipped for the delighted spectators. "What do you think, Suzanne?" Abigail asked.

Bringing herself abruptly back to the present, Suzanne answered vaguely, "I'm sorry. I didn't hear what you said."

"We were talking about the possibility of traveling together to Baltimore over the Christmas holidays. Your Grandfather Hanson might prefer that, as opposed to coming here, especially if you were to cancel the wedding."

Suzanne dropped her lashes to hide the hurt. She gulped hard, hot tears slipping down her cheeks. "Father approved of Thaddeus. It seems simpler to continue with my plans. And who knows, I may grow to love Thaddeus. He will, after all, be able to advise me," a slight shudder ran through her, "and I'm ready to settle down and have children of my own."

Suzanne spoke calmly, trying to hide the sadness that passed over her heart. "Besides, Grandfather's trip is all arranged. I've convinced our good friend Captain Neal Franklin to come along, too. He's taking care of the final details. They're arriving in time for the Harvest Ball and will not return to Baltimore until after the New Year.

"Now, if you will all excuse me, I must get over to Mr. Will's. Forgive me. I know I haven't been very good company. I have a lot on my mind, but I promise to let you all know of my final decision as soon as I can think it out."

As she turned to leave, loneliness and confusion welded together in one upsurge of all-consuming yearning. Spontaneously, she swiveled back and reached out to touch Jesse's cheeks. "Thank you for telling me about yourself. I'm so glad we are family."

His gray eyes darkened as he held her gaze. "We have all known a great loss. Don't be hasty in deciding your future. If Thaddeus is worth your devotion, he can wait until you are sure of your feelings."

The Bandit's Lady

* * * *

John Will, a tall and still distinguished-looking man, despite his sixty-odd years, approached the long display case. He gave Suzanne a warm, beaming smile. "My, my, how good to see you. I'm so happy to see you fully recovered. We were all concerned when we heard you were so ill after your father's tragic death."

"Who was your informant, Mr. Will?"

"Jesse Owens came in to purchase a ring for his bride. I had read about the *Annebella* and knew Jesse had recently been in Baltimore. I asked after you, but now my dear, how may I be of service to you?"

Suddenly shy, Suzanne struggled to explain her need for jewelry, then embarrassed said, "I am to be married to Thaddeus Stuart at Christmastide. I'm looking for the perfect necklace and earrings to compliment my gown."

"That should be easy enough," John Will said as he began pulling out tray after tray of strands of precious gemstones.

The brilliant jewels were delicately strung and boldly displayed. Some were mixed with tiny diamond clusters. There were beads and lockets and pendants and long chains of gems and chokers. Suzanne looked longingly at the emeralds, but finally selected a dainty two-strand sapphire, diamond and seed pearl necklace, with a matching bracelet and tiny earrings. To go with the gown for the Harvest Ball, she chose a tiny, but resplendent heart pendant of diamonds and rose quartz on a gold rope chain.

"That will be all for today, Mr. Will. You may wrap them up."

"Would you like for me to deliver them to Royal Oaks Manor after you return to the plantation?"

"Yes, thank you. It's dangerous for me to carry them on my person. They are much too valuable."

"I will put the jewelry in velvet casings to protect it and send them along with my man a few days before the ball."

* * * *

Suzanne stood up straight and stretched her aching body. She looked out over the land. The acres pale with cotton bolls had a somber, profuse beauty. It was a lush land and a cruel one, in which man could live off a heavy bounty of nature, or suffer destruction in a day from disease, fever and boll weevils.

She had returned to join the slaves three weeks before. She spent the days tenderly picking the soft fleecy cotton and depositing it with the rest in the woven wicker baskets at the ends of each row. They had been working five and a half days a week, as opposed to the normal six. Suzanne felt secure she had made the right decision as the slaves were content and growing in numbers, although freed by the emancipation. She felt thankful the harvest was almost complete. It would be another month, at most. The Harvest Ball was three days away and Thaddeus had arrived the evening before. Suzanne sighed as she remembered the angry dispute they had in the library after dinner.

Her rebellious emotions had got out of hand. "You can demand of me to your heart's content," she had said viciously, "but I will see the harvest through. This is my plantation and in your absence, I took full possession of my land. And, by the by, I also took control of the rest of my money."

His face paled with anger. His eyes blazed icy blue fire and his voice, though quiet, held an undertone of cold contempt. "We'll see about that when you've taken your marriage vows."

"What makes you so sure I've not changed my mind?"

His angry gaze swung over her until the silence between them became unbearable. The long deep look they exchanged had infuriated her, but when he spoke again, he was more agreeable, almost regretful. "We shouldn't quarrel on my first night home. Come here, Suzanne."

The smoldering flame she saw in his eyes startled her. She found herself extremely conscious of his virile appeal. They calmly, then, discussed their future. She had consented to the announcement of their engagement at the Harvest Ball. "It's good you agreed, my dear," Thaddeus had murmured in her ear, "because I stopped at Judge Pope's chambers on the way out from town. He gave me permission to declare our intentions and publish the date of the wedding."

She had no desire to back out of his embrace and had settled back, enjoying the feel of his arms around her.

* * * *

Suzanne closed her eyes and tipped her face to the sun before looking back to her land. *I have known true love once,* she thought. *It can never be the same again. I must settle for what will be.*

Chapter 30

In the distance, wending its way toward the plantation through the pathway of weeping willows, Suzanne saw a carriage approaching. She dropped the cotton out of her skirt into the nearest basket and started toward the manor.

She passed the gin shed where baskets of cotton were being readied for market. Tommy was tending the gin, a wooden cylinder with spikes like porcupine quills. As the cotton rolled by them the seeds fell out and the lint went into a press for baling. Young Jed was covering each bale with cotton bagging and clamping them shut with metal ties for security. As she passed the bins where the cotton was stored she wondered idly who would buy this year's bountiful crop and risk getting it past the blockades.

Suzanne felt untidy; she was sweaty and red in the face. She arrived at the driveway in time to see John Hanson alight from the carriage. Although she had not had time to clean up, she threw her arms around him and buried her head in his neck. "Grandfather. Grandfather. Oh, how I've missed you, but you are looking so very fit."

He put Suzanne at arms' length and stepped back to look at her. "And, you my dear, if you will allow me to get a word into this conversation, are looking healthy as a young lady should."

Suzanne whooped with laughter. "I'm filthy, of course, and you must be exhausted from the long trip. I'll have Sadie show you to your room for a short rest while I see to my bath. Then you can catch me up on all of the news."

Suddenly remembering, Suzanne turned to embrace her other guest. "And, my dear Captain Neal, won't you join us?"

"The pleasure will be all mine," he said as he caught her up in a big bear hug. He gestured his pipe out over the land. "While I'm waiting for the two of you to return to normal, I'll take a short stroll around the place, if that's all right with you."

"Go wherever you wish. We'll all meet back in the library in an hour," Suzanne said as she waved him away and started toward the door.

* * * *

John was sitting quietly in Aman's big leather chair when Suzanne entered the room an hour later. "Ah, there you are, my dear. Before I forget, James sent you a message. He tried to make me memorize it. He said it's a riddle and that you would know immediately what the message means."

Suzanne crossed the room and planted a kiss on the top of his head. "Good. We haven't played that game since we were youngsters. What are the lines?"

"It was something about…holiest holidays kept…in silence…secret anniversaries of our heart. Goodness, I don't remember."

Suzanne smiled with remembered pleasure. "He funs you, Grandfather. It simply means James will be here for the holidays and the wedding."

"You're right about that, but how you knew I can't even hazard a guess."

"It's not too complicated. It's a favorite Longfellow poem of ours. We played a lot of games with poetry. When is he coming?"

"His Christmas break starts December twelfth. Frank Reilly will travel with him."

"Oh, how fun. I can hardly wait to see them."

"Which reminds me," Captain Neal said, "Will Snooks and Clay Long sent you their regards. They said you were a real trooper on the trip home."

He looked fully into her eyes, his own twinkling with amusement. "Will said you'd never marry that Thaddeus bird. He bet me a silver dollar. Said he and Clay would be down for a short visit to collect his winnings."

Briefly, Suzanne's face fell as she remembered her vow to marry for love and the adventurous anticipation she had known before she went to Baltimore. Even later, when she fell in love with Tyrone, she held fast to the dream that happiness could be worked out. But she smiled calmly. "Would you please get word to Will and Clay they are welcome to attend my wedding? However, it looks like you are the winner, and have only to collect the prize when they arrive."

She watched the captain's expression take on a look that was compassionate, troubled and still. "We will see," he said quietly.

Strange and disquieting thoughts began to race through Suzanne's mind before she masked her inner turmoil with a deceptive tranquility. Turning to John, she asked, "Is James happy, Grandfather?"

"Completely. He has decided to live with me in Baltimore. It will be nice to have a young person in the house. Someday my practice and the estate will go to James, and future generations of Hansons will grow up there."

"I'm so happy for you, Grandfather. It must be a big worry lifted from your shoulders, but right now, you two must be hungry. Let's go to the dining room and see what Josy has cooked up for our supper. Abigail, my former governess will be here; she's living with me until after the wedding." Catching her grandfather's puzzled look, she grinned. "Chaperon, you know. Thaddeus has been staying here since his plantation was destroyed by the fires set by hostile runaways. I have a surprise for you. Uncle Stephen is here. Polly and Jesse, too. They'll be staying until we leave for the Harvest ball."

John's brows lifted. "Won't they be attending the ball?"

"Uncle Stephen will. Free Negroes are not allowed to mix with whites here, Grandfather. Don't worry. We have a beautiful friendship and more. I will tell you about it one day. We see each other often, although discreetly, because it is not generally acceptable, and Polly and Jesse could get harassed if we're not careful to protect each other. Come on, now. Let's get in there before Josy has a fit."

Suzanne watched tears form in her grandfather's eyes when he saw Polly enter the dining room on Jesse's arm. Polly flew to embrace him. "Don't feel sad, Granddaddy. I'm the happiest bride south of the Mason-Dixon line."

"But, my dear, I just learned you can't attend the Harvest Ball."

"Oh, but you've been misinformed. We wouldn't miss it for the world." She gave Suzanne a triumphant grin. "Jesse and I can't be guests, but there's going to be more than a hundred

The Bandit's Lady

people to cater to. Judge Pope is Jesse's friend. He asked Jesse if we would be willing to help out. He knew we were dying to be there because of Thaddeus' announcement."

"But it seems so unfair."

"We are fine, Granddaddy. We'll stay in Charleston and help change the terrible conditions of our people. Remember, the emancipation has already freed them. When this war is over, our work will begin in earnest."

"And I'm going to help," Suzanne said.

"Never!" Thaddeus said in a voice brimming with distaste.

Suzanne intentionally kept her voice low, but the words whipped like steel between them. "I will be your wife as I have promised, but my life will always be my own. Let there never be any doubt that I will not be told whom my friends shall be, nor what I shall do with my time."

He stared at her, quick anger rising in his eyes, but when he spoke his tone bordered on mockery. "Ah, my dear, you are so young and zealous. You will grow up to be supportive of slavery. How would your plantation survive without niggers? Maybe Jesse could set up his smithy shop here at Royal Oaks; the proceeds would help out during the rough years ahead. Polly could be employed in the big house."

Suzanne felt the blood begin to pound in her temples. "Stop! This whole conversation is preposterous. Now, let's enjoy this delectable roast beef and savory shrimp scampi."

She shot her grandfather a grateful look when he innocently asked, "And, my dear, what's for dessert?"

* * * *

The next two days sped by. Suzanne and John resumed their morning rides as though nothing had changed, except the scenery. "Oh, Grandfather, look at this beautiful land. It's all mine, and I plan to take very good care of it. Father would be so proud of our harvest."

"Proud of you is what he would be, my dear," John answered, "but if I may be frank, Thaddeus' attitude troubles me. Are you very sure of yourself, Suzanne?"

Suzanne spoke slowly. "I have decided to marry Thaddeus, Grandfather. Father always thought he would be good for me and since Tyrone's death I have come to the conclusion it is the best course for me."

"I do wish we all felt more confidence for your future, but I will say no more, my dear. I wish you every happiness."

"Thank you, Grandfather. I will try to be a good wife, and someday I hope to give you some great-grandchildren."

They rode back to the house in silence. The breakfast table was swarming with hungry guests. John and Suzanne took their place in line at the sideboard and joined in the banter. Excitement was running high for the Harvest Ball. Thaddeus, too, was congenial, and gave Suzanne tender looks.

Later, dressed in the French beige lace and swirling dress, Suzanne sat in front of the mirror while Sadie brushed her copper curls to a bright shine. Polly, in a simple straight, floor-length black serving dress, adorned only with a white, starched pinafore, peeked around the corner of the door. "May I come in?" she asked.

"Of course," Suzanne said. "Oh, you look so sweet, but I do wish you could wear one of your new gowns. At least you can wear the powder blue one at my wedding." She handed Polly the heart-shaped pendant. "Please help me with this clasp."

The Bandit's Lady

"There," Polly said when the necklace was in place. "Oh, Suzanne, you look beautiful, but I wish you didn't look so sad."

Suzanne gave her friend a hug. "It's all right, Polly. I feel a little sad, but this is for the best."

"I wish I could dance with Jesse tonight, but at least we'll be there to watch the whole thing. Come. Let's go downstairs. The men are waiting for us."

Like old times in Baltimore, hand in hand, the girls went down the wide, winding staircase together. Standing at the bottom, Jesse and Thaddeus watched. Thaddeus spoke first, "You look devastating, my dear Suzanne."

Jesse said, "Ravishing is a much more apt description, don't you think, Polly?"

"Much better. She is going to be the charmer of the ball."

Suzanne felt the heat rising in her face. "Come on you two."

Jesse's gray eyes sparkled. He swung Polly into the circle of his arms. "Ah, but I wasn't finished. My compliments also to my favorite bride. You are the most breathtaking maid I have ever met."

"Bride? We've been married almost two years."

Suzanne watched their shared happiness with a tug of regret. *They are blissfully happy, fully alive,* she thought. It seemed to her to be something wonderful, beyond her.

Thaddeus broke the spell as his thigh barely touched hers. His gentle nudge brought her back from her daydreams. She swallowed hard and squared her shoulders. "It really is time for us to leave. Grandfather, Uncle Stephen and Abigail have already gone."

* * * *

The Judge and Amelia Pope lived in an old-time Charleston mansion. It stood boldly against the shore line of Charleston Harbor. It faced its gardens and presented its shoulder to the world. The first floor was raised to provide greater coolness and protect against floods.

Suzanne wondered at the age of the house. It stood in heavy foliage that had taken decades to grow to its present state. Polly followed her through a delicate, intricately designed iron gateway that led to the gallery, and assured that the inhabitants would remain in private, half-hidden from the outside.

Suzanne noted the rich, elaborate house had handsomely arranged windows and doors. Its many arched columns and roofed galleries were ablaze now with candlelight and gas lamps. Polly laid her arm around Suzanne's shoulder. "We'll see and hear it all, my friend. Have a wonderful evening," she said before she and Jesse slipped quickly to the back of the house.

Inside, Suzanne was awed by the thick rugs and fine silver pieces that lined the mantel. Magnificent oil paintings, flanked on either side by candle sconces, adorned the walls. Thaddeus and Suzanne were presented to their host and hostess.

Judge Pope bent low over Suzanne's hand. "My dear, it's so good to see you. I want to be the first to wish you happiness. The surprise announcement is planned for the first thing after the midnight dinner."

Suzanne's dance card was rapidly filled. Thaddeus claimed the first dance and the last. He was in a generous, indulgent mood. "I want this to be the best night of your life," he said in Suzanne's ear as they whirled around the dance floor. "We will do nothing to spoil this wondrous evening for you. I've waited too long for you, my dear."

He let her go then, and the hours sped away in a haze of dances until Suzanne found herself in the arms of Captain Neal Franklin. "Oh, Captain, I'm exhausted from dancing. I see by my card we are favored with two dances in a row. Would you mind terribly if we sit this one out?"

Captain Neal's bright eyes searched Suzanne's face with a grateful look. He pulled her to him and kissed her forehead. "Or go out on the veranda to get a whiff of fresh autumn air?"

"Perfect! Let's go to the back piazza where we can look out over the harbor and breathe in the ocean's fragrance."

"And miss both dances? Oh, thank you, Suzanne. You know I miss the aura and the mood of the sea, don't you?"

She was silent as they walked through the clamor. At the balcony railing, Suzanne felt the cooling breezes gently tousle the loose tendrils of her hair. "Don't give me too much credit, Captain Neal. I need the tranquil quiet of this night ever as much as you do. When we must go back, it will be time for the last dance and the dinner hour. My life will never be the same."

"Suzanne, I am anxious for you. You need more time to find your true beloved."

"Don't fret, Captain Neal. I let my beloved go, but I have cried my tears and thought everything through. Thaddeus may not be perfect, but he will help manage my affairs and see to my welfare to the best of his ability."

She turned to face him squarely and lowered her voice. "And he will father my children."

When they entered the ballroom again, Thaddeus was waiting to claim the last dance.

Dinner was a gala affair, beginning with an offering of a choice of soups. Suzanne selected okra soup, but mischievously dipped into her grandfather's crab soup. Appetizers of roast oysters, tiny crackers with cheeses, artichoke relish, and a variety of preserves followed the soup course. Then along with bowls of a variety of vegetables, platters of entrees were passed along the huge tables. When Suzanne felt stuffed to discomfort, Polly was beside her. She served Suzanne a wedge of warm pecan pie with a thin dab of creamy cheese melting into the sugary thick sauce. Polly touched her shoulder and whispered in her ear. "Jesse and I are finished until the guests ask for their cloaks and carriages. We are going to stand behind you so we won't miss a moment of the excitement."

Abigail smiled across the table, and John patted his granddaughter's knee. When the tables were cleared at last, Judge Pope nodded to Thaddeus. He squeezed Suzanne's hand, then stood up and tapped his glass with his spoon.

Those closest guests to the couple quieted down first. The silence spread across the room until the hush was complete. "Our host," Thaddeus said, "has graciously given me a few minutes to make a very important announcement." He looked down and took Suzanne's hand. "Suzanne, will you please stand up."

Suzanne rose slowly to her feet, staring in the direction of the veranda. Thaddeus' voice dimmed into the background as she disengaged her hand and walked toward the open doors. Framed in the doorway was a tall man wrapped in a tattered cape. He had a sliver-thin scar above his bushy left eyebrow. The expression in his deep-set, ebony eyes quickly captured the crowd. Tormented, they seemed to plead for understanding. At the same time they brimmed with tenderness and held a glint of wonder.

"Suzanne!" Thaddeus bellowed. "Come back here. You wouldn't want me to tell your friends all of your ugly family secrets, would you?"

Unhurried, Suzanne pivoted back to face Thaddeus across the huge room. Very gently, without raising her voice, she said, "You may say anything you wish. I have nothing in my past to apologize for. However, I would remind you of your recent transactions at my father's bank. Mr. Johnston assured me I could sue you for the fifteen thousand dollars you took under false pretenses."

Suzanne felt Thaddeus' sharp eyes boring into her as she turned away. She felt the color drain from her face as she sought Tyrone's eyes. Suzanne's last conscious thought, *I never have the vapors,* came seconds before she felt strong tender arms scoop her up and carry her into the darkness of the night.

Chapter 31

Suzanne stirred. Tyrone gently eased her down onto the bed. Her eyes fluttered open. "Where am I?"

"You're on the *Sea Queen*, hidden between Charleston Harbor and Royal Oaks, on the Ashley River, and your father lives. You will see him soon. Shush, now, my cherished beloved."

Suzanne felt a bottomless peace and contentment.

Leisurely, Tyrone loosened the tiny silk ribbon that fastened the lace bodice of Suzanne's gown. His large hands slid the dress over silky shoulders and down slim hips. Lovingly, he stripped away the petticoats. Suzanne squirmed and lifted her arms to cover her breasts, but Tyrone removed them. His dark eyes never left her body for an instant. They softened at the sight of her, caressed her silkiness, then melted into her own eyes. Tyrone rose and covered Suzanne with a fine wool blanket. Heart hammering in her ears, she did not move as he took off his cloak, then his shirt and breeches.

He lay down beside her, so close she could feel the heat from his body. His nearness, the sweetly intoxicating musk of his body, overwhelmed her.

A shudder passed through her. She was filled with a

strange inner excitement; her whole being seemed to be charged with the waiting. Explosive currents raced through her. She tried to speak, but Tyrone's mouth covered hers hungrily and when he lifted his head, his voice was low and husky. "We have the rest of our lives to sort out the mysteries. This night is ours alone."

Pausing, he gazed at her for a sign of an objection. Suzanne crept into his arms, snuggled there. "I thought you were dead. I wished...I...I'd let you make love to me, but I want to go to my husband, be untouched when—

His mouth moved over hers with exquisite tenderness, then parted her lips in mute invitation. His flickering tongue pushed her toward new sensations, and she opened her mouth with a small whimper. A wild surge of pleasure surprised her as Tyrone's hands explored the soft lines of her back, her waist, her hips. His lips brushed her taut nipples worshipfully. The magic of his mouth and fingers triumphed, sweetly draining all her doubts and fears. Suzanne surrendered then, completely, to his masterful seduction. He whispered her name and endearments over and over. The feeling was much more than sexual desire. As her body melted against his, the world was filled with the love that flowed between them.

Their legs intertwined and she arched her hips to meet him, welcoming him into her body with one sharp intake of breath that turned quickly to a gentle moan of craving as his body claimed her. Their bodies meshed with the reverence of tender love and the fervor of seduction. Fire bolts of desire raced through Suzanne as her virgin body discovered the cadence of his rhythm.

The starburst of ecstasy started deep inside her. Patiently he brought her to the brink of a spiraling climax and she couldn't control the outcry of delight as the rapture exploded around them in a downpour of passionate sensations, a dizzying uncontrollable burst of joy, until contentment and peace surged through them, and Suzanne was filled with an amazing sense of completeness. Afterward, they lay in silence. Tyrone held her through the night as they slept and woke and loved again. And slept.

* * * *

"Come, my darling, we must get you back to the plantation before daybreak or your reputation will be ruined."

Suzanne smiled shyly up at Tyrone. "A lot you care about my reputation. You steal me away from my betrothed, carry me off into the darkness, and seduce me on your ship. Please, Tyrone, tell me about Father."

"Get dressed. I'll tell you on the way." He grinned down at her. "Your Uncle Jesse lent me a carriage and team; Rufus is waiting for us.

"How did Jesse know you were here? Why didn't he tell me?"

"I threatened his life and swore him to secrecy. I didn't want Thaddeus to destroy you and your father's good name. He became suspicious of Aman and myself. He even discovered that Jesse is your half uncle. Thaddeus had threatened terrible things if your father wouldn't disappear so he could marry you. Jesse told me your engagement was to be announced at supper. I watched you through the window all evening. You seemed melancholy, but I had made up my mind. Oh, my darling, I would have loved you all of my life and been jealous of Thaddeus for that same period of time, but I had decided we must lead separate lives far apart."

"You weren't going to give me a chance to make my own choice?"

The Bandit's Lady

Tyrone pulled Suzanne into his arms. He kissed her softly and held her tenderly. "You never were to know how I felt and neither would anyone else. Oh, I was so brave inside and so dramatic. I was going to seal my love for you away, and there it would stay forever."

Suzanne nestled against his subtle strength. "What made you change your mind?"

"I was on the terrace, in the shadows of the gardens, when you and the Captain came out on the veranda. I was so close I could have touched you. I heard the captain's concern and elected to let you decide. Thank God, my love, you picked me. I can't think what I might have done if you had not."

"Please tell me about Father. Why didn't either of you let me know you were alive? And how did you escape the fire?"

Tyrone moved away, laughing. "You never could ask your questions one at a time."

At the carriage, Suzanne threw her arms around Rufus. "It's so good to see you!"

Rufus gave her a crooked grin. "Yes, 'um, and it be good to see you, too. Didn' I a'ways tell you quit fussin'?"

As the horses began to move, Tyrone spoke. "Your father is in a safe place. The explosion did not destroy the *Sea Queen*. It was the *Annebella* and the *Sea Dog* that went up in smoke and fire, but I already had the crews on board. We were finishing up some plans for abolitionist activities when it happened. The newspaper accounts erroneously reported the *Sea Queen* burned."

"I won't wait a minute longer, Tyrone. Where is Father? Don't you know that Abigail is mad to see him? Has he contacted her yet?"

Tyrone pulled Suzanne into his arms and pressed her close

with relentless enjoyment. His mouth twitched with amusement. "I was hoping to simply hold you for the duration of the ride out to Royal Oaks, but I see you will have none of that. Your Father is in Havana, Cuba. We escaped there to deliver a hold of sugarcane we had picked up in New Orleans, and to get some vital supplies, and also a few luxuries. In West Indies' waters we got into the middle of a violent storm. A sail rig collapsed, so when we arrived the damage to the ship had to be repaired. By the time we got ready to come back, we had decided I should come alone and find out what was going on. Thaddeus' threats were very powerful and we had been gone so long we thought it better this way."

"Now what?"

"You, my beloved, are going home. I'm going back to get your father. I'll be leaving in about three days, after I can make some other minor repairs and pick up a load of exchangeable goods."

Suzanne felt a momentary panic as her mind raced on. "But what of me? What will Thaddeus do to me?"

She watched a spark of humor light Tyrone's eyes. "What of you, indeed? You have more than enough to do, getting in the harvest and getting the plantation chapel ready for a wedding. Your father and I will be back in time for your wedding. After last night I can only assume you are still going to have a wedding."

He gave her a conspiratorial wink. "Only the bridegroom has changed. I wouldn't worry myself overly about Thaddeus. It seems you put him in his proper place before you passed out in my arms. Too bad you missed the cheers from your devoted followers."

Happiness filled Suzanne as his gaze roved and lazily appraised her. "You seem to have everything all thought out." She leaned lightly into him, tilting her face toward his.

Tyrone pressed his lips to hers, caressing her mouth, then he brushed a gentle kiss across her forehead. His deep voice held barely checked passion. "I must not stay close to you, or I'll never be able to leave you, but before I go I want to return a gift."

He held out a small package and Suzanne took it in wonderment. "For me?"

"For you. Open it. We are almost at Royal Oaks."

Inside the black velvet case lay Suzanne's own emerald-and-diamond ring and matching pendant, exquisitely arranged in the delicate gold settings. Suzanne felt tears tremble on her eyelids as she looked into Tyrone's eyes. "You saved them for me?"

"Please wear them on your wedding day. The whole truth is that your father asked me to see that you arrived at your grandparents' safely. We were on our way to Norfolk when we saw the carriage and decided to do a good deed on the way. We needed funds to help supply food to one of the new Underground Railroad stations..."

"But if you were supposed to protect me, why did you attack the stage I was traveling in, and why did Will and Clay kidnap me later?"

"I recognized you immediately. Your father had shown me a portrait of you, but I had no way of knowing you were delayed because of the broken wheel. I didn't tell Will and Clay they were to help take care of you. I never dreamed you would not arrive safely. Once you boarded the *Bianca,* Captain Neal was to see to your welfare. I had to report for my commission before you arrived in Baltimore, but I had asked for the jewelry as my cut of the job. Later, I gave them its value in silver and saved these precious pieces for you."

The touch of Tyrone's hand tingled up Suzanne's arm. She felt her heart skip a beat. "Won't you stay at Royal Oaks for a few days before you leave?"

"I'm sorry, my cherished one. If I don't leave immediately, I won't get back in time for the wedding." The coach had pulled up in front of the manor and stopped. "You must get out now. Enjoy Abigail's expression when you tell her Aman is alive. I'm going to write to Mother and ask her to come down for the holidays, and our wedding. I'll have her come directly to the plantation. Is that all right?"

"Yes, my love. Everything will be ready." She grinned mischievously. "Just don't forget the wedding is the day after Christmas. If you're not here, I have one waiting in the wings, you know."

His lips met hers with a deep affectionate promise, in a gentle lingering kiss. Suzanne clung to him, wishing the kiss would last forever, but he pulled away with a tearing reluctance. "Enough, my beloved. You must go now and change your clothes for breakfast."

* * * *

The days shortened into December. Thaddeus had left immediately after the Harvest Ball to establish residence in Columbia, "...where my political future lies," he had said with a touch of bitterness.

Harvest was complete. The happy slave-laborers were paid. Anticipation of the holidays excited the whole plantation. Polly and Jesse moved to Royal Oaks. Polly had dismissed her students until after the festivities. Jesse left a sign on his blacksmith shop saying he could be reached at the plantation. "If it's all right with you, Suzanne," he had said, "I'll set up temporarily in your old smithy shed. Folks won't mind driving out here with their work."

Two weeks before Christmas, Suzanne, Abigail and Polly, joined by Sadie and Josy, and by the two new housemaids, Pearl and Flora, met at Royal Oaks Chapel. They brought buckets and rags, scrub brushes and lye soap.

When they arrived at the Chapel, Jesse Owens, Jasper, Jimbo and half a dozen others were waiting for them. Will Snooks and Clay Long joined them. Will said not a word, but gave Suzanne a lopsided grin and held up a silver dollar as he acknowledged her presence.

The women scrubbed ceilings and walls, windows and floors and the altar and benches. They polished the bell and the candelabrum until the whole place sparkled and shone. The men scraped the rough boards and brushed on a fresh coat of whitewash.

As they wearily trooped back to the house, Suzanne saw a carriage approaching. *Who can that be at such an hour?* She ran to meet the guests.

Mrs. Jane Sterling, as regal as Suzanne remembered her, stepped down. Right behind her, dressed in cornflower blue, was Bridget, who looked for all the world like she had just stepped from her morning toilet. For an instant, Suzanne stared in disbelief before she threw her arms around Tyrone's mother. "Welcome to Royal Oaks. Your son and my father have not yet arrived, but we will wait for them together."

In her soft, kindly voice, and gesturing toward Bridget, the gentle Quaker woman said, "I hope you don't mind that I took it upon myself to invite our dear friend Bridget. I needed a traveling companion for such a long trip."

Behind them, a baby cried. Impishness sparkled in Jane Sterling's eyes. "As it turns about, we brought Bridget's husband and their new baby, Billy, as well."

Suzanne turned to watch a well-dressed young man step out of the coach and hand the child to its mother. "We won't be a bit of bother, Suzanne," William Barclay said as he grabbed her around the waist and gave her a brotherly kiss. "We wanted to join your friends in wishing you well, and to thank you and Tyrone for introducing us."

In the excitement that followed, Suzanne learned William had finished serving his time in the muddy war-torn battlefields. He had secured a position in the banking house of Philadelphia and married Bridget a few months later. "The baby," he said with a grin, "is already a seasoned traveler at four months of age."

James' arrival three days before Christmas was an equally gala affair. He was no longer gangly, but tall and straight. His voice no longer cracked in youthful immaturity, but was deep and strong with confidence. "Come on, Cousin," he said with a tug at Suzanne's sleeve. "Let's ride together to get my father."

Changed into a chocolate-brown, velvet riding habit and mounted on Ginny, Suzanne challenged James to a race. Later, breathless, they rode quietly, reminiscing, until they stopped by the pond. "I'm so proud of you, James, and Grandfather is so happy you will be staying with him."

"I'm going to miss all of this, Suzanne, but we are two lucky young people. We have known the best of two worlds. I'll not forget my southern heritage, but I gratefully accept my grandfather's gift for healing."

The Bandit's Lady

****

Christmas morning dawned mild. The sun was a peaceful burst of light across the misty fields. While Sadie was brushing Suzanne's copper curls, she said, "What you be gonna do if'n de groom don' gets here?"

Abigail, with a deep sadness in her voice, had asked the same question yesterday afternoon, and Polly, plopped in the middle of her bed last night, had repeated the concern. The question burned in Suzanne's heart, tormented her mind. Except for the fact that the two people she loved the most had not arrived, the days had been glorious. The house was full to overflowing. Expectations lingered in every room, like the brightness of holly berries, the smell of fresh pine boughs, and the odors of warm baked breads, fruit pies and roasting turkeys and roasted beef from the kitchen.

Now Suzanne smiled with remembered pleasure. She recalled Tyrone's lips claiming hers in a gentle, drugging kiss and the moment of ecstasy exploding around her. She gave Sadie the same answer she had given the others. "Tyrone will be here. He promised to be here on my wedding day."

"Wise girl, my sweet."

Suzanne whirled around, and stepped into the circle of Tyrone's arms.

****

Suzanne found Abigail and Aman in the study. Father and daughter held each other close, tears of happiness glistening on their cheeks. "Oh, my darling daughter, I'm so sorry for all your sadness. We couldn't let you know we were safe; it would have spoiled our plan."

"Father, did you know Thaddeus stole money from us?"

"I suspected he would if he could, but I understand you found him out and put a stop to it. In fact, Jesse tells me you have handled the business like an expert. I'm so proud of you. Come here, Abigail."

Aman gave her a loving look as he put his arm around her waist. He turned to Suzanne. "Do you mind very much if we marry and live at the plantation while we grow old?"

Suzanne's undiluted laughter rang through the room.

* * * *

On December 26, 1863, there were two weddings in Royal Oaks Chapel. Suzanne and Tyrone stood proud, one on each side, while Aman Willoughby and Abigail LaFontain took their vows.

Finally, surrounded by the same family and friends, Suzanne Willoughby and Tyrone Sterling pledged their own love.

Hours later, as Suzanne snuggled into Tyrone's arms, he said, "I had in mind, my beloved, to live on the *Sea Queen* and to cruise the blue waters and gentle rolling waves, until we are saturated with its beauty and its balmy ocean breezes. Then we will spend a year or two in Baltimore, where I will design and build my mother's ship. After that..."

"After that, sweet love, we must sail with your mother to her homeland, so your son may learn of his heritage at an early age."

"My son?"

"Yes. Or daughter. The one you gave to me the night of the Harvest Ball." Without waiting for his answer, Suzanne pressed her form against the length of him and instinctively arched her body with the promise of fulfillment. Gentle rain drummed against the deck overhead.

The bandit didn't notice—nor did his lady.

ABOUT THE AUTHOR

Irene O'Brien lives in Columbus, Nebraska, where she was a freelance writer for twenty-five years. Later, she wrote and published *Christian JoyRide (Marked by a Reckless Driver)*. She then became a Licensed Lay Minister, and served a small rural church for several years before retiring. A voracious reader, Irene has four other books in various stages of unfinished. Widowed, she has five grown children and twelve grandchildren.

For your reading pleasure, we invite you to visit our web bookstore

WHISKEY CREEK PRESS

www.whiskeycreekpress.com